Jeanin   novels
The Outside Boy, *The Crooked Branch* and *American Dirt*
and one true crime work, *A Rip in Heaven*. She lives in New
York with her husband and two children.

Praise for *The Crooked Branch*:

'Wonderfully written, with strong, compelling characters,
it is a deeply satisfying combination of sweeping historical
saga and modern family drama, a gentle reminder of the
ever-reaching influence of family, both near and far' *Booklist*

'Even before you come to care about Jeanine Cummins'
rich and intricately drawn characters, before you become
enmeshed in her skillfully tangled plot lines about the hard
and wondrous task of mothering children in times both
catastrophic and ordinary . . . Before any of that, this is what
you have to look forward to: the first page, Ms. Cummins'
luminous prose, and that feeling we're all hoping to find
when we sit down to read: "This is it – a book I'm going to
love"' Carolyn Parkhurst

'Exploring the effect of a secret from the past on a woman
who is truly on the edge – of motherhood, of her future, of
sanity, of happiness – Jeanine Cummins has written a story
that truly resonates. Insightful, suspenseful, and sometimes
bitingly funny, with characters the reader will think about
for weeks, this bittersweet novel is emotional and immensely
satisfying' Simone St. James

ALSO BY JEANINE CUMMINS

A Rip in Heaven
The Outside Boy
American Dirt

THE

CROOKED

BRANCH

JEANINE CUMMINS

TINDER
PRESS

First published by New American Library

First published in Great Britain in paperback in 2020 by Tinder Press
An imprint of HEADLINE PUBLISHING GROUP

4

Cataloguing in Publication Data is available from the British Library

ISBN 978 1 4722 728 50

Printed and bound in Great Britain by Clays Ltd, Elcograf S.p.A.

Headline's policy is to use papers that are natural, renewable and recyclable
products and made from wood grown in well-managed forests and other
controlled sources. The logging and manufacturing processes are expected
to conform to the environmental regulations of the country of origin.

HEADLINE PUBLISHING GROUP
An Hachette UK Company
Carmelite House
50 Victoria Embankment
London EC4Y 0DZ

www.tinderpress.co.uk
www.headline.co.uk
www.hachette.co.uk

For my mama

THE
CROOKED
BRANCH

Prologue

IRELAND, AUGUST 1846

I t all happened in one night. One wicked, godforsaken night in August, and they couldn't believe it. The way they took to their beds in the evening, and everything was grand and ordinary. Hungry, yes, but ordinary. They'd already been hungry for a year; they were getting by, hanging on for the coming crop. So that whole doomed island of people, they slept, naive in their myriad dreams. Their limbs tangled around lovers, their sleeping children twitching and murmuring nearby, the dying turf-fire shadows stretching along the thatching above. They slept.

For no one could imagine the horror they would waken to. Not a one of them could have foretold that noxious, murderous fog that came in the night, and strangled the light from their moon-bright skies. It rolled in from the sea, from God knows whence it came, but it was the Atlantic waves that heaved that fog up onto the western shores of Ireland. From there it crept and slithered, low to the ground like a vaporous serpent. All along the soil, up hills and ridges and mountains it climbed, breathing itself into every hollow. And then down again it rolled, into the slopes and glens and valleys, staying low, low, all the time, clinging to the ground, hugging to the knobby roots of trees, skulking across the lifeless skins of lochs.

They didn't notice that pungent bitterness in the dark, beyond their walls, and turf fires, beyond the milky breath of their sleeping children. They slept, while that mortal fog stole into their bright, green country, and grew like a merciless stain across the darkened land. It killed every verdant thing it touched.

It was silent when Ginny wakened in the morning. No cock crowed. No dog barked. Most of the country's sheep and cattle had already been slaughtered or sold for food, but those skinny specimens who remained were silent in the fields. Even the birds were struck mute. She stirred herself from sleep, startled by the lateness of the daylight. She arose without waking the others.

Now look: there she is, standing in her doorway, the golden thatch drooping low above her in the moist morning light. Her red petticoat hangs down her legs; her bare feet are pressing into the cold flagstone beneath. She's gazing out. There's a lone magpie in the blackthorn tree, speechless with terror.

The first sound is a strangled cry that escapes her throat. It's not a word—just a simple, unadorned cry, an anguish-sound. And then her babbies are stirring behind her, still innocent for these few moments. But Raymond is on his feet now, untangling himself from the blanket. He is beside his wife, his hand on her shoulder, his voice a terrible gasp in her ear. "God help us."

And there they are, their fingers roped fiercely together, their bare feet leaving the flagstone, stepping out, their weight sinking slightly, the leftover dew from that lethal fog licking their toes and ankles, until they are in the middle of their slaughtered field. They are decimated. The black and broken, reeking stalks of their potatoes are all around, as far as they can see, up to the ridge and down through the sloping glen. Ginny turns in circles, looking for any trace of life, a single green leaf, a purple blossom, a breath of prayer. But there is nothing, only the stench of death now, rising up from the soil, clinging to the thick air like a fetid warning. Everything, everything is rot.

She looks back at her children, the four of them gathering now in the doorway, already hungry for their breakfast. They are stretching sleep from their warm little bodies, they are shaking the dreams from their eyelids.

She might have closed their blameless eyes that very moment, might've saved and sealed those lingering dreams inside their heads, for sustenance, for nourishment.

But she didn't know, even in that moment of bottomless panic. She could never conceive of the kind of suffering that would follow.

Chapter One

"I think I should go see someone, try again," I whisper in the dark.

Leo and I have our best conversations when he's asleep.

"Maybe you're right, that it just wasn't the right fit," I say. "It would be good to get some things off my chest."

"That's great," Leo says, rolling over to face me.

"Oh. You're awake."

He props up on one elbow. "Well, yes. Did you think I was asleep?"

I don't answer him. He leans in toward me until our foreheads are touching. His skin gleams in the faint moonlight from the window. Okay, it's not moonlight—it's our backyard neighbor's motion-sensing, super-megawatt back-porch spotlight, and it blinks on and off incessantly throughout the night, whenever a cat or a raccoon wanders by. Which is often. It's like trying to sleep in a lighthouse.

"Majella?" Leo whispers.

"Yeah?"

He squeezes my hand. "I think it's a good idea. I'll even go with you, if you want me to."

I squeeze back. "No," I say. "No, I think I have to go by myself."

He kisses me, and then flumps back down on his pillow.

"You'll feel so much better," he says. "You'll see."

And then he is snoring again, because he really believes it; he's not that worried. He believes I can get better.

"So what brings you in today?" Dr. Zimmer asks.

There is a desk, but she doesn't sit behind it. Instead, she chooses a red leather chair, and gestures for me to sit down on the couch opposite her. It's a dark brown faux-suede couch, and I perch on its edge.

"Am I supposed to lie down?" I ask.

"However you're comfortable," she says, and then waits, but I will never be comfortable in this room, on this couch.

I pick up one of the tawny pillows and hold it in my lap. The lamplight is nice, at least. The fluorescent overheads are turned off, and the tasteful standing lamps give a much warmer glow to the small office. It could feel cozy, with all its dark wood built-ins and its well-trimmed windows, if it weren't for Dr. Zimmer with her notepad and her patent-leather shoes.

"Majella?"

"Hmm?"

"Why did you decide to come see me today?"

"Oh," I say, picking at the gold rope edging of the cushion. "I don't know, really."

Dr. Zimmer waits some more.

"I think . . ."

She's a professional waiter. She doesn't even fidget.

My voice is so small I can barely hear it myself. "I think I might be going crazy," I say. "I'm scared that I'm going crazy."

Dr. Zimmer frowns at me. She turns her head on a slight angle like dogs sometimes do, when they're really considering you. There are leafy, green ferns lining the windowsill behind her, and their brightness seems to make light of my confession.

"Like actual crazy," I say, for clarification. "Not fun-crazy."

"Okay." She nods. "Okay. Let's see if we can figure out where that fear is coming from."

During my twenty-seventh hour of labor, I realized I would need therapy. I pulled so hard I feared that the bar would snap and splinter, and nurses would be stabbed in the head with the shrapnel and killed instantly, falling to the floor with their mouths and eyes open in horrified Os. Their last act of motion in the world: the release of a ballpoint pen from a lifeless hand, the languorous roll of a Bic across the laminate floor.

It was shift change again. My third nurse was leaving to go home for the night. She was sporty and olive, with almond eyes and swingy black hair. She could have been anyone. But she was my third nurse and she was going home for the night to eat a Lean Cuisine and stretch out on her couch and pretend to read Borges while she watched *The Bachelor*. Tonight was the finale: would Sebastian choose Crystal or Shenandoah?

I passed out. The contractions were ferocious because the doctor had turned off my epidural so I could *feel* them. As if I was in danger of *not feeling* the eight-pound child who was attempting to exit my body. He was a male doctor, and he thought the pain would help me push, which is like the philosophy that waterboarding helps people confess to hiding weapons of mass destruction. Between contractions, I lost consciousness. Or maybe I just went to sleep. I was likely very tired, though I couldn't have said so with any conviction, because all I could really feel was pain. Like fire and knives and every other cliché of pain that's ever been muttered, all of it patched up together in a big ball, like in that video game where you start off with a little teeny ball that rolls around the room and picks up thumbtacks and paper clips until it gets big enough to start picking up buckets and small dogs, and then eventually cows and then barns and then skyscrapers and then planets. My pain picked up incongruous, unrelated, worldwide pains in the exact same way. So that first I could feel stubbed toes and paper cuts and smacked funny bones. And then I could feel the farmer in Ipswich twisting his back in spasms under the weight of some greasy machinery, the child in New Delhi who had just run her hand under the sewing machine at the factory where she worked, the twenty-two-year-old Hollywood waitress who didn't get The Part, even after she lap-fucked the paunchy casting director (no easy feat) within easy earshot of his assistant and two other hopefuls. And then finally: facial burns, chemotherapy, suicide.

My new nurse came in and she wasn't a new nurse at all. She was an old nurse, my first nurse, who had gone home the evening before, slept all night, gotten up in the morning, measured and eaten her Special K with skim milk, gone to the gym, had a manicure, lingered in a coffee shop with an ex-boyfriend (now married), and finally returned to work, where I was STILL IN LABOR, TWENTY-SEVEN HOURS LATER.

"Still here?" she said. "My goodness! Going for a record, are we?"

I hated her. I thought about the violence of this beginning, so different than I had imagined. My birthing ball mocked me from its corner. I pushed. Well, not me—my muscles pushed. I grunted and strained and prayed. The nurse held my knee open on one side, and Leo held the knee on the other. They tried to comfort me. They told me I was brave and I was doing a great job. I didn't have much choice. I squeezed my eyes shut so that my eyeballs wouldn't spring free of my head. My baby would be born, and during the big, beautiful moment of arrival, it (he, she) would get hit in the head with my runaway eyeball. An inauspicious greeting.

"Welcome to the world, baby!" PING! "Oh, don't mind that, sweetie—no, no, don't cry. It's just Mommy's eyeball."

Another contraction. I curled, I heaved, I pushed, I pushed, I pushed. It was the twenty-eighth hour now. I passed out again, and the nurse put a damp washcloth over my face to cool me. I tried to breathe in and I was sucking terry cloth. My nose was blocked. I panicked and tried to shake the washcloth loose.

"YOU'RE NOT HELPING," I wanted to scream. "I'm claustrophobic! Get that fucking thing off my face!" But I was unconscious again. And then another contraction. I was crying now, the tears just slipping down my face, indistinguishable from all the other fluids.

"C-section," the doctor said.

He was talking to Leo, and I'm pretty sure there were more words in the sentence than that. Their voices were traveling over and back now, in front of me. They were saying more words.

"You told me you could see the head," I cried, with my real, out-loud voice. I was sobbing, wasting precious energy on that. "Three hours ago," I sobbed. "What happened?"

Leo moved back toward me, toward my face-end. He put his hand on my forehead. I was so fucking hot. "I'm sorry," he said. "I'm so sorry. I think this is the only way."

It was seventeen more hours before the anesthesiologist came. Or okay, it was seven minutes, but really, that's only a technicality because my ball of pain was so big now that it was picking up *galaxies.* I was feeling alien pain. Blind, one-legged, orphaned Martian pain.

You'd think that after all that crescendo of horror, its release would be spiritually epic, that there would be a heroic, unblemished afterglow, a sepia portrait of love. After twenty-eight hours of labor, three hours of pushing, and finally a C-section, didn't I deserve some damned afterglow?

But instead of sepia, there was only the fluorescent, overhead buzzkill. It shone down on my baby's red face, her red head, her tiny red fists. And then my teeth started to chatter, and my arms started to twitch and flutter, and my whole body was shaking, and one of the nurse-voices told me that it was just the anesthesia wearing off, but that they'd better take the baby, just in case. And then they scooped her little red-wrapped body out of my arms and gave her to someone who was a much better mother than me, or at least to someone who wouldn't shake her and drop her, splat, on the hospital floor in her first hour of life. I watched her ascend from my arms, and the weight of her absence was like a brand-new grief, a hysteria.

Leo sat beside me on a spinny chair, holding my greenish shaking hand. He tried to smooth back my ridiculous hair, but it was no use. I hadn't seen a mirror in days, but I knew what I looked like: that school photograph, the one from the eighth grade, with the hair that managed to be both greasy and fluffy at once. I'd worn a royal blue cable-knit sweater, too, for God's sake. I shuddered and shivered and clattered.

"Is she supposed to be shaking like that?" Leo asked the nurse.

"It's normal."

"But that much?"

The nurse came around the curtain and moved some wires around.

"Oooh, blood pressure not great," she said.

She was wearing pink scrubs. Leo looked at me and smiled with his lips closed.

"I'm so proud of you," he said.

"I couldn't do it," I said.

"You did do it. She's perfect."

"But I couldn't do it, I couldn't push her out."

He shook his head at me.

"You did great, you cooked her for nine whole months."

"Ten," I whispered.

"She was stuck," he said. "That wasn't your fault."

"She only weighs eight pounds. Why would she get stuck? My hips are massive."

"Shhhh," he said. "You're just tired. You're exhausted. You did great."

And then I was shaking again, awfully hard, and I was afraid I might actually pull some of the tubes loose from their machines. I hoped they weren't vital. I waited for it to pass.

"I heard a horrible story," I said to Leo when my teeth stopped clattering momentarily. "About a woman who fell asleep with her baby, in the hospital bed."

My throat was shaking now, too. I didn't know your throat could shake, but there it was, and the words were coming out all quivery and distorted. I tried to keep my voice down, but I couldn't control it. Leo was looking at me strangely.

"And she dropped the baby," I said. "He fell right off the edge of the bed. She just fell asleep and she dropped him."

"Why are you telling me that?" Leo said. "Don't even think about that." He leaned in and kissed my forehead.

"He died, just from falling off the bed."

"Shhhhh," Leo said again. He stroked my hand.

"They're so fragile. That's all it takes."

The nurse pulled back the curtain, I could tell by the metallic sound of the rings scraping along their track. But my eyes were closed against the wicked light, and I was shaking again, and I don't know where my battered body found the energy to shake like that, like some primal, tribal bone-dance.

The morning after Emma was born, I woke up in my hospital bed and tried to sit, but I couldn't move. I had to roll over on my side first. Ow. Slowly. First roll, then hoist, roll, hoist. A long series of miniature, agonizing movements until I was half-seated.

"You all right over there?" A voice behind the curtain. "You were whimpering in your sleep."

I tried to pull back the curtain to get a gawk at my roommate, but when I reached, I felt like the incision across my abdomen would open up, and all my insides would strew themselves unattractively across the bed.

"Yeah," I said. "Thank you. I just had a bad dream. A horrible dream."

I shuddered. It took me at least four or five minutes to reach and press the nurse-call button on the wall behind my head. Then a loud crackle and another disembodied voice.

"YES."

I looked around.

"Hello?" I said.

"Yes?" the voice said again.

"Oh," I said. "Hi."

I couldn't tell if the voice could hear me, or if I was supposed to be talking into a microphone or something. I hesitated.

"Yes, hi," the voice said again. "Just calling to chat?"

"Oh," I said. "No. It's awkward—I didn't. I didn't know if you could hear me."

My roommate was chuckling behind the curtain. I thought I

could hear her rolling her eyes, but I couldn't, of course, and that was probably just another weird symptom of all the morphine and rampant hormones, thinking I could hear a thing like a rolled eyeball.

"I can hear you," the voice said. "What do you need?"

Was there a volume switch somewhere? The voice was so loud it gave me goose bumps. I jumped in my skin every time it spoke.

"I need my baby," I said. My roommate snorted. "I mean I just woke up here. I haven't seen her. I haven't seen her since she was born. I wanted to . . . I'd like to feed her."

The speaker crackled and there was a metallic switching noise, but no voice.

"Hello?" I spoke into the air around my head. It was like talking to God, but with less assurance. "I couldn't hear you."

"I said it's shift change right now." The voice was back. "Nurses are taking report. But someone will be in to see you within a half an hour or so, and you can request the baby be brought from the nursery then."

"Oh," I said. "Okay."

The final crackle indicated the end of the conversation, and I didn't expect it, but I started to cry, great heaving, shuddering racks of tears. Crying hurt, and now my small intestine would fall out for sure, but I couldn't stop. I reached for the phone, and I had to sort of collapse onto my elbow in order to punch in the numbers, but then I couldn't right myself again, so I just stayed like that, half-tipped-over in the bed, clutching the receiver against my ear. Leo answered on the fourth ring.

"Are you coming?" I said.

"What time is it?" he asked.

He sounded confused. I looked at the industrial school/hospital/jail clock on the wall.

"Seven thirty."

It was really only seven twenty-three. I could hear rumpling sheets. He stretched.

"Yeah, I'm coming, for sure, of course," he said. "I can't wait to see my girls!"

I couldn't answer him because I was crying again.

"Are you okay?"

I shook my head. A giant, voluminous sniffle. "Not really," I said. "I'm all alone here." Roommate flicked on her television, as if to contradict me. "I haven't seen the baby. They haven't brought her to see me, yet. I don't even know if she's okay." Leo was running water.

"I'm sure she's fine," he said. "You only gave birth to her four hours ago. They're probably just expecting you to get a little rest. Visiting hours don't start until nine."

"I can't sleep," I said. "Everything hurts. I can barely move." God, I was whiny. I knew three-year-olds who weren't this whiny. I couldn't help it. "I just want to see her. I want you to be here."

"Well, I'm coming, okay?" he said. "I'm getting showered, and I'll stop and get you some breakfast on my way so you don't have to eat hospital food. I'll be there waiting when they open that door at nine o'clock, I promise. Will you be okay until I get there?"

"Sure." I nodded.

"Okay."

"It's just not what I expected," I tried to explain. "To wake up alone here, in this room. It doesn't seem right that we're finally a family, our first morning as a family. And none of us are together. And everything hurts. My body . . ."

I sniffed again, and there were more tears. Ugh—more tears!

"I know," Leo said. "But it's going to be okay, right? I'll be there before you know it. And they'll bring that baby in any minute, you'll see."

"Okay," I whispered.

I guess that's when I started to hate myself a little bit—that was the beginning of it, when I hung up that phone and sat there all trembling and helpless in that hospital bed. And I don't mean *hate* hate, like the way I feel about control-top panty hose or anything. But more like a Condoleezza Rice kind of hate, like where you know she's culpable and a little bit shady, but damn, she's just so smart and full of promise. And anyway, she has plenty of time to redeem herself, doesn't she? That's how it was with me. Because I knew I was stronger than this. I was a black belt in jujutsu, for God's sake.

"Do you have any history of mental illness?" Dr. Zimmer asks.

"Not personally, but my family grows crazy like they can sell it for profit," I say.

"That's funny," she says without laughing. "You're very witty." She says it like it's a diagnosis: witty. "What kind of mental illness have you encountered in your family?"

"Oh, mostly your garden-variety types," I say. "Depression, manic depression, alcoholism. Nothing too unusual. Just ordinary crazy."

"It's interesting that someone with your substantial vocabulary would choose to use the word *crazy*," she says. "Rather than *mental illness*."

I wonder what I've said in the twelve minutes she's known me to make her think I have such a substantial vocabulary.

"Maybe that word just makes it feel more like fun," I say. "Less terrifying."

She watches my face while I talk, looking for symptoms, probably. A tic or a tremor.

"Like a carnival," I offer. "Crazy!" With jazz-hands.

"Hmm." She nods.

I try watching her face, too, but I'm distracted by her puffy, frizzy halo of gray brown hair.

"So what does that word mean to you?" she asks. "Crazy?"

She scribbles something down on her notepad without ever taking her eyes off my face. It's unnerving, like being dissected without anesthesia.

"What, like a definition?" I say.

"Well, just your impressions."

I wipe my hand across my mouth, and then take it down again, in case that gesture has some kind of latent crazy in it.

"I guess, my strongest impressions of crazy are my memories of my grandmother," I say. It feels like a powerful admission and/ or betrayal, but Dr. Zimmer only nods.

"What was her diagnosis?" she asks.

"I don't know," I say. "I'm not sure she was ever diagnosed—it was the 1950s. But she was in and out of institutions most of her adult life. She had all kinds of electroshock therapy and stuff. But mostly, I think she was just mean. She didn't know how to love her kids."

"How many children?"

"Four. My dad was the oldest."

Dr. Zimmer writes the number 4 in her notebook.

"Do you have any children, Majella?"

"Yes."

"How many?"

"Just one."

"How old?"

"Three weeks."

"Aha." She stops writing, and closes her notebook, as if she's just cracked the case, and there's no need for any further investigation. She leans back in her chair and folds her hands in her lap. "You have a tiny baby at home?"

"Yes."

"And you're suddenly worried about your crazy grandmother who didn't love her kids?"

I nod. Why does this make me feel guilty, like I've duped her? "But it's really not that simple," I insist.

Dr. Zimmer has twisted in her red leather chair to open a low drawer in her built-in filing cabinets. She flips through the files and pulls out a single sheet. It's a checklist, and she hands it to me. I don't want to take it from her, but it would be rude not to. I take it, but don't look at it.

"Are you experiencing any of these symptoms?" she asks, gesturing to the page in my hand.

I'm suddenly completely, unreasonably enraged, like an angry teenager. I don't want to look at a goddamned checklist. I take a deep breath, and close my eyes for a moment. I have to read it like a grown-up. I open my eyes and look at the paper:

Do you feel sad or low? Are you more tired than usual? Do little things upset or annoy you? Do you have trouble concentrating or making decisions? Do you feel like you have no one to talk to? Do you feel numb or disconnected from your baby? Do you feel scared that something bad might happen?

I don't mean to, but I roll my eyes.

"Why are you rolling your eyes?" she asks.

I want to punch Dr. Zimmer in the face, but I refrain, which feels like a noteworthy triumph, even though I've never punched anyone in the face in my entire life. I haven't even considered it. I'm not a face-puncher. If you gave me a thousand dollars to punch someone in the face, I'm not sure I could do it. Unless that person was Dr. Zimmer.

"Because this isn't what I'm here for!" I say instead, struggling to keep my voice at an acceptable volume. "Of course I'm more tired than usual. Of course every little thing upsets me. I haven't had a good night's sleep since my second trimester."

Dr. Zimmer has finally stopped staring at me, and is scribbling furiously on her notepad. I look back at the inane checklist. *"Do you feel scared that something bad might happen?"* I read aloud. "Are you kidding me? Show me a new mother who doesn't stand over her baby's crib for hours a day, just willing that kid to keep breathing. Of course I'm scared that something bad will happen. I imagine a thousand different deaths a day for my daughter. I'm obsessed with mortality, that she is growing older, even now." My voice is rising in pitch. I can hear the hysteria creeping in. "She will grow up and die, my baby will die. We will all die. I'm a hormone freak show, I'm obsessed with death. But this is not why I'm here!"

I'm clutching the checklist in my hand and shaking it at her. I tear it in two, crumple the halves together into a ball. I love the crashing loudness of the paper destruction, but my tirade has exhausted me, and I'm spent. Now that it's totally quiet in the breathless room and I'm grasping the ruined paper ball in my fist, I begin to feel embarrassed. I lean back against the couch and shake my head.

"I'm sorry," I say. I feel unhinged, completely deranged. I didn't even know that about myself until I heard it coming out of mouth—about being obsessed with mortality. But it's true. It's all I think about since Emma was born—how my life is whizzing by, and soon I'll be gone. But Dr. Zimmer just waves her hand like it's a wand, and it will banish whatever badness has come into the room. My teenage self will retreat, and I will be restored to adulthood because she bids it so. She folds her notebook closed and tucks it into her lap, leans toward me.

"You're obviously deeply frustrated," she says.

Man, she is *astute.* I bite my lip.

"Maybe this was a mistake," I say.

"Maybe it was," she concedes. I wonder if she'll ask me to leave now. "But you'll never know unless you stay and give it a chance. I won't condescend to you, or make any assumptions. We can just talk."

I stuff the ball of paper down in between the couch cushions. "Okay," I say.

She nods. "So let's just forget about the checklist."

"Yes, let's."

The ferns on the window ledge behind her are waving slightly in the draft from the air-conditioning vent overhead, and so is Dr. Zimmer's hair-halo.

"It's just. It's not postpartum depression," I say. "There's more to it than that."

"Okay," she says. "Like what?"

I take a deep breath. "I just feel totally lost. Like I don't know who I am anymore. I've never felt this way. I've always been to-tally grounded and ambitious. I've always had a very strong sense of myself."

Dr. Zimmer looks completely unintrigued.

"And—" I hesitate. There's so much I don't want to tell her. I guess those are probably the things it's most important to con-fess. "I've started to hear things."

She perks up. "What kinds of things?"

"Crunching."

"Crunching?"

"Yeah, crunching," I say. "Crrrrrk, crrrrrrk, crrrrrrk. At night, when I'm in bed, I hear it. At first I thought it was coming from the attic, but then it just seems to come from all around. Like it's coming from inside my head."

"Couldn't there be some logical explanation?" she asks.

"Like a tumor?"

Dr. Zimmer frowns. "I was thinking more along the lines of a squirrel in the attic."

"We've checked and checked," I say. "There's nothing up there. And my husband doesn't hear it, even when I wake him up. And it's so *real*. It's loud."

"Okay." Dr. Zimmer nods. "Any voices?"

"No." I shudder. I'd never even thought of that. "No, thank God."

"Okay, what else?" she asks.

Isn't that enough?

"I don't know, I just find myself doing things and saying things that are insane. I can't seem to control myself. Like what just happened here, that outburst? That checklist made me so damned angry. I'm not usually like that. Or I didn't used to be."

She waits for me to continue. She knows there's something more coming—it feels like I'm in a confessional and I'm about to go for it. It's that awful swelling moment of terrified shame before you admit your lusty buffoonery to the shocked and kindly priest.

"Last week I told someone that the baby died," I whisper.

It's the same whisper I use when Emma's sleeping and I don't want to wake her, a hope of not being heard. I can't meet her eye now. I'm too ashamed to look up, but I imagine I hear something like empathy in her one-syllable response.

"Oh."

At home, the baby monitor is propped against the window frame, and I'm padding around the attic in my fluffiest (quietest) socks, careful not to wake Emma, who's napping in the nursery below. The window is thick with grime, but that's no match for the hard, gushing light of a September afternoon. I'm sending up rockets of dust through the sunbeams, and trying hard to avoid sneezing. Three weeks after I gave birth, my incision is still prone to frequent spasms of icy pain. Right after we bought this house, I started cleaning out the attic, but then I got too pregnant to move, and I abandoned it half-finished. I still have dreams of making it lovely, maybe a playroom for Emma, or a quiet reading nook. But in the meantime, it's a mess, filled with semiorganized piles of junk. In one pile, clothes. In another, old newspapers, journals, and scrapbooks. In a third, rusty things: a birdcage, an old-fashioned bellows, a manual typewriter with a missing *L*. I feel like this is the pile for me.

If there is a squirrel living here in this attic, tormenting me with his elusive crunching noises, making me think I'm going crazy, I will find him. I will make him pay. I look around at the stacks of stuff. It's like a squirrel's paradise. He could be anywhere. There is a heap of old handbags nearby, and I nudge it uncertainly with my toe. Nothing scurries out from beneath it. There is no sound of crunching. The steamer trunk stands alone near the window and the diagonal light cuts across it, slicing it into shadows. Could there be a nest inside? Of course not. There's no squirrel door. But I cover my nose from the pending dust cloud, and open the sticky lid anyway. Inside, the stale scent of mothballs, some long brocade skirts, and two woolen coats. I lift the items out one at a time to throw them on the clothing pile. A small clothbound book must have been stitched into the lining of one of the coats, because there's a gap there, just at the hem, where the threads are worn brittle and loose, and the diary just slides out from between the folds of fabric. It comes to a rest on the floorboards, in a small puff of dust beside my filthy, fluffy socks.

In this moment, I am pierced with foreboding: goose bumps, a cold breath across my neck. There is a damp, quiet *presence* in the hushed and sun-clogged room. I can feel a distant suffering, before I even bend down slowly to retrieve the battered book, before I open it to its first fragile, yellowed page, before I see or understand the significance of the name emblazoned in mad, familiar handwriting fourteen times across the inside cover: Ginny Doyle. Ginny Doyle. Ginny Doyle.

There are all different kinds of crazy, but mostly I think it's ancestral. Sometimes you can even trace it back along the dead branches of your family tree; you can find *evidence* in family anecdotes or documents. A sepia-stained photograph. A diary. You might think you've escaped its reach—you might think you're okay. Because it can lie dormant like a tumor, until some gentle, private trauma pushes it loose inside you.

Chapter Two

IRELAND, SEPTEMBER 1846

Ginny was on her hands and knees at the edge of the potato pit, staring in. Moisture seeped up from the soil and stained damp circles onto the knees of her petticoat. Her fingernails were caked with black earth, and a stink of rot saturated the air. She covered her nose with one hand to keep from retching. In the chilly dampness, her breath came out from behind her hand in puffy white blooms.

"Mammy, I thought we weren't supposed to open the pit again until spring, only as we needed them." Her daughter Maire was beside her, talking in her granny voice. "Sure, we only pulled these up last week, and we still have loads in the shed. Shouldn't we leave them covered?"

Ginny looked across the pit to where Raymond was digging on the other side. She tried to catch his eye, but he wouldn't look at her; he was staring into the opened ground.

"Maire, you're eleven going on seventy-three," he said to their worried daughter without looking up.

"But isn't that right, Daddy?" she said. "The air isn't supposed to get at them."

"Yeah, that's right," he said. "Usually, Maire."

"But not this time?" Now it was Michael talking, jumping at the chance to prove his big sister wrong.

"No, not this time, son."

"Why not?" Maire asked.

Raymond finally looked up at Ginny with his deep brown, half-moon eyes. The first time she'd met him, she'd been caught by those eyes, by the beautiful curl of them, the way he looked like he was always dreaming. But now she could see only naked fear in his face. She hoped Maire wouldn't notice.

"What's wrong, Daddy?" their daughter said.

Ginny shook her head at him. He was a good man, funny and handsome, but he never was much good at pretending, even for the sake of the children. Ginny smiled at her daughter.

"Never you worry," she said to Maire. "Your father and I will sort it out."

"Sort what out?" she said.

"Never mind," Ginny said, standing up, brushing the dark clumps of earth from her hands. "Take Michael and your sisters inside for a few minutes. Let Mammy and Daddy have a chat."

Maire twisted on her feet but didn't go. Her long, fair hair was stringing across her face in the late-morning wind, and her mouth was screwed up with worry. Her face was bright and clear, with only a dusting of freckles across the bridge of her nose.

"Go on, love," Raymond said softly.

Maire's shoulders drooped, but she grabbed Michael by the hand, and then she turned and trudged toward the door, calling for her sisters to follow. Maggie went running, but Poppy was still squealing in the hazy fields, flinging her arms out to her sides while she spun in circles.

"Come on, Poppy!" Maire called again. "Inside!"

Poppy stopped spinning, but toppled over, laughing. Then she stood, and ran dizzily after the others, her moppy golden curls bouncing against the back of her neck. Ginny winced, watching her baby run, thinking she might zigzag into the doorjamb, but Poppy corrected her course and disappeared inside with the others.

"How bad on that side?" Raymond asked without looking up.

Ginny shivered and looked down at the hole by her feet, where she'd dug into the fresh pit to check the potatoes from the early harvest. They'd dug them up a few weeks premature, at the first sign of blight in the fields, hoping to save them. Even as they'd pulled them out from under their wasted stalks, a good portion of them had already turned to slime, black and spongy in their beds with an awful gag of an odor to them. But they'd managed to save and store more than half, and they'd been living the weeks since on hope.

This morning when they opened the pit, they found a horrid, stinking, squelchy mess. Those salvaged earlies were decaying altogether.

"Any savers?" Raymond asked.

Ginny shook her head, kicked some dirt back over the hole. "Maybe three out of ten if we're lucky," she said. "What about over there? Anything?" Raymond scratched the back of his neck, and then folded his arms in front of him.

"Maybe a few, Ginny," he said. He walked the rim of the pit, and put his arm around her shoulders.

She tried to breathe deeply, to refute the tears that were coming. She looked toward the cottage door and felt the fear clawing up the inside of her throat like a monster. Raymond put both arms around his wife, and she collapsed her forehead against his shoulder.

"We'll manage," he said.

"Gale day is coming, Ray," she said. "Rent will be due."

He nodded his head.

"Thanks be to God, the oat harvest looks to be in strong condition, at least," he said.

"Touch wood," Ginny answered.

"It's the heartiest crop of oats I ever did see," Ray said.

"Isn't it strange, to have the oats that thick and the blight won't touch them," Ginny added, "when the potatoes are all in ruin?"

On a good year, they wouldn't save but a small stock of oats for their family—they sold nearly all of them, and the pig, to pay the rent. They lived all the time on potatoes, with the odd turnip or cabbage from the kitchen garden, a few eggs from the hens. They were better off than most of their neighbors because they had the old cow for milk. But she wouldn't last, not now. "That's all our food for the next six months," Ginny whispered, looking out over their scalped field. "Gone." She snapped her fingers. There were tears in her eyes, she couldn't help it.

Ray squinted off into the foggy damp. "We haven't sold them oats yet, Ginny. We have the pig, still, and a decent crop of turnips and cabbage besides."

"And we owe most of that to Packet," she said. "You know what'll happen if we don't pay."

Every year on the gale days, there was always a family or two who couldn't manage the rent for whatever reason, whatever hardship had befallen them. Packet took no pity on those people. His agents and the constables would be dispatched to drag whole families out of their homes. Those men would tumble the cabins down into the road before the very eyes of their inhabitants, never mind the wailing of the women, or the wild panic of the screeching babbies. A rope would be fixed to the roof beam, and the whole house just tumbled down in front of them, until all that was left was a mess of stone and thatch, a big, choking hot cloud of dust. The neighbors would be warned against taking the family in, and the poor wretches would be destitute then. They would take out to the roads in misery. Ginny shook her head.

"Whatever happens, we've got to pay."

Ray nodded. "You're right. If we're going to be hungry, we may at least be hungry with a roof over our heads."

The stink from the pratie pit was so sharp they could taste it, bitter in the backs of their throats.

"We'll get a good price for the oats," Ray reasoned. "We can keep a decent stash back from that."

"We can sell the cow," Ginny said. "We'll manage without milk for the winter."

"We'll get by," Ray said.

They tried to believe each other.

The children loved going into Westport town. They never minded what reason, or the long walk. Poppy, Maggie, and Michael skipped on ahead, flailing their loose, warm baby limbs around them. But Maire kept solemn watch beside her parents. Ray held Ginny's hand and tried to quell her fear, so Maire wouldn't sniff it out. You couldn't hide anything from their eldest daughter— if you wanted her to believe something, you had to believe it yourself.

Ginny squeezed Ray's hand, and started talking for a distraction. "Michael's getting a bit big for the petticoat."

The boys usually wore them only until they were eight or

nine years of age. Michael was on the small side for his age, but even so, his lean legs were beginning to stretch out beneath the skirts. He looked more like his father every day, the only one of the children who'd inherited Ray's half-moon eyes.

"I reckon that's right," Ray said, watching their son on the road ahead.

"He's nearly ten now. Time for some knee breeches and a coat and vest, like a proper little man."

"He needs a hat, too, Mammy," Maire said.

"He does," Ginny agreed. "But sure, he'll be grand in that getup for now anyway. Won't do him the bit of harm."

The roads were eerily quiet, only for the sound of their gathered footsteps falling against the packed dirt of the road, and the high voices of the children in the distance. It was a mild, clammy day, and the rain wasn't falling, but it was hanging in the air so you had to walk through it nonetheless. The ends of Ginny's hair were damp when she tucked them in under her bonnet. She looked out from under its brim at the fields on the sides of the road, usually a heavy, bloated green at this time of year, just ready for harvest. Now they were a cankerous, weeping brown, and the stink of blight was so strong you could nearly see it hovering over the land. The farms they passed felt abandoned of their food and people, the fields empty of living things. On a stile in the distance, a lone figure sat up, curled over himself, with his head in his hands. Ginny called the children back to her, and they turned and skipped toward their parents, till they all approached the sitting figure together. It wasn't until they were upon him that they recognized him.

"Well." Ray stepped out away from his family, extending his hand. "James Madigan. How're you keeping?"

The man lifted his head from his knees and looked up wild-eyed at Ray. They knew him well—he was a young enough fella, with a family of his own, but the way his scraggly hair stood out from his head put the weight of years on him. His knee breeches were worn soft, and patched. His coat was frayed about the cuffs and collar. He was unshaved, and he kneaded the knuckles of one hand with the other. Ray's hand was just hovering there in the air, until finally James took it in his own.

"Sorry, sorry there, Ray, I nearly didn't see you there," he said.

Maire snapped a look at her mother, but said nothing.

"Are you right there, James? You look awful shook," Ray said to him.

James's eyes fled from Ray's face to Ginny's, and then, in turns, to the children. He opened his mouth, but made no reply. He rocked himself a small bit, turned then to look back over his shoulder, to his own decimated field. And then his hands were in against his scalp, pulling at his hair, and the tears stood in his eyes as plain as day. Ginny looked down at her feet, to give him a moment. Poppy was pawing at Maire's skirt, and Maggie and Michael were inspecting a grasshopper who'd emerged from a gap in the wall.

"It's all gone." James's voice was a choked whisper.

"Ah, here," Ray said, but James was shaking his head, still kneading his knuckles with his fingers. His eyes were pink and rheumy.

"No," he said. "There's nothing for it. When gale day comes, we'll have nothing to give Packet. He'll throw us out."

"Ah, James," Ray said. "Surely there's something, something you could sell? Or maybe Packet will give you credit until the spring rents?"

"Ha!" James spat into the road. "You'd sooner get credit from the devil himself."

Ray drew up his hand and scratched his chin. "Things being

what they are now, surely the landlords might compromise. They can't drive the whole population into destitution. They have to see reason."

But despite these hopeful words, a look of desperate resignation passed between the two men. They knew the absentee landlords over in London didn't care about the natives, so long as their plum Irish land continued to yield hearty profits, so long as the grains and cattle they extorted from Ireland continued to fetch their English fortunes.

"He'll take my house." James Madigan's miserable voice climbed in pitch while he talked. "That blaggard Packet will turn my family out into the roads. We will starve. My hand to God, my children will starve!"

Maire drew in a sharp breath, and Ginny turned to her, steered her over toward Maggie and the grasshopper.

"Never worry, love," she said to her daughter.

"Never worry?" Maire looked at her mother like she was mad. "We're well past that, Mammy." Maire lifted her chin, just enough to remind Ginny that there was no baby fat left there. She was slimming down in her jaw and her cheeks, and the lashes grew longer and softer over her pale blue eyes. Soon she would be a young lady.

"All right, so." Ginny nodded at her.

"Look, Poppy," Maire said then, crouching down to her little sisters. "See the way its back legs are bent, for jumping?"

Raymond wasn't long talking to their neighbor, the men's heads bent toward each other, Ray with his hand on James's shoulder, James with his arms folded gravely across his chest. Ginny talked loudly to the children, hoping they wouldn't hear the notes of hysteria in the poor man's voice. He slipped inside the stile and was staggering off through his bald field when Ray returned. They walked on to Westport town.

"The poor man sowed no oats this year," Ray said quietly when the children were out of earshot.

Ginny could only gasp in response.

"They're in a bad way, Ginny. It's the road, for them." He shook his head. "God save them."

"You don't think Packet will postpone the rent for them, just this once? Give them a pass until spring?"

Ray didn't even bother answering; he didn't need to. He just looked at Ginny with one eyebrow arched.

The road before them wound down through the fields, and then pitched itself steeply uphill again as it narrowed into the town. The children dropped back and gathered in around Ray and Ginny as they entered the streets. There was a bustle in Westport, people hurrying all around, some with a horse and trap, or a donkey, but mostly on foot. Poppy was tired from the walk, so Ginny lifted the child onto her hip, and carried her as they crossed over the Carrowbeg River onto Bridge Street.

In town, the noise of the people was frantic, as if all their voices had been drawn out of the surrounding farms and fields with a thirsty dropper, and then unleashed like a wild thing into the clamoring streets. The urgent volume pressed in and gave Ginny a fright. She drew in against a shop wall to collect herself for a moment. People streamed past in frenzied clusters and her red petticoat flittered on the passing breeze. She grabbed Maggie by the hand. Raymond was talking, but in the din, Ginny couldn't make him out.

"What doesn't look good, Daddy?" Maire answered him.

"By God, Maire, would you ever stop with the bloody questions!" he snapped, loud enough for Ginny to hear over everything. "Just for once, and be quiet. Let me think."

Maire looked at her mother for comfort, but Ginny only shook her head.

"Why don't you take Michael and go look at the ducks," she said to her daughter. "Go on. We'll meet you on the mall, after."

"I want to go, too, Mammy!" Maggie squealed.

"No, love, you stay with us."

"But, Mammy!"

"You're too small, *mo chuisle.*"

"I love the ducks!"

"We'll see them after."

Maire and Michael had already slipped off into the crowd. Maggie sulked, so Ginny had to rightly drag her down the street toward the open market. Two-and-a-half-year-old Poppy had her warm body wrapped around Ginny, her legs clamped tight around her mother's waist, and her mop of goldy curls tickling her mother's chin. Ginny kissed the top of her head. She was a pretty child, with big, reverent brown eyes—her only reverent feature, perhaps. Her big sister tugged and leaned from Ginny's arm.

"Maggie, don't pull on me," Ginny said, and the child turned to scowl at her mother. For an instant, a certain twist of expression, Maggie looked exactly like Ginny: the black hair and vivid blue eyes, the arched brows and full lips. But it was something more than that. A trick of God's magic, the way a mother can trace herself sometimes, beneath the skin of her children.

All around them, animals bleated in their pens, and men's voices competed over one another in their haggling. Ginny could smell the animals, the manure underfoot, the press of men's bodies, the sweetness of burning tobacco, and then behind all that, out beyond the streets in every inch of soil surrounding Westport, that awful, sharp and curdling rot. On a crowded corner, an old fella sat playing the fiddle, and a small gathering of children stood quietly staring at him. Maggie tugged at Ginny's arm and pointed.

"Isn't he lovely, Mammy? How does he do that?"

There was another tug then, at her waistband, and it was Michael. Himself and Maire were back already.

"I thought you were going to wait for us on the mall," Ginny said.

"Ducks are gone," Michael announced.

Maggie's blue eyes grew wide.

"That's odd," Ginny said quietly.

"But the ducks are always there, Mammy," Maggie said, with an edge of worry in her voice. "Where've they got to?"

It was true that there were usually ducks in that walled stretch of the Carrowbeg—almost always. The children loved to quack and waddle after them.

"I don't know, love," Ginny said. "Maybe they're off at a duck meeting, up at Westport House."

Michael grinned. "Like a quacker council?"

Ginny laughed. "Yes, just like that."

Raymond wasn't listening. He approached one of the merchants, John McCann, who was known for doing a stiff trade with the English ships. He always offered a fair price to the locals. There was a small crowd of men around him already, some talking, some only leaning in, listening. Ginny pulled in as close as she could, and strained to listen, too.

"It's no skin off my nose if you don't want to sell the pig for that price, if you want to hang on a bit," McCann was saying to a lean, whiskered man. "But I'd hide him fast if I was you, before your hungry neighbors find him."

The gathered men laughed, but the whiskered fella only waved an exasperated hand at McCann, and turned on his heel to go. The man pushed past Ginny through the crowd, and McCann called out after him. "You watch, that pig will go the way of the ducks!"

On the mall, there was a young fella, only a child really, no more than maybe fifteen years of age, sat on a bench reading out of the newspaper to a group of stern-faced listeners. Maggie and Poppy wheeled over to the canal wall to peer over at the missing ducks. Indeed, the gray and swift-flowing water beyond was empty of them. Michael stood between his sisters, pointing out the places where the ducks would usually be mucking about.

"I told you," he said. "They're *disappeared*."

Maire stood beside Ray and crowded in among the others, who jostled to hear the young lad reading out of the paper in his unfaltering voice. He had it spread open across his knees like a blanket, and his voice rang out clear enough, despite the way he hunched over to squint at the words.

"'Serious food riots in Dungarvan led to the pillaging of a baker's shop in the town center. The baker fled, and was uninjured. Authorities now fear that the nationwide devastation of the potato crop will be permanent and absolute, in all provinces of the country. Indeed, no corner of Ireland appears to have escaped the ravages of this year's annihilation.'" The boy looked up from his paper and eyed the growing crowd nervously.

"Go on, son!" someone encouraged him from the back.

"Read it out, child!" an old woman added.

Maire was staring at him, her eyes as wide as the sun. The young man rearranged his grip on the paper and cleared his throat.

"*Panic reigns in Ireland,*" he called out, and then he closed it, folded it up on his knee.

"What else does it say?" a man from the back of the crowd urged him.

The boy shrugged, his eyes no longer flicking over the words on the page. "More of the same," he answered quietly, standing up from the bench and glancing back down at the folded paper.

"The Queen is sending men of science to analyze the extent of the destruction."

"God save the Queen!" a lone voice shouted, and this sentiment was met by a round of hissing and jeering.

"Devil take the Queen!" someone else shouted, and then everyone cheered.

"She's not our Queen!"

The crowd was growing rowdy.

"God save us," said an old woman beside Ginny.

"Sure it was God Himself that did this," said another old woman, her companion. Their arms were linked through each other's at the elbow. Perhaps they were sisters. They were dressed like townies, no muck of the roads on their feet. They sighed heavily together, almost like one beast. "Divine Providence has finally seen fit to punish our wastefulness. 'Twas a sin, the way we'd that many praties in the good years, the farmers were using them to manure the fields."

The other old woman clicked her tongue. "We never took any heed when times were good."

They turned as one and tottered off down the mall, shaking their heads and tutting at each other. The lad with the paper started to push his way out through the crowd, but a young mother with an infant at her breast pressed her hand against his arm.

"But what are we to do?" she asked. Her eyes were pleading all over the young lad's face. "What good are these *men of science*? Will they help us?"

He shook his head. "I don't know, missus."

"But surely there must be something to be done." Her voice was rising in pitch, and she tightened her grip on the boy's arm. "A lad of good learning like yourself must know. There has to be an answer coming, please God."

The young lad bit a sharp breath into his lungs and wrenched his arm back from the desperate young mother. "I'm just like the rest of ye," he insisted. "I don't know anything!"

The woman began to wail. "Winter is coming, God help us! Merciful God save us!"

The boy slipped away as quick as he could through the scattering crowd. People were drawing away from the young mother, wary of her shot nerves and her swift panic. There was a contagion to that kind of madness that no one could afford. The cracked and hollow sound of her cries followed the Doyle family as they crossed back over the Carrowbeg River, and found their road home.

Maire herded the other children in front of her as they walked, and only looked back at her parents now and again. Ginny carried Poppy, and she and Ray spoke to each other in fits and starts. He was mostly deep in thought.

"We'll slaughter the hog that's left," Ray said as they walked. "Never mind the rent, we'll slaughter the hog."

"Never mind the rent, Ray, have you lost the plot?"

He shook his head and his mouth made a small twitch, but he didn't answer.

"That hog is going to Packet," Ginny said. "No question about it. I'll not give him an excuse to throw us out into the roads. Anyway, we've the cabbage and turnips, and we still have the three hens, the eggs from them. We still have the cow."

In truth, the hog wasn't in great shape—he was hungry, too. But regardless, he was owed to Packet; he was rent, and there was nothing to be done about that. Any other food was only supplemental, little things Ginny grew in the kitchen garden just for the odd bit of variation. It was a paltry inventory, and it would never be enough to survive on. How would they even feed those hens?

Ginny and Ray reared up their children on potatoes, as

everyone did—and those children were fit and pudgy off them. Look at them there in the road ahead: their strong, loose bodies, their glowing skin. Their free little hands like birds, flitting and soaring. Michael poking Maggie in the ribs, and she lunging back, like fencers at play. They were the picture of grace, those small, nourished people with their bright eyes. Even after a whole year of slim crop.

The Doyles had never really been troubled before, even when times were bad; they'd managed to escape the worst of the blight until this. Ginny thought of their two scarce mounds of saved potatoes at home. They were catastrophic, those heaps. Maggie started to fall back from Michael and Maire, exhausted from the long walk, and Ray hoisted her onto his shoulders. She tucked her feet into his armpits.

"How come you get so tired, missus?" Ray asked his little daughter.

"Because I'm only five, Daddy, and my wee legs are only small," she said.

"Lazy, that's what you are."

"I'm not, Daddy. I have to work twice as hard as you. Even harder. For every step of yours, I take three. Do you know what that means?"

"What?"

"I've walked ten times farther than you today. I walked all the way to Dublin."

"Is that so?"

"Yep."

"And did you see the castle?"

"I did."

"That's my girl."

Maggie stuck her fingers into Ray's ears and wiggled them around.

"I'VE GONE DEAF!" he yelled.

Poppy giggled over at them. "You're not, Daddy—it's Maggie's fingers!" she said.

Except for the solid knot of dread that had settled somewhere near the top of Ginny's throat, things seemed almost normal.

After the children went to sleep, Raymond and Ginny left the lantern burning and went out into the dark night. There was a smattering of stars smeared across the blackened sky, and a cold wind rattled through the ruined fields. She pulled her shawl tighter around her shoulders and crossed it over itself, tucking it into her waistband in front. They turned their backs to the cottage and stepped out together among the crunching stalks. Ray kept his arm around her, and she floated her opened palm above the withered brown crop. He hadn't said much all afternoon, and she wondered if his heart felt as tight as hers. It was a new moon, and well dark in the fields. Only the faintest glow in the western sky whispered the lamps and hearth fires of Westport town. She couldn't see his face. They were quiet for a time, and she was the first one to speak.

"It won't be enough." She said the words for both of them. "The eggs, the cabbage. It's only September, Ray."

She heard him cracking some of the potato stalks next to her. He crinkled them in his palm and took a sniff, then dusted his hands off. Maybe he hoped, if he kept checking, he might find something different.

"The next harvest is June at soonest," he said, thinking out loud.

She stopped walking and turned to look in his direction. He already knew, they both knew. There was a queer, silvery fog like a veil over the land, even in the dark, and that blanket of fog kept the stink of rot tamped down beneath it.

"Please God, let the sun come tomorrow," she said, "and burn all this dankness away."

"Amen to that," Ray whispered. His hand found hers in the darkness, and they avoided it for another minute—the horrible thing they had to say to each other. She was the one, in the end.

"We'll have to go, Raymond." Her voice was like the rattle of those lifeless stalks in the stiff night breeze.

"We can't afford passage for six," he said.

"No," she admitted.

"So one of us will have to go. Get work and send money back," he said.

There was just enough light from the cottage to outline the shape of his face. She reached out to feel the stubble on his chin and cheek, sticky beneath her fingertips. He leaned in to kiss her, and she locked him into her arms, his face buried in her neck. They stayed like that for a long time.

"I'll go," he said, and he pulled away, straightened himself up. He glanced back to the cottage, and Maire was standing tall in the open doorway, watching them. She was backlit by the warmth of the lamplight. He nodded, tucked his lips inside his mouth. "We're lucky, Kevin is gone this two years. Maybe he can help me find work in New York—he's already set up. Lots of folks have no brother, no family over there, nobody to go to."

"Most folks couldn't even manage the price of a ticket," Ginny said.

But Raymond and Ginny could. They could pay the rent, buy a single steerage ticket, and then still have food enough—maybe—to keep the children until Ray found work beyond and started sending money back. Ginny clamped her arms together in front of her, but it was no use—there was an emptiness already, howling up from inside her. She couldn't remember how to live without Raymond. Twelve years they'd been married—thirteen, nearly. She could feel his absence already, like some sacred part of herself had been stripped savagely away. He leaned into her, bumped shoulders and foreheads with her, as if to remind her that he was still here. She could hear him smile, the way his lips framed his beautiful teeth.

"It's going to be all right, Ginny," he said, really trying. "We'll get through it." He squeezed her shoulders.

She sniffed, and slapped her two cheeks lightly with her hands, willing color into them. Willing faith. How many young Irish lads had gone out before Ray and crossed that ugly ocean to America? How many of them had ever come back? She wanted to fling herself into his arms and sob. She wanted to plead with him not to go. She wanted to scream and cry, and batter his chest with her fists. But there's never any use in despair when you're a mother; it's a fruitless endeavor entirely. Instead, she breathed. She looked back at the cottage again, but Maire had disappeared inside.

"We will, we'll get through it," she said, with such a surprising degree of strength in her voice that she nearly believed it herself. She ventured on. "The passage takes ten weeks or thereabouts." She counted out the time in her head, as if Ray leaving Ireland, leaving her and their babbies, were just some tricky sort of mathematics.

He beat her to it. "Say February," he said. "March at the latest, I should be able to get some money back over by then. And the turnips and that should keep you ticking over until then."

She nodded.

"We could slaughter the cow instead of selling her," he said. "It's meant to be a cold winter, so you might be able to keep the meat."

"A cold winter," Ginny repeated.

They were talking about weather.

"Listen to me," Raymond said. "I don't care what it takes. I don't care how many people have trod this path before us. That ocean goes two ways. Do you hear me? I will be back."

She closed her eyes and shook her head. "Raymond . . ."

"I will be back for you," he said again. "No American wake for this ould paddy. No sir, I will be back."

"You can't . . ." But he interrupted her again.

"If I have to *swim* it," he said, and then he took her chin in his hand, like she was a child. "Wifey."

Her eyes found his in the dark.

"I will not be parted from you," he said.

And in that singular moment, there was no question in her mind or her faith. She believed him. Yes.

"I believe you."

And then there was the slightest welling of grateful tears hidden in the corners of his eyes, and she could feel them, even if it was too dark to see them.

"Raymond Doyle, if you cry right now, I swear I will follow you to America just to divorce you. I hear a girl can divorce her fella no problem, over beyond."

His laughter in those last days was miraculous, a kind of nourishment in itself.

Chapter Three

I press a button, and my daughter's image pops up on the tiny monitor screen in grainy black and white. She's lying on her back, with her two fists up over her head like she's celebrating some clandestine victory. At three weeks old, I feel like Emma could already have a life that's so separate from mine, so covert and mysterious, that she could in fact be celebrating a secret triumph—something she'll never tell me about. I know more about her, and less about her, than anyone else I've ever known. I feel like my own heart and brain and all my vital organs are jammed inside those two tiny fists of hers. I turn the volume way up, until I can hear her breathing.

I walk out the front door, careful not to let the screen bang behind me. I sit on the top step, where the brick is warm despite the sloping shade of the afternoon. I try several different angles before I find a spot where the monitor can sit without static.

Sometimes I enjoy the interference—I can pick up two different families when I change to channel B or C.

The B family is amazingly jolly, and they speak to their child with the enthusiasm of Elmo, despite the guttural tones of a language I can't place. Something Balkan, maybe. The image on channel B is just a close-up shot of the crib, and occasionally the dark-haired, smiling little baby who seems rarely to sleep there. There is a lot of clapping and squealing and all-purpose merriment on channel B, and I often try to guess which nearby house they live in. I feel like they should have rainbows and unicorns on their mailbox, but I don't see a single neighbor who could even fake the kind of delight I hear on channel B.

Channel C is much more sordid, like a story on *Dateline*. There are four cribs on channel C, and I haven't been able to discern, yet, if there are really four babies (are they selling them on the black market?), or if it's just twins and a mirror. I rarely hear any voices at all on channel C—only crying, footsteps, sighing, toilets flushing, a loud television in the background. Those two or four babies spend an awful lot of time in their cribs. It's grainy and dark. You can't see much.

But channel A is where the real action is: my sleeping girl and her glorious fists. I check the volume and then stretch my legs carefully in front of me. I'm determined to spend every possible moment outside before the weather turns. The leaves are changing colors already and as the days grow shorter, the heat begins to falter as well. Soon we'll be trapped inside for months. Just me and my baby girl. Channel A.

I dial three different friends, and nobody picks up. They have jobs, lives. Finally I try my mother's number.

"Majella," she sings. "How's our grandbaby?"

"She's good," I say.

"Great!"

For a half a second, I wonder if she'll ask how I'm doing, too. Ordinarily, I wouldn't wonder; she never asks that, probably because it would require her to stop talking long enough to listen to my response. But I sorta thought me giving birth to her first grandchild might result in the occasional glimmer of curiosity about my well-being.

"Oh, I've been so busy, I'm just exhausted!" she says, and then she plows headlong into a detailed description of her week. And when I say *detailed*, I'm talking she includes how many times she pooped on Tuesday. And how many times she tried, but failed. Seriously.

I start to lean back on my elbows, but my abdomen is still too tender to stretch, so I just examine my legs in the sun while she talks. She's on to the weather now. Apparently they had some strong winds last night, and their dog, Cocoa, got so nervous she peed on the new carpet in the den. Thank God they went with the green, it really hides the dirt! I stop listening after that, and just wait for her to be finished. I take the phone away from my ear every few minutes to check on the time. Yes, I'm timing her. At about twelve and a half minutes, she takes a breath.

"All right, well, I don't want to keep you," she says.

And my mouth falls open—not from shock exactly. This isn't shocking—it's the same conversation we've been having for years. But Goddammit.

I almost explode on her. Really, I almost say: I don't care if your fucking bank teller is taking his granddaughter to the Buccaneers game this weekend. What about ME? I just had a baby over here! But I am deeply cowardly, and the words stay buried somewhere in my solar plexus. After all, it's hard enough in therapy, being honest with the woman I'm paying to be the receptacle of my deepest fears; how am I supposed to be honest with the woman who's the harbinger of them? My mouth closes slowly, like a drawbridge inching up from the moat. In the background, I can hear my father mumbling at her.

"What's that, Stu?" she says away from the phone. "Well, I don't know. Is she still keeping you up nights? Pop wants to know."

"Well yeah, Mom, she's three weeks old," I say irritably.

"You slept through the night right away," she says. "You always did, and when I would tell people, they didn't believe me! But you did. You were a great sleeper."

I yawn loudly enough for her to hear me.

"Anyway, it doesn't last forever," she says. "The sleep deprivation."

"Yeah, it's fine." Her pep talks tend to make me suicidal. "In fact we're just getting ready to head out to the market. I only called because I wanted to ask you something." I hadn't intended to ask her anything, but I need a diversion.

"Sure, what's up?" she says.

"I found this diary in the attic."

"What were you doing up there?"

"Nothing, just having a look around, and—"

"Majella, you should be taking it easy. You have your hands full enough with the new baby and your recovery, without climbing those steep stairs all the way up to the attic."

"Mom, PLEASE, stop lecturing me," I say, in the horrible, ungrateful bitch tone that I reserve only for her, a tone that's inevitable, but steeped in immediate regret. "I didn't call to ask your advice about sleep deprivation or whether or not I should be hanging around in my frigging attic!"

In my defense, I know I'm being nasty. Is self-awareness a passable defense for bitchiness? I'm *aware*.

"Oh," she says, and I can actually hear the deflation in her voice, like an untied balloon. It seeps down the phone line and into my shoulders.

"I'm sorry, Mom," I say, shaking my head, my eyes welling. "Really, I don't mean to be so cranky."

"I know, it's okay."

"I'm just so tired," I say, rubbing the heel of my hand into my eye. "And I only wanted to ask you about this diary."

"Go on," she says.

"Who was Ginny Doyle? I think it belonged to her. Was she like a great-great-grandmother or something?"

"I'm not sure. There was a Virginia Doyle somewhere in there." I can hear her drumming her fingers on something. "You know we actually considered that name for you—Virginia? There were a lot of Virginias, on my side and your dad's, too. But then we both just loved *Majella*. Did I ever tell you how we came up with *Majella*?"

"Yes, Mom." Seventeen thousand times.

"We were on our honeymoon in Montreal, and the local church we attended on the Sunday was called after St. Gerard Majella, and I just thought the name was so unusual and so pretty, I always remembered it."

"I know, Mom." I try to strangle that awful bitch-tone out of my voice, I really do. But why does she always bother asking me if I know the story, if she's just going to repeat it anyway? Why? WHY?

"I'm glad you didn't name me Virginia," I say then, because I want to say something nice to her. "But what about Ginny Doyle?"

"Yeah, I'm not sure. I'll have to check my genealogy log."

"Great, yeah, if you wouldn't mind."

"Sure thing, honey. You know I just love all that stuff. It's so interesting, all those family stories just waiting to be discovered."

My mom has been an amateur genealogist ever since my sixth-grade family tree project, and in recent years, she's gotten serious about it. She's traced certain branches of our family back to like the eighth century or something. She has this ravenous curiosity about dead people's lives. But I'm less interesting, and her other line is beeping in. She's about to drop me like a fad diet.

"Hey, is Pop still there, can I say hi?" I preempt.

"No, he just left—they're having a casino day down at the clubhouse."

My parents are taking full advantage of the programs on offer at their Floridian retirement village. They tackle the weekly events schedule like a military campaign, and she reports back with precision.

"Oh, and I have to run, too," she says, possibly tapping her watch in the Florida sunshine. "I don't want to be late for my luncheon! It's candied ham on Tuesdays!"

"Okay, Mom," I say, wondering if she knows that I can *hear* when the other line beeps in. I know she's ditching me so she can talk to somebody else instead, but I guess I can't blame her. I would ditch her, too, if there was candied ham on the line.

Sometimes, after she hangs up, I stay on the line and listen to the dial tone, and then the please-hang-up lady. Just to depress myself, really, to face the harsh buzz of my mother's absence and feel sorry for myself. But today I don't need extra self-pity—I'm full up. So I turn off the phone and stay on the front steps wishing I had a friend who lived nearby, wishing I still smoked, to give my poor nails a reprieve from my biting. I try not to cry, but the tears are jammed up tight in the back of my throat. I blink.

When neighbors walk past with their dogs or their children, I give them my hopeful smile, which, in New York, is code for *I'm demented, you should probably cross the street in case I try to speak to you.* Why can't someone just smile back? I wish we'd never bought this house from my parents. We should've stayed in Manhattan. I'm not cut out for this outer-borough life, for motherhood.

"I wish I never had a baby."

It's not true, that wish. I don't know why I said that thing out loud—it's just another symptom that I'm coming undone. I mean, it's at least ninety-three percent completely untrue. I love Emma. More than anything. I love her in a way that is so acute that it makes me physically aware of my heart beating inside me, the vessels carrying blood out to my fingers and toes, the milk swelling in my breasts. I love her so much that her breath can bring tears to my eyes. So here is my real confession: all that love? That vast and powerful, terrifying love? I don't know if it's enough. I don't know if I love her the way I'm supposed to. Because I miss my old life. A lot. My apartment, my job, my firm and reasonably sized breasts. I miss romance and coffee and television. I really miss television.

I catch up on *The Price Is Right* while Emma sleeps, because I've made the decision that there won't be any television while she's awake, which feels like enough of a sacrifice to make me a good mother-all by itself. Taking television away from an already lonely, isolated person is like robbing a tired swimmer of her life preserver. I am a martyr. I watch Drew Carey wistfully, heroically. He's good, but I long for the spaying and neutering of the Bob Barker days.

After nap time and feeding, I strap Emma into her car seat, and the car seat into the stroller. I check all the straps twice, because I have an irrational fear that the stroller will get struck by a car, and Emma will come flying out of it like a Hail Mary pass to the end zone. In fact, that is only one of *many* awful fantasies I have every day, every hour, like a freaky horror show in my mind: Emma's stroller rolling into traffic while I bend at an intersection to tie my shoe; me passing out from exhaustion while I bathe her,

Emma's little head slipping under the water, bubbles coming up; Emma pulling her blanket up over her face in the bouncy seat while I shower, unaware of her suffocating just beyond the curtain. Sometimes I even imagine that I can see a hand on the monitor, someone standing over her crib. The terror that seizes me is so paralyzing that I have to stop what I'm doing and go to her, to reassure myself that she breathes, she lives.

I check her straps again, tuck her blanket under her chin, and set off walking the streets of Queens, the graveyard borough. This is where I grew up, where I was determined to return and raise my daughter. Queens is the most solidly middle-class and residential of the five boroughs. Well, okay, of the four boroughs at least, because no one really counts Staten Island, except the people who live there. And sometimes, not even them. Queens is a place where people are civic-minded, and entirely without pretense, where the neighborhoods are proud and distinct. It's the I-don't-give-a-shit borough. It's not trying to be cool. It's not trying to be anything. It has terrific ethnic food, large, crowded parks, and decent, affordable square footage. People here have grass—not enough to own a lawn mower or anything, but still, authentic green grass that they grow in neat little squares behind their rows of brick two-family homes. My childhood here was happy and wholesome, and that's what I want for my kid.

Emma and I round the corner and pass a neighbor we don't know, who's busy sticking bat decals in her windows for Halloween. She already has a veritable gang of scarecrows stuck to her front door, and it's not even October yet. She was probably friends with my mom before the big move. She pauses in her window and waves out at us. That confirms it: crazy. I wave back and hurry on.

"The market closes at four on Thursdays," I say to Emma, reaching into my pocket to check the time on my phone. "It's already three thirty-two. Think we can make it?"

Emma stares at me.

"I can't wait until you can talk. I'll probably have to stop cursing before then."

Sometimes when you say this sort of thing out loud in front of other grown-ups, they tell you not to wish the precious babytime away, and then you have to restrain yourself from punching them in the throat. So it's best just to whisper it to Emma when no one else is around. The phone in my hand rings, and I fumble it, almost drop it. Leo.

"Hello?"

"HONEY!"

Oh my God, what is he so happy about?

"Hi."

"How are my two girls?" he says.

"Fine, we're good. We're out walking to the Amish market so I can make us a real meal tonight." We've been ordering in, gigantic fried sandwiches with waffle fries, Chinese food, and even Tex-Mex "salads" in edible bowls. Extra ranch dressing, please. My inner foodie shudders.

"Oooh, honey." I can hear him making a sort of sucking-air-through-his-teeth sound that usually indicates news he's reluctant to share.

"What?" I say.

"Yeah, it's just that I'm not gonna be able to get out of work tonight. The restaurant is slammed."

I stop walking.

"You what?" I ask.

"We have a full house, and I just don't think Mario is ready for a full dinner service without me."

"Oh."

Mario is Leo's dinner sous-chef, and he's been at the restaurant for almost two years, but according to Leo, he'll never be ready to run the kitchen alone. Leo is so busy with the business side of the restaurant that he hardly even cooks anymore, but he just can't let go of that kitchen. Real tears spring to my eyes, and my nose starts that wet, swelling feeling. It's a horrible admission, but I actually count the hours that Leo is away from the house, and that's not hyperbole. I literally count them: *four hours to go. Three hours to go. Okay, just two hours to go now, I can do this.* I'm lonely without Drew Carey for company, but when Leo's home, it's completely different. I watch him with Emma and I feel *happy*, like the decisions we made were the right ones. When he's home I don't even remember the deserted panic of these empty afternoons. It's like I have revolving brains, each one amnesiac of the other.

"I won't be too late. I'll get out of here as soon as the first wave is over, once Mario finds a good rhythm," he says. "I'm just nervous about business here now that you're not working. We're relying on the restaurant income more than ever."

I feel sick to my stomach, like a tightrope walker watching the safety net collapse. I'm not prepared for this.

"She's only three weeks old," I say. "You weren't even supposed to go back to work until she was one month, that's what we agreed. You have such a good team there now. You need to trust them more."

"But I have an even better team at home," Leo says. "You guys are doing great!"

Great? The sensitive, articulate, successful man I married . . . is he stupid? We're doing *great*?

"It's only a few hours, honey. We just can't take any risks with the restaurant now that you're not working."

If he says the words "now that you're not working" one more time, I swear I am going to walk into traffic.

"Okay?" he says.

I have to hang up the phone. I don't want to become a woman who hangs up on her husband, but there are lots of things I didn't want to become. I'll just add this to the list. Because I can't answer him. I literally can't speak. I press *end call*. I will give myself a few minutes and then phone him back. I will tell him I lost the signal, or maybe even the truth, that I momentarily lost my voice. The phone rings immediately and I send the call to voice mail. I concentrate on deep breathing and walk to the end of the block. It's a windy day, and in the graveyard across the street, the oak trees are scattering the season's first leaves among the headstones. My neck is sweating. My armpits are sweating. Emma is making a face that means she might soon begin to cry.

I bend into her stroller and tickle her cheek with my hair, because even a mama in crisis comforts her baby. That's the minimum, automatic human response. Emma's arms flail out and then she snuggles in. She is fuzzy and smells like pie, but she cries. A lot. And mostly, I still feel like that doctor just sliced me open yesterday, like I might physically split in half with one wrong twist or a significant hiccup.

At first, Leo was enormously supportive. Our second night home from the hospital, I needed his help in the shower. I felt helpless, mortified. But he opened the shower curtain brandishing a razor, and asked, "What do you need me to shave?" And the two of us laughed so hard I thought my stitches would spring loose and I would bleed out in the tub. But now his patience is beginning to run short, and yesterday, when I told him my incision was throbbing, he asked when it would stop being an incision and start being a scar.

"When I can throw sharp, heavy objects at your head without wincing," I answered.

The phone rings again, and I retrieve it from the stroller's cup holder.

"Sorry," I say evenly. "Bad signal."

"Do you need me to come home?" Leo asks.

"No, no, we'll be fine. It's just a couple of hours, right?"

"Yeah, hey," he says. "You know, I really love you, Jelly. You're doing great." Like if he repeats it often enough, he can make it be true. *I'm doing great.* I look down at Emma staring up at me, sucking on her fist. I bounce the handle of the stroller lightly—this is what I've learned from three weeks of motherhood. Constant motion is paramount.

"I know," I say. "We love you, too."

The market feels almost familiar. My panic ebbs. I am like a regular human, walking the aisles with my human baby, browsing and purchasing foods to cook and eat. Normal. In my previous life, I was a food writer—that's how Leo and I met. I went to his restaurant one day, and he seduced me with wild mushroom risotto. Food was the foundation of our universe. Before we had the baby, we could spend a whole day together—roasting, sautéing, chopping, boiling, reducing. There was something incredibly sexy about that, like tantric cooking. Now we eat ramen, and if Leo thinks to throw a piece of ham up in there for me, I weep with gratitude.

Emma has drifted off in her car seat, so I'm able to take my time at the butcher counter, selecting the veal chops. I'm going to cook anyway, just for something to do. I squeeze plenty of produce before adding two lemons to my basket. When I finish shopping, I take two more laps around the shop just to fill up some extra minutes with people and food and comforting public noises. The thought of returning to the empty, aching house terrifies me. Emma begins to stir and stretch. She will be hungry. She is always hungry. I pay for the food and stuff the ingredients into the storage basket under the stroller.

"Oh, what an angel," the cashier says to me, leaning across her register to get a better look at Emma.

"Yeah," I say, rearranging her blanket.

"How old is she?"

"Three weeks."

"Oh, she's brand-new! God bless you!"

"Thanks." I smile. "Do you want to come over for dinner?"

The startled cashier looks up at me and leans away from us, back into her comfortable little work space.

"I'm kidding," I say. "I kid!"

The cashier tries to chuckle.

"NEXT ON LINE," she says.

The whole way home I mutter to myself about what an idiot I am. I hadn't really meant to invite the cashier over for dinner. I meant to *say* it, but I also meant to laugh afterward, to indicate that I wasn't serious. My voice is getting into an awful habit of doing things I haven't sanctioned.

"She thought I was a total freak," I say to Emma, whose eyes are now open and blinky. "Mommy's not a freak, baby." I can't tell if she believes me.

It's late afternoon now and as we walk down Seventy-eighth Avenue, two kids skateboard around us single file. Most of the street is shaded by trees, but in the sunny patches, the skateboarders cast fast-rolling shadows along the uneven pavement beneath. They shriek and call out loudly to one another. They make kissy-face noises at a young couple who are smooching against the railings of P.S. 119. At the corner ahead of us, the boys kick up their skateboards and carry them over the crosswalk and into the deli. I round the corner and unstrap the car seat to lug Emma up the steps to the front door. Across the street, my hot neighbor, Brian, is pulling his slick, black non-dadlike car into his driveway. My parents loved him, when they lived here. My mom called him "an old soul," which is the highest praise she can bestow on anyone under the age of sixty.

He scrunches on the parking brake with virility, I swear. I try to wave a casual hello, but with my shopping bags hanging from one elbow, and Emma's car seat from the other, I may actually appear to be signaling for help. He waits on a passing car and then skips across the street. Here is a man so inherently masculine that he can *skip* without fear of ridicule. He can cross his legs elegantly, at the knee. He can drink a cocktail of a pinkish hue without irony. He is that manly. He takes the eight stairs in two strides, and lifts all of the shopping out of my hands.

"I won't touch the baby until I receive instruction!" he laughs. I want to kiss him.

"Thanks," I say. "I wasn't flagging you down or anything, just saying hello."

"Hello!" he says back. "No, you just looked like you could use an extra set of hands." Emma is starting to whimper loudly in her seat. She has a big voice for a tiny newborn.

"I could use an extra set of boobs, too," I say, immediately regretting the breast-feeding humor that is funny to no one on earth except me. But he laughs. He laughs!

"Aw, she's hungry, Majella. You're hungry, aren't you, beautiful?" he says, peering over the edge of Emma's car seat while I fiddle with the keys in the lock. "She's gorgeous. Looks just like you."

I blush. Which is totally stupid. Because he is only being kind, saying the sort of automatic thing that people say about squished-up, squalling newborn babies and their haggard-looking mommies.

"Thanks," I say.

The door swings in and bangs the wall inside while I lumber through the doorway, gracelessly dragging Emma behind me. Brian follows us down the long hallway into the kitchen, sets the shopping bags down on the counter, and goes back out for the stroller. Emma begins to wail, and I begin to sweat. I need to pee. My incision throbs from carrying the car seat up the steps. But Emma's hunger trumps all my would-be biological urgencies.

I always wanted to be one of those effortless, French-style women who can breast-feed discreetly anywhere, but I'm not. For me, breast-feeding requires a Boppy, a footstool, a glass of water, and substantial nudity. I look around wildly, wondering if I can put Emma off eating until Brian leaves, but she is hollering the house down, and my skin is crawling. I can actually feel my blood pressure climbing as she cries. My boobs begin to leak. Brian is coming back down the hallway with the stroller now. There's no way around it. I hike up my shirt, unsnap my nursing bra, and collapse onto the couch with Emma. It's a minimalist couch, and it feels judgmental in this living room, like it's afraid to touch anything else for fear of contamination. Leo and I ripped up the linoleum tile in here and replaced the subfloor before we moved in, but we haven't installed the shiny new hardwoods yet, so the sofa is sitting on some plywood in front of a spackled and unpainted wall. The floorboards sit a few feet away, still in their boxes.

Emma latches on like a champ, and I'm so grateful for this small, ordinary miracle. Breast-feeding is like a gift after the C-section, like evidence that my body isn't biologically opposed to motherhood, even if my brain seems to be.

"At least I can do this right," I whisper to the top of her soft little head.

Brian leans the stroller up against the counter.

"Wow, thanks," I say.

He's even managed to fold it up, which took me *days* to figure out. Brian is an engineer. I look down to make sure that my shirt is draped over as much of my boob as possible.

"Yeah, no problem." He looks over at us on the couch, and then snaps his head away, as if I've slapped him across the face.

Brian is one of those progressive, gentlemanly types who believes in breast-feeding, but only theoretically. In practice, he is completely undone by it. He doesn't know where to look, so he studies my kitchen ceiling. I glance down at my engorged boob. It's bigger than Emma's head. Disgusting. I feel a hot blush creeping up my neck.

"The kitchen looks fantastic," Brian says, staring at the light fixture. "The place is really coming along."

"Thanks," I say, stretching my shirt halfway across Emma's face while she tries to eat. "It's not like yours—I wish we had the patience to restore all those great historic details. It was a mess when we moved in, needed so much work. My parents just didn't have the energy to keep it up when they lived here."

"Well, it was homey," he says kindly. "But it sure looks a lot different already." I don't think it would be an exaggeration to say that he's *fondling* my poured-concrete countertops.

"Well, much as I enjoyed the linoleum paradise of my childhood, those yellow appliances were ready to retire," I say. "They limped to their deaths."

The kitchen was the first room we renovated after we bought this house from my parents—the only room we've finished, with a cork floor and a Sub-Zero, over-and-under, built-in fridge with a glass door. That fridge is so beautiful that sometimes I actually embrace it, and then I have to spritz off the leaky breast milk stains from the glass door afterward, with Windex.

Brian opens one of those glass doors now, and deposits both of my shopping bags inside the fridge without unpacking them. He's wearing dusty jeans and Timberland boots, and somehow he looks elegant in my immaculate new kitchen. We are a before-and-after picture: I am *before*, all sweaty, disheveled, and bloated in the unfinished living room, and Brian is *after*, standing in my flawless kitchen like some sexified, twenty-first-century version of a Norman Rockwell painting.

"I really miss the grape-motif wallpaper," Brian jokes from the kitchen. "But I guess your aesthetic has a certain appeal, too."

Conversation! Complete with sarcasm and humor! Hallelujah! Emma sucks noisily at my boob, and thwacks my chest with her free-flailing arm.

"Don't tell my mom," I say, laughing. "She'd be heartbroken if she heard you weren't a fan of the grape wallpaper."

Brian takes a break from his breast-feeding-eye-contact boycott to flash me a grin.

"How are they settling in, in Florida?" he asks.

"Good, they love it. I just talked to my mom this morning."

"They coming up for a visit soon, to meet Miss Emma?"

And suddenly my eyes are filling up again, and I am mortified. I will not ruin this. I will not frighten my hot and kindly neighbor with my bizarre, uncomfortable tears. I will swallow them. I shake my head, glad I didn't switch on the lamp before I sat down. It's still light outside, but the sun has dropped behind Brian's roof across the street.

"No, I don't know," I say, and I'm encouraged by my voice, which sounds unaccountably solid. "They're still getting used to everything. They'll probably come in the spring, after the bad weather."

They moved to Florida just six months ago. At the same dinner where I told them I was expecting their first grandbaby, they made their own announcement: "We're moving to Tampa!" Which felt, at first, infuriating, and then fortuitous. On the subway home that night, I asked Leo if we could buy their house.

"In Queens?" he said, like I'd just suggested we should move to Libya.

"Yes, in Queens. Where I grew up. Where lots of nice, normal, nonelitist people grew up," I said, in my most elitist voice.

"No, I know—Glendale is great," Leo said.

"There's so much green space in Queens," I said. "I miss that, living in Manhattan. All the trees and grass and sky."

"But there are dead people under that grass," he said. It's true that Queens has a lot of graveyards. That's always sort of creeped Leo out. "And isn't it kind of far?"

"From what?"

"You know, from Manhattan, from work. From stuff."

But Leo was already defeated. I was barely nine weeks pregnant then, but I'd already acquired the habit of placing my hand suggestively across my belly in an argument, to illustrate the righteousness of my position. And my position was this: I wanted out of Manhattan. I hadn't even known until that very moment, but it was true. I wanted out of our tiny, sterile, teacup apartment. I was tired of paying $3,500 a month for eight hundred (beautiful) square feet in a glass box that we didn't even own. We'd been talking about buying a place anyway, and now I wanted a house that had windows you could *open* in the springtime, with screens that would collect buckets of pollen and dead insects. I wanted neighbors who could annoy me horizontally instead of vertically. I wanted a weed-whacker and a garden hose.

"I want an education for our kid that's somewhere in between *Gossip Girl* and *Gangland*," I told Leo, while our train rumbled north through Midtown. To his credit, he didn't roll his eyes at me, but he did say, "I think you're being *slightly* dramatic."

I didn't care. Pregnant people are entitled to be dramatic. The suburban city was singing to my new-sprung maternal ferocity, and in the end, Leo couldn't escape. We bought the house—my childhood house—from my parents, and now here we are, in

Glendale. Or here I am, at least. And here's Brian, standing grace-fully in my new kitchen.

"Ask your mom to bring some of her famous brownies when she comes to visit," he says. "Are you allowed to bring brownies on airplanes now?"

"I'll ask her."

"You need anything else before I get outta here?" he asks, stuffing his hands into his jeans pockets.

Get outta here? I begin to panic. I hadn't thought about him leaving. I glance at the clock on the DVR. It's only twelve minutes past five. Leo won't be home for hours. I think of the two veal chops in the fridge. I think how much I like hot Brian, how he's probably going home to order a pizza, how inappropriate it would be for me to invite him to stay for dinner. I bite my lip. I'm lots of things I don't like now, but I'm not an idiot.

"Nah, I'm good."

Chapter Four

IRELAND, SEPTEMBER 1846

Before Ray left, they harvested and threshed the oats, and sold enough to John McCann, along with the hog, to make rent. They sold him the cow as well, and used some of that money to buy Raymond's ticket. So that left a decent stock of oats, cabbage, and turnips, a small sum of money, and the three hens, to last until the promise of Ray's American dollars. Across Ireland, hunger was falling into famine, but the Doyles were managing better than most of their neighbors. Ginny and her family were getting off lucky.

His last night, Raymond and Ginny stayed awake while the children slept. They didn't speak. They hardly moved. It was more wrestling than lovemaking, really. That's how tightly they clung to each other. They were like a hard knot, fixed at the eyes, his elbow locked round the nape of her neck, her thighs clenched round his hips. She gripped his hair, his shoulder blades, his knuckles. Her fingers would remember him, every inch of him.

They stayed like that until the dread dawn. When he finally spoke, his voice was a promise.

"I will never let you go."

They were all up early, and when Raymond was dressed and ready, he lingered by the cottage door. He had been insistent that there would be no American wake, that his neighbors would not gather to see him off, that his family would not mourn his going. So Ginny tried to honor his wishes by hiding the worst of her terror from him.

"I'll be back in the summer, sure, when the crop comes good," Raymond said to his wife. He kissed her mouth, and then he held his nose against her neck. He breathed her in, the scent of her. Their children stood around them in silence. Husband and wife tipped their foreheads together for a moment, and when Ray leaned away, he only nodded at her, and she nodded back. She turned away quickly, before he could notice her tears.

"You'll be a good girl, Maire, you'll help your mammy," he said then, giving his eldest daughter a squeeze around the shoulders.

"I will, Daddy, of course," Maire said, and her eyes were shiny, but she never betrayed herself any further than that. She was solid.

The two littler girls were blubbery and sad. They clung round their daddy's neck, and begged him not to go, but he kissed their cheeks and landed them down on the floor with a thump and a tickle.

"If you're good, I'll bring ye back something from America," he said. "But not if there's tears."

Poppy did her best to dry her face with the back of her hand. "Like sweeties?" she asked. "Or a doll?"

"Something like that," Ray said, but Maggie couldn't be won over so easily. The big, sloppy tears were still rolling on her pink cheeks.

"Go on," Ray said, swatting her backside. Maggie scampered away to her mother.

Michael was the worst. He was inconsolable.

"Why can I not go with you?" he asked his father for the hundredth time. Ray was down on one knee, and Michael stood in close to his father. "I'm big enough to work."

"You're big enough to work the farm, all right," Ray answered him. "That's why you have to stay, son. Your mother needs you here, to keep things ticking over until I can get back. We can't leave the girls all on their own, right?"

Michael shook his head. He was nearly ten now. He hadn't cried in two years. He wanted to show his father how grown he was. He wanted Ray to be proud of him. But in this moment, it was all too much. He crumbled in against his father's broad chest. He fell in like a rag doll, and when Ray put his arms around him, he felt tiny there, curled up on his father's knee.

"What time is the ship sailing?" Ginny asked, to cover the sound of Michael's sniffles. "God forbid you should miss the boat."

Ray nodded again. He gave Michael one last squeeze, and then kissed the top of his head.

"I'd better be off, all right," he said.

But Michael wouldn't let go. Ginny had to peel her son off Raymond. It was a horrible scene altogether: Michael was wretched, writhing. Any thought of wanting to please his father was abolished entirely by grief.

In the yard, Ginny held on to Michael so he wouldn't chase his father down the road when he had to go. Her son was almost too strong for her, getting big as he was. But he wept like a little baby, and in truth, Ginny wept along with him. Their three daughters followed Ray to the top of the ridge in their front field, and there they stood, staring after him as he went, their eyes already stretching, trying to cover that growing distance. Poppy and Maggie cried over each other, holding hands, their little faces turning all puffy and red. And Ginny sat on the three-legged stool beneath the crooked branch of the blackthorn tree, with Michael wailing and thrashing about on her knee. She pinned his little arms into his sides.

"Daddy's gone, gone," she said. They all needed to believe it, to accept it. "He's gone."

And then a grief stole over her that was so pure it was nearly like the chaste agony of losing a child, a sickening feeling of horror and panic. Ginny had suffered that kind of anguish only once before in her life, when she lost a baby in between Michael and Maggie. That time had been bottomless in its despair, and it was hard to believe that Raymond's departure could feel that brutal. Ginny hadn't been prepared for the enormity of it. But there was something primal in the farewell; maybe it came from Michael, from the immediacy of his pain. But whatever it was, it inspired a feeling of near certainty that she would never see Raymond again, the sweet corners of his half-moon eyes. It caught her by surprise, rendered her senseless. She held on to Michael, and she cried until her head pounded, until Maire put her hand on her mother's hair. She patted her mammy's neck.

"It's all right," Maire said. "Stop crying now, Mammy."

And Ginny felt like such an *amadán* then, that Maire could be brave when she wasn't. So that was the thing that snapped her out of it, at least in her body. Ginny snuffled and heaved, and then after a moment, she shuddered quietly. She wiped her tears with the corner of her apron, kissed Michael on top of the head, and after a few minutes of rocking, he, too, stopped fighting and turned toward his mother. He buried his face against her, and cried just loosely and quietly until he slept. She laid him inside on her own bed to recover, his face like her own: all pink raw, and covered with snot and tears.

Those first days without Raymond were like learning a new way of breathing for Ginny, like her lungs had been folded in half, and she had to discover how to get by without air. At nights, she shuddered and shivered under their blanket. She prayed for sleep that did not come. Her eyes yawned open in the dark, and she imagined Raymond stretched out on some bunk or berth, sleeping heavily in the steerage of that America-bound ship. She imagined him rocking gently on the waters, like a baby in its mother's arms, and some nights, she cursed him for that imagined comfort. She wished to trade places with him, to be the one whose grief and terror might be allayed by adventure. If she was gone to America, all full of purpose and energy—to save her family—well, wouldn't that be all right in the end? Better than staying here, waiting in fear and sorrow, all the joy gone out of life entirely, watching her children grow tough and skinny. America would be the greatest distraction.

What would the light be like there, among the tall ships in the harbor, the teeming city streets? In the letters they took to Father Brennan to read, Raymond's brother, Kevin, said there were more languages on the streets of New York than he ever knew existed. Ginny wondered what they might sound like, those unknown tongues, fighting for space, cleaving their singsong through the air. And all the families from right round the world, all packed in tight, living in beside one another, cooking their foods, spicy foreign steam billowing from their New York City windows. She wondered at the girls and women inside those windows, sweating at their hearths and cauldrons, swiping loose hair from their sticky foreheads. She wondered if Raymond would meet a beautiful young thing who smelled of chutney or pepper.

In those first days, she lived more in her mind, with Raymond, than she did in their cottage, with their too-quiet children. That was how the remainder of September passed, unspooling itself into October, when the cold punched in and stayed. Michael hadn't spoken a word since the day Raymond left. His little voice had gone dry in his throat, so there were two fewer voices now, instead of just the absence of Ray's. Maggie took to building a cairn in the yard for her father—each day that passed, she added a stone to her mounting pile. By mid-October, her little monument was no larger than an upturned pail, but it grew day by day, and its smallness was a comfort, somehow.

The first week of November was gray. There was no break of blue, no crack of sunshine in the heavy, slate sky. It pressed down on them, damp and grave overhead. In the morning, Ginny threw two sods of turf on the fire and stoked it up. The smoke drew up to the thatching, some of it pulling out through the smoke hole, and the rest tucking in under the eaves to warm them. Michael was leaning back on the tick of straw where he slept, his bony knees sticking out from beneath the hem of his petticoat. He seemed not to notice the chill, though Ginny could see the blue veins in his ankles and feet. He had one piece of scraggly straw in his fingers, and he was twirling it, watching it spin.

"Michael, love," Ginny called out to him, but her words didn't even bump against his face. "Michael," she tried again. He stared at the spinning straw. "Go on out to the shed, love, and bring us in the eggs for breakfast."

He stayed there long enough that she nearly repeated herself, but finally, a heavy sigh rolled over his shoulders, and he pushed himself up to his feet, and went out silently into the yard. He was gone so quiet that even his footfall failed to thump against the packed earth. The door wouldn't rattle beneath his hand. And when he returned a few minutes later, he spooked his mother, appearing beside her like a specter with empty hands.

"Where are the eggs, love?"

Michael shrugged as the door swung shut behind him, but Maire caught a sight in the door gap, and lunged to swing it open again. She staggered outside, and Poppy followed behind her.

"Mammy!" Maggie called, tumbling to her feet, and chasing after her sisters. "It's snowing!"

The thick white flakes in Michael's hair were turning clear and dropping into cold streaks that ran along his scalp. His eyes were as flat as the sky. He trudged back to the tick, and Ginny followed him, knelt down, and leaned over him. She ran her hand through his moppy brown hair, cold with the melted snow.

"I know you miss him," she said. "We all do. But you've to be the man of the house now, Michael. I need your help, *mo chuisle*."

He rolled over to face the wall. Ginny sighed and stood up.

"Fine, I'll get the eggs, but you get yourself scrubbed up. You know it's gale day. We'll head over after breakfast to pay the rents."

She went out the door, and passed Maire swinging Poppy round by the arms in the side yard. Poppy was squealing, as usual, and had her tongue stuck out, trying to catch snowflakes. Maggie was out in the field a small pace, and Ginny could tell by the seriousness on her daughter's face that she was rock-hunting, looking for the perfect stone to add to her father's cairn.

In the shed, the hens seemed awful nervous. Two of them were out in the center of the shed, flapping and scratching about. The third one was missing, and the baskets where they ordinarily roosted were empty. No eggs. Ginny backed away and stared into the empty baskets, her fists planted firmly on her hips.

"Where?" she whispered.

She spun around to watch the two remaining hens behind her. They were stood in the doorway, where the faint light of the early winter's morning was stretching their cold shadows across the floor.

"Where's your friend got to?" she asked them.

Her presence seemed to have calmed them a small bit. They clucked and pecked, waiting for their feed. She usually fed the hens on the skins of potatoes, but the praties were all gone now, and Ginny was trying the hens instead on what oats and scraps they could spare. They were growing skinny, and she knew they'd have to be slaughtered soon, but she hadn't expected them all to stop laying in the one night.

She stepped toward the doorway, to go out and scour the yard for the missing fowl, but she stopped short when she heard a strangled screech coming from a dark corner of the shed, behind a bushel of oats. The petrified creature came flapping across the shed, screaming its head off. It landed nearly at Ginny's feet, and recovered itself at once, as only a hen could. In a moment, it was like nothing had ever happened to it at all. Ginny bent down to look at the bird: her feathers were still puffed and startled, but apart from that, she seemed unharmed. She bobbed her head.

"What the devil were you doing back there?" Ginny said to her, and then straightened herself up at once, fearing a fox. She grabbed the hayfork beside the door and called out to Maire. The girl came in at the doorway.

"What's the matter, Mammy?"

"Take the hens inside the house for a minute, love, and your sisters, too."

"What is it?"

"I don't know, I think we might have a fox."

"In the daytime?"

"I don't know, love."

"If it was a fox, wouldn't the hens be gone already?"

"Maire, for God's sake, stop asking questions and get the hens in!"

Maire stooped and swept the three of them up in the blink of an eye. She had two of them hanging by the feet in one hand, and the third in the other. She could talk for Ireland, but she had a lovely quick grace to her all the same. After a moment, Ginny heard her daughter's voice calling out quietly to Poppy and Maggie, and then the cottage door clicked shut behind them. Ginny held the hayfork low to the ground, and stepped in behind the empty baskets. It would be no bad thing to catch a fox now.

"How would you cook a fox? I wonder," she said to herself out loud. She did a lot of talking to herself, with Ray gone. "A stew, I suppose." She shuddered at the thought of eating fox meat, but she'd be glad of it all the same.

She crept forward and drew her breath in. She didn't want to startle the beast, exactly. She wanted it to know she was coming. She didn't want it flying at her face. They were fierce animals when they were cornered.

"I wish Ray was here," she muttered.

She drew the hayfork back then, and up to her shoulder. Her hands were trembling, but she tightened her grip and took a deep breath. She could sense a presence there, in behind the oat bushels—maybe she could hear it breathing, or smell the alien musk of its pelt. She crept forward. She wanted to catch it, and she didn't want to catch it. She lifted the hayfork with both hands, and yelled as she stormed forward, plunging the fork down through the air.

"Faith, don't hurt me! Merciful God!"

She twisted the fork up just in time, and its tines clattered against the wall. Her hand flew up to her heart, which was beating now like mad. She shook, from the legs up.

"Mary Reilly, I nearly had you for supper!" Ginny gasped.

Her neighbor was sitting crouched in behind the oat bushels there, her ragged red petticoat draped over her knees, and her head cradled down in her two hands. Her fair brown hair was thin in its braids, and the knuckles stood out of her hands like an old woman's. She was close to the same age as Ginny.

"God forgive me," the woman said. "I'm sorry, Ginny Doyle. I'm awful sorry. I never meant to startle you."

Ginny held the hayfork in one hand, and leaned back against the wall to try and catch breath into her lungs. Her heart was still lunging around in her breast.

"But what are you doing here, Mary?" She looked at her neighbor crouched down there like a cowering animal. "I thought you were a fox. I nearly poked you full of holes."

Mary Reilly opened her mouth to speak, but her face contorted, and she drew the apron up from her knees to hide herself behind it.

"Here, come here, Mary," Ginny said, leaning down to her. "Come out of that corner, pet."

Ginny tried to pull the woman up by the arm, and was startled to feel how slight and loose the flesh was there, hanging away from her bones. She struggled to her feet, and Ginny pulled the apron away from her face. Ginny drew the poor woman out toward the middle of the shed and sat her down on the milking stool. The woman's eyes stayed stuck to the earthen floor. Outside, the snow was falling harder, the little flakes eddying along the frozen dirt. Maggie's cairn had a white veil over it. Ginny waited for Mary to recover herself. When she finally spoke, her voice was so strained, Ginny had to step forward to listen.

"We've nothing left," Mary whispered, and for the first time, she glanced up at Ginny, their clear blue eyes locking on to each other for just a moment. She was shaking her head. "I came here to thieve one of your hens."

The woman dropped her head into her hands again, and Ginny thought she would begin to wail, but she didn't seem to have the strength. She only shuddered instead. After a moment, she looked up again.

"What has become of me, Ginny? I would never have done it if the children weren't so weak and so hungry, I promise you that. But I've tried everything. I made boxtie for the first while, out of the rotten praties, until the children got sick on them. And then I made a soup from nettles, and it brought Kathleen all out in hives. I couldn't take it no more, seeing how they're wasting in front of me, and now young Mick has the cough, and he getting awful bad all the time. I'm in fear of his life, and I thought a good chicken soup might cure him, might put some life back into him. So I gave in to a weakness, and I came here in the night, while everyone was sleeping, and I might've taken the hen and stolen away home with it, but I couldn't. I couldn't do it."

Her face twisted up with such miserableness then that Ginny couldn't even find her own voice to respond—she was that tormented by the closeness of the woman's pain. The effort caught in Ginny's throat.

"I had every intention of doing it," Mary went on. "I said to myself, *God has forsaken us, and there's nothing else for it. He can take me, but I'll do what I can to save my children before I go.* And so I came here, because I knew you weren't as bad off as all that, and I thought you might spare the hen. But I was here for an hour, that hen clutched into my hand, and it getting on toward dawn, and the light coming into the sky, and me thinking of Mick at home, ailing and coughing. And me knowing that the hen just there might save him. But my conscience wouldn't allow it, and all I could think of was being close enough to my own end, and having to face Saint Peter with that theft on my hands, that I was taking food out of the mouths of your own hungry children as well, God forgive me. And then I heard your young ones coming out, and I hid into the back there, behind the bushels."

Mary crossed herself, stood up from the milking stool, and began to pace, but that effort was too much a strain for her, and she nearly tumbled when she sat back down. Ginny caught her before she went backwards off the stool. The woman's whole body was shaking.

"Ginny," she gasped, pulling at her hair. Her face was twisted into a wretched grimace. "Young Mick. You won't believe."

"Here," Ginny said, crouching down and taking the woman's hands. "Calm yourself."

"Ginny, I nearly smothered him. Oh!" Mary's face was all vivid agony now, and Ginny tried to quiet her, but she was bent on confessing. "I nearly smothered him, Ginny, my firstborn son. I said it would be kinder. God will take him from me. God will take him regardless, and this way, he won't have to suffer no longer. Why should he have to go slow, with the wicked coughing and the hunger both? Why should he suffer, when I could help him along, just to sleep now, and he'd be at peace then. He could be with his father, God rest him."

Ginny caught herself recoiling in horror, but she forced herself to stay, to draw closer, even. She squeezed the poor woman's fingers. She knew Mary Reilly to be a good woman, a soft woman, even, and God-fearing. Ginny knew Mary's love for her children, the depth and veracity of it. And she thought of her own ones inside, how horrific and slow the end would be for them if the food ran out before they heard from Ray. What would she do, if the time came? Wasn't it possible that Mary was right, that a quick end would be the compassionate thing? Surely God would forgive a mother for that sort of tender brutality? Ginny trembled in her very soul. She put her arms around Mary.

"There, you're all right," Ginny said. "It's only the hunger talking."

"I could never do it, I don't think I could really do it," Mary whispered. "I only thought. I thought it might be kinder."

"Shhh, now," Ginny said, letting go, leaning back to look Mary in the face. "You leave that to God. His will be done."

Mary nodded weakly.

"When did you eat last?" Ginny said.

Mary shook her head. Her cheeks were so sunken, Ginny could see the shapes of her teeth in behind them.

"Come into the house, we'll get you a bite," Ginny said.

Mary was too weak to argue, and when she came inside the cottage, she slipped her hand into her pocket and drew the three eggs out. They wobbled on the table, and Ginny said nothing when she saw them, only scooped them into her apron, and then dropped them into the water to boil. Afterward, Mary protested only slightly when Ginny insisted she take one of the hens home with her, for Mick and the others, to keep them ticking over for a few more days.

"Maybe that will be just the thing he needs," Ginny said. "And he'll be back on his feet in no time."

They were standing in the doorway, and the hens were still clucking around, in beside the hearth.

"Ginny Doyle, may all the blessings of heaven rain down on this house," Mary said, gripping Ginny's hand with all the strength she could muster. "I never met such a generous soul, God bless you. My children owe their lives to you this day."

"It's nothing you wouldn't do for us," Ginny said, and then she called over to Michael. "Bring the red one."

He stood, and scooped the flapping red hen up from the floor.

"See Mrs. Reilly home safe, love, and then hurry back."

"Ah, there's no need of that now, to send the poor little dote out in the snow and the cold, Ginny. I'm grand," she said, but Ginny waved her off.

"It'll do him good, the fresh air," she said. "But you won't get much chat out of him. Been awful quiet since his father left."

Michael stood beside them with the hen turned up in his hand, staring out into the snow, as if he couldn't hear them at all.

"We'll wait for you, love," Ginny said, kissing his cheek. "When you're back, we'll head over to pay the rents."

He pushed open the door and went out into the cold. Mary Reilly kissed Ginny on the two cheeks, the prayers and gratitude falling from her lips the whole time, and then Ginny watched her son and her neighbor walk out together into the snow. She waved after them, when Mary turned to look, and she couldn't help noticing that Michael's petticoat was as sad and shabby as Mary's. Mounting the ridge, they were like two fading drops of blood against the snow.

Ginny was combing Maggie's black hair when Michael returned, trailing Willie and Thomas Harkin, and Father Brennan behind him. Ginny stood up from the hearth, and handed the comb to Maire, who took over, working at Maggie's knots. Michael's lips were purple, and there were bright rings around his eyes from the cold.

"Get in beside the fire there, love," Ginny said, and he scuttled over, went down on his haunches to warm himself.

The two Harkin boys were standing in the doorway, still, but Father Brennan came striding into the room.

"Ginny Doyle, how're you keeping?" Father said, taking her hand for just a moment. "How are you getting on with Raymond gone?"

She looked over at Michael's round, vacant face, the glow of firelight lamping his features.

"Ah, we're managing, Father."

"God bless ye," he said. "It's hard times that's in it."

"It is," Ginny agreed, and then she turned to the Harkin lads. "Come in outta the cold, boys, come in beside the fire."

Willie was the larger of the two brothers, but they had both grown into fine, big lads, with rosy cheeks and strong jaws. They were handsome, just getting on to the age where they might start looking for wives. They drew themselves into the room, closer in beside the fire.

"Thank you, Mrs. Doyle," Willie said.

"Can I get you lads anything?" she asked. She hoped they'd refuse, but she had to offer. They both looked lean, but healthy, escaping the worst of the hunger, at least for the moment. "I've some oatcakes just pressed, I can fire one up for you."

"No, thank you, Mrs. Doyle, don't trouble yourself, we're grand," Thomas said.

"Father?"

"No, thanks, Ginny," Father Brennan said. "You've enough with your own mouths to feed."

She tried not to show the relief in her shoulders or face. There was so little to spare.

"What brings you lads out in this weather on gale day?" she said then.

There weren't stools enough for everyone, so they stood in a bit of a circle beside the fire, the children down below them in the warmth. Thomas looked at Willie, and the older brother nodded back at him.

"We're trying to get talking to everyone in the parish before they pay the rents." Thomas dropped his voice low in the room, even though there was nobody else to hear. Ginny leaned forward. "Myself and Willie, and then a good few of the other young fellas, we've got together, and came up with a bit of a plan, but we need everybody to agree on it."

Ginny looked at Father Brennan, who was staring severely into the fire. His whole face was a frown, and he'd his fingers drawn up to his lips.

"Agree on what?" Ginny said.

"Not to pay the rents."

Michael snapped his head up from the fire, and stared at the older boys. Maire kept brushing away at Maggie's hair, pretending not to listen. Willie stepped over to the door, and opened it a crack to look out. Then he closed it again, and came back to the others, with a fresh breath of the cold on himself. Ginny folded her arms in front of her.

"How do you mean, not to pay the rents?" she said, trying to keep the tightness in her throat from creeping into her voice. She shook her head. "You know what happens to families who don't pay their rents, lads. Raymond's off to America, now. Would you see me evicted, turned out onto the roads in this weather, with four babbies to look after? Are you mad, altogether?"

"Just hear us out, Mrs. Doyle," Willie said then. "I know it's frightening. But if everyone does it, if we all stick together, we'll be grand. Packet can hardly eject everyone, can he? He'd have no tenants at all, then."

"There's plenty of families would be lined up after us, to take our place," she said. "And them all too willing to pay Packet his rents."

"But no one can pay," Thomas argued. "It's not a matter of willingness, with the pratie crop gone. It's a matter of survival."

Willie looked around the cottage, gestured at the three bags of meal hanging from the tie beam. "You're going to be all right, Mrs. Doyle," he said. "You're better off than most. You had a great harvest of oats this year, I know, and you've always had that kitchen garden, with the turnips and cabbage and that. It's well you know that most people don't have that kitchen garden—they only sow the praties for to eat. And you managed the price of a ticket for Mr. Doyle as well."

"Most families in this parish never planted anything, only the praties," Thomas said. "Sure that's all they had space enough to grow, after sowing most of the land with oats for to pay the rents. And now, with the praties gone, there's nothing standing between the people and starvation—only them oats Packet demands for rent. He'll take the food from our mouths and sell it out to England to please his lordship, for to fatten his wife and his wallet. They will profit from our starvation!"

Ginny looked to Father Brennan again, but he was mute. Michael stared up from the fire with his father's half-moon eyes. She bit her lip.

"If our rent leaves Ireland, Mrs. Doyle," Thomas went on, "we will *all* starve, make no mistake. Our neighbors, our children, everyone. Sure, there's people starving enough already. But God help us, this is only the start of it."

Ginny wished she could cover Michael's young ears, but it was too late for all that. He was taking it all in. Then Willie spoke up again. "O'Connell and the commission appealed to Lord Heytesbury in Dublin just this week, and they were turned away," the older brother said. "This is what they asked for, exactly this— the prohibition of exports. O'Connell knows it—everyone knows it—that if they keep exporting our food for rent, all will be annihilation. Even those like yourself, lucky enough to have a surplus or a bit of money, you won't be able to buy food where there is none."

Michael was still staring up at his mother, his eyes watery, the melting snow dripping down from his hair. She wondered if he knew the word "annihilation." Before his voice went, he was always asking the meanings of words, looking to learn newer and bigger ones. He was a clever boy. She leaned down to stroke his face.

"They don't care, Mrs. Doyle," Thomas went on. "They're only too glad to be rid of us. There was talk of government aid, but it's not forthcoming. The Queen has washed her hands."

The cold was stealing into the room now, even though the door was shut and the fire crackling away. Maire laid down the brush and began plaiting Maggie's black hair. Poppy had fallen asleep beside the fire, exhausted from chasing snowflakes. How she wished for Raymond in that moment, for the comfort of collective thought.

"What do you say about all this, Father?" Ginny asked.

Father Brennan reached inside his coat, and drew out a newspaper. "It's the *Freeman's Journal*," he said.

"And?"

He cleared his throat, and read it out in a most terrible, somber voice. " 'They may starve! Such in spirit, if not in words, was the reply given yesterday by the English Viceroy, to the memorial of the deputation, which, in the name of the Lords and Commons of Ireland, prayed that the food of this kingdom be preserved, lest the people thereof perish.' " Father Brennan looked up from the paper, his eyes and the pate of his head gleaming. "It's just as Willie says, I'm afraid. O'Connell went to Heytesbury, to plead with him for Ireland, for mercy. Not for a handout—we don't need help from England. We produce enough food on this island to feed our people ten times over. If the lords and ladies would only stop taking that food off us and exporting it for profit. Even just for one season of hunger! But Heytesbury wouldn't hear of it. He turned O'Connell away." Father Brennan drew his lips in tight.

Ginny's stomach gave a great twist and a heave, and she was afraid she might be sick right there on the hearth. She put a hand to her mouth, and after a moment, the feeling washed out of her. Father Brennan was folding the paper back into his jacket.

"I cannot, in good conscience, counsel you to heed the advice of these fine boys, Ginny," he said. "I know you're on your own here now, with your own good parents deceased, God rest them, until Ray gets work and sends back for you. I can't say what Packet might do, when he meets with treachery on his watch. He could very well turn you out into the roads. Knowing Packet, I'd say he might evict the whole lot of ye, every last child of God."

The priest turned to survey the Harkin lads, who were standing quietly now. "But I've known these two brave lads all their lives, and I like their gumption. Who knows? Maybe Packet would agree to delay the rents until the summer gale, seeing what kind of condition the poor people are in. He could convince his master surely, just to put off the collection for one season. It's a fine idea they've cobbled together. If it works."

"It will work," Thomas piped up. "There's a great strength in our numbers. No violence, but we have to stand together. It will only work if everyone does it."

"Please, Mrs. Doyle," Willie said, touching her arm. "At least think it over."

Ginny nodded. "I will."

The lads began to bundle themselves then, clapping themselves up to greet the cold. She saw them out through the door, and watched as they pitched themselves up the ridge toward the road beyond, their bodies all full of youthful hope and purpose. When they were gone, the cottage felt quiet and empty. Ginny looked at the silent faces of her children for only a moment before she made up her mind. She didn't have the courage to risk them to the road, to wager the demolition of their home, to face Packet's men and the constable armed with crowbars and torches at their door. She had to pay the rent.

The queue at the Big House was the same as any gale day. Ginny Doyle wasn't the only coward in the parish. All the hungry families waited their turns to step in, and hand over whatever Packet demanded of them. For many, since the ruin of their potatoes, handing over their pigs or oats for rent would mean utter destitution to follow. They would starve. And still, they queued up for it—they all did. Fear of the road was worse than the fear of hunger. Mary Reilly was there, empty-handed. That portion of her potato crop that would've paid her rent was gone, along with all the rest. Ginny didn't know what Mary would do, what she might offer to Packet in return for a stay. She tried not to wonder.

They trooped home after like a sad parade. It was usually a bit festive, gale day. There was a weight took off your shoulders by paying the rents, and afterward, there'd be a lot of merriment, and all the young people would gather up by the crossroads and there would be a great song and dance, once in the early winter and once in the early summer when the rents were due. But it wasn't the same now, with Ray gone, and all the hunger in people's throats and faces. It was uncommon cold, for November, with the snow and everything, and Ginny was glad to get the children home before sunset. Inside the door, the girls scattered, but Michael turned to look back at his mother.

"Mammy," he spoke.

The miracle sound of his voice after eight weeks of silence brought a rush of blood swishing through her. Ginny went down on her two knees beside him, and gripped his hands in her own.

"There you are." She smiled.

He cleared his throat, like his voice was rusty after not being used. "We should clear out the shed, bring everything inside the house," he said.

There was no question, no sentiment. His voice was solid. He was right. They would have to keep everything under watch now, things being the way they were. Ginny should've thought of it before. She stood up.

"Come on, girls," she said. "Poppy and Maire, you clear space in here—make as much room as you can. Michael and Maggie, come with me. We'll start hauling it in."

"Hauling what in, Mammy?" Maggie asked.

"Everything."

Winter deepened, and the novelty of snow fled. It was the worst weather Ginny ever remembered having, and they stayed inside the whole time. They went out most Sundays, for mass, and the church was half-empty like she'd never seen it before. The people of the parish were disappearing. The Doyles' cottage was tight and close, packed as it was now, with their provisions. The weeks went by like an oblivion. They seldom had visitors; everyone drew into themselves, their own little families. The hungry ones were too shamed to show themselves. The lucky ones even more so. They all became suspicious of one another, so they stayed inside and barred the doors. It was like all of Ireland was asleep, like the country thought it could outwit the famine by a trick of hibernation.

But Maggie never missed a day—never mind the winds blowing the rain sideways in lashing ropes across the frozen fields, never mind the drenching lonesomeness of her task—she went out and tended to her cairn. It grew fat and bloated, and she had to venture farther and farther from the cottage to find suitable stones. Christmas went, and then the year ticked over to the new one, and as Ginny watched that cairn growing larger, and their oat bushels dwindle, she began counting the weeks until she might get word from Ray.

Chapter Five

NEW YORK, NOW

Things have not improved with Dr. Zimmer, but I keep going, mostly because Leo watches Emma for an hour before I leave, so I can take a shower. My hair dryer has acquired a luxury status I never imagined before motherhood, so I run it until my scalp is hot, until I fear that my hair will scorch. I think about canceling the therapy session and not telling Leo, so I can use my free time to go out with my good, clean hair, and window-shop or sit on a bench somewhere and feed pigeons like a proper crazy person. But then I remember the crunching, so I go.

On my way out the door, Leo grabs my hand. He has Emma snuggled effortlessly in the crook of one arm, in a way I haven't learned how to do yet.

"Hey," he says. "I'm really glad you're doing this for yourself."

"It's important."

"It is," he agrees, "and I have no problem babysitting while you—"

"Babysitting?" I interrupt.

"Yeah, I have no problem babysitting while you go and do this, however long it takes."

Leo is smiling warmly at me. His face is completely without guile, and I wonder if mine is reflecting the degree of enraged disgust that suddenly engulfs me. I close my mouth, measure my tone carefully. "It's not *babysitting* when it's your own kid, Leo."

He looks at me quizzically. We're standing in the open doorway, and his hand is on the knob. "You know what I meant," he says.

"No, I know what you *said*."

He sighs, and I see the effort, but it fails: he rolls his eyes. "Oh, Majella, come *on*." He is exhausted by me. I am exhausting.

I don't want to be hypersensitive. I don't want to be a bitch. But come the fuck on. *Babysitting?*

"Did I give up my life and friends and boobs to stay home and babysit?" I ask. "Seriously, is it babysitting when I do it, or just you?"

Leo shakes his head. He leans to kiss me, but not on the lips. "I'll see you after," he says.

"At the end of our first session, you mentioned your baby dying," Dr. Zimmer says, flicking the button on her ballpoint pen like she's reading back her grocery list. "You told someone the baby died, and we've never really revisited that." I cringe. "Do you want to dig into it?"

"Not really," I say, smiling so she'll know I'm nice and I love my baby abundantly. I wonder about doctor-patient confidentiality, and what the rules are about when to call child services. She's not a real doctor anyway. I mean, not the medical kind, even though she likes to be called "doctor" because of her PhD. I wonder if she's still bound by the same rules, to keep my disgusting secrets. "I kind of never want to talk about it again, but I guess I should, right?"

"Probably." She settles back in her chair, crosses her patent leather pumps at the ankle. I wonder if she owns other shoes. "So who were you talking to when this happened?"

I take a deep breath.

"My therapist," I say. "A different therapist—I tried one other time before this."

"And why didn't it work out?" Dr. Zimmer says, with no indication that she might be kidding.

"Because I told him my baby died," I answer.

"Yes?" She looks at me as if there should be more to this explanation.

"You know, once that kind of lie is out there, you can't really take it back," I say. "You can't exactly stuff it back into your purse like an escaped vibrator."

Dr. Zimmer smiles, which might be a breakthrough.

"So you never told him the truth?"

The truth? What an outlandish idea!

"No, I mean, how could I? *Woopsie, my baby's not actually dead at all—just kidding!* I was afraid he'd have me committed."

Dr. Zimmer shakes her head, and her hair-halo bounces lightly. "So what happened?"

"I called you," I say. "I came here instead."

"And did you tell your husband what happened, about saying the baby died?"

"No, I just told him it didn't work out, I wasn't comfortable."

Dr. Zimmer takes the kind of deep breath my mother takes when she's worried about me.

"Do you think I'm pathological?" I ask.

"I think you're overwhelmed."

That seems like a fair appraisal.

"But what about the crunching?"

She holds a hand up. "One thing at a time. I want you to walk me through how it happened with this other therapist. How did the conversation go, when you told him the baby died?"

I cringe again. I wish she would stop repeating it. Can't we move on?

"Well, it's not like I planned it. I didn't plomp down on his couch and go *I'll just make up a bunch of crazy shit and see what happens*. I don't . . . I don't know." But now I'm thinking back to that day in his office. I'm remembering that awful conversation, the feeling in my stomach. "I was telling him about a dream."

Dr. Zimmer writes down *dream* in her notebook. I watch her underline it.

"In the hospital, the night I had Emma. It was horrible, it was so real." I close my eyes. "When she fell, it happened so slowly that I should've been able to catch her. That's what I told the therapist, that I saw her fall, I saw her slip from my breast and roll toward the edge of the bed."

With my eyes closed, I can see it happening again, like it's real, like it's happening right now. It's terrifying. I clutch my chest, take a sharp breath.

"I grabbed for the blanket," I say. "But I only grasped the corner of it, and it unrolled, unraveled, like a burrito. So slowly, sickening slow, but she came loose from it like the meat of the burrito, and her ten little fingers splayed out in terror. Her startle reflex worked, because she screamed when she fell. And then, after she landed on the floor in a heap, she didn't scream anymore. She was like squashed fruit on the laminate floor, her soft, tiny, newborn head caved in—no blood, just a rumple of small, naked death."

I open my eyes, and Dr. Zimmer is staring at me.

"It didn't start out as a lie," I say. "I was just telling him about the dream—this horrible dream that was so real and so haunting, and he misunderstood. I guess I let him misunderstand."

"You still seem quite alarmed by it," Dr. Zimmer notes.

"I am."

"Have you had the dream again?"

"No," I say, but then I stop. "Well. Not when I'm asleep."

"So you think about it during the day?"

I nod. "I'm besieged by that image, of Emma falling. It comes to me constantly—at the sink washing dishes, at the grocery store choosing avocados, in bed kissing my husband, I suddenly see Emma coming loose from her swaddle and plunging toward the floor, her tiny gums bared open to the world."

"What you're describing sounds very much like a flashback," Dr. Zimmer says. "When you have these incidents of memory, do you almost lose track of yourself, where you are, what you're doing, when the memory comes on you?"

"I guess so."

"And for that moment, the memory feels more real to you than whatever you're actually doing?"

"Yes." I feel this swooping sense of relief, that she understands. "Once, the vision was so strong that I actually cried out, and startled Leo. He was dozing on the couch, with Emma on his chest, and I woke them both. She started crying and Leo couldn't figure out what was wrong with me, why I'd screamed like that."

"You didn't feel you could explain it to him?"

"I didn't want to scare him."

It's quiet in the office now, too quiet for New York. I can't hear traffic noises or the hiss of the steam radiator or quarreling neighbors. No pigeon pecks the ledge outside the window. Dr. Zimmer's pen is poised silently above her notepad.

"Was there anything else about the dream?" she finally asks. "Anything else you remember?" I close my eyes again, and it's like going back into a place of dread, slipping under. I can still see it, her tiny fingers stretched out in the naked air.

"There was a monkey-creature on the wall above my bed, and the nurse came in with a dustpan and a little broom, and she swept the baby away," I say, opening my eyes. "Silly, right? And the nurse just pressed that lever on the trash can with her squeaky white sneaker, and when the lid popped open, Emma's body slid off the dustpan and into the garbage. The nurse said not to worry—they'd get me another one."

Dr. Zimmer is writing again.

"Then the monkey scampered down the wall and tried to pry open the trash can, and that's when I screamed myself awake. But I didn't tell the other therapist, and I don't know why." I'm crying now. Dammit, I'm always crying.

Dr. Zimmer considers me for a moment. "Perhaps you needed that imaginary death to explain your tears," she suggests kindly. "You're a new mother, you're supposed to be filled with exuberant joy, right?"

Maybe I've been too hard on Dr. Zimmer.

"And instead, all you could think about was this awful dream, the possibility of losing her," Dr. Zimmer says. "You said it yourself, that you're obsessed with mortality."

I nod again, and then a fresh round of boring tears.

"Majella, trauma can account for itself, however plain."

"But I haven't had a trauma," I say.

Dr. Zimmer smiles. "Becoming a mother can absolutely be a trauma, both physically and mentally."

"But I wanted this baby. More than I've ever wanted anyone."

"And now you have her. And it's probably nothing like you imagined."

My shame feels bottomless. How can she know this, when I haven't told her?

"No, it's not. . . . I mean, I imagined my body would take a beating, but not like this, not this total annihilation. I didn't think I would need a C-section. I thought I was tougher than that, and then . . ."

"Lots of tough women need C-sections," Dr. Zimmer interrupts. "Please tell me you know that has nothing to do with toughness."

I shrug, and then I shake my head.

"So your physical recovery has been difficult?"

"It's shocking," I say. "My body is a disaster."

"But you're improving?

"I don't know. I mean the pain is improving. But that's not the thing. I mean I feel like my body failed the first test of motherhood, which sucks." Dr. Zimmer shakes her head, but doesn't interrupt, so I continue, "But it's my mind that is most startling." I reach carefully for each word, like a kid swinging arm-to-arm across the monkey bars. "My mind is in tatters. I didn't expect this. I feel just totally . . . adrift."

Dr. Zimmer lays her pen down on her notepad.

"I love her so much," I say, and my voice feels strangulated. "I don't mean to sound like I don't love her. It's fucking macabre how much I love her."

My heaven-scented need-factory. I am entwined with Emma in ways I never saw coming. My love for her has the bared teeth of a wild animal. Fangs. Slaver. So what does it say about me, that I was able to deliver that nightmare lie, that harrowing, horrible, terror-gape of a lie, so easily? It slipped out of me, exactly in the precise way that my reluctant daughter did not. There was no preparation, no struggle, no push. It tumbled forth unbidden.

"How could I say that about her? That she died?"

Dr. Zimmer is watching me twist the Kleenex around my

knuckles. I can see my distorted reflection in the toe of her shoe. She doesn't answer.

"It's like this kind of love that obliterates everything else in the universe," I say. "Like there's nothing else left. It's postapocalyptic, motherhood. Like I'm just a shell that's left."

"It does feel that way sometimes," Dr. Zimmer concedes. "And it might for a while. But not forever. Parenthood is tough. But it gets easier."

I don't believe her, but it doesn't matter because the bell on her cell phone dings, and our time is up.

There's always a crazy guy on the subway, but it's not usually me. Or maybe it would be more honest to say that people don't usually *know* that it's me, because at least I'm self-aware. Usually, crazy on the subway is obvious: an out-loud iPod singer, a twitcher, or a crotch-on-pole rubber, complete with revolting funk and moans. Or a Jesus-shouter, angrier and more unkempt than the son of God ever was. But today it's me. I'm the obvious one.

There, all the way against the wall, alone on the two-seater. No one wants to sit next to me because I'm leaking tears and milk, see? I forgot to change my nursing pads before I got on the train, so I start to leak through my shirt three stops before home. September is drawing down, but it's still too warm for a jacket, so I cry to cover the wet spots. It's like biological pyrotechnics.

"I'm such a fucking mess," I say out loud. I'm grateful to live in New York, where no one cares if you mutter and curse to yourself on the subway.

At home, I change my shirt and bra, stuff fresh nursing pads against my itchy nipples. Leo is in the office, on the computer, and Emma is sleeping in a basket by his feet. I stand in the office doorway and watch them for a moment. He's poking around on Facebook, answering e-mails, but he keeps looking down at

Emma beside him. He leans over her with his phone, and snaps a picture.

"God, you're beautiful," he says to her.

And my heart wells up with guilt and gratitude. Leo is such a good father, such a natural. *He should be the mother, not me,* I think. He is touching the tip of her sleeping nose softly with his finger; he's not terrified of waking her. I take the two steps down, into the office, and he turns to greet me.

"I didn't hear you come in," he says, and he pushes the rolling chair away from the desk, and grabs me onto his lap. "How was it, was it good?"

"Yeah, it was fine."

"Jelly?"

"Yeah."

"I'm sorry about the babysitting crack."

I shake my head. "It's fine."

"It's not fine," he says, and he turns me on his knee so that I'm facing him. He touches my cheek, and I recognize the love in that gesture—I just saw him do that to Emma. "I want you to know that I don't really think that," he says. "I know it's not babysitting, she's my own daughter. It was just a poor choice of words."

I lean my head against his.

"I'm sorry, too."

"For what?"

"For being such a raging hormone monster."

Leo kisses me, on the mouth this time.

"I love you," he says. "You're the only raging hormone monster for me."

Emma wakes up just as Leo is leaving for work. He kisses her, and whispers to her, and then hands her off to me. She smells like Dreft, with a sour backnote of spit-up. I put my nose right against her skull and I breathe her in. We wave at Leo through the front window, as he heads off to catch the bus. Well, I wave, really. Emma can't wave yet.

In the living room, Drew Carey is clutching his microphone on the screen. I tell myself that it's okay to watch while I nurse, because Emma's not facing it, and she won't even know the television is on if I keep it muted. I sit down on the couch and cradle her in my arms. Her cloudy little eyes blink up at me, and I blink at the showcase showdown.

"Seriously, Drew? You call that a prize package?" I say. Emma is eating. I stare at the middle-aged blonde who is struggling to maintain her enthusiasm for her shitty showcase. She smiles and claps. "Next, he'll be giving away bus fare to Hoboken," I tell Emma. She only slurps in response.

The blonde overbids by fourteen thousand dollars, and it is appalling. I am truly aghast. So today, that is the thing that saves me from plunging into permanent madness—because I recognize it: that no one should be emotionally invested in *The Price Is Right*, especially if they're not even a member of the studio audience. Self-awareness is key, in staving off the crazy.

I slip Emma into her bouncy seat right before the phone rings. She's too little yet, to bat at the monkey and toucan that hang down in front of her, but she has taken to staring intently at them, and when I swing them for her, she makes faces I can't decipher. I pick up the phone with one hand and flick the monkey with the other.

"Hello?"

"Hey, sweet pea!" It's my dad.

"Hi, Pop!"

"How's it hangin'?" My dad started trying out slang when I was in high school, but he hasn't progressed beyond the early nineties. Sometimes it's endearing.

"Good? Hanging good," I decide.

"How's the munchkin?"

"She's awesome, Dad. She's so cute, and getting more alert now—she still sleeps most of the time, but when she's awake, she's really *awake*. You should see her." I smile at Emma, and she gurgles.

"Ah, I wish we could be there," he says. And then there's this long uncomfortable beat, because there is nothing preventing him from being here. Nothing at all. "You know how your mom hates to fly."

"Yeah."

"And it's a long haul up there in the Prius, but we'll do it! We'll do it soon!"

"Yeah, no, I know."

"So how's motherhood treating you?" he asks.

"Good, I guess. It's hard. Harder than I expected."

"Yeah," Dad says. "The women have it so much harder than the men. Such a tough job, and so easy to get it wrong."

I take a deep breath.

"But not for you, Majella," he quickly corrects himself. "You'll get it right, kiddo. I have every faith."

"Did Mom tell you about the diary I found?" I ask.

"Yeah, she's been looking up a bunch of stuff in all her gene-ometry crap."

"Genealogy," I correct him, but only under my breath.

I wander into the kitchen and look around like I'm going to find the diary on the counter, even though I know I left it in the attic. I can hear some birdsong on his end of the line. He must be outside on his condo balcony, overlooking the golf course.

"So talk to me about the house, how's the house coming?"

"I don't want to talk about the house, Dad," I say. "I'm exhausted. I know it's boring, but all I really want to talk about is how hard this mommy-thing is, how much I miss you and Mom."

There's a snag in his breath. I can hear him scratching his neck. He plomps down in a chair, I can hear him rearranging his limbs beneath him.

"Yeah, it wasn't great timing, I guess, the way we left," he says.

"No."

"But you're doing all right, hey? With Leo, and everything?"

"Not really, Pop," I say. "I feel so isolated. It's not natural, living like this. It made more sense the way people used to live back in the day, all in little villages with lots of family and the rest of the tribe around, and everybody would pitch in at whatever they were good at." I'm leaning my elbows onto the concrete countertops, staring out the kitchen window and into my neighbor's shower. "If you were a bad mama back then, it probably didn't matter, because there were all these women in the tribe there to show you, to help. I don't know what I'm doing, and there's nobody I can ask questions. I'm so on my own."

"You can always call us, Majella, me and your mother."

Emma squeaks in her bouncy seat, and I turn to look at her.

"Come on, Dad, you know what Mom's like," I say, walking back to Emma and bouncing her little seat with my toe. "Mom will tell me the exact shade she had her toenails painted last week (*Totally Toffee*), and how many kids the pedicurist had (*four!*), and how much she paid (*only seven dollars, can you believe that? Not including tip, of course, and she forgot her cash, so she had to put the whole thing on her debit card*), but she never wants to talk about real stuff. I can't tell her that I'm lonesome."

There is a crackling noise as my father's hand passes across the mouthpiece of whatever phone he is holding in Florida.

"You're lonesome?" he says, and I can hear a split in his voice, all jammed up with emotion.

I shrug. He cannot see me shrug. He is in Florida.

"Yeah, you know," I say. "It's just, I'm home alone all day now. Leo's great, when he's here, but he has to work. And all my friends. They work."

"But you'll be back to work before you know it. And hey, you were alone a lot before—you're a writer. Don't writers spend loads of time alone?"

"I guess so, but no, Pop, this is different. I used to be out all the time, doing my research and stuff."

Emma coos, and I bend down to kiss her toes. She kicks automatically at my waiting hand. She's beneath the window, and the sunlight glows down on her perfectly round head, her sloped nose, her full cheeks. *How am I not going to ruin you?* I think, and then we both begin to cry. My dad hears me sniffling.

"Pop, I gotta go, Emma's crying," I manage.

Before I hang up, I hear him say, "Call me later, hon."

There is no thinking, no rationale, and certainly no conversation when Emma cries. My body responds to her in a way that is purely primal, that I have no willful control over. She cries: my blood pressure climbs. My limbs become tense, my neck locks into a rigid posture. My uterus contracts, the stitches in my incision do their best to give with the spasms. My breasts fill with milk. My brain shuts down, replaced by some kind of repetitive variation on the mantra: *please stop crying please stop crying please stop crying.* Sometimes Leo tries to talk to me during these times, and I look at him, desperate to find words on my tongue, desperate to locate myself in my brain, so that I might respond to him in some appropriate way. It's impossible.

I lift Emma from the bouncy seat and swing her in my arms. I walk the house with her, swinging, shushing, singing, crying. I watch the clock, just to give my brain some other focus, something outside this biological circle of friction. The minutes tick by. Forty-seven of them. While Emma mewls and whimpers and screams and then whimpers and wails again.

"I didn't mean it, Emma, it will be fine," I try to tell her. "We'll be fine—I'll be a good mama, I won't ruin you, I promise. I'll take good care of you."

She stops crying and makes a tiny, shuddering sigh in my arms. Then a face that threatens.

"No, no," I say. "I will, I'll take care of you."

And that is the thing that calms her. I make a song out of it—an "I'll Take Care of You" song—and I sing it until she falls asleep in my arms. This moment is my greatest victory of motherhood, and also probably of my life. Better than the day I got my first byline in *Gourmet* magazine. Better, perhaps, than my wedding. It is so wonderful that I don't want to put her down, in case she wakes up and starts screaming again, which will obliterate my triumph.

I lift her gingerly to my shoulder and we walk some more around the house. We walk upstairs, and then upstairs again. It's probably not a good idea to bring her into the attic. It's filthy, and there are tripping hazards everywhere. I turn around to head back down, but first—there's the diary, sitting atop the old steamer trunk, still drunk on sunshine and dust. I navigate carefully across the floor and pick it up. I jam it into my back pocket so I can hold the railing and won't somersault down the stairs and land on Emma at the bottom.

After a while, I manage to settle her into the crib without waking her, and then I head back to the unfinished living room, where I can now permit myself to unmute the television. There are no words to describe what a lucent feeling of pleasure it is to unmute the television. Some soap opera is on, and I don't want to watch it, but the sound of an adult human voice is like an anchor. I think about calling Dad back, but I'm not ready.

Leo has been encouraging me to pick up a writing job or two, to start freelancing again. He thinks I can do research during the days and the evenings while Emma sleeps, and then write during the mornings when he's home, before he goes in to the restaurant. Before Emma, I had more work than I could manage. But Leo doesn't seem to understand what's happened to my brain. Writing requires focus, and I have none. I can't imagine I'll ever be able to form a coherent written sentence again.

I ponder all of this from the couch. The office doors are open, the computer just beyond. The baby monitor is silent. I haven't even checked e-mail in almost a week. But my brain refuses. It's like concrete. I don't even want the frustration of trying. For a few minutes, I watch the laminated couple on the television screen, with their silent, well-dressed baby. The mother is lipsticked and ironed. Her hair has a bouncy shine. I flip the channel.

I'm still too sore to maneuver my hips off the couch beneath me, so I lean forward to pull the diary out of my back pocket. Then I lean back, and arrange pillows all around me. I flip open to the inside cover, and trace my fingers along the name written in uneven scrawl over and over again: Ginny Doyle. The madness is so viral it has leached into the childlike handwriting of its host—the loops of the letters look frenetic, they lean a little too precariously. I flip to the first brittle, yellowed page and begin to read.

12 March 1848
The infernal crunching, it's followed me here.

I stop reading and sit up a little too quickly on the edge of the couch. My incision throws a quick jab, which I barely register, because I'm so astounded by what I have just read. I don't know why, but I flip back to the inside cover—what am I looking for, a hidden camera? I shake my head to try to sluice out the confusion. Then I lean back, and flip again to the text. I read:

12 March 1848

The infernal crunching, it's followed me here. I thought coming to New York would be the answer for us, like it would wipe things clean, but it's been so much harder than I imagined. I've lost so much, and that's all I can think of. Not what we've left, but what's gone. My children need me, but I'm all hollow for them. All that's in me is sorrow.

I'm tormented by so many memories. I wake up sweating in the nighttimes, and I have to throw open the windows to the chill night air, just to calm me. And the children do be waking up, and crying and shivering, and asking me to close the windows, but I can't. I need to open them, and to sing and clap loudly, to strangle out those memory-noises: of screaming, of struggling. Of wicked crunching. I'm going mad in the head altogether. I need to be strong for the baby, for the children.

Everything I've lost. God help me.

18 March 1848

I've confessed. I thought it would be a tremendous balm for my soul, but I'm still plagued by my conscience, even though the priest here is lovely and friendly— nothing like the sort of commanding fellas we get at home. So much softer than Father Brennan ever was. He never asked me for any details about what happened, only gave me a penance, and said that it must've been an

awful weight for me to be carrying around. He said God
would forgive me if I did the penance, but forgiveness
seems too much to ask.

The phone rings while I'm reading, and I glance up at the caller ID on the television screen. It's Leo. He's probably calling to see if I'm getting any writing done while Emma naps. I let it go to voice mail. I know he'll be too busy to chat when I ring him back later, but I just don't feel up to my unwieldy explanations. I feel the tiniest prickle of guilt, but I shrug it off.

25 March 1848
  Even now, the crunching persists. I think the baby can
hear it too, because he cries at night right after it starts,
and he won't settle again until I lift him out of the cot
and sing him back to sleep. Maybe it's not in my head
then, if he can hear it, too? It's so difficult to sort things
out in my head.

1 April 1848
  Tomorrow is Good Friday. I can't imagine what
Easter will be like this year, after so much terror and
grief. If it weren't for the children, I don't know could I
go on. Even after everything that's happened—when I
look at the baby especially, I know I've done my best, and
that's all I can do, the rest is up to God. I had no choice
but to save him, surely. Surely my hands were tied.

The red light on the monitor begins to flicker. Emma is awake.

Chapter Six

IRELAND, MARCH 1847

The day was warm despite the damp, and as the sun climbed higher into the midday sky, Ginny stepped out of the cottage and climbed toward the ridge at the top of their field. Saint Patrick's Day had passed in hunger and silence, and there was still no word from Ray. Maggie's cairn was beginning to look like another small house beside their own, and the meager spring sunshine leaked down over it. Ginny stood at the top of the ridge, shadowed her eyes with her hand, and peered down toward the bottom of their land at the road beyond, but it was empty. Not a soul walked there; no shadow of a bird fluttered down from overhead. The only sound was the thuggish wind raking down over the barren fields. Ginny stepped over the ridge and started down the slope on the other side. The lower field was soppy, and when she neared the road, her footprints began to squelch, and fill with water. At the high rock wall, she leaned her elbows up, happy to be away from the cottage, just for a few moments. Her children were hungry inside.

Winter had been savage. Willie and Thomas Harkin had been brought up on charges, along with four other young lads from the parish, and they'd all got transported to Australia. They were the lucky ones, who got gone before their parents and sisters all perished from the hunger. Mary Reilly and her brood were evicted, their house destroyed, and all the neighbors warned by Packet's men against taking them in. Where they'd vanished to, Ginny hadn't the heart to imagine.

There was a time when she had known every bit of news and gossip from this parish—every wedding, every child born, every passing. Now the people were gone in great troops, men and women Raymond had known all his life, just gone. Like flocks of geese, lifted up into a skyward vee, and then vanished.

Ginny turned and leaned her back against the rock wall, to stare back up at the ridge above her land. She was making a habit of this, of coming here every day for a few minutes, just to stretch her limbs, to move her body over the land, to get away from the seeking mouths of her desperate children. Their need had grown too strong for her in these last days, their hunger too acute to endure. The very sight of her children pained her now—how gaunt and wasted they were. She couldn't abide their needful eyes.

They had eaten the rotten potatoes until they were indigestible, even the seed for next year's crop. They had eaten all the turnips and the cabbage. Then Michael began to disappear for a day at a time, and he'd come back with a fish he'd poached from God knew where. When he did that, Ginny was overcome by terror and gratefulness. They would eat the fish in great secrecy and fear—nearly raw. She was in dread that the smell of it roasting would give them away, and Packet's men would come and seize

Michael, and take him to jail or transport him for thieving. Two grown brothers in the parish had already been hanged for stealing a sheep to feed their starving children. Ginny and her children had eaten everything, all the oats and meal and veg and borrowed fish, until there wasn't a crumb of food left in all the world. Then they ate a water soup she made from dandelions and nettles.

Ginny closed her eyes, squeezed them shut hard, until she could see a floaty mass of colored specks inside her head. She tried to conjure Raymond's voice, the sound of his confidence before he'd left.

Say February. March at the latest. That's what he'd said. March was drawing to an end now. Any day, they would get word from him. He'd send a letter to Father Brennan. He would send money inside. If her children could only hang on a few more days. Please God.

The wind carried a stifled song to her ears and she turned, stepped toward the gate in the wall, and leaned out so she could see up the road. There was a figure approaching, an impossibly thin man drawing toward her. As he drew closer, she could see: he was so rickety, he'd hardly the strength to stand upright. On his back, he carried a roughened sack, its top gathered together with a bit of twine. His eyes were like open graves—they didn't see her, didn't latch on to her, even after she waved, she saluted him. He didn't even know she was there. She shrank into the wall, pulled her body into a knot. He was raving as he passed.

"Mo leanbh," he wailed. "My baby."

Ginny flinched from him, but he never even glanced her way, just continued trudging on, and as he went past, she could see the bony fingers of a little hand protruding from the sack slung over his shoulder. Her hand flew to her mouth, and she crushed the skin of her face with her fingers. She tried squeezing her eyes shut, but it was no use. She couldn't unsee his face, those fingers. She couldn't unhear his cries.

She watched the horrible specter of a man until he disappeared over a rut in the road, and then she bent down beside the wall and she retched, but nothing came up—not even the sticky yellow bile that was normal now. She was empty.

She stood absently for some time in the vacant yard, staring back at the ridge with her stomach quivering. She began to dread going back to the cottage, to her hungry children. Time passed so strangely now. Without the regular busyness of food, the hours were drawn and purposeless. Mealtimes came and went without any chatter or preparation or cleanup. Ginny tried feeding her children on songs and prayers instead. But they were growing listless. The most terrifying thing was when they had stopped complaining of the hunger. Even Poppy no longer asked for food. They had ceased growing as well, and now their skulls were starting to look huge on their little bodies. Their hair was falling out. Still, they were her children, and she could feel their souls, strong and glittering inside their withered bodies. She could sense them in there.

Ginny heaved her body away from the wall and started back toward the ridge, and the cottage beyond, but a voice from behind called out, and she spun on her foot, hoping to God that whoever owned that voice was bringing news. A letter from Raymond.

"*Dia duit*," a woman hailed her from down the road. The woman waved her hand overhead, and Ginny waved back.

"*Dia is Muire duit*," Ginny replied, and then waited until the woman drew level with the gate. She didn't recognize the woman, but she was well dressed, her petticoat black instead of red, and she'd a traveling bonnet curled over a fine head of shiny black hair. Even for all that, she looked weary and her brogues were well-worn, covered with the muck of the road. Her young face was damp with sweat.

"Have you far to go?" Ginny asked her.

"Coolnabine," the young woman said, pointing north, "up the far side of Beltra Lough."

"That's a fair old walk for you," Ginny said. "Hope the weather holds out."

"Please, God."

"Will you take a drop of water for yourself, for your journey?"

"I will, thanks," she said, following Ginny in through the gate and up through the boggy lower field toward the ridge.

"I'm Ginny Doyle. You're very welcome," Ginny said as they neared the top of the slope. "The cottage is just there." She gestured down to her tidy little home, gleaming against the rugged bleakness of the landscape.

"Anne Cassidy," the woman said. At the door, she wiped her brogues on the flagstone before stepping in.

It seemed dim inside, after being out in the high light of a spring afternoon. Anne pulled off her bonnet, and Maire stood up to give her the stool. Ginny handed the visitor a mug of water, and she gratefully gulped it down.

"I wish I'd a morsel to offer you," Ginny said.

Anne shook her head, but then she looked at Ginny, dead in the eye. It felt like years since anyone had looked her in the eye. "You've had a bad time of it?" Anne asked, without any guile.

"Like everyone else," Ginny said, then turned back to Maire. "Take the children outside for some fresh air, love, it's a nice dry day."

Maire tucked her shawl around her shoulders and herded the others outside wordlessly. They were like a crowd of slips, the way they flitted from the room. Some deep horror crept over Ginny while she watched them go. She turned back to her guest.

"There's nothing to give them this two days," she confessed. She stayed leaning in the doorjamb. "Their father is gone to America." She tried a smile. "Since September. We'll hear from him soon, with some money."

"Please, God," Anne answered.

"Please, God," Ginny echoed.

But that expression had lost its meaning. It was hard to believe in beseeching God anymore. Ginny changed the subject.

"We don't often see strangers out walking these days. The parish is near empty now. Is it home you're going to?"

"It is," Anne said, wiping a dribble of water from her chin. "I was working at Springhill House these last months—I was chambermaid. Then this morning Mrs. Spring let me go."

"Ah, God love you," Ginny said.

The girl shook her head. "I can hardly believe it myself. I don't know what we'll do now. It was a good post. Kept my family going."

"Family?" Ginny asked.

"Three sisters, two brothers," she said. "I'm the eldest."

Ginny looked back over her shoulder and out at her skinny children in the yard. The others were helping Maggie find a good stone for the cairn.

"What age are you?" Ginny asked.

"Nearly seventeen."

"You're awful young for these kind of worries."

Anne shrugged. "I don't suppose there's any good age to be, for them."

"And your parents?"

"My dad's at home with the little ones. My mam died in January, God rest her. The fever."

"Ah, God love you," Ginny said, and she crossed herself, sent up a prayer for the girl's dead mother.

Anne stood up from the stool quickly and handed Ginny back the mug. She was uncomfortable talking about her mam. It was an awful thing that'd happened, the way this hunger had undressed death, and made it common. Ginny had nothing for this strange, weary girl, only platitudes. It didn't matter how many people had died of starvation or the attendant fever, it didn't make the pain of real, meticulous grief any less. It was all over Anne's pretty young face, the mournful blackness of her hair.

"No rest for the weary!" the girl said brightly, trying on a brave smile.

"And do you mind me asking, why did they let you go, at Springhill House?" Ginny said. She was anxious for her guest not to go, not yet. It was so nice to have a visitor, someone to talk to. She hadn't meant to upset the poor girl. "Are they finally packing it in, heading back to London?"

"No." She shook her head. "They would if they'd any sense. But the missus, she's a nutter—I don't know what she's hangin' around for. She's not right in the head. She just takes a notion one day, and that's it—you're gone. She never keeps any of the staff on for long, only the old housekeeper."

"I heard that all right," Ginny said, refilling the girl's mug with water. Anne waved her off.

"I'm grand now, thanks," she said. "I'd better be off. I've a long journey ahead of me yet."

Ginny poured the water back into the pail, and followed the girl back out the door into the yard. The children stood around the cairn, watching them. Their eyes were as big as saucers. The girl stopped short in the yard, looking at them.

"What's your name?" she said to Maire.

"Maire."

"I'm Anne."

"Anne," Maire repeated, without smiling.

Then Anne reached into her satchel and drew out a cold block of cheese and a small hunk of grainy bread while the children watched.

"Here you are, Maire," she said.

Maire tried not to show how eager she was, stepping over to the older girl, while the little ones clamored around them. Anne handed the cheese and the bread to Maire then, who broke everything into five equal pieces, careful to save a portion for her mother. The children were all so patient and quiet, God love them, while Maire passed the bites around. They fell on the food in silence. Ginny's sight had gone blurry from tears.

"God bless you," she said to the visitor.

Anne smiled. "God bless and keep you," she answered. "Good luck."

When she turned to go, Maire caught her hand and squeezed it. "Thank you, miss," she said.

Anne nodded, and made for the road. When she got to the top of the ridge, she waved back before she disappeared over the other side. Maire came to her mother in the doorway, to hand her a portion of the cheese and bread.

"You have it, love," Ginny said, but Maire pressed it forcefully into her mother's reluctant palm.

"I'm not hungry, Mammy," Maire insisted, pushing the food at her mother's hand.

"I'll have it!" Michael piped up behind her.

Maire reeled on him, smacked him in the back of the head. "You will not," she hissed.

"Are you hungry, pet?" Ginny asked him.

Michael looked at Maire, who glared ferociously back at him.

"No, Mammy." He shook his head.

Ginny brought the three-legged stool out, and sat beneath the blackthorn tree, nibbling the corner of the cheese. She chewed slowly while her stomach yawned and groaned in anticipation. That little bit of nourishment had been enough to cheer the children, at least in their spirits, and Michael and Maggie were lying on their backs now, pointing up at the passing clouds.

"Look, that one's like a ship with a dragon's head," Michael said.

Maggie twisted her head and squinted. "I see a selkie."

Poppy was creeping around by the cairn, running her little fingers along the gaps in the stones. Maggie sat up and looked at her.

"Don't touch it!" she warned her sister.

Poppy drew her hand away.

Maire sat beside her mother on the ground, quietly watching the others. She folded her legs beneath her and leaned her head on Ginny's knee. Ginny combed her fingers through her daughter's long, fair hair.

"Mammy?"

"Yes, love."

"Maybe they'd be hiring a new chambermaid at Springhill House."

"Mmm."

Then they were both quiet again, for a moment.

"Were you listening at the door?" Ginny asked.

Maire only shrugged in response. "Would I be old enough?" She lifted her head to look at her mother.

"Ah, no, love," Ginny said, rubbing her hand along the softness of her daughter's cheek, her chin. "You're too young to go out working."

"But I could do it," Maire said. "I'd be a tremendous chambermaid." She put her head back down on her mother's knee. "What if Daddy couldn't find work straightaway, in America? Or what if the money got lost on its way here? What if it doesn't get here in time?" She didn't say in time for what, but Ginny shuddered. She put her arm around her daughter, and leaned over her, kissed her.

"Shh, don't worry," Ginny whispered into her daughter's hair. "It's my job to do the worrying."

But Maire's posture stayed rigid while Ginny sat up and chewed thoughtfully on the last nibble of bread. Ginny licked her fingertips, then brushed them against her petticoat to dry them.

"I'm still hungry, Mammy," Poppy said.

Maire lifted her chin from her mother's knee.

"Me, too," Michael admitted, ignoring the look Maire was giving him.

"Tell you what." Ginny stood up, lifting Poppy onto her hip, and taking Michael by the hand. "We'll all have a drop of warmed water. Come inside now."

They took turns with the mug.

"Better?" Ginny asked.

Michael nodded, but not believably, and Ginny watched his back as he returned outside. She looked at his little shoulder blades standing up in his back, and for a moment, she imagined she could see him withering in front of her, like the stalk of some diseased potato. She had the sense that if she stood still for a time, she would actually watch him disappear. It seemed like a certainty in that moment: they would die here, one by one. Not in some distant, tentative, theoretical way, but soon, presently. Her babies would die. And she might even go first, leaving them to fend for themselves. She imagined them gathered around her body in the morning, trying to waken her, Poppy curling in for a cuddle. That thought seized her with horror, like a hand on her throat. She couldn't breathe for grief.

"Mammy?" Maire's hand was soft on her mother's.

Ginny turned toward her daughter.

"D'you know what I need you to do, Maire?" Ginny said, crouching down and taking her daughter by the two hands. "D'you think you could manage to look after your brother and sisters?"

Maire's eyes widened, but she answered bravely. "I can of course."

Ginny brushed a loose strand of hair away from her daughter's face. Maire had always been a serious child—wise beyond her years. But looking at her now, Ginny could only think how young she was, how much life she hadn't yet lived. Eleven years of age. "Not just today, but for a little while?" Ginny said. "Until we hear from your father? A few weeks maybe?" She needed to be sure her daughter could take it on. It was an awful lot to ask.

Maire gulped, a tiny quiver in her throat. She nodded.

"You're the best girl," Ginny said, giving her a squeeze. "Daddy will be so proud of you when I tell him."

Ginny stood.

"Are you going to get the job, Mammy?" Maire asked. "At Springhill House?"

"I'm going to try."

Ginny splashed water on her face, and pinched color into her cheeks. She removed her kerchief and knotted her hair into fresh plaits while her children sat quietly on the floor, watching her. Poppy was crying, but Ginny wasn't moved by her baby's tears. She felt renewed. She had a fixed plan. She could shut away her fears, and concentrate on the task at hand. At least for now there was something she could *do*.

"You'll be all right," Ginny said, stooping down to kiss Poppy on top of the head. "Maire's going to take great care of you, aren't you, Maire?"

"I am." Maire stood up, and, with some effort, hoisted Poppy up onto her hip. Poppy flopped her blondie head against Maire's shoulder.

"I'm going to call in to Mrs. Fallon as I'm going past and ask her to look in on ye," Ginny said, tying a bonnet over her tidied hair.

The Fallons were about the only nearby neighbors left. Ginny fluttered around the cottage while she talked, stoking up the fire for them, looking for things she could set to rights before going. There was nothing. No chores left, no animals, no food in the house, no crop in the ground outside. Until she could get food to them, there was nothing else to be done. She breathed deeply.

"I'll stop and ask Father Brennan for a reference on the way," she said to Maire. "You may start preparing the ground in the turnip patch. If I can get some seed, we'll plant that as soon as the weather turns."

Michael was watching his mother with a hardness in his jaw. His eyes were dry.

"Help your sister, Michael," she said to him.

He only nodded. She was ready to go, ready to walk out the door and down the road, away from her four babies, ready to leave them on their own. Maire allowed Poppy to slide down to the ground and run to Ginny. Poppy wrapped herself around her mother's legs.

"Michael, take Poppy and Maggie outside for a few minutes," Ginny said, standing. "Let me talk to Maire."

Michael unfolded himself from his spot beside the fire, and herded his sisters out into the sunshine. Maire turned from the doorway to face her mother.

"You know what to do if Poppy wakes up crying in the night?"

"Give her a bit of warmed water and a cuddle."

"That's right, and sometimes she likes a song," Ginny said. "If you can sing to her, that always settles her right down."

Ginny was amazed by Maire's solemnity, and she could see that it wasn't a performance. The courage in Maire's face was not for her mother's benefit—it was authentic. Maire could do this.

"And you're not to tell anyone that I'm away, except Mrs. Fallon—she'll know. But if ye have any other visitors call in, say nothing. If they ask where your father is, you can tell them he's gone to America, but if they ask for your mother, just tell them I'm gone to see a neighbor, and you expect me back presently."

"Of course," Maire said.

"If anything happens, if you need help, send Michael to Mrs. Fallon, or up to Father Brennan," Ginny went on. "I don't want you leaving Poppy and Maggie. You send Michael, understand?"

"We'll be grand, Mammy," Maire said, crossing the floor to where her mother stood.

Ginny embraced her eldest daughter. She would not cry. She would be stalwart, like Maire. They clung to each other for a full minute, but Maire was the first to let go. Ginny stood, fluffed her petticoat out beneath her, went to the doorway, and looked out. Maire stood beside her mother, and Ginny noticed how tall she was—that the top of her head came nearly to her shoulder now.

"Mam?"

Ginny turned to look at her.

"What will I feed them?" she whispered.

Ginny caught a thick breath in her chest. What a leap of faith she was asking of Maire, to stay calm while her mother walked out the door and away. She was turning her back on them, Ginny was. That's what it must have felt like, leaving Maire alone with three hungry babies, and not a morsel of food left in the whole of Knockbooley. Surely Maire knew that Ginny would never abandon them; she wouldn't leave them to perish.

"Oh, Maire, you poor darling, I'll send food right away," Ginny said, lifting her daughter's chin. "I promise, as soon as I get there, that's the whole point in me going. So I can send food back at once."

"But how, Mammy?"

Ginny shook her head. "I'll find a way."

Ginny kept her legs moving swiftly beneath her, pushing on to Springhill House. When she was fit and healthy, she could have walked this distance in two hours, but now she was weak and her body felt wilted and warm. Her legs were shaky beneath her, and a few times, she was tempted to rest, but she feared sitting down, in case she couldn't get up again. Tears kept brimming her eyes, but she pushed them away. She felt like a sweet left on a rock in the sun, melting. In the last weeks, there was a strange gnawing sensation in her belly that she initially put down to hunger, but today there was a distinct fluttering there, too.

"It's only my nerves," she said to herself, though she knew, in that instinctive way that women know, that it wasn't her nerves at all.

Her stomach flipped and swooped as she tramped the road. Each step felt more like a struggle, like she'd a yoke on her shoulders, a rope stretching home to her babies that grew taut as she ventured on. There was part of her that hoped she'd be turned away, an icy slice of terror in her gut when she thought of her children at home without her. But then she pictured Maire's stern and determined little face, and she knew that somehow this might work.

"I've no choice," she reminded herself. "If I go back, we starve. That's it."

In truth, she wasn't sure she was fit to walk home again. She'd heard stories of people falling over dead in the road from the hunger. She took a deep breath and straightened herself from the shoulders. After three arduous hours, Ginny Doyle arrived at the gates of Springhill House. There were two men and a woman already waiting beside the gates. One of the fellas looked to be in fair enough shape. He was lean, but tall, and he still had a color in his face, a bit of animation about him. He was dressed in a swallow-tailed coat and a hat. The brogues on his feet were worn but not broken. He nodded at Ginny when she drew close to the gate.

"All right?" he said. She nodded back.

The other two sat in a fixed heap, leaning against each other for the strength of their combined posture. They were so feeble and gray that a stiff breeze might have blown them away like a scattering of ash. The man's head hung limp from his neck, his dry mouth agape. The woman stared at Ginny with unblinking eyes. She moved her lips in greeting, but no sound came out. Ginny couldn't look at her for more than a moment. Beyond the gate, a fat, sweaty man was hustling down the long drive from the house. Without opening the gate, he addressed the older couple first, gesturing toward them.

"What's your business here?" he said.

The woman's eyes reeled on to him, and she licked her lips in effort, but there was no voice in her throat. The man beside her never moved, never even twitched. Ginny wasn't sure he was breathing. The fat man looked at Ginny.

"You know these two?" he asked. She shook her head.

"Nor do I," said the man in the swallow-tailed coat, "but I can guess their business here as well as you can, Mr. Murdoch."

The fat man glared through the bars.

"And you, Mr. Brady?" Murdoch said to the man in the coat. "What is it you want?"

"My family and I are going to America," Brady answered, "and we need to settle our affairs before we go."

"So you're packing it in, eh? Calling it a day?"

"There's little choice now."

The woman on the ground was becoming agitated while the men talked; she was trying to speak. Ginny watched in horror, the flutter in her stomach growing into leaps and plunges.

"And you?" The fat Murdoch was looking at Ginny now, but before she could respond, Brady interrupted.

"Mr. Murdoch, please," he said, with a quiet insistence. He gestured to the woman on the ground. "They've no time to lose. Couldn't you send down a bite, for pity's sake?"

Murdoch's red neck quivered. "You'd want to mind your insolence before you get to America, sir," he said. "It doesn't stand to you."

"No, sir," Brady agreed. "But it stands to them."

The woman on the ground looked up at him, and for a moment, her face changed with gratefulness—Ginny could see what she might have looked like before hunger had robbed her voice and her body. Murdoch had his key in the gate now, and he was opening the lock. He swung it open and gestured Mr. Brady inside.

"Wait for me in the library."

Mr. Brady stood his ground.

"If you're not coming in, get off my land before I call for the constable," Murdoch seethed.

Brady shook his head, and glanced dolefully at the ghosts by his feet. He shook his head, and shoved past Mr. Murdoch. But Murdoch grabbed him by the arm and hissed into his ear as he went past, "Have you any idea the havoc it would cause, if we started handing out food to every beggar who had the nerve to disgrace our gate? It's well for you to feign righteousness, but I don't see you forking over the price of your American ticket to feed your fellow paupers out there."

Brady freed his arm from Murdoch's grip with a violent shrug and, turning his back, started up the drive toward the house. Murdoch muttered after him, "Empty-headed fool," and then he turned to Ginny. "You?" he said.

She cleared her throat, tried to infuse herself with some of the bravery she'd just witnessed in Mr. Brady. She drew herself closer to the gate.

"I'm Ginny Doyle, sir, from Knockbooley, and I heard you had an opening for a chambermaid. I'd like to inquire after the position."

Murdoch scowled in his eyebrows while he scrutinized her.

"Where's your husband, girl?"

She tried not to show her shock at the boorishness of the question. She cast her eyes downward. "America," she answered quietly.

"Children?"

She didn't answer, but shook her head only slightly. Murdoch opened the gate again, just wide enough for her to pass through.

"Around to the back corner, there's a green door, across from the stables. Ring there and ask for the housekeeper." He gestured up the drive with his head while he swung the gate shut behind her.

Ginny didn't look back at the couple heaped on the ground beyond. Instead, she fixed her eyes uphill, on the huge and daunting house, while Murdoch twisted his keys in the lock behind her. Her heartbeat felt like a small riot in her breast, and her lips moved in a quiet prayer of gratitude. Yes, she was grateful. Even though Raymond was gone, gone, and she was on her own with nothing to feed her vanishing children. Even though it was still nigh on impossible she would get this job that might save them. Even though that heavy gate yawned shut between herself and her hungry babies beyond, and she could feel that clang in her bones like an amputation.

"Thanks be to God," was what she said.

Chapter Seven

Dr. Zimmer and I are having a bit of a stare-down. Sometimes she does this to me when I first come in—she just sits there and looks at me from beneath that great, voluminous swell of gray hair. If I stubbornly refuse to break the ice, will we just sit here and mock each other with our eyes for the entire hour? I pull a strand of hair out from behind my ear, and sniff it. So clean. So dry.

"How are you feeling today?" she finally asks.

Her jacket and hair are the same color as the building across the street, out the window behind her. If I blur my eyes she almost disappears.

"How's the baby?" she tries again.

I nod. "Emma's good."

"Getting easier?"

"Sure," I lie.

"Perhaps this week we should talk about your mother," she says.

I snap my eyes back into focus. She's wearing glasses, and I can feel her eyes behind them, studying me for a reaction to this suggestion.

"Why my mom?"

"Oftentimes, when a new mother finds the transition into parenthood uncommonly difficult, we can trace at least some of that struggle back to the relationship with her own mother."

"Yeah, I guess that doesn't seem like rocket science," I conclude. I expect Dr. Zimmer to leave it there, to wait for a moment while I ponder my mama, while I flip through memories, and zero in on a good place to get started. But she surprises me instead.

"She seems like a decent woman, from what you've shared with me so far."

"Yeah, she is. Of course."

"So then where do you think all the hostility comes from?" she says.

I feel the air squeezed out of my lungs like water from a sponge. I try to suck it back in. Is this what a panic attack feels like?

"What hostility?" I splutter. "What are you talking about?" I glare at Dr. Zimmer, who is raising a hand in protest.

"Perhaps *hostility* is too strong a word?" she says. "I didn't mean to upset you. It just seems to me that there is some clear animosity there."

I can feel my jaw clenching and unclenching. How is it that she can reduce me to this—this insolent, enraged teenager feeling—with just a peppering of words? *This* is what hostility looks like.

"Why do I keep coming here?" I accidentally say out loud.

Dr. Zimmer takes a short breath and purses her lips.

"Because you want to feel better?" she asks. "And even though sometimes I say things that anger you, deep down, you know we're on the right track. And the reason you respond so strongly is because I'm touching a nerve?"

I pick up the gold pillow and stuff it into my lap like any self-respecting fourteen-year-old would do. I study my fingernails, select one to chew.

"Listen, Majella, mother and daughter relationships are some of the most complicated on earth," she says then. "It's perfectly natural for you to feel a degree of tension there. Every woman I know thinks her mother is annoying in some way or another. Surely you can admit that much, at least?"

"What, that she's annoying?"

"Yes."

I shrug. "Of course she is," I say. "She's incredibly annoying. That doesn't mean I hate her."

"Okay, how?" she asks. I pull on a hangnail with my teeth. "If you had to pick one thing about her that annoys you the most, what would it be?"

The hangnail rips loose, and the little pocket of my nail bed fills up with blood. I grab a tissue from the cry-box that Dr. Zimmer keeps beside the couch, and blot the tiny wound. Then I look Dr. Zimmer in the face.

"I guess the worst thing is probably the way she talks to me."

"How does she talk to you?"

"The same way she talks to everyone," I say. "I mean absolutely everyone. The ladies at church, the bank teller, the grocery store clerk, the guy who pumps her gas. They know as much about her as I do. Last week she told me that her neighbor's dog has cataracts. She talked about it for like ten minutes. I don't even know this neighbor, let alone the dog. It's a Pomeranian, by the way, named Luke. He's almost fourteen."

"I see."

"It's like she's an open book, but all the pages are blank."

"I imagine that's quite frustrating."

"Of course it is," I say. "Because I know it's not real. I know she has depth, somehow. She has interests. She's a smart lady. But it's like she can't access her feelings unless they're immediate."

"Or at least she *won't* access them," Dr. Zimmer says. "Or share them with you."

"Right."

She shifts her position in the chair. "That's difficult, because we can't change your mother. It's not your job to change her. We can only change you, how you cope and respond."

"Yeah." And then it's quiet, and something pops into my head, so I just say it out loud, because that's how therapy works, right? "Last week I was watching some baby show on television, after Emma went to bed and Leo was still at work."

"Mm-hmm." Dr. Zimmer nods encouragingly.

"And the woman just had this baby, and she was holding him, in the hospital delivery room, and she was all sweaty and swollen, and happy. So happy. And her mom was there with her, and she looked at the mother, and she said, *Mom, I never knew you loved me this much.*"

As soon as these words are out in the room, I very predictably and insipidly begin to cry. Dr. Zimmer watches silently for a few minutes, while I snuffle myself back together. I pat at my bleeding fingernail some more, to distract myself.

"And what do you think about that?" Dr. Zimmer finally asks. "What's making you so upset?"

I blow my breath out heavily, from my puffed-out cheeks, and drop my head back on the couch to look up at the ceiling. I picture Emma. Fuzzy, squeaky Emma. My voice comes out in a whisper. "When I hold my baby, I guess the thought I have is: *I don't think my mother loves me this much.*"

"Oh boy," Dr. Zimmer says, and it's the most human thing I've ever heard her say. She closes her notebook and leans slightly forward in her chair. "What if she's just not able to show it?"

"I'm worried that she's not even able to feel it."

"What about the other women in your family, other mothers? What about your grandmother? Was she like this, too? Sort of glossed over?"

"No," I say. "I mean, my dad's mother was a crazy bitch, but my mom's mom was amazing, tremendously warm and sweet." And then I remember the diary. "But there were others."

"Like who?"

"Well, there was some great-great-grandmother or something. . . . I don't really know how she was related to me, but I recently found her diary in my attic, and I started to read it."

"And?"

"She seems more than a little crazy, actually. Even her handwriting. She had some kids, but she only refers to them obliquely, and she's just totally obsessed with herself, like she's just living inside her own head."

"Well, sometimes a diary can just seem like that," Dr. Zimmer says. "It's a bit like therapy. Navel-gazing. Maybe she wasn't as crazy as she seems, if the diary was just her outlet."

"She heard crunching, too," I say, as if that proves everything. But Dr. Zimmer ignores this, so I carry on. "Apparently something horrible happened when she was leaving Ireland or something, and she came here hoping for a fresh start, but she just seems completely haunted and tragic and fucked-up."

"When does the diary date from?"

"From 1848."

"Oh, so she came during the famine times." Dr. Zimmer's eyebrows are up a little, over the tops of her glasses. "Seems like that would be enough to traumatize anyone."

"Yeah, I never even thought of that," I say. "The famine."

"I bet it's fascinating, that diary."

"Yeah, I've only managed to read a few pages, because every time I sit down with it, Emma wakes up, or something interrupts. But it's really something. I wonder what happened to her."

"Do you believe in genetic memory?" Dr. Zimmer asks.

"What, like I could remember something that didn't happen to me, just because it happened to some ancestor of mine?"

"Well, that's a rather literal interpretation, but yes," she says. "I was thinking more along the lines of you, looking for an ancestral excuse to be a bad mother."

My nail has stopped bleeding, so now I look for another one to assault. "I hardly need an excuse," I mutter.

Leo is standing at the kitchen counter when I come in, fiddling with the baby monitor. Behind him, I can see through the glass doors of the refrigerator that he's been shopping. How does he always manage to get so much done when I'm gone, even with Emma here? He makes it look so damned effortless. I throw my bag down on the counter.

"Hi, honey." I sling my arm around him, but he shushes me.

"Listen," he whispers, pointing at the baby monitor.

I lean my elbows down on the counter beside his, to look at the tiny screen, but it's not Emma there. It's channel C: the four cribs, their wooden slats glowing green in the night-vision light of the dim room. The baby nearest the monitor weeps and wails, like he's acting in a Greek tragedy. He gnashes his gums together, and I reach across Leo to the far side of the monitor to turn the volume all the way down. I can't stand the crying.

"We can pick up other channels on this thing," Leo whispers gleefully. "We can watch our neighbors."

"Yeah, but why are we whispering?" I whisper.

"Because if we can hear them, they can hear us, too, right?"

Strange that I hadn't thought of that.

"Sure, but only when we're upstairs, in Emma's room, right?" I say out loud.

Leo stands up straight and sets the monitor back on the counter. "Yeah, yeah." He clears his throat. "And there's this other family, on channel B, my God. . . ."

"Oh, the Elmos?"

Leo laughs. "They *do* sound like Elmo. Hungarian Elmo!"

I giggle, too. "I always wonder where they live," I say.

"You already knew about this?"

"Of course, I found it out like the first day," I say, and I feel a tiny thrill of pride because I'm beginning to recognize these slivers in Emma's world where I'm the expert, where I know more than him. I *need* this. "The first day, I was flipping around the channels, and I heard them singing the alphabet. Like they were at a Phish concert. Who the hell is that happy?"

"I'm exhausted just *listening* to it," Leo agrees. "One day that kid is going to wake up and say, *Yo, Ma! Dad! Shut the hell up, you're driving me insane with the baby talk!*"

I laugh, and Leo kisses me again. For a split second, it feels like the old us, from before we were parents. He looks sexy, and I'm suddenly self-conscious in my floppy clothes. I'm in second-trimester maternity pants, and a baggy T-shirt. I keep waiting for my waistline to spring back like the women in the pages of *Us Weekly,* but it's been almost six weeks since Emma was born, and there is no evidence that any part of my body will ever spring again. My C-section belly is still distended, my breasts droopy and drippy. I turn from Leo and open the fridge, take out a Diet Coke, and pop the top. He flips the monitor back to channel A, and turns it up. We listen to Emma breathe.

"I got a few groceries together while you were out," he says. "And some diapers. We needed everything."

"Yeah, I hadn't had a chance to stock up," I say, and now I feel self-conscious about that, too. "I guess Emma had a good morning?"

"Yeah, she was great. She's snoozing now." Leo pretends to look at his watch, but he's not wearing one. "You know, I have over a half an hour until I have to leave for work." He snakes his arms around me. "Baby's sleeping, Mama and Daddy are alone." He begins kissing my neck. He smells so good. I feel so gross, so leaky and globular. I'm wearing jeans with a five-inch elastic waistband, for God's sake. How could he possibly want to have sex with me? That *is* what he's suggesting, isn't it? It's been so long, I can hardly remember how one initiates these things.

"The doctor said six weeks," I say, pulling away from him, wrapping myself around the Diet Coke instead.

"It'll be six weeks on Friday," he says, running a finger along my neckline.

I gulp at the Coke in a panic. I'm still so sore, so fragile. Sometimes, when I sit on the toilet, I'm afraid important body parts are going to fall out with a splash. Clean, blow-dried hair can only do so much for you. Leo takes the Coke can out of my hand and sets it back on the counter, and I'm suddenly terrified, that he's going to take me by the hand, and lead me up the stairs, and that there will be smooth jazz playing while he undresses me. Smooth jazz! And stretch marks! And a nursing bra! The *horror!*

But instead, he just kisses my hand. He rubs my knuckles with his thumb. "Hey, no rush," he says. "Whenever you're ready."

And he wraps his arms around me, and I press my head against his chest, and I feel tremendously guilty, because I fear that I will never be ready again. He's so loving and patient, and I'm so relieved; I don't want to kill the kindness of this moment by explaining it to him, that my body is permanently altered now. These boobs have finished phase one of their biological job: in perky innocence, they attracted a mate. Now they have obviously matured to their second biological use: to *suckle*. To feed our child, as from an udder. Yes, I am bovine, entirely.

"Moo," I say to Leo.

He draws back and looks at me. "What?"

"That was a cow joke," I explain. "I feel like a cow."

"God, Majella, you're beautiful, would you stop?"

"Moo," I say again, softly.

After he leaves for work, I take the monitor, and flip it back to channel C. That baby is still crying, and now there is even more crying—at least two screamy little voices, maybe more. Man, if I was that mother, I would lose it. It sounds like someone is murdering Smurfs over there. I turn the volume all the way down again, and watch the red volume light flicker and dance along the bottom of the screen. After a moment, the light in the channel C room changes, like someone has opened a door, or turned on a lamp. I quickly turn the volume back up. The babies stop screaming, and strain their necks to see who has come in. One of them flips from his back to his front, and I can see now, from that movement, that it's definitely just two babies, and that their cribs are pressed up against a large mirror.

The flipped-over baby is on his hands and knees now, rocking, trying to crawl, but he's not quite there yet. He wills his arms and legs, but they're stuck to the mattress beneath him. I stare, mesmerized. I wonder how old they are, how long until Emma does that. Maybe it will change everything, when she begins to flip over. When she begins to do *anything*.

Now I see a pair of feet, just the feet, coming into the picture, and the babies are rapt, silent, hopeful, watching the feet approach.

I hold my breath. I'm afraid to even blink, in case I miss something. And now there's a hand, a shoulder, a bottle, dropped into the crib. The hands-and-knees baby flails at the nearby bottle. The other baby begins to wail again. The arm reaches into the crib, nestles the bottle into the baby's mouth. The baby's hands come up by instinct. He holds his own bottle. And the human shape moves over to the second crib; the arms reach in and flip that baby over onto his back. He smiles up at the camera. He grabs the bottle that's pressed into his hands, and he drinks. Greedily. Noisily.

The arms and the hands disappear. The feet retreat from view. And now the babies are quiet, eating, and I can hear something else, beyond. I turn the volume all the way up. It's a woman, I hear. She is sobbing.

I grab the phone and dial Tampa. "Mom, thank goodness I got you," I say when she picks up.

"Hey, Jelly!" she sings. "Listen, I don't have long, I'm about to run out to water aerobics. What's up?"

I chew the inside of my lip. I mean, what *is* up, exactly? Now that I've got her, I'm not sure what to tell her.

"Yeah, hey, Mom—you knew most of the neighbors around here, right?"

"Sure," she says. "I mean, everybody who's been in the neighborhood for a while, but that six-family apartment building always had people coming and going. I could never keep track of the tenants. There was this one guy who lived there, and he used to stand in front of his kitchen window and shave his legs at the sink *stark naked*." I press my lips together, shake my head. "And all the women would talk about it at book club, and they'd pretend to be shocked and appalled, but nobody would call the cops. I think they enjoyed the sneak-peek. . . ."

"Mom!"

"Yes?"

"Did you know anyone around here who was expecting twins, before you and Dad moved out? Like the babies are . . . I don't know, maybe four or five months old now, so she probably would have been pregnant when you lived here, right before you moved."

"No, honey, nobody I can think of," she says, even though she doesn't seem to have given it much thought at all.

She doesn't ask *why* I'm asking, so I just tell her. "Because there's a woman I'm picking up on our baby monitor who has twins, and I think she might be in trouble."

"What do you mean you're *picking her up* on your baby monitor?"

"Like, when I switch to one of the other channels, I can see her," I say, "with the twins."

"*See* her? I thought baby monitors were just like little walkie-talkies?"

"Ours has a picture, too."

"Oh," she says, "like a little television screen, so you can see Emma when she's in her crib?"

"Yes, Mom."

"Wow, that's so neat, I didn't even know they—"

"Mom, focus, please!"

"I just think it's interesting, honey, we didn't have all these doodads when you were little."

"Anyway, Mom, this lady must live close by, for me to be able to pick up her signal, but I can't figure out which house she's in, and I'm worried about her."

"Worried how?"

"Like, she seems pretty overwhelmed."

"Well, that's probably normal for new mommies, honey. Especially with twins. Can you even imagine?"

"No, Mom, I don't think this is normal," I say. "Like just now,

I heard the babies crying and she came into the room, and gave them their bottles, but she wouldn't even pick them up. The babies are feeding themselves, and then I could hear her crying."

It sounds incredibly not-ominous when I say it out loud. I begin to wonder if the creepy, greenish night-vision light on the monitor is making things appear more menacing than they actually are.

"Hmm," Mom says.

"What do you think? Should I call 911 or something? No, that would be totally crazy overreacting, right?"

"I don't know, maybe not," she says. "I just saw a story on *Dateline* last week about a mother of infant twins, who got so freaked out, she took a hammer to them, and then threw herself off her seventh-story balcony."

"That's great, Mom."

"But she landed in her complex swimming pool, and she survived, but she's paralyzed from the waist down. It probably would've been better if—"

"Mom, this isn't some homicidal woman on *Dateline*."

"Tragic," she says.

"Mom, this is a real person, a neighbor. What if she's really in distress?"

"Yeah, I donno, honey. Maybe ask Vera Wimmer, in the green house. She knows everybody, the way she's always stuck in that front window of hers, watching all the goings-on."

I walk to my front door, and open it. I step out into the sunshine, and lean on my wrought-iron front-porch railing. I look across the street at the green house beside Brian's. Vera waves out at me. I wave back, and when a bus passes between us, I scuttle back inside.

"Yeah, okay, Mom," I say. "Maybe I'll talk to Vera."

"Oh, honey, I'm late!" she says. "I'll call you later."

Leo comes home early because it's Tuesday, and the restaurant is quiet, but I don't hear him come in because Emma is screaming. She has been crying since twelve minutes past five o'clock, and it is now seven thirty-eight. When I see Leo's face appear, I am so happy I could weep. So I do. I weep. And he sweeps heroically into the room, and scoops that baby out of my arms, and he's talking to me, but I couldn't tell you what he's saying, not for all the money in the world. And I look down at myself, now that Emma is safe in her father's arms, and I notice how I'm shaking, and my shapeless green shirt is all wet, and I don't even know what that liquid is. Snot, tears, saliva, milk. I don't even know who that liquid came from. I go through the kitchen, and open the door into our little mudroom, and I go through that mudroom, with its strange, sloped ceiling and low-hanging light fixture, and I open the back door of our house. I don't flip on the back-porch light, because I don't want to attract mosquitoes. I step outside, and I try to close the door firmly behind me, but I end up slamming it instead.

I sit on the top step, and plant my elbows onto my knees. Everything is shaking. How long have I been shaking? It is twilight in my back garden, and the painted white brick of the apartment building next door is glowing a soft purple. Leo and I haven't managed to clear out this garden yet. It's overgrown and wild beyond the square patch of concrete where our little table and chairs sit, our deluxe barbecue. That machine was one of the only things that excited Leo about moving to Queens. A real, honest-to-God, macho, sleek, oversized, suburban barbecue. I stare at it now, blurry because I'm still crying. My head is pounding. How could I have been so wrong about all of this? About how it was going to be, living here, raising a family?

A lone cricket creaks pathetically somewhere in that tangle of mad foliage. I tell it to shut the fuck up. Then, a giggle. I look up at one of the windows in that white-painted brick, and a little face is shining down at me.

"I heard you say a bad word!" He's a kid, maybe five or six, in one of the second-floor apartments.

"Yeah, sorry," I say.

"I liked it!"

This kid is the best thing that's happened to me all day. Maybe Emma will be like this one day. Bright and smiley and not-screaming.

"I'm supposed to be asleeping," the kid tells me. "My name is Franklin."

I nod. "I'm Majella."

He stares down at me for a while longer, and we don't talk, but I feel like he's the best friend I've ever had. "G'night," he says after a few more minutes.

"Good night," I tell him, and I hear him yawn as he drops away from the screen.

I don't want to go back inside in case Emma is still crying. But the mosquitoes are starting to swarm, so I stand up and take some deep breaths before heading back in.

It's quiet, except for the sound of Leo's voice. I make my way to the office, and Leo looks up at me.

"Hang on," he says to someone on the computer, and then to me, "She's asleep."

"Are you fucking kidding me?" I think but do not say. To Leo, I say, "Wow."

"Yeah, I'm just talking to Jeff on Skype."

"Hi, Majella!" I hear the voice of Leo's brother coming from our computer speakers.

"Hi, Jeff," I say, without stepping in front of the camera, because I am such a disgusting mess I cannot possibly appear on

Skype without a shower, a whiskey, and hundreds of dollars' worth of spa treatments.

"I'll be out in a minute, I brought you a bottle of wine in the fridge," Leo says.

For this, I will give him sex.

"Thank you," I say, and I slip out of the room and back toward the kitchen.

I can still hear them chatting as I work the corkscrew into the bottle top.

"So it's totally amazing, being parents, right?" Jeff says. He and his wife have been thinking about starting a family, too. They live in Colorado.

"Yeah, it's awesome," Leo says.

"But has it just completely turned your whole world upside down or what?" Jeff asks.

"Nah, not really," Leo says.

Not really? I put the bottle down so I won't drop it. I step closer to the door to eavesdrop.

"You know, life is pretty much the same. Now we just have a baby!" Leo is saying.

Pretty much the same? What is he, insane? Or maybe he's just lying because he wants parenthood to seem *fantastic* so that Jeff and his wife will hurry up and do it, too. Maybe he wants to trick them. But I hear him saying that the biggest change of all, really, is living in Queens, and I just don't feel like you could make this shit up. I step back to my wine bottle, and attack the cork with renewed vigor. It pops, and I take a large gulp straight from the bottle before finding myself a glass.

I install myself on the couch with the remote control and the baby monitor, and I begin flipping through the channels on both. Channel B is the usual exuberant bullshit. And someone is whimpering quietly on channel C when Leo closes up the office and joins me on the couch.

"You're home early," I say.

"Just in the nick of time," he says.

"Yeah, you're telling me."

"How long was she crying?" he asks.

"Before you came in? I don't know. Two and a half, three hours?"

In fact, I know exactly how long it was because I watch the clock when she cries. It was two hours and twenty-six minutes, but I always round up when Leo asks because I need him to understand the enormity of it. I could, in fact, tell him that she had been crying for seventeen thousand hours, and that would feel closer to the emotional truth of the situation.

"Oh, that's awful," he says. "I guess she wore herself out. She conked out after about five minutes when I came in."

I grip my wine so hard that the pads of my fingers turn yellow beneath the glass. He takes it from me and tries a sip, hands it back. Then he walks into the kitchen to find himself a glass.

"Hey, Leo, let me ask you something."

"Yeah?"

There's nothing so beautiful as the sound of a wine bottle glugging into a glass, to soothe a frazzled, exhausted mind. I close my eyes and listen to him pour. He plomps down beside me on the couch.

"Did you mean what you said to your brother? About life being pretty much the same, except now we just have a baby?"

Leo takes a sip of his wine and thinks it over. "Yeah, I guess I did."

"Oh."

But now he is looking at me thoughtfully, like it's just dawned on him this moment. "I guess it's not like that for you, huh?"

"No," I say.

"It's hard," he says.

"Yeah." And then we both sip at our wine for a few minutes, while the baby whimpers softly on channel C. "I guess I'm just not the mother I expected to be," I confess. "I thought I would be so super-nurturing and easygoing. I love kids. But with Emma, it's like. I don't know, I can't even think. When she cries, I just. I'm a fucking mess. I thought I'd be so good at this."

Leo has taken my hand. "You're exactly the mother I want you to be," he says. That should be such a comfort to me, but the words fall into my chest with a hollowness. I can't *feel* them. "There isn't another woman in the world I would want to be Emma's mother. It's just a learning curve, Majella, that's all. It's the toughest job there is. But you'll knock it outta the park. You just need some time to adjust."

I sniff and blink. I'm determined not to cry again. I'm so bored of tears. "Thanks," I say.

The baby on channel C starts to cry a little more loudly, so I tell Leo about what I witnessed this afternoon, the feet and the hands, the bottles, the sobbing. I don't feel like I'm fully able to articulate my alarm. I'm also acutely aware of my own recent sobbing. How can I explain my fear about channel C without inspiring a similar worry about all *my* sobbing? Can I really tell Leo that it's different for me? That I would never leave Emma in her crib, alone with a bottle? That I would always pick her up, if she was crying, that my instincts are sound?

"Well, are you actually worried about this?" Leo asks, when I'm done talking. "Because it sounds like maybe the channel C mom just had a rough day. Or you don't know, maybe she just had a terrible phone call and got some bad news or something."

"Maybe," I say. "But I don't know, there was just something about the way she was crying."

Maybe it was recognition. Familiarity. I shudder.

"I want to find out where she lives," I say.

"Yeah, I'll keep an eye out for her, too, around the neighborhood. How many twins can there be, living on our block?"

"Yeah," I say.

I hold the monitor up over my head, as the channel C baby starts to cry louder. I stand up from the couch and walk into the office with it, watching the picture on the screen. It goes staticky.

"Switch it back to Emma," Leo says.

"I will," I say. "In a minute."

And then I have this great idea, and I pass back through the living room, and plant my wineglass down on the coffee table, and I walk out through the kitchen, down the long hallway, and out the front door. On the stoop, channel C buzzes and flickers. I walk down our front steps in my socks, and make a left. I walk two houses down, holding the monitor up over my head all the time. The signal fades and falters. I swivel around and walk back, past our house, toward the six-family apartment building. As I approach the building, the signal on the monitor crystallizes. The buzzing stops. One baby is babbling softly, and the other is back to the low whimper. There is no sign of a parent in the room. I look up at Leo, who is standing on our front porch, watching me with what might be a look of concern on his face. His hands are in his pockets. I point up at the apartment building.

"They live here," I say.

Chapter Eight

IRELAND, MARCH 1847

Ginny couldn't see Springhill House from the gate, but she followed the drive uphill, where it wound through a stand of shade trees and skirted a neat little pond. There, the landscape flattened, and Ginny could see that her path would lead her through a line of hedges, to where she could discern the shapes of a gabled roof beyond. She paused—not to gather her thoughts, which could only lead to terror and distress, but rather, just for a moment's rest before she would step through those hedges, and face whatever awaited her. There was a breeze stiff enough to ruffle the brim of her bonnet, and she breathed it in.

"The same air Maire is breathing right now," she said to herself. "Only six miles down the road."

She shivered slightly as she stepped past the hedges, as if she were passing through a portal, an elemental shift. And indeed, on the other side, it was as if all the world brightened with promise. There was no suffering here, and Ginny felt the shame of betrayal already. Her children were still out there. Beyond the gate.

But here was Springhill House, staunch and impeccable, perfectly symmetrical, with its three rows of shiny glass windows, five across. Here was salvation. At its center was a cheerful red door with a gleaming scalloped fanlight above it. Buds of spring ivy were beginning to steal across the facade, but they were neatly trimmed back from the windows and doors. The house wasn't massive, but it was opulent. She ventured cautiously out onto the tidy circular drive, and then detoured to the side of the house, guessing at where the stables might be. To this side, she heard voices and laughter coming from an open gate. She peeked through and saw the stables and a number of outbuildings. She could smell the gathered horses, manure, and hay. She struck back to her path, and followed it behind the house, where the gardens dropped into manicured tiers. She marveled at the perfection of the spreading lawns, dotted with primordial trees and bright little pools of flowers. A high wall separated the bottom tier of the pretty pleasure gardens from the fields and pastures beyond. Inside the wall, men were working in busy clusters, some trimming hedges, others down on their knees picking weeds and stones. Someone was lime-washing that bottom wall. Every man here looked strong and well fed, handsome. Several of Springhill House's chimneys were smoking against the sky, and the heady smell of hot food permeated everything. It was like Ginny had stepped into another country, or no—it was still Ireland. Rather, it was like she'd stepped into another year, before famine and the English had pillaged the land.

She screwed up her courage, turned her back to the elaborate gardens, and pulled firmly on the large iron handle of the doorbell at the small green door. After a few minutes, a young girl of about sixteen opened it, and stared at her without speaking.

"I'm looking to speak to the housekeeper, please."

The girl looked Ginny up and down, and then nodded, ushered her silently into a dark corridor, and then into a large dining room at the back.

"About the position, is it?" the girl finally spoke.

"For chambermaid, yes," Ginny replied.

"Wait here."

The room was splendid and quiet, with tall glass windows and central French doors that opened out onto the shadowy top lawn. The walls were painted a pale blue, with plaster angels looking down from the scooped cornices. Ginny untied the bonnet from under her chin and pulled it off her head, set it on the chair behind her. A gilded mirror hung from one wall, and she stood up to examine her reflection.

She hardly recognized herself. Her black hair was thinning and the luster was gone out of it completely. She smoothed it back, her scalp still hot from the closeness of the bonnet on her long walk here. Her neck looked ropy and weak, and dark circles ringed her bright blue eyes. The skin of her eyelids was papery, fragile. She touched her cheeks, shocked by the dry looseness of the skin beneath her fingers. She thought of that woman on the ground outside the gate, and her whole body shuddered with recognition. She'd been watching her children wilt and wither, even Maggie, who looked so much like her. But she just hadn't noted the change, how severe it was, in her own self.

She turned quickly from the mirror, and sank back into the chair, holding her bonnet on her knee. Even through the thick velvet cushion, she could feel her bones protruding beneath her. She shifted uncomfortably.

After a few minutes, a door swung open in the back corner of the room, and a woman, the housekeeper, appeared with a laden tea tray. As the door swung shut, Ginny saw the deep gap of a darkened staircase behind. The newcomer sat down across from Ginny, poured out two cups of tea, and handed one to Ginny on a smart little saucer. Ginny studied the woman's clipped fingernails and tidy gray hair, and tried to keep her glance from lingering on the tray, which had a selection of scones and biscuits and fresh fruit. She took a sip from her tea instead, and tried to sit up without squirming.

"I'm Miss Farrell," the woman said, and then she paused to take a sip of her tea. "I suppose you heard we're shorthanded?"

"I did."

"And have you a letter of reference?"

Ginny frowned, peeked accidentally at the tea tray.

"Don't be shy, dear," Miss Farrell said, gesturing toward the tray. "Help yourself. It's no sin to be hungry in these days—you look like you could use a nibble." She smiled, took a small, gold-rimmed plate from the tray, and handed it to Ginny. "Go on."

"Thank you," Ginny replied. She took a scone from the tray and broke it open, slathered it with butter. It was still warm, and she forced herself to leave it on the plate for a moment, so as not to betray too much hunger. "I didn't bring my reference, but I can get it," she said. "I didn't want to waste time stopping for it on the way, in case someone else got here before me, and the position was filled."

She felt a hot blush on her cheeks as she fibbed. In truth, she'd stopped in at the church, and Father Brennan had told her she was mad in the head. He'd told her to hang on, that she'd no business going out to work and leaving her children alone. He'd promised she would hear from Raymond soon, that a packet of money would come from America.

"Soon isn't soon enough, Father," she'd pleaded. "My children are starving now. They won't last the week out."

But Father Brennan had shaken his head, sealed his lips in a frown that was so stern she had nearly given up. She had nearly turned around and marched home empty-handed. She had nearly given her babies over to the will of God. So maybe it was the will of God, then, that pointed her stubborn feet onto the road to Springhill House instead, reference or no.

As she walked, she had planned it all so carefully, what she would say, what she wouldn't say, how she would manage without a referral. But now that she was here, she was sure she reeked of desperation. She could smell it on her own skin, on her breath. She was sure this woman could see the images of her hungry babies imprinted on her, on the insides of her eyelids. She saw their faces every time she blinked.

"All right, then. Tell me about your previous situation," Miss Farrell prompted.

Ginny bit into the scone so she'd have time to think while she chewed. But she found that she couldn't think at all, at that moment, because she had scone and butter in her mouth, and she was overcome by the raw, natural relief of food, followed immediately, of course, by the guilt, that she was sitting in this fine house, eating off a gold-rimmed plate, while her children were starving just a few miles away. She watched the housekeeper's bright blue eyes boring into her, and she couldn't think at all. She swallowed the bite, and her stomach gave a trembly, indebted heave.

"Were you working elsewhere?" Miss Farrell tried again. "Nearby?"

Ginny set the scone down on her plate. "I've been out of work for some time."

"Never mind that—just tell me about your previous situation. What house were you in?"

She had already planned this out; she had chosen a town a safe distance away, but she was so nervous. She could feel the bite of scone sticking in her throat. She swigged her tea to wash it down.

"Bingham House?" she finally answered. "In Castlebar?"

"Oh?" Miss Farrell's face looked suspicious—she had to be careful. "And what was your position there?"

Ginny cleared her throat. "Nursery maid," she answered, with forced conviction. "I was nursery maid to the youngest."

"How many children were there, in the family?"

She felt she was being tested now, that Miss Farrell knew these answers already. If she got this wrong, the jig was up. She had to guess.

"Four," she answered decisively. "Three girls and a boy." She tried to hold the teacup steady, but her hands were shaking something mighty.

Miss Farrell leaned back in her chair and smiled. "Relax," she said. "You're awful nervous altogether."

Ginny tried to smile. "Sorry, missus," she said, and she took a deep breath.

"Call me Roisin, dear, I'm nobody's missus." She smiled, and Ginny felt entirely washed with relief.

"Roisin, then," she said, lifting the half-gone scone from her plate to take another bite. Two bites. She gobbled them down.

"Why did you leave Bingham House?"

She took one more bite while she practiced her prepared answer in her mind. "The family went back to London," she said, after she swallowed.

Roisin nodded. "As many are, in these times, I suppose."

Ginny pressed the last bite of scone onto her tongue, and took another draft of tea. Her stomach was beginning to feel unwell. There had been too much food today, too much richness after so many days of want.

"Well, you do know it's a junior position; it's not really chambermaid. I mean that's the title, but really it's a bit of everything. There's only three staff in the house, not including Mr. Murdoch. Well, two now that Anne's gone, only Katie and myself," Roisin was saying, but her voice was beginning to sound warped. Ginny tried hard to concentrate. "There're no children in this family, and limited indoor staff, despite the size of the estate. Most of the work is in the gardens. The man of the house is in London—it's only Mrs. Spring here, so we all chip in, whatever needs doing. It's very informal, this house."

Ginny tried to breathe deeply through her mouth, but suddenly the meaty, floury odors of the house filled her up like a tidal wash, and she clapped a hand over her mouth. She stood up and lurched across the room toward the French doors.

She managed to get to the door and force it open, before she vomited on the flagstone just beyond the threshold. The housekeeper was behind her in the doorway now. Ginny could feel a hand on the small of her back.

"There there, now, you're all right," Roisin was saying.

Outside, Ginny stood up and placed one hand against the thick gray outer wall of the house. It was gritty beneath her fingers. She felt herself tremble, and she closed her eyes for another deep, fresh breath. They were both quiet for a moment, and in the distance, Ginny could hear the singsong call of sheep. She tried to remember the last time she'd heard the baa of a sheep. It was before Raymond had gone, anyway. They'd all been slaughtered for food since. For months now, the countryside had been silent of its animal voices, but not here. The famine hadn't reached Springhill. She pulled a sticky stray hair from her lips.

"I'm sorry," Ginny said again. "I haven't eaten. All I've had is a bite of bread this two days. I think the butter was too rich for me."

She placed a hand on her small belly and waited for another shudder to pass. She bit the insides of her cheeks.

Roisin stood back and observed. "Just the butter?" she asked. The two women locked eyes. "You're sure that's all it was?"

Ginny licked her lips and stared out across the gardens and the fields beyond. She could see the Sheeffry Hills in the distance. "Of course," she whispered, brushing the loosened hair from her sweaty forehead, and tucking it behind her ears.

Roisin was staring at Ginny, at the small swell of her stomach where her hand was resting. She tried to fluff out her petticoats, but Roisin reached over and placed a hand on Ginny's bent elbow.

"I hope you're not fooling yourself, dear, because you're certainly not fooling me."

Ginny could feel her jaw beginning to tremble. Her shoulders dropped, and she tipped her head back against the wall behind her. She leaned all her weight on that wall, felt its pebbly roughness through the gauzy fabric of her shirtwaist. Her blouse was so worn that the wall scratched at her bony shoulder blades, beneath.

"You have to help me," Ginny said. "Please. I'm willing to work. I'm not asking for a handout. I'll do anything. I'm desperate."

"You're having a baby?" Roisin asked.

Ginny tried to shake her head, but she couldn't.

"It's all right, girl, but you have to face it," Roisin was saying. "You won't get anywhere pretending it's not happening."

Ginny could feel the color draining from her face, her only chance to save her children slipping away.

"You're having a baby," Roisin repeated, more insistently this time.

Ginny's shoulders shook. "I am," she finally admitted.

"And where is your husband?"

"America."

"And how far gone are you?"

"I'm not sure." She trembled. "He left in September, so over halfway gone, anyway." She rocked forward, planting her hands onto her knees. She thought she might retch again.

"Well, you're hardly showing at all," Roisin said.

"There hasn't been enough food."

"Here, it'll be all right, you'll hear from that husband of yours in no time. Come back in and sit down."

Ginny shook her head. "I can't wait for him. I can't wait any longer," she said, rubbing her head at the temples to try and stop the thudding. She stood up straight again. "I have to do something, before I lose this child. I have to try, please. I can work. I need the work."

The housekeeper folded her hands in a gesture of prayer and brought them to her lips. "God above, I wish I could, woman," she said. "If it were up to me, the job would be yours, but Mrs. Spring . . ."

"Mrs. Spring would insist that you stay." There was a new voice now, interrupting, as Alice Spring herself emerged into the garden.

She was stunning in a bold blue gown that she gathered up in one hand so it wouldn't drape into Ginny's vomit as she passed. As Alice Spring stepped between them, the two women both straightened their posture, and Ginny tried not to gape at the clean display of splendor. The price of that dress would've fed her family until the next harvest. That one gown could have saved them from hunger. Ginny had never seen anything so fine up close. It was embroidered along every seam with a delicate vine of violets. The color was vivid, saturated.

Alice Spring was beautiful, a linear and austere kind of beauty that might have been ordinary in London, but was almost exotic here in the west of Ireland. Her jaw, her nose, even her eyelashes, were impeccably straight. The stem of her neck was a perfect perpendicular to the angle of her shoulders. Her waist didn't nip in, to the hourglass most women aspired to, and neither did it bulge outward, the way that happens after the accommodation of growing babies. Her figure was flat and smooth, like the simple lines of Springhill House. Even her hair hung in thick golden ropes that didn't curve or tangle in the breeze. The feminine shapes of Ireland framed her; behind her, out beyond that lowest garden wall, the rowdy land swooped and bulged with raucous colors. The sunless Irish sky was bloated and churning above her. In the foreground, Alice Spring was precise, immaculate.

She stood with her back to the others now, and cocked one hand up to shield her eyes while she surveyed her sprawling parklands. Her waist and her rib cage were tidy inside her corset, and the bustle tumbled out theatrically behind her. Roisin looked flabbergasted, her mouth standing open. She was speechless.

"Did I hear you're with child?" Alice Spring said brightly, twirling around to face Ginny.

Mrs. Spring had the strangest smile on her face. Ginny had heard stories of Alice Spring's eccentricities ever since her arrival from London four summers ago—everyone for three parishes around had heard those stories. But hearing rumors was an entirely different business from staring them in the face. Ginny tried to stand away from the wall, but found she still needed the extra bit of support. She leaned back.

"Yes, mum," she said. "But it won't interfere with my ability to work."

Ginny tried to ignore the absurdity of the scene. She tried to pretend that the three of them weren't standing around a puddle of her vomit discussing her employment prospects.

"Of course it will, you silly girl," Mrs. Spring responded. "But that's to be expected, in your condition. We can work around it. I'm terribly fond of babies."

Ginny nodded, but wasn't sure how to respond. The housekeeper was still standing with her mouth open. Mrs. Spring strode out a few paces, then turned back again.

"Are you from this parish?" she asked.

"A neighboring one, Knockbooley," Ginny answered. "This side of Westport."

"And have you family? Aside from your absentee husband?"

Again, Ginny wasn't sure how to reply. Her parents and Raymond's were dead, and she was in the unusual position of having no siblings. Raymond's only living brother was in New York. But did she mean children? Ginny hardly dared to breathe. Alice Spring was watching her like a chicken hawk. Ginny nodded again, almost imperceptibly.

"Visiting them will be out of the question," Mrs. Spring said, and Ginny tried not to grimace. "We're quite isolated here. I don't like to mix with the outside. Fever! The fever is everywhere," she whispered, clutching Ginny's arm queerly for a moment.

Ginny looked down at the woman's fine gloves gripping her sleeve. The sour smell of vomit clung in the air.

"Yes, mum," Ginny stammered.

"Roisin will show you around. She'll instruct you in your duties," Mrs. Spring said, and then, turning to Roisin, added, "Close your mouth, you're like a lighthouse."

The housekeeper snapped her mouth shut.

"I think I'll go for a promenade, get some fresh air," Mrs. Spring said then, clasping her hands behind her back, allowing her blue skirts to billow beneath her like a sea.

Ginny held her breath. For the first time in weeks, she felt a faint thrill of hope, a reprieve. She might save her children. She still couldn't believe what was happening, the strangeness of it.

She was afraid she would awaken from this, to find her babies moaning of hunger. Or worse, to find them not moaning at all.

"Thank you, mum," she said, bowing her head. "Thank you. I'll work. You'll be so glad of me."

Mrs. Spring waved her off with one hand. "You can start by cleaning up that mess." She gestured to the stink at their feet. "Roisin will get you cleaned up. And Roisin?"

"Yes, Mrs. Spring?"

Mrs. Spring gestured to Ginny's red petticoat. "Get her something more appropriate to wear."

First, Ginny scrubbed the sick off the flagstones, and then doused them with a pail of fresh water. The shabby afternoon sun was fading into a drippy mist, but the breeze was still clean enough to scour away the bad smell quick. Ginny was feeling a bit wobbly and worried, and entirely stunned by her luck. But she was determined to get straight to work, before Mrs. Spring could come to her senses and change her mind. She still had to figure out how she could get food to her children, fast.

Roisin gave her a jug of clean water and a towel, and then took her up three flights of stairs to a small attic room, with a bare mattress and a three-legged table where the stub of a candle remained. There were no windows in the little room, and the gables sloped down low overhead.

"You'll sleep here, nights," Roisin said, stepping inside so the sound of her brogues rapped loudly against the gappy floorboards. "But never worry that it's a bit bare; you won't spend much time here besides."

Ginny gave a measured nod, careful not to betray the awful swell of tears she felt, looking at that lone, bare mattress. She tried not to think of the cozy little bed she shared with the girls at home, now that Raymond was gone. The sunny patch of clean straw for Michael in the same room, where they all slept together. There was a warm reassurance in all that shared breath in the nighttime. She couldn't imagine how she would sleep here, alone, without the whispered dreams of her children all around her. Sometimes Maggie giggled in her sleep, even since the hunger, even now, when she never laughed in her waking life. Ginny took a deep breath and held it for a moment. The trick, she would learn, was to relieve her mind of the burdens of adjustment, and convince her body to take over that work instead.

"Get yourself washed," Roisin was saying. She opened the glass trap on her lantern, and lifted the little candle stub from the table to light it. There was a black skirt and fresh white shirtwaist folded neatly at the end of the mattress. Roisin pointed to it. "Get dressed and come down to the kitchen, after. You can help me get the tea on."

"Will I be able to find it?" Ginny asked. "The kitchen?"

"Back to the dining room—you know the door I came through?"

Ginny nodded.

"In that door and down the steps, in the basement."

"Right."

When the housekeeper closed the door behind her, Ginny sat down for a moment on the mattress. The flame from the candle threw close-dancing shadows overhead.

"I have to get food to them," she whispered to herself, her face screwed up with anxiety. "Straightaway. Tonight."

Thank God they had that small bit of food today, to keep them ticking over. Thank God that girl Anne had passed by the cottage and stopped. Ginny knelt for a moment, gave a few further prayers of thanks, and asked God to watch over her children and keep them safe. Then she stood, careful not to bump her head on the gables above, and unbuttoned her worn shirtwaist. The skin of her belly was stretched taut, and the bump was fairly pronounced when she was undressed. But not the size it should be.

Outside she could hear the wind scraping itself over the roof of Springhill House, and she reached a hand up to touch the cold wood overhead. She hoped her babies were warm enough at home, in the cottage. "Don't worry, Maire," she said. "Just hold it together."

The kitchen at Springhill House was enormous, by far the biggest room Ginny had ever seen, outside of the parish church. Copper pots and ladles lined the walls, and still more hung from racks that were strung to the ceiling. Wooden storage bins stood along the walls, and atop these were countless little clay pots and small glass bottles with oils and dried herbs in them. There was a deep larder at the far end of the room, and two massive fireplaces along another wall that shared a chimney. One of the hearths was raised up off the floor, at waist level, so that you could cook in it without having to kneel down on the stone floor. The other was the ordinary kind, down low to the ground, but there was a great spit affixed above that hearth, and the girl who had answered the door earlier stood there now, turning a large leg of mutton on the spit. The chimneys were well vented, but the scent of roasting meat filled the hot, dark room. There were no windows, as the room was in the lowest level of Springhill House.

Roisin stood at a long, central worktable, kneading some dough in a trough, and she looked up at Ginny when she came in.

"You met Katie, before," she said, gesturing at the girl beside the hearth.

"I did, at the door, but not properly. How're ya, Katie."

The girl kept turning the spit, and gazed back at Ginny without a word.

"She's our scullery girl, a great helper. She's been with us this five months, nearly."

Roisin smiled at the meek, dark-haired girl, but Katie only turned her big, mournful eyes toward the mutton.

"Misses her family something awful," Roisin whispered. "Her mother was my only sister. Passed away last autumn, and Katie came here to me. Her brothers and sisters all got shipped out to various places. She's been a great addition to our little number. Haven't you, Katie?"

The girl still didn't answer, and Ginny tried not to scratch at her neck, but the uniform was terrible itchy.

"It's just the starch, dear, you'll get used to it." Roisin glanced up again. "There are knives in the drawer just there, in the larger press. You may get started on those carrots." She nodded at a large bunch of thick orange roots.

Ginny found a knife, and lifted up one of the carrots by its leafy stem. Roisin was watching her, still kneading the dough.

"Give it a quick scrub, use that bucket there"—she pointed with her chin—"and then just peel it, the same as you would a potato."

"Right, so," Ginny said. She had never seen a carrot before.

The three women cooked for the better part of two hours, and while they did, Ginny asked Roisin about the daily operation of the house. Although the estate had a substantial acreage and numerous outdoor staff, the house itself was rather on the small side, despite its flawless Georgian facade and pristine walled gardens. Ginny learned that, apart from herself and her two kitchen mates, it was only Murdoch and Mrs. Spring who were resident in the house. "A tidy little number," was what Roisin called it. Ginny thought it odd. She had never heard of an estate with such a small house staff, and she wondered whether that would mean less work for their limited number, or more. Not that it mattered in the least. While she scrubbed and chopped, she moved her lips again, thanking God for her strange turn of excellent luck.

The feast that was laid on when they finished cooking would have served a village. Ginny thought of her hungry neighbors in Knockbooley, her skinny children at home. The amount of food in Springhill was perverse.

"Are the meals always this grand?" she asked Roisin, as they prepared the plates to be carried up to the dining room. They used little clay domes to keep the food warm.

"Only the evening meal," Roisin said. "Breakfast is usually fairly simple, just toast, maybe a boiled egg, unless there's guests. And Mrs. Spring likes to keep the supper in the daytime fairly light. A bit backwards if you ask me. But then who asked me?"

She was so pleasant, Roisin—so easygoing and lighthearted that you could nearly forget about the horrors going on outside the gates of Springhill House. You could nearly forget about that man who'd passed by the cottage in Knockbooley just this morning with his starved baby wrapped up in a sack for the graveyard. It was a sort of madness inside these walls, a determined forgetfulness. The length of the worktable was covered with food: boiled carrots with butter, roast mutton, fresh bread, and a mushroom soup with barley and fennel. Ginny wanted to scoff at the extravagance of it, but she couldn't gauge Roisin yet, what her loyalties might be to Mrs. Spring. She couldn't risk offense.

"It's some feast," she said instead, trying to sound admiring. "What about the staff?"

Roisin was loading the prepared plates onto a tray. Katie added a basket with the steaming bread wrapped up in a cloth.

"Well, as I said, it's really only us in the house," Roisin explained. "We usually serve Murdoch and Mrs. Spring together. They ordinarily dine together because Mrs. Spring doesn't have anyone else for company, God bless her. And then it's only the three of us, after. And the jarvie. The odd time he joins us for the evening meal instead of eating with those ruffians in the stables."

"Jarvie?"

"Mrs. Spring's driver," Katie piped up. It was the first time she'd spoken, and a blush came to her cheek straightaway. He must be handsome, this jarvie.

"But what about the grounds staff?" Ginny asked.

"The head gardener's wife cooks for the outdoor staff, there are so many of them," Roisin explained. "She even has her own scullery girl, because there's a whole army of gardeners and stable hands. I couldn't even keep count of their number. But they eat much simpler than this, more like the tenant farmers. Just potatoes and eggs, mostly. Of course this year it's different, with the praties gone. They're having to make up the difference with grains and vegetables out of the house gardens. Mrs. Spring has spent a small fortune feeding them already, since the potato crop failed. I tell you, Murdoch is none too happy about it."

"Murdoch is the agent?" Ginny asked.

Roisin nodded.

"I met him earlier at the gate. What's he like?"

Roisin looked up warily. "What are they all like?" she whispered. "You'd think he was English, the way he carries on. He doesn't mind selling out his own people to please the gentry." Roisin glanced up at the staircase and then shook her head. "Ruthless," she muttered.

Just like Packet, who'd been the agent at Knockbooley so long that he fancied himself a landlord now. The tenants in Ginny's parish knew their real landlord's name was Lord Crofton, but they had never clapped eyes on him. He had never set foot in Ireland. Instead, the absentee landlords in London would hire in these local Irish agents like Packet and Murdoch to run their estates for them, to squeeze out every last drop of profit they could from the land. The agents would rent out the acreage to tenant farmers like Raymond and Ginny for exorbitant prices. And then God help them if they couldn't pay. God help them. Some families got evicted even if they did pay. The agent might turn a poor punter out for some other reason, on a whim. If a tenant had the gumption to improve his plot of land, for example—to irrigate or build or expand—the agent would seize these improvements for profit. He'd turn the tenant out into the road, and then let his land to a neighbor for a steeper rent because of the effort and ingenuity the first tenant had put in to make it better.

Nobody could blame a man for doing what he must to survive in times like these, but there was a certain class of a scoundrel who would do this sort of work with glee. The Murdochs and Packets of the world seemed to enjoy lording this kind of power over their own neighbors and kin. These agents were a hateful sort of specimen altogether, a wicked disgrace to their countrymen.

"You needn't worry about Murdoch," Roisin said, "so long as you keep your head down and stay clear of him. He keeps mostly out of the household affairs. He leaves all that to me. Just be thankful you're not one of his tenants."

Ginny sighed, looked at the elaborate spread of food covering the table. "But all of this food . . . it's just for us, then? Just for five people?"

"That's right, dear," Roisin said, hoisting the tray firmly. "It's not our job to question."

Ginny cringed at herself, slightly. She'd ventured too far.

"Katie and I will serve," Roisin went on. "There is fruit and cheese in the larder. Prepare a tray from that for afters, will you?"

"I will, of course," Ginny said, wiping her hands on her apron.

"I'll be back to put the tea on." Roisin and Katie disappeared through the arched doorway, and up the darkened steps.

Ginny took a lantern and went into the cold larder, where she marveled at the store of food. Along one wall were large barrels of salted fish and flour. Some cured pork hung from the ceiling, and everything smelled salty and pungent. The other two walls were lined with shelving from floor to ceiling, and every shelf was neatly stocked, with milk, buttermilk, eggs. Ginny could smell the sharp tang of all the different cheeses, even covered, as they were, in cloth and twine. It was all so rich that she had to breathe through her mouth, in case it would overwhelm her and she'd be sick again. There were fruits she'd never seen before, not even in the shops in Westport, and their skins were so bright they glowed. She set the lantern atop one of the barrels, and began selecting some of the fruits to lay into her apron.

"Hallo!" A man's voice behind her.

She spun, and her apron came loose from her hand. The fruit tumbled to the ground, and an orange rolled across the floor, where it bumped against the man's foot. He was standing in the little doorway, and he rightly filled it up. He was grinning at Ginny.

"I didn't mean to startle you."

"You didn't," she said, stooping to collect up the scattered food. "I mean I just didn't see you, I didn't hear you come in there."

He bent down and picked up the orange that had come to a rest beside the toe of his brogue.

"You must be the new chambermaid."

She fitted all the fruit back into the sling of her apron, and lifted the lantern back into her hand.

"I must," she said.

He moved out of the doorway and back into the large kitchen so she could get past. She took the fruit back to the long table, and began to arrange everything onto a copper platter. He went back into the larder, and returned with a small wheel of cheese, already cut. He lumped it up onto the table and fetched a knife from the press. He cut himself a small wedge, and then left the knife down for Ginny. She could feel him staring at her, and she was anxious for Roisin and Katie to return. She glanced at the stairwell, but couldn't hear any sign of them.

"I know you," he said to her then, taking a bite of his cheese.

He sat up on a high stool beside the worktop, and she lifted the knife, peeled back the layer of cloth on the cheese wheel.

"Do you, now?" she said, without interest.

"You're Ginny Rafferty."

She paused to look at him. She gripped the knife in her hand.

"No," he went on, "hang on, that's not quite right." He was still grinning, showing all his teeth. "You're Ginny *Doyle* now, aren't you? Née Rafferty, and then you married that Raymond Doyle, from Knockbooley, didn't you, around about the time your parents passed away, God rest their souls? Must've been ten years ago."

"Twelve," she whispered, staring at him. He was tall and broad in the shoulders, with keen blue eyes that were made even brighter by the dusky tint of his skin. He'd a strong jaw and cheekbones, and hair even blacker than hers. She couldn't place his face. "You must be the jarvie," she said.

"Seán Lyons," he said.

"You're never." She set the knife down on the counter.

"I am," he said.

"My God, you've changed a small piece since I seen you last." She stared hard at him, and his smile tapered off modestly while she looked. He'd only been a child then, only slightly older than Maire maybe, when Ginny's parents died in the same bad winter, and she left her home in Doon to marry Raymond. His mother,

Kitty Lyons, had been her childhood neighbor, one of her mam's dearest friends. Ginny studied the lines of his face for a trace of the boy she had known.

"You haven't changed a hair," he said, staring her boldly in the face without smiling. "Still the most beautiful girl in Mayo." He shook his head, looked down at his hands. "Oh, I was heartbroken when you went off with that Raymond fella," he laughed.

"Ah, wouldja stop," she said. "You were only a boy."

"A boy with a savage heart!" He clutched his chest with his hand, and she laughed at him, she couldn't help it. She was sure she was blushing. He stood, and lifted the knife out from under her hand, began slicing the cheese for her. "Where is he now, our hero, our dashing Raymond Doyle? I reckoned you'd have a lock of childer and be off in Knockbooley living the sweet life."

She bit her lip. "He left for New York in September." She took the cheese as he sliced it, and arranged it on the platter with the fruit.

"Ah, it's bad times," he said. "Bad times for dear ould Mother Ireland."

"It is," she agreed.

But it was good times for Ginny Doyle, she reckoned. Awful lucky times altogether. "You drive for Mrs. Spring?" she said.

"I do," he said. "All her messages, her elegant appointments, her step-and-fetch." There was no small hint of mockery in his voice. "When she sends for new silk slippers from the Continent, I hasten into Westport to collect them for her. I'm vital! Important work, that." He tossed the cheese knife into a nearby bucket of water, and sat back up on his stool. He glanced at the stairwell before leaning in toward Ginny. "It's a load of bollix," he whispered. "But what are you going to do?"

She leaned across the worktable, and looked at him. "Jesus, I'm awful glad you're here, Seán."

The quick and earnest blush of his cheek shocked her, but still, she reached over to squeeze his hand. They could hear footsteps coming down the stair.

"Can you meet me tonight?" she whispered.

He took her cue, and whispered back. "In the stables, after the house goes dark."

She nodded, just as Roisin swept back into the room with the empty dinner tray, trailing Katie behind her.

"Ah, you met our jarvie, then," Roisin said.

Katie's whole shape changed when she saw Seán there. She straightened herself, and her face went pink with joy.

"I did," Ginny said, squeezing a wet rag out over a bucket. She started to wipe down the worktable.

"Katie, fix four plates, then, for us, while Ginny tidies up," Roisin said, inspecting the cheese-and-fruit platter, picking off a piece here and there that failed to meet her standard. "I'll bring this up, and then we'll eat."

Seán stole a grape off one side, while Roisin slapped at his hand. Katie was stretching to reach some plates from a high sideboard. Roisin turned back to the stairs. Seán swiveled on his stool, caught Ginny's eye, and winked.

Chapter Nine

"Hey, honey, look at this." Leo is at our office desk, clicking around on the computer. He swivels the flat-screen monitor so I can see it through the doorway, from where I'm sitting on the couch breast-feeding Emma.

"I don't think I can read it from here," I say, and if he has any response to my sardonic wit, he doesn't show it. "What is it?"

"There's a mommy meetup group right here in the neighbor-hood," he says, swiveling the monitor back around to face him.

"I really prefer the word *mama*," I say thoughtfully, adjusting Emma's weight on the Boppy, and sitting up a little straighter. "Or even *mom* is fine. *Mommy* just sounds so . . . I don't know. So enthusiastically infantile. Like the mothers have just completely identity-dived into the brains of their bald-headed little spawn."

Leo leans around the monitor to look at me.

"*Anyway*," he says, settling back into his chair, "it says they meet up at least once, sometimes twice a month, always at a local venue, usually a playground or a library. And there are like forty-three members."

"Huh," I say, tipping my head back onto the pillows behind me.

"You should go to this," he says, pushing his chair to the side, so he can talk to me through the open French doors. "I really think the hardest part is probably just that you're on your own, here, and most of your friends are still in Manhattan."

"And they don't have kids."

"Right, and they don't have kids," he says.

"And they have jobs."

"You still have a job, you just have to *do* your job."

"Ouch," I say.

"I'm not rushing you," he says. "But don't complain about it when it's your own choice."

I pick up the remote control and attempt to mute him, but he rolls his chair back to the desk and keeps talking.

"It would be good for you to meet some new people, local people, who are in the same boat as you. Some women who can relate to what you're going through."

I close my eyes. "Read me the group description part."

He scrolls and clicks for a minute, then clears his throat.

"*Welcome! I'm Tanya, mommy to Tabitha and Toby, the cutest toddler girl and baby boy in the whole universe, at least to me! Come meet up with other Glendale mommies and our cutest baby boys and girls in the whole universe. We don't do much, just talk and laugh and play. Who says playdates are just for the kids? Mommies need fun times, too.*" Leo pauses to look at me.

"Shoot me in the face," I say.

"Just try it," he says, standing up from the desk, and coming into the living room. He sits down on the coffee table across from me. "If you hate it, what are you going to lose, except an hour of your time?"

I can't explain why Leo's painfully reasonable logic makes tears spring up behind my eyes. It's like when I was in seventh grade, and my dad used to sit with me over my prealgebra homework for *hours*, and I would be so frustrated and angry that even after I'd have the breakthrough to understanding, I would refuse to admit it. I would sit and glower. For some reason, I never could meet an epiphany with joy. How dare he try to steal my despair? I'm entitled to it, dammit. Leo lifts my feet onto his lap.

"They're having a meeting on Friday afternoon," he says, massaging my foot, trying to entrap me. "Just think about it?"

I sigh as heavily as I can with Emma on my boob and my stitched-up belly.

"I will," I say. "I'll think about it."

On Friday, Leo leaves early for work. It's one of his busiest days of the week, so he's gone by nine o'clock. The lunch chef will do all the early cooking, and Leo won't even step foot into his kitchen until midafternoon. But it's autumn now, and the holiday season is approaching. There are banquets to plan, clients to meet, schedules to make, bills to pay. We're getting close to the time of year when Leo makes his best money. The restaurant will be packed every day from Thanksgiving until January. I lay out one of Emma's blankets on the thick carpet in our bedroom, and spread some toys around her. I don't know why I do that, with the toys, because she can't reach for them yet, but I know there'll come a time when she can, and I want to be prepared.

I open my closet door bravely, like a mercenary, and I stride up to my hanging clothes almost as if I were not terrified. I choose several of my roomiest prepregnancy outfits, and lay them out on my bed. These were my fat-clothes once, the ones I would reserve for periods of severe bloating or eating at a churrascaria. I pull off my tank top, wiggle a blue jersey dress free of its hanger, and slip it over my head. I step out of my stretchy maternity jeans, and gingerly approach the mirror.

"Oh good God," I say out loud at my enormous fun house reflection, and I slam the closet door, almost hoping to hear the mirror shatter to the ground inside, just so I will never have to meet with such a sight again. The mirror rattles, but holds. Emma is startled, and looks up at me, so I smile, but she only blinks back. "Maybe it will be better if I can wash my hair?"

Emma moans.

"Yeah, can't count on it," I say. "That's a good point." I peel the dress off over my head, and stand over the bed, reviewing the options. I shake my head. It's better not to even try them on. Trying them on is just an exercise in anguish. I step back to my maternity jeans, and yank them back up over my hips.

"Maybe a cute top," I say, gathering up all the hanging clothes to go back in the closet. I open a dresser drawer and pull out a flattering purple top from late in my first trimester. I hold it up to me. "What do you think, Emma?" She doesn't answer me. She's so unsupportive. I wriggle into it, step back to the mirror. It's not terrible. I can be seen in public like this. A little mascara, some lip gloss. I'm hardly glamorous, but perhaps I can be presentable, with the right shoes.

Three hours later, I am ready. My toenails are painted, my shoes are open-toed and platformy, but not so tall as to risk falling. My hair is clean, if somewhat damp. Emma is dressed in polka dots, and has extravagant, multicolored ruffles on her bottom. We look good. We are not stained or smelly. At the bottom of the steps, I strap Emma into the car seat and stroller, and then drape a blanket over her. We're running early, so we stop at a deli on Myrtle Avenue for a coffee. "Half decaf, please," I say, because I don't need Emma getting all hopped up on my caffeinated breast milk.

I sip while we walk, and I'm half wondering if Emma can sense my nervousness, because my mom has mentioned that babies can feel their mothers' tension. In fact she says this whenever I tell her that Emma is fussy. She says, "Well, she can probably sense how uptight you are, and that makes her uptight, too," which is obviously a very helpful observation.

But now Emma has fallen asleep, so I feel like the babies-feeling-their-mothers'-tension thing is probably horseshit. I've left some sticky red lip gloss hickeys on the rim of my paper coffee cup, so I stop on the sidewalk to wipe them off with a napkin, because that's not the kind of first impression I want to make. It's a glorious, chilly, blue-sky autumn day, and we crunch through leaves as we walk. Before we reach the playground, I fish my *Food & Wine* magazine—the July issue, with my story about pears—out from my diaper bag. I tuck it nonchalantly under my arm as a conversation piece.

I feel like a kid on the first day of a new school—excited and terrified. I hope I meet someone nice. When we reach the playground at Eightieth Street, I try not to appear too eager. I glance through the bars as we skirt the fencing, and I notice that there are already several moms with strollers chatting by the monkey bars. There's another small group sitting at the benches. I find the gate, open it, and push Emma through. I'm trying to decide which group to approach first, when I notice that all the moms at the benches have fallen silent, and are staring at me. I try a smile.

"Are you going to close that?" one of the mothers asks me, in the bitchiest voice I have ever heard. And holy cow, it *is* like the first day of school—junior high school—when that nasty peroxide-blond Nicole Davis, who was a year older than me, threw an apple at my ass when I bent over to get something from my locker. Before I can even answer the evil mom, she stands up, strides past me, and slams the gate I've just come through.

"Forget it," she says, shaking her head.

My mouth is still hanging open when she installs herself back on the bench among her troop of mean mommy-friends and starts talking loudly about "amateur mommies, whose children, *thank God*, are still too small to run through an open gate and into traffic, because God help that kid when it can walk."

I am so shocked at this moment that I respond with a sort of reactionary coma, exactly like I did with Nicole and the seventh-grade apple. I shut down completely. I can't leave yet, not with any degree of dignity. I have to stay at least a few minutes to prove to myself that though I might be a chubby, whiny, angry, despondent, drippy mess of a woman, I'm not also completely spineless. So then why do I mumble, "Sorry," as I scamper past the mean bench-mommies? Fuck.

I approach the monkey bars, and no one really looks at me. These are mommies of newborns—I can tell. They are disheveled and unsure of themselves. More than one is leaking through her bra. There are spit-up stains and maternity pants everywhere. It feels like an outdoor ward—you can almost smell the desperation. Plus, they all have small babies with them.

"Hi," I venture, when there's a big enough gap in the nervous conversation. Several of the moms turn to look at me, and one steps aside to make room for me to join their circle. I want to kiss her, to make a sticky red lip gloss hickey on her mouth.

"Hi," they all say at once, as if we're at an AA meeting.

"Is this the meetup group?" I ask.

"Yeah," one of the cleaner-looking moms says. "I'm Amanda," and she sticks her hand out to me.

I shake it. "Hi, I'm Majella."

There are "nice to meet you's" and a couple of "that's an unusual name's." And then we all just stand around smiling uncomfortably at one another for a few minutes, until I have the brilliant idea to start asking about their babies.

"How old is your little one?" I ask Amanda, who is wearing her baby strapped to her chest like an enormous tumor.

She strokes the top of his head, which is covered by an aggressively striped hat. "He's eight and a half weeks."

"Oh, he's adorable," I lie, because I can't really see him in there, but he's probably cute, right? "Is he your first?"

"Thanks," she says. "Yeah, little Henri is my first."

She pronounces it *Awn-ree*, like a Parisian.

"Oh, Henri," I repeat, "what a lovely name. Are you or his father French?"

"No," she says, and offers nothing more, so I stop asking.

I pull back the hood on Emma's stroller a little bit, hoping that the light will wake her, just so I'll have an excuse to pick her up, to give myself something to do. Maybe she'll even be fussy, and we'll have to leave. I have never hoped she would be fussy before. The mom standing next to me leans down to look at Emma in the stroller, but she stands back up without saying anything. Weirdo.

After a couple of awkward minutes, the bitchy mom from the benches stands up, and walks toward us. I'm horrified. What the hell could she possibly want from me now? I haven't even looked in her direction since the gate incident. Hasn't she berated me enough already? If she attacks me again, I will stand up for myself. I will let her have it. Fuck her. I square my shoulders. Maybe I can pretend that all these meetup moms are my friends now. Yeah. I have friends, too. Yeah!

There is a blondie kid hanging almost upside down from the top bar of the slide, dangling dangerously. "Tabitha, get down from there," the bitch mom yells. Then she stands at the edge of our little circle, and her mean-looking cohorts from the benches approach, too. It's like a scene from *West Side Story*. Like there's going to be a musical, hyperchoreographed fracas. We're about to *throw down*. But now she is smiling. A big, fake, ugly, toothy smile.

"Welcome to the Glendale Mommies Meetup!" she says, in a singsong, cartoon version of her bitch-voice. "I'm Tanya, the group leader."

Holy shit.

"And this," she says, grabbing the blond monster from the slide as it tries to rush past her, "is my daughter, Tabitha." She leans down to give Tabitha a kiss, but the kid shrieks and wriggles away, and is back hanging upside down at the top of the slide before I can even blink. "And this is my little man, Toby."

She produces a stroller from behind her as if by magic, and there is an enormous, pie-eyed, fuzzy-headed baby sitting up inside. He blinks at us like a benevolent overlord. The mommies *awwwwww* respectfully. I feel like I'm going to throw up. *Please wake up, Emma, please wake up. Now is the time to scream.*

"I see we have a few new mommies joining us today," Tanya says, looking at me with her eyebrows pointing up into her forehead, "and a couple of *very* new mommies."

The newbies giggle nervously and turn to smile at me, as if we're all in on the joke. *We are totally not in on the joke. This woman is a witch, why can't you all see that?* My cell phone makes its text-message noise, and I'm delighted for the distraction. I take it out of my pocket and read Leo's message: *How's the meetup going?* I type back with my thumbs: *hell hell hell.* But my iPhone corrects me to: *he'll he'll he'll.* Annoyed, I jam it back in my pocket without hitting *send*.

In the short time I was distracted, the women have begun taking turns introducing themselves.

"I'm Rebecca," says one of the harried new moms. Her red hair is threaded with gray, and it has a moplike quality. She has deep purple rings under her eyes. "My little Jayden is three months old, and I'm a SAHM."

I notice a lot of the other moms bobbing their heads enthusiastically, and I whisper to a nearby mom, "What's a SAHM?"

"Stay-at-home mom," she whispers back.

There is almost nothing I hate more than people who talk in acronyms. I make a mental note not to get too friendly with Rebecca, despite the rings under her eyes.

"It's *so much better* for the children," Tanya is saying, "to stay at home with them full-time."

I can see panic in the eyes of a few of the other moms, the guilty, job-having moms. They immediately begin to fuss over their babies. One little man is beginning to whimper loudly in his seat. His mom reaches into her diaper bag, and retrieves a bottle with water in it. She dumps the premeasured powdered formula into the bottle, and begins to shake it up. Her eyes are glued to her crying baby, and she doesn't notice that everyone else has stopped talking to stare at her. She's unstrapping her hungry little boy; she's lifting him onto her shoulder.

Tanya points to the bottle. "You're *formula feeding*?" she says.

The mom looks at her bravely, stares straight into her eyes. She's not scared of Tanya. The baby boy in her arms is content now, sucking happily on his formula bottle.

"What's it to you?" the brave mom asks. She's like a firefighter, an astronaut, and a midwife all rolled into one—that's how fearless she is. I watch in awe. Tanya purses her lips, and exchanges knowing glances with some of her underlings.

"Just curious," Tanya says. "You know, with all the research about how much better it is to breast-feed, I just find it peculiar when mothers choose to feed their babies chemicals instead of the real thing."

The courageous mom straightens herself up tall. Well, as tall as she can—she's only about five feet two, with cascading black curls, and gorgeous skin, and Latina hips. I think she's going to lay into Tanya. I think I'm about to watch a bona fide smack-down. Who knew there was so much potential violence in suburban parenthood? But what the brave mom does is *so much better*. She drops her voice to a near whisper. She takes a step forward, to make sure Tanya doesn't miss a word.

"Some women can't breast-feed," she says.

Tanya tries to interrupt. "Anyone can breast-feed, if you try hard—"

But the brave mama plows ahead. "Some women are on experimental drugs for cancer, you nosy, judgmental bitch. And it's none of your business what anyone chooses to feed, or not feed, their kid."

We are watching like it's a tennis match, me and all the other moms. We turn back to Tanya, to await her stunned, apologetic retreat, but it doesn't come. It does not come! Instead, she snorts.

"Well, there's no need to get all bent out of shape about it," she says. "I was only asking." And then she waves her hands in front of her, as if to erase the whole ugly incident from our minds. "*Anyway*," she says.

But the brave mom isn't done.

"Fuck this," she says, slinging her diaper bag into her empty stroller. "What a joke."

Tanya is sweeping her arms around in elaborate, circular gestures, trying to distract us, trying to win us back. But now more than a few of the moms are packing up. I stuff the *Food & Wine* magazine back into my diaper bag, and double-check Emma's straps. I turn the stroller, and point it toward the gate. The brave mom is already halfway across the playground, her baby boy still in her arms, still eating from his bottle. She turns and yells back at the group.

"You know, the whole point of this shit is that new moms need to support each other. We need *support*. That's why we came here today."

There's nothing else for Tanya to say, so she just laughs in response. This is the single most awkward, horrible exchange I have ever witnessed between adult humans, and that includes my devout consumption of many seasons of *The Bachelor*. I chase after the brave mom. I want to be her friend, or maybe even her wife. I love her. I meet her at the gate, and she's struggling with the baby in one arm, trying to push the stroller with the other. I open the gate, and hold it for her.

"Thanks," she says, pushing her stroller through.

I smile. "You were so great back there," I say. "That Tanya is a total bully, it's like being back in school. You were so right to stand up to her."

The brave cancer-mom is shaking her head. She makes a disgusted noise; she's all out of words.

"I'm Majella," I say, following her through the gate.

"Hi," she mumbles, and sticks out her hand, but she forgets to tell me her name back. "Nice to meet you."

"Hey, you want to go grab a coffee or something?" I ask her.

She stops walking and puts the brake on her stroller. It's hard to hold and feed her baby with one hand. She looks at me and takes a deep breath.

"Thanks," she says. "But no, I'm just . . . I think I just want to go home, after all this. I need to get home."

"Sure," I say, even though my heart is sunk. "Okay."

"Yeah, thanks anyway, though. I gotta go."

She walks away, pushing the stroller with one hand, and holding her son's bottle pinned between her cheek and her shoulder. Emma is still asleep, and another mom is trying to get out through the gate behind us now. I'm in her way, but she hasn't even asked me to move. She's just waiting. I scuttle out of the way. "Sorry, excuse me," I say.

She nods, and pushes her huge stroller out onto the sidewalk without saying a word. She has short, spiky blond hair, and her arms are lined with tinkling bracelets. A tattoo snakes out from beneath one sleeve of her fitted T-shirt, and reaches toward her elbow. I slam the gate behind her, and it makes a loud, satisfying clang. She starts to push her stroller down the street, and I follow her until we reach the first intersection. We pause at the crosswalk and wait for the light. She looks up at me, and her eyes look completely hollowed out, the whites of them laced with swollen red veins like she's been crying for decades. Her cheeks are puffy, and her stroller is oversized and awkward. She looks like a baby herself, almost too young to have a child. I didn't notice her at the playground.

"Were you at that horrible mommy meetup group?" I ask her. "I didn't see you in the playground."

She takes a deep breath. "Worst. Mommy group. Ever."

I laugh, "Yeah, it was seriously awful, right? What is wrong with people?"

"I went one other time, and it was just as bad," she says. "I don't know what possessed me to go back." She runs her hands through her spiky blond hair, tugs it away from her scalp. "I guess I just needed to get outta the house."

The light changes, and we push our strollers out into the crosswalk.

"I should've known not to come, from that huge fight on the message board," she says.

"Message board?"

"You don't read it?" she asks.

I shake my head.

"Ugh. One woman suggested that because it's grown into such a large group, maybe we should subdivide into smaller groups. You know, based on the ages of our children."

"And that caused a fight?"

"You wouldn't believe it. They ripped her to shreds, telling her she wasn't the organizer of the group, and she had no right to go mixing everything up, and if she didn't like things the way they were, she should start her own group. It's like Tanya has them all brainwashed. And then the one woman who did come to her defense said, *Oh, you know, I think we actually should subdivide by the kids' ages, because my son is almost two now, and I don't even bother talking to the new moms, because I have nothing in common with them.*"

"Good God," I say.

"I know," she says. "Like the only thing these women could possibly have in common is the age of their children? Give me a fucking break. What about movies, books, travel, sports? *Interests?* What about who you were before these little sprogs were born? Jesus, it's like these women, they have no identity of their own, beyond what the little shits have reduced them to. They're just a bunch of fucking *mommies.*"

I know I should be shocked by her calling all those defense-less babies "little shits" out loud, but I'm not. It's like she's inside my head. I'm almost afraid that I'm hallucinating her. I touch her arm, and she doesn't disappear, but she does seem slightly star-tled. She pulls away. My cell phone makes its swoopy text-noise, and I remember that I never got back to Leo. I pull it out of my pocket: *Still there? How's it going?*

"Hang on," I say to the other mom, and then I stop walking for a moment to type back: *It was awful. Bitchy mommies. Heading home.* I can forecast Leo's disappointment. I wonder if he'll think it's my fault, that I didn't give it a chance. I'll have to explain it to him, how terrible it was. He'll understand, right? I stick the cell phone in my cup holder, and sip my now ice-cold coffee. Gross. It's gone bitter in the cup.

"I'm Majella, by the way."

"Yeah, I'm Jade."

We don't shake hands. She sniffs, and I notice the tiny silver ring in her nose. I want to ask how old she is, but I know that's rude, so I ask how old her baby is instead.

"They're five and a half months," she says. "Almost six."

"They?"

She pulls back the hood on her enormous stroller, so I can see inside: two babies. *Two! Twins!* I think of channel C, and my heart races. I've been talking to this woman for three city blocks, and I didn't notice that she has two friggin' babies in there. Way to go, Sherlock.

"Boys or girls?"

"One of each," she says.

"That's great, you got one of each!" I say, and I realize the stupidity of it even as the words escape my mouth.

"Yeah," she says, "great."

I stare at the babies, and try to determine whether they could be the ones from the monitor. They do have dark hair, but it's so hard to tell, without the grainy green night-vision light that makes the monitor-babies' eyes glow like little goblins'.

"It must be tough, having two," I say.

Jade shrugs. "Having any is tough, right?"

"Yeah."

I can sense her drawing into herself, the plates of her armor shifting and clicking down. I don't know what's happened, what has changed, but her little outburst is finished, and she is done talking unless I can draw her back out.

"Are you from here?"

"Nah, Miami," she says.

"Been here long?"

"A year," she says. "What about you? You sound like a New Yawkah."

"Yeah, I grew up here," I say. "But I was living in Manhattan for fifteen years. My husband and I just moved back to Queens to have the baby."

Jade nods, but doesn't ask any more. I feel a little desperate; we've been walking for almost six blocks now, and we're nearing my turnoff. I wonder if she'll turn off, too, if she's that sobbing mom from the monitor. But she can't be; she seems so strong, so hard—even her body is fit and solid. She must be a size two, and her arms are toned and tan. She has that kind of effortlessly lean body I had once, before my pregnancy blurred me into a new, permanently swollen shape (like parentheses). I wonder how she got hers back after twins. She's so young. She can hardly be twenty years old.

"Hey, you wanna go somewhere for a coffee?" I ask, afraid of her answer because that brave cancer-mom already rebuffed me, and I don't know if I can take two rejections in one day. "I'm all gussied up with nowhere to go," I joke, and then I look down self-consciously, because I realize that to any sane human being, I wouldn't look *gussied up* in the slightest. Since when does a clean shirt and maternity jeans constitute *gussied up*? And who the hell says *gussied up* anyway? "I just, I'm not ready to go home yet," I say, "so I'm probably going to head down to Salamander's for a coffee and a scone if you want to join me. I'm going any-way."

We come to another red light, and Jade seems to be weighing me against whatever her other options might be. If she has other options—any other options—I will lose. Why would she choose me over an actual friend, or *The Ellen DeGeneres Show*, or scrub-bing her toilets? I bite my lip, and try not to care while I await her verdict.

"Yeah, okay," she says, unenthusiastically.

My heart soars.

Chapter Ten

Ginny blew out the candle in her little room, and lay down on the mattress in the dark, the whiff of squelched smoke still trailing through the air above her. Roisin had given her a heap of blankets, but it was still cold and dark in the attic room, with no cheerful turf fire for warmth. It wasn't hard to stay awake, never mind how exhausted Ginny was.

After a time, the house seemed quiet. She could hear only the sound of the determined wind hauling itself savagely across the roof above her. She crept from her mattress, and stooped by the door, listening. She grabbed one of the blankets and folded it around her shoulders. Then she carefully turned the doorknob. In the black-ened corridor, she carried her brogues in one hand and groped her way along the wainscoting with the other. She crept backwards down the steep attic stairwell, wincing with the creaking of each floorboard underfoot. She didn't know which chamber was Murdoch's, and she didn't fancy bumping into him in the middle of the night. When she reached the first floor, she went into the dining room and sat down in one of the soft chairs to lace up her brogues. She went out through the French doors, and left them unlatched behind her.

Ginny drew the blanket more snugly around her, and studied the darkened upper-floor windows of Springhill House as she walked, but the sound of her footfall on the gravel path didn't rouse any curiosity to the windowpanes. Seán Lyons was waiting for her in the shadowy stables, and she was glad to get in out of the wind. There was a lamp going in one of the bottom stalls, and she could hear men's voices, slurry speech.

"You're looking to get in on a card game, is it?" Seán said, as she approached.

"Hardly."

"So it's romance, then." He grinned. "But, Mrs. Doyle, I needn't remind you that you're a married woman. Though it may grieve my heart to slight you, I am not the breed of wicked man who would deign to take advantage of a woman in your position." He clutched at his breast again. "Oh, sing, treacherous heart!"

"Shhhh." She pulled him into the quieter light of one of the stalls. "Seán Lyons, when did you get to be such a trier?" she admonished him.

"When my heart was broken at the tender age of thirteen." He smiled.

The mare who shared their stall leaned down to nudge Seán for a sugar cube. He flicked one out from his pocket, and she licked it up quick.

"Come on, we'll walk out," Seán said then, and he led Ginny back into the cold, dark night.

The sky above was a mess of stars, and the moon was nearly full. The wind fairly howled through the fields, whipping Ginny's ropy black hair around her head, but those stars were as fixed and still as God Himself. Seán was watching them, too.

"Ah, here!" he said, pointing up. "This one's making a run for it," as one of the stars arced frantically across the sky. Seán whistled low. "Think he'll make it?"

"For dead certain he will," Ginny said.

They walked to the back of the stables, and started down a stone path that was canopied by a thick arcade of trees. Their boughs stretched and swayed above, protecting the walkers from the worst of the wind, and blotting out the starlight. There was a stone bench cut into the trunk of a big oak tree, where Ginny and Seán sat down.

"There's nobody here?" she asked.

Seán hummed in response.

"You're sure?" she said. "Nobody would overhear?"

He sat forward. "Jesus, Ginny, you're awful nervous."

"I am."

"What is it, woman?"

"I need your help, Seán."

"Anything."

"Don't say that until you hear what it is," she said. "It could cost you your life, your job, everything. What I have to ask you."

He leaned forward on the bench and planted his elbows on his knees. She could see only the outline of him, in the dark.

"Go on," he said.

"Raymond is gone this six months, nearly," she said, shivering, and pulling the blanket tighter around her shoulders. "We were meant to hear from him by February, with money."

Seán took a breath out of the wind, and sharpened it in his lungs. "It's nearly April now, Ginny," he said.

"I know."

"So he's what, six, eight weeks overdue?"

"Something like that."

"Is there anyone you can write to, to ask after him?"

"Yes." She nodded. "His brother, Kevin, is there, and I sent him off a letter last week, to find out, before I came here. But I couldn't wait any longer. We have a family, we have four children. I had to leave them, to come here for the job."

"Who has them, then, who's looking after them?" he asked. "Are they with his parents?"

Ginny shook her head, and an awful lump of a thing came into her throat so that she found she couldn't answer him.

"Where are they?" he asked again.

"Raymond's parents are dead, too," she said. "There was no one."

Seán sat up, and she could see his blue eyes moving over her face in the darkness.

"They're at home, still," Ginny whispered. "I had to leave them."

Seán gulped. "On their own?" he said.

She nodded.

"Jesus, Ginny."

"I'd no choice, Seán. They were starving, we were all going to starve. Dammit!" She stood up, and the blanket fell from her shoulders so that she could pace the width of the path. She was grateful for the wind now, because it dried the tears quickly on her face and neck.

"How old are they?" Seán asked. His elbows were planted on his knees, and he cracked his knuckles while they talked.

"Maire is the oldest," she said. "She's nearly twelve, but she's very grown. Very responsible. I know she can manage." But Ginny's voice had a creeping edge of hysteria, and she knew it wasn't Seán she was trying to convince. He stood up, and found Ginny's hand in the darkness.

"Sure twelve is ancient," he said. "Calm down, Ginny. You did the right thing."

But her throat felt all choked and petrified, thinking of them out there in the cottage on their own.

"But the little ones," she said. "Poppy isn't yet three. God, what have I done?"

"Only what you had to do," he answered. He was tugging on her arm, steering her back to the bench. He groped around for her blanket in the darkness, and heaped it back onto her when she sat. He handed over his handkerchief, too, and she honked her nose into it. Then they were both quiet, listening to the wind rifling through the branches above.

"I'm having another one," she said, after a while. "Soon, I think. A couple of months more, maybe."

"I wondered if you might be," he said. "You look well."

Ginny tipped her head back and rested it against the tree behind her. "It's too small, this child." She felt for the swell beneath the blanket. "But he's kicking in there, still. I can feel him moving around."

"Ginny, I don't mean to frighten you," Seán said then, "but you know what they're saying about them American ships."

She leaned over and bundled the blanket all around her like a suit of armor.

"They're calling them *coffin ships*, Ginny, because so many on board are dying before they even get to New York. Conditions are dire, and the fever is rampant on them ships."

Ginny shook her head, shook his words out of her ears. She'd heard that before, all right. She'd heard it from the gossips in Westport town, and in the churchyard on a Sunday.

"But Raymond is young and fit," she said. "He can do anything."

Seán nodded quietly beside her. "I'm only telling you, you did the right thing, coming here, for your children—finding work. I don't want to upset you. I'm only telling you to be prepared for whatever happens."

Ginny drew the blanket up over her head and face, then, to save Seán the discomfort of watching her sob. She rocked herself, and wept and heaved. The baby in her belly seemed encouraged by all the bustle, or maybe it was the good meal she had eaten. She could feel the child rolling and stretching inside. Then Seán's arm was steady on her shoulder. He didn't try to stop her crying. He let her go.

When she was calm enough to speak again, she told him, "She won't let me go. Mrs. Spring knows I'm expecting, but she has no idea about the other children, and there's no way she'd let me off to see them, even if she did."

"She's terrified of the fever." He nodded. "She's nearly deranged over the fear of it. But sure she's half-deranged anyway, at the best of times."

"She does seem a bit odd." Ginny sniffed, blowing her nose into his handkerchief again.

"Oh, she's mad as a March hare," he said.

"She'd want to be, to take me on in this state."

Seán hummed again, stood up, and clasped his hands behind him in the dark. "I'll do it," he said.

"You'll do what?" Ginny looked up at him. "I haven't even asked you yet."

"I'll look in on your children, make sure they're all right, keep an eye out," he said. "I'm out on the roads at least every other day, I'm the only one from Springhill who's allowed free travel. She keeps everyone else under lock and key. But I can run messages for you."

Ginny breathed carefully, her heart flying like that arcing star. "They need food," she said.

"Of course."

It was dangerous, what she was asking him to do. If Murdoch or Mrs. Spring got wind of it, he'd lose his job no question—they might even see him transported. But even worse, carrying food in these times was downright unsafe. Since the famine had deepened, there had already been drivers killed by starving natives in Mullingar and Strokestown, just for a chance at the provisions they might be carrying.

"You're sure?" Ginny said. "It's an awful risk, Seán, and nobody would fault you—"

"I would fault me," he interrupted, and then he sat down again, by her side. "How could I live with myself if I didn't do this? Of course I'll do it."

"Thank you," she whispered, and she had nothing more to give him, only that.

"Yeah, to hell with it," he said, slapping his thighs. "Where's the fun in living a safe, easy life anyway?" He stood up abruptly from the bench. "We should get you inside, Ginny. Jesus, with the baby coming and all, and you out here in the freezing cold."

"I'm all right," she said, but she stood up, too, and it was true that her teeth were chattering. They started back up the path toward Springhill House, and Ginny could see the light dancing out merrily from the stables. Before she crept back up the lawns toward the French doors, she thanked him again.

"Do you think you might go tomorrow?" she asked. "I wouldn't press, only they're so hungry. I'm awful worried over them."

He shook his head. "Tomorrow, no," he said. "There's no messages tomorrow."

Her heart plummeted, but she couldn't push him any further. She'd already asked for so much.

"Ginny," he said, and then he waited until she looked up at

him. His blue eyes flashed in the windy moonlight. "I'm going tonight."

She slept. Ginny slept deep and hard and guiltless and dreamless, and when she awakened, the room was lit gray, with a dusty shaft of sunlight leaking through the gap beneath her door. Someone was knocking. She sat up and smoothed down her hair, wrapped the blanket around her, and went to the door. Roisin was in the corridor, already dressed and smiling.

"It's laundry day," she said, "no time to lose!"

Ginny nodded. "Right, I'll just get dressed."

"Quickly, dear." She clapped her hands, and disappeared down the corridor toward the stairs.

In the kitchen, the women ate eggs and cheese and toast with butter, and Ginny attacked the food with vigor. She was too hungry to feel guilt.

"The laundry is heavy work," Roisin said, mopping up the yolk on her plate with some bread. "But we'll be able for it if we're well fed, hah?"

Katie ate silently, without looking up from her plate.

"You're looking better already, dear," Roisin said, studying Ginny's face across the table. "Fuller in the face, and a better color in you, your eyes a bit clearer. After only one day! Imagine after a week here, that baby will be fat in your belly. You won't be able to move, with the grows of him!"

"Please, God," Ginny said. "That'd be a fine problem to have."

It was true that she felt stronger already, able for the work ahead. They bent to it without complaint. They stripped the beds in Mrs. Spring's room, and Murdoch's as well, and brought all the table and chamber linens down to the basement. Two enormous wash boilers were already bubbling in the laundry room, and the air inside was steamed, damp and warm.

"Thank God there's only the two of them here to look after, Murdoch and Mrs. Spring," Roisin said, as they loaded the sleeping linens into the first copper boiler. "We'd never manage the washing for a full house. We'd need more help."

"But why is that?" Ginny asked. "It seems awful unusual, the way Mrs. Spring is here on her own in such a fine house, with the agent managing the estate. Where is her husband? You'd think she'd prefer to be in London."

"Oh, she would," Roisin said, plunging the linens deep with a wooden paddle. "She'd be off to London in a flash if she could. She keeps a brave face on it most of the time, but in truth, she hates it here. She's miserable."

Roisin stopped in her work and stood straight for a moment to look at Ginny. "I say too much," she corrected herself.

"Not at all," Ginny answered, taking the paddle from the older woman, and pitching the linens herself. "I'd never breathe a word of it, you needn't worry about me. I'm only interested. It seems so curious, a man leaving his wife here on her own in these times." And as soon as she said it, she thought of Raymond, and blushed. "I'm sure they have their reasons."

"Oh, he has his reasons, all right," Roisin tutted, as she started loading the table linens into the second boiler. "It's easier for him to carry on with his other women if his eccentric wife is tucked well out of the way, at the end of nowhere in the west of Ireland."

Roisin paused and went to the door, opened it to look out. All was quiet beyond. She closed it, and returned to their work.

"Mrs. Spring never comes down the stairs," she said. "Still, it would be just my luck."

"Did you ever meet him?" Ginny asked. "Mr. Spring?"

"When they first came here four years ago, I did. I was the first one they hired in, before Murdoch, even. Mrs. Spring took a shine to me straightaway," she said. "I don't suppose she'd yet given up on him when they arrived. She was hoping for a baby, I reckon."

Roisin reached for a second wooden paddle, her face already pink and sticky with sweat. "And who knows? Maybe a child could have saved the marriage," she said, leaning into her work. "But I don't suppose we'll ever know. After just one summer, he abandoned her here, went back to London on his own."

"How do you mean *abandoned*? Surely she could've gone with him?"

"No." Roisin shook her head. "He never gave her the chance. I didn't know he was going—no one did. Perhaps Murdoch. He left her a letter."

Ginny stopped churning her paddle and stared at Roisin. "He never."

"He did," Roisin said. "Just up and left, in the middle of the night. Didn't even tell her good-bye."

"Bastard."

"Nearly four years ago," Roisin said. "He's never been back. Hardly even writes."

"The poor woman."

"Sure if she wasn't mad in the head before that, who could blame her for coming a bit undone after?"

They worked on for a while in silence, and Ginny thought about Alice Spring. It was hard to imagine she had anything in common with a rich Englishwoman like her, and Ginny knew that Raymond had left because he loved her, he loved their family. He hadn't abandoned them at all; on the contrary, he had gone to save them—precisely for that. But he was gone, all the same, and Ginny knew how that felt. She knew the terror of lonesomeness and longing. While they worked, Ginny listened for any sign of Seán, for his footstep on the stair above. She was desperate for news of her babbies. There was no sign of him all day.

That night, she sought him out again, and found him in the stables playing cards with some of the other young fellas. They whistled and catcalled when he excused himself to join her, but Seán told them to shut their gobs.

"Well?" Ginny asked him, as soon as they were outside the door.

"They're grand, Ginny," he said. "Maire looks just like you, except with the fair hair. She's gorgeous. And smart. She wouldn't let me in, at first."

Ginny stood back and crossed her arms in front of her. She rested them on her bump. "How do you mean?"

"I knocked on the door, and she shouted out to me, she said, 'We have no food, and there's fever in this house, so you're best to move along down the road!'"

"She didn't!"

"She did, and when I told her I wasn't looking for a handout, and I was a friend of her mother's, she interrogated me before she would open the door."

"What did she ask you?"

"How I knew you, where I came from, what was your mother's Christian name. Jesus, Ginny, it's lucky I have a good memory."

"Clever girl." Ginny smiled.

"She is," he agreed. "She's doing a fine job looking after the little ones, and they tore into the food you sent. They were well fed."

"Thank God," Ginny said. "And thank you."

"Ah, it's nothing."

"It's everything."

He stuffed his hands into his pockets. "I told them I'd be back tomorrow, I'd try to come every other night, so make sure you pack extra, Ginny. Give them two days' worth."

"I will," she said. "Grand."

So that was how the rhythm started. How, by the grace of God and Seán Lyons, Ginny fell into the rituals and routine of saving the lives of her children. After a time, it began to feel normal, to be rent from them. When she prayed at night, she spent time trying to conjure their faces, the sweet and breathy timbre of their voices. With each passing day, that magic was harder to summon. She wanted to remember the way they'd been when they were happy, before the potato failed, before Raymond left.

Days drew into weeks, and Seán became like a pivot in Ginny's life. Everything turned around him. She would awaken in the morning, and the hours would stretch and unfurl toward him, until his brief appearance. And then at night, when he was gone back to her children, with the food she'd pilfered and packed them, she would climb the steps to her attic room, and lie awake, feeling the minutes unraveling until she could see him again. She would work all day, at the cooking and the washing and the serving. Throughout the day, she always looked for little gifts she could send to her children along with the food. Whenever she could, she tucked in a bluebell for Maire, or a smooth stone for Maggie. Ginny lived for those night-bright minutes with Seán, when he brought news of home: Poppy still cried sometimes, missing her mammy, but mostly she was very brave, and her curly hair was getting longer and fuller. Maggie had started a second cairn now, on the far side of the cottage, for Ginny. It was easier for her to tend the cairns now that the weather was beginning to hint toward spring. And Michael had stepped up to help, now that his parents were both gone. Maire was well pleased with him. The children all worked together to prepare the turnip patch for planting, and they were wanting seed for it, so when the time came, Ginny gave Seán all of her paltry wages.

"I don't know if it's enough, if you'll get any seed with that."

"Don't worry, Ginny," he said to her. "I'll get it."

It was May, and Ginny's stomach swelled properly. There was still no word from Raymond, and her terror over that grew by degrees, like Maggie's stone sculptures, like her own round belly. She asked Seán to send Michael to see Father Brennan, for to write a second letter to Kevin in New York.

She was on guard against contentment, in case that same willful forgetfulness, that refusal to bear witness, that she'd noticed when she first came into Springhill House would invade her own mind as well. Now that her children were safe, at least for the time being, she didn't want to forget the suffering of her neighbors, the real and acute starvation beyond the gate. But the absence of her family was reminder enough, her isolation from them a sort of secondary starvation.

Ginny saw little of Mrs. Spring, and thankfully, even less of Murdoch. She worked mostly in the kitchen and the laundry with Roisin, but she cleaned the upper chambers as well, and one late afternoon, when her belly had grown heavy enough to sway her back, Mrs. Spring noticed, and had Ginny installed in one of the empty bedchambers not far from her own. There was an enormous four-poster bed that Roisin helped make up, and a domed ceiling above. The walls were covered in striped silk, and heavy swaths of gold fabric hung from the tall windows. There was a cheerful fireplace at the foot of the bed, all dressed with dancing plaster angels. Roisin brought up a pail of turf and set it beside the hearth. Ginny watched her companion's face for signs of resentment, but there wasn't a trace of it. They stood by the window together, and Roisin lifted and patted Ginny's hand.

"Strange," Ginny said, "the thought of sleeping in a room like this."

Roisin released the drapes from their belts, shook them loose, and helped Ginny pull them across the darkening windows. "It's beautiful, isn't it?" Roisin said. "Has always been one of my favorite rooms in the house. I love the stripes." Roisin touched the silk on the wall.

"It is," Ginny said, and she sank down on the edge of the bed. "I'm grateful. Still and all, I'd rather be at home in my own poor cottage with my Ray."

Roisin swept across the room to where Ginny sat. "He'll be along any day now, dear," Roisin said, looking at Ginny's belly.

"I reckon that's right." Ginny took Roisin's hand in her own, and placed it low on her bump, so she might feel the baby kick.

"Oh!" Roisin said. "And strong. Brilliant! He can help with the cleaning." She clapped her hands, and they both laughed.

Ginny slept well in the room, her spirits encouraged by the amiability of the turf fire. Mrs. Spring watched her day by day, the brightness in her gaze trained always on Ginny's growing belly. Mrs. Spring insisted that Ginny take it easy, but for her part, Ginny kept working, worried about what might happen when the baby was born. She couldn't allow herself to become burdensome in this house. She would have to spring back on her feet, get back to work in haste. She would have to mind the baby easily. She prayed to God for an easy birth, an easy child. Maire had been difficult, but she cleared the way for the others, and all of Ginny's children since had practically walked out. It was nearly three years now since her last baby was born, slipping out so fast that Ray joked, when he first held that baby girl in his arms, that she had popped out like a cork from a bottle. So they christened her Pauline, but they only ever called her Poppy.

On her knees at night, Ginny prayed, "Please God, give me another Poppy."

Ginny was in the cold larder, preparing a basket for Seán to take to the children, when her water broke. She found herself standing in a spreading lamplit puddle.

"No, no, no, no, no," she said. "Not yet. Not yet."

And she swayed from hip to hip, to ease the cramps, while she finished packing the food. She left the basket down on the kitchen worktable, and went to the laundry room for some rags. She had to clean up the puddle first, so no one would suspect that she'd been down in the larder raiding food when the baby started to come. She was a few minutes late meeting Seán at their usual spot.

"What kept you?" he asked, as he leaned down from his saddle to take the basket from her. He never took the carriage on these night runs, only the horse on her own. Ginny winced, and Seán leapt down from the saddle, nearly tumbled the basket of food. "The baby's coming, is it?" he asked.

Ginny bobbed her head, breathed through the cramp, as deep and fresh as she could. Seán turned in circles. "I'll go for . . . a . . . Here." He turned around again. "What am I supposed to do?"

Ginny felt her muscles relax as the cramp eased. She laughed. "You're not meant to do anything, just the same as you always do. You take the food to the children," she said. "I'll have the baby."

He nodded his head, and the horse mimicked him. They were both dipping and waggling like puppets in the moonlight. Seán threw his leg up and over the saddle, and Ginny watched from below, shifting her weight in circles over her loosening hips. This baby would come fast. Seán turned his mare in a circle above her.

"Godspeed, Ginny, never worry about a thing," he said. "If you're off your feet for a few days, I'll mind out for them, I'll take care." He leaned down from his saddle and Ginny squeezed his hand.

"I know you will."

"Are you sure you're all right there, Ginny?" he said. "You can make it back to the house on your own?"

"I'll be grand," she said. "And Seán?"

"Yeah?"

"Tell Maire that I love her."

The baby didn't pop out, exactly, but he did arrive in style, on pressed bed linens in a grand four-poster bed in that stripy, silky room, attended by Roisin, and Mrs. Alice Spring herself. Before dawn lightened the windows of Springhill House, baby Raymond Doyle was born. And he brought with him a great festive, joyful feeling that glowed on the faces of all the women in that house— Ginny was sure of it—not only on her own.

Roisin stoked up the turf fire cheerily in the hearth, even though Ginny and the baby were both drenched with sweat. He went to the breast straightaway, and Mrs. Spring couldn't take her eyes from him. She sat on the edge of the bed and stared at the mother and new child, her lips parted in a smile. She kept repeating herself.

"Oh, isn't he lovely? Isn't he the loveliest little thing? Look at the size of him, he's so small," Alice Spring said, over and over again. She watched him eat.

"Mrs. Spring, perhaps we should give them a bit of privacy now, some time to rest," Roisin tried tactfully.

"Nonsense," Mrs. Spring said, waving her off. "Ginny doesn't want to be alone at a time like this, do you, dear? No, of course you don't!"

Mrs. Spring leaned forward on the bed, and touched the baby's head, where he was eating, and Ginny felt very uneasy, the way the woman fondled the back of the baby's head while he suckled. But she said nothing, because she was so very grateful for the comfort of a good, clean birth, and this lovely room and bed to recover in. It was all so odd, and Ginny had a nagging fear that Mrs. Spring would snap to her senses, and toss them out into the road before the day's end.

So when Alice Spring leaned even closer, and grazed against Ginny's swollen breast, in order to peer down at Raymond's perfect little face, Ginny allowed it. And when Mrs. Spring asked, the moment he was finished eating, "May I hold him?"—well, what else could she say? "But of course."

That evening, Roisin brought a tray of food up to Ginny's bedchamber, as if Ginny were the lady of the house herself. Ginny found it very discomforting.

"I could come down for it, to the kitchen," she said to Roisin.

"Nonsense," Roisin said. "Enjoy it while you can. It won't last, you lazy thing!" And then she laughed at her own joke.

Raymond was asleep in a neat little curl on his mother's legs, and she stroked his tiny red fingers while she sipped her tea. Roisin sat down on a blue cushioned chair beside the bed, and rubbed her hands together.

"Mrs. Spring is awful fond of him altogether!" she whispered. "I thought we'd never get her out of here!"

"Ah, I know, isn't it lovely, the way she doted over him?" Ginny said.

Roisin shook her head, took a deep sigh into her. "Such a tragedy, the way she was never able to have her own. Poor wee duck. She might have made a fine mother. Might've changed everything for her, sort of cleared the lunacy out of her muddled head, the poor dear."

"Ahh," Ginny tutted. "Perhaps it just wasn't meant to be."

Ginny leaned her head back on the thick pillows behind her. She felt exhausted and happy, relieved.

"Perhaps," Roisin said. "I suppose we can't all be so lucky as you, the way that fine, healthy child came out of you—so neat and quick-like."

"Ah, well, it gets easier each time."

Ginny realized immediately what she'd said, and from the look on Roisin's face, she knew she'd been drawn into it. The whole conversation had been a trap. Ginny clapped a hand over her mouth, sat up quick, and startled the baby. His arms gave a wild little flap.

"I only meant . . ." She had no idea what kind of uncultivated lie was about to come out of her, but Roisin put a hand up to excuse her from the effort.

"Calm yourself, woman," Roisin said. "I've known for weeks."

Ginny eased herself back to the pillows. "How?"

"You think I don't know when food starts disappearing from the larder beneath my very nose?" Roisin said. "Besides, you're far too old to be having your first child. What are you, twenty-six, twenty-eight years of age?"

"Thirty." Ginny stared at her.

Roisin nodded. "I knew there must be other children. What harm?" Ginny heaved a deep prayer of relief. "Mrs. Spring likes you, you're a great worker, and you're good company for me. God knows we have enough to spare."

"I wasn't trying to hide them," Ginny said, but Roisin looked at her skeptically. "Well, I suppose I was. I just, I needed this job so badly, and I didn't want you to have to share the burden of my secret. It wasn't that I didn't trust you. I just . . ."

"It's fine, dear," Roisin said. "It's exactly what I would've done."

Ginny relaxed into the conversation then, and started to feel glad for the accidental confidence. It was a blessed relief to speak about her children after so many watchful weeks of hiding them, in her mind. Roisin stayed and kept them company for another hour, and after she left, Ginny got up from the bed and threw another sod of turf on the fire. She never bothered with the lantern that first night with baby Raymond. She drew back the gold drapes, and watched the sky deepen to a purple bruise through the tall glass windowpanes. Her room faced the side of the house, and down below she could see light blazing out in the stables. She placed her palms flat against the cold glass, and then watched while the ghosts of her handprints glowed and then faded.

Her new baby shuddered and sighed in his blanket on the bed. Ginny curled herself around his little body, and sang all their life to him, their real life, away from Springhill House. She sang him his father, and his brother and sisters. She sang them all home again, in their little cottage. Together.

Chapter Eleven

NEW YORK, NOW

Salamander's is always pretty crowded on Friday afternoons, and by the time we arrive, all the good, stroller-friendly couches are already taken. The only seats left are a couple of the tiny café tables, barely big enough to hold two mugs of coffee. Jade's double-wide really is enormous. She bumps every single seat on our way to the counter. We stand in line, and she looks around nervously.

"This isn't gonna work," she says, biting a nail while she surveys the layout. "I only ever sit outside when I come here. The stroller won't fit. Is it too cold out?"

"No," I say, "we can sit outside—I don't mind."

"Yeah, okay," she says, and I wonder if she was actually just looking for an excuse to jet.

She orders two espressos and a vegan cookie. I ask for a decaf, and then we find a table on the sidewalk where it's easy to park the strollers.

"Hey, could you keep an eye on them while I run to the ladies' room?" she asks.

"Sure!" I answer without even thinking, and then, an instant later, I am alone at a sidewalk café with three babies.

Please stay asleep please stay asleep please stay asleep, and they all do. Emma stirs but does not open her eyes. I pull back the hood on Jade's stroller, and watch her babies sleep for a few minutes. Then I become worried that she'll return to find me gazing at her babies and think I'm creepy, so I push the hood across, and sip at my decaf.

And that's when I begin to worry that Jade is never coming back. I mean, what kind of mother leaves her two babies alone on the streets of Queens with some woman she just met? I'll tell you what kind of mother: a mother who does not want those babies anymore. A mother who has probably skipped out the back kitchen door, and is catching the Q55 bus down Myrtle Avenue at this very moment, from where she will hop on the L train with all the Williamsburg hipsters, never to be seen again. Does she even remember my name? My God, I would *never* leave Emma with a stranger!

Oh, here she comes. Never mind.

"Sorry I took so long."

"It's cool," I lie.

She is scraping her heavy metal chair back from the table. She doesn't even glance into the stroller, to make sure her twins are still safe inside. The waiter has delivered her espressos, and she knocks one of them back like it's a shot of Jack Daniel's.

"I need all the caffeine I can get," she says, biting into her vegan cookie. I *almost* say, *Oh, are you not breast-feeding?* but catch myself in the nick of time, and settle on "I hear ya," instead.

Salamander's is on one corner of a pinwheel intersection on Myrtle Avenue, across from a McDonald's, a great old-timey

Queens bakery that's been owned by the same Italian family for eighty-six years, and a famous German restaurant with a Tudor-style facade that is often featured on television shows on the Food Network. (They have an obscenely delicious pork shank that you have to just ask for, because it's not listed on the menu.) Outside the front door of that restaurant, two young Ecuadorian men in lederhosen are ashing their cigarettes into the window boxes. At the bus stop next to Salamander's, every single person is engrossed in his or her smartphone, except for one little kid who is staring up, astonished, at the two mounted NYPD who are clopping their horses slowly along the avenue in front of him. Jade and I watch the uninteresting late-Friday traffic stacking up at the intersection, in order to avoid looking at each other. It's all incredibly awkward, like a bad first date. I so want to like her.

"So what brought you to New York?" I ask.

"The usual thing," she says cryptically.

"A job?"

"Nah, a boy."

"Oh." This is good. Boy talk! Good. "So who's the daddy, what does he do?"

Jade downs her second espresso. "His name is Paul, and hmm, what does he do? Yeah, he mostly impregnates his girlfriend with twins, and then fucks off to L.A. to go *find himself.*" She twists her face into an approximation of a smile, and I am at a complete loss as to how to respond.

"Wow," I say.

"Yep."

"Shit."

"Yep."

"So do you have any family here or anything?"

"Nope."

I manage to refrain from saying *wow* again, but just barely.

"So you're totally on your own with these two?" Jade shrugs, and I lean down and peek into the stroller, where one of the babies is stretching and yawning. He blinks his black eyes, and rubs a hand across his sticking-up hair.

"I guess so," she says.

And before I can stop myself, I say, "I would die."

Jade laughs, crosses her arms in front of her, and looks into the stroller for the first time since she sat down.

"Look who's up," she says. "Hiya, Max!"

The baby looks up at her and smiles with his whole face, his whole body. His mouth curves open, and his cheeks bunch, and his black eyes glimmer, and his chest puffs up, and his fists thrash, all in response to his mother's simple, rather uninspired greeting. Please God, let Emma do this one day. I peek into her stroller, where she is still sleeping—not even half the size of Jade's stalwart little people. Next to her, Max is reaching out for his mother. She pops his buckles with one hand and hoists him onto her lap. He immediately tries to grab her empty espresso cup, and she instinctively swivels her knee away from the table so he can't reach. She has the quick and quiet grace of a ninja. What kind of man would leave this woman?

"So what do you do?" I ask.

Because how the hell does she pay for two babies, and possibly child care, on her own? Does Paul send money? Does he help? Does she stay home with them? Is she on welfare? *How does this work?* Jade spins her espresso cup like it's a top, and Max is mesmerized. I am intrigued by her, but it's all so personal, so dicey. I suddenly realize that there is no safe topic of conversation among new mothers. There is no question that doesn't sound prying and potentially critical.

"I'm a receptionist at a law firm in the city."

I nod. "Sounds fun."

She looks up at me. "It's awful. The lawyers are a bunch of self-important pricks. But the pay's good, and they have half-day Fridays and free on-site child care, which is crucial."

I nod some more.

"How 'bout you, you work?"

"Yeah, I'm a writer," I say, and then I remember the *Food & Wine* magazine in my bag, my pears article, and I wonder how the hell I ever thought that was going to work. Was I just going to whip it out and start bragging to all the other moms about my awesome, exciting, successful, defunct career? I'm so lame. But Jade seems to perk up, slightly. I can almost detect a hint of interest.

"What kinda writing, like, are you a journalist?"

Why do people think all writers are journalists?

"A food writer," I say.

"Huh," she answers, signaling the death of her fleeting curiosity.

In my experience, most people don't understand what a food writer is, so I decide to explain it to her, even though she didn't ask and no longer seems the least bit interested. "I started out doing restaurant reviews, but now I mostly write articles for foodie magazines and Web sites. And I've consulted on a few cookbooks."

"Cool," Jade says, by which I gather she means, "That could not be more boring."

"Yeah, it's fun," I say.

"I'm not much into food," she answers. "I'm one of those people who forgets to eat."

I have never understood those people, and frankly, I believe that they are all liars, people who say this. But hey, there are worse things you can be than a liar.

"I *wish* I could forget to eat," I say. "I spend all of my time between meals thinking about what I'm going to eat next. I'm obsessed with food. My husband is, too. He's a chef."

Max is getting squirmy on Jade's lap, and she hands him a sugar packet to play with. He immediately balls it up in his fist and begins slobbering on it.

"Yeah, maybe I'd like food more, too, if I had a chef in my life," Jade says. "My mom wasn't much of a cook, so I never had real food growing up. A lot of garbage. I probably became vegan just out of self-defense, so I wouldn't have to eat the crap she fed me anymore."

"Oh, so you're all-the-way vegan?" I ask. "Like, no dairy, nothing?"

"All-the-way vegan," she says.

"That is impressive," I say, though I don't really mean *impressive*. What I really mean is something like *tragic* or *dire*. "I could probably give up meat if I had to, but I would die without cheese. Or eggs. And I really love shellfish. And meat, really, if I'm being honest. I couldn't survive without meat."

Jade laughs, and her face is beautiful when she allows herself that lightness. Her bottom teeth are crooked. Her second baby is waking up—I can hear squeaking coming from the stroller, and the smile flees from Jade's face at once. She begins to juggle Max on her knee, even though he's still quiet, content with his wet sugar packet. She reaches in, and pops the buckles on the baby girl's harness, but how will she lift her, with one hand? Should I offer to take Max? He is grunting now, his face turning red with effort. I'm moderately sure he is pooping. Jade fails to hide the defeat in her shoulders, a tiny sigh that escapes her slightly caved-in chest. She places Max back into the buggy, and he immediately begins to wail.

"I know, I know," Jade says, and now she is so focused on

those babies, it's like everything around her has disappeared. The baby girl begins to cry, too, and Jade shushes them desperately. She swivels the stroller, and her arm disappears underneath, then reappears with a small bag. She places two bottles on the café table in front of her, and the babies lock their eyes onto the bottles. The babies are both reaching and squirming and whimpering. That whimper. I know that whimper. Jade dumps powdered formula into the two bottles and shakes them up while the babies watch, transfixed. Max is bouncing a little, in his seat, and his sister swings her arm around in big arcs, thwacking him in the head beside her. He doesn't mind.

"What's the baby girl's name?" I ask, but Jade is so centered on the bottles that I don't think she hears me. Max begins yelling loudly.

"Okay! Okay, it's coming," Jade tells him, and she gives him the bottle, even though the liquid is still slightly clumpy inside.

Max takes it, drops it, and it rolls off his lap and onto the sidewalk. There is chewed-up gum down there, hard black splotches of it, ground into the pavement beneath our table. I wince at the wasted bottle, but Jade doesn't even blink. She leans down and hands the bottle right back to him, holds it in his mouth for a minute. She reclines his seat a little, and then helps him wrap his fingers more firmly around the bottle. Max sucks noisily.

"Now, Madeline," she says, scooping the baby girl out of her seat. The baby arches her back and kicks angrily at the second bottle, but Jade catches it with one hand just as it rolls off the edge of the table. She is like a circus performer. I can feel prickles of sweat in my armpits, just watching this shitshow. Jade holds Madeline sitting up, with one arm laced beneath the baby's armpits, and pops the nipple into her waiting mouth. Madeline immediately slumps back against her mother and stops wriggling. Jade slumps back, too, in her chair, and the collective relief at our table is palpable. I hadn't realized I was holding my breath.

By the time the babies have finished their bottles, Max's diaper is so ripe that I feel like there is a green fog hanging above our little table, even though we're outside. The stink has not dissipated, but rather has hunkered down around us in a very determined manner. A young hipster couple, with their hands tucked cloyingly into the back pockets of each other's skinny jeans, emerges from the café with their to-go cups. They sit down at the table beside ours, but only for a moment, because then they smell the crazy funk that is Max's poop, and quickly dart to another table. Jade doesn't seem to notice.

"Maybe we should go," I say. "Emma's gonna need a feed soon, too, and I still haven't mastered the whole breast-feeding-in-public thing."

"Yeah, cool," Jade says, and she plops Madeline back into the stroller, straps her in. Max is still gumming the bottle, even though it's empty now.

"Which way do you go, from here?" I ask.

Jade points back up the road. "I live on Seventy-fifth Street, by the library."

"Me, too!" I say. "Small world."

And now my heart is racing, because how many sets of twins can there be on Seventy-fifth Street, by the library? Jade is *definitely* channel C, there's no doubt about it. I can hardly wait to tell Leo.

When we get to my house, I stop the stroller and put the brake on while I fish into my bag for my keys.

"No way, this is your house?" Jade says.

"Yeah, why?" I say. "Which one is yours?"

She points next door to the six-family, and I feign enormous surprise.

"That is *crazy*," I say. "We really are neighbors!"

Jade nods, and then yawns. "I should've gone for a third espresso," she says.

"You can never have too much caffeine!" I hear myself say, and then, "Hey, why don't I give you my number? Maybe we can get together sometime, have a playdate?"

"Yeah, cool," Jade says, taking her cell phone out of her back pocket. She programs in my number, and I wait for her to offer hers in return, or maybe even to press *send* on her phone, so that her number will pop up on my screen, too. But instead, she just pockets the phone, whips out her keys, and heads for her front door. I feel like I've just gone in for a kiss and gotten the cheek.

"See you round," I say, in an attempt at a cheerful voice.

"See ya," Jade says. There is only one step up, into the apartment building, but it might as well be an entire flight for Jade with her double-wide stroller. She tries to hold the heavy door with one hand, while she bumps the stroller up the single step with the other. It's painful to watch.

"Need a hand?" I ask her, from where I'm standing now, with Emma's car seat looped over my elbow, halfway up my own front steps.

"Nah, I'm good," she says, so I make myself turn back to my door, but it's a physical effort, like peeling your eyes away from a car crash or a particularly discomforting episode of *The Bachelor*.

"I hope she's gonna be okay," I say to Emma, once we're inside with the door shut safely behind us. She just blinks at me. She doesn't reach or wriggle or squeal. Just blink, blink.

I take the monitor to the couch with us, and immediately flip it to channel C. I can't hear anything. I set it on the coffee table while I feed Emma. Afterward, I roll my yoga mat out on the unfinished floor, and put one of Emma's baby blankets on top of it. I feel like she spends her whole life in contraptions. She's always strapped into the car seat or the bouncy seat, or else she's propped up in the Boppy on the couch beside me. She's six weeks old now, and I want her to stretch out into the world. The pediatrician wants her doing tummy time. I lie down on the floor beside her.

"Hey, you're six weeks old today!" I tell her. She blinks at me. I sing "Happy Birthday," and flap my hand above us like a pterodactyl. Or at least that's what I'm going for. She watches the pterodactyl-fingers, and makes a sound I've never heard before. It's like a coo. I roll to my side.

"Did you just coo?"

She blinks at me, and I make the pterodactyl-hands again.

"Coo," Emma gurgles.

Oh my God this is so exciting.

"You did! You cooed!" I squeal, and I sit up quickly, and I wince, but the pain in my abdomen isn't as sharp as I expect. "Wait until we tell Daddy!"

After ten minutes of tummy time, including three more coos, Emma is spent. She falls asleep in her bouncy seat, and I am so encouraged by the wild, unaccustomed success of my day that I decide to tackle some work. I haven't even checked e-mail in weeks. I take off my shoes and pad into the office to flick on the computer, but as soon as I sit down, I notice that the red monitor light is flickering from where I left it on the coffee table. I go back to the monitor and turn the volume up. Max and Madeline are both back in one of the cribs together, and there are some toys in there with them. They are sitting up, facing each other, and I can see a drum, a rattle, and a stuffed panda bear in there, too. Madeline grabs the rattle and begins waving it around, precariously close to Max's nose.

"Maybe I shouldn't watch," I say.

Now that I've met Jade, it seems like my voyeurism may have

slipped from natural curiosity into weird spying. My hand goes up to the power switch, and I am *just about* to turn it off—I swear I am—when I hear the unmistakable sound of muffled sobs. The babies hear it, too, and they both turn toward the noise. Max lunges for the side of the crib, laces his one arm through the bars. He reaches for his mother. His chubby little hand strokes the air.

I don't do any work. I don't even open my e-mail. I just sit there at the desk, staring helplessly at the monitor until the phone rings. It's Leo.

"So how horrible was it?" he asks.

"On a scale of one to ten?"

"Yeah," he says, "one being like that time we had to go to the Hamptons for your cousin's wedding, and ten being an adulterous case of genital herpes."

"I'd go with a solid seven."

He whistles.

"Yeah, it was bad."

"What happened?"

"Nothing really *happened*, just the women were awful to each other."

"Ugh," Leo says.

"For real. They were all so judgy and mean. And there were like warring factions. The breast-feeding moms versus the bottle moms, and then the working moms versus the SAHMs."

"The SAHMs?" he says.

"Don't ask." I'm rubbing my temples. "Oh! But guess what, I almost forgot to tell you! Emma cooed."

"She what?"

"She cooed."

"Like a pigeon?"

"No, Leo, like a baby. Like *coo*." I try to do the gurgle as cute as Emma did it, but I sound like an insane person. "Forget it, you'll hear it tomorrow. It's this new thing she's doing. It's cute. And guess what else."

"What?"

"I met the mom from channel C."

"No way," he says.

"Yep."

"Did you go find her? Did you like ring her doorbell or something?"

"What am I, a stalker?"

"No, I'm just asking, because I know you were concerned. . . ."

"No, I didn't ring her doorbell," I say disgustedly, but secretly I'm glad I didn't think of it sooner, or I might have. "How would I even know which doorbell?"

"I don't know."

"She was at the mommy group."

"Oh, was she one of the awful mommies?"

"No, she was actually really nice, I mean she seems nice. We went for a coffee afterward."

"Oh?"

"Yeah."

"And how was that?" he asks.

"It was good. I mean, it was kind of awkward. I don't know how much we have in common. Not a whole lot, I think, but we might have the same sense of humor, and a similar potty mouth. Anyway, it was just nice to go out during the afternoon, and sit and talk with another adult for a little while, even if it was sort of weird."

"Good, honey!" Leo says. "See, something good did come of the awful mommy group!"

"Well, we'll see." I don't want him jumping to conclusions. "And anyway, she's still, I don't know. I mean, I'm still worried about her."

204 · JEANINE CUMMINS

"Why?"

"After we got back, she was still crying on the monitor."

"Majella, you're still listening in on her?" Leo sounds appalled.

"What? No. I mean, just for a minute, it was on the wrong channel, I just overheard. I wasn't spying or anything."

Leo sighs. "All right, well, now that you've met her, maybe you can talk to her. See if she needs some help or something."

"Maybe," I say, but I'm already trying to imagine how that conversation would go. *Hey, listen, Jade, I've been eavesdropping on you and notice you seem to weep a lot.* Her response: *Nah, I'm cool, you crazy bitch.*

"All right, I gotta run," Leo says. "I'll be pretty late tonight. We have a full house."

"Okay!" I say readily, because I want to show him how well I am adapting to my new life.

Emma and I have a good night. The cooing helps. After she goes to sleep, I pour myself a glass of wine, find Ginny Doyle's diary, and run myself a bubble bath. I lean against the bathroom sink while the water foams up and the air steams warmly around me. I want to read the diary in the tub, but the pages are so fragile, I'm afraid. What if I drop it in the water? A charge runs through me, just holding that weathered book. It's like the woman embossed her grief onto its very pages, and now it's stained there, animate beneath my fingertips. I can *feel* her anguish. I crack the book and reread the first few entries. When the tub is full, I lay the diary down carefully on top of a towel on the closed lid of the toilet. I twist off the squeaky taps and immediately hear the crunching.

Shit. I crack the door to the bathroom and peek out. "What the hell is that crunching?"

My heart feels rickety, my breath shallow. *And why does it scare me so much?* The monitor. Where is the monitor? When Emma is asleep in her room, I always have it nearby on a table, or clipped to my enormous waistband. Shit. I've forgotten it downstairs. I tighten the belt of my bathrobe, and scamper down the hall in the direction of the crunching, but now it seems like it's coming from behind me. I spin around in the dark hallway and try to listen. *Crunch.* I flip on the light switch, run to Emma's room, and push open the door, so the light from the hallway brightens the carpet inside. Emma is breathing steady, a soft little rhythm, a reassurance. My own breath deepens, and I strain to listen past the sound of small lungs filling and emptying. The crunching has stopped. I step into the room and stand over her crib to watch her features in repose. She's so beautiful like this, her cheeks all full and soft, her tiny hands thrown up over her head, and the light through the crib slats falling in stripes across her peaceful face. I touch her velvety forehead, and her lips make a seeking motion in her sleep. I tiptoe out and pull the door mostly closed behind me.

I retrieve the monitor from downstairs, and bring it back to the bathroom with me, but I'm too uneasy to sink into a hot bath now. The crunching has me unsettled. I step into the tub just long enough to soap and splash myself clean. Then I pull the stopper, towel myself dry, dress in my baggiest pajamas, and take the monitor and diary down the hallway with me, into my bedroom. The monitor is turned up loud, and I set it on my nightstand. Our bed is one of those high platform ones, so I use a cushioned footstool to climb up, and then I lean back onto my pillows and open the book. A shiver runs down my spine.

7 April 1848
    The children are grand, they're so much more resilient than I am, as if they don't even remember the hunger,

the grief. They don't speak of who's missing. I feel like a ghost of myself, but my babbies are bright little nuggets of resolve. Whatever sorrow has haunted them no longer weighs them down in this new place—they seem to have swallowed it, digested it. It becomes a part of them, and they move on in lightness. I wish I could know their secret, and thieve just a morsel of that lightness for myself.

Easter was gorgeous. The way the sun shines here is so different from Ireland. It's closer, somehow, and heavier. The light really stays on your skin. The children glow with it. New York is a good place for them, after everything.

15 April 1848

I think I might be expecting, and I'm happy. I'm trying. I know it's a joy and a blessing, the idea of bringing a new child into this reinvented family. But I miss our old life at home. I'm as happy as I can be here, but not as happy as I once was. And maybe that's as it should be. I have to pay somehow, for what I've done. And still I feel that our new life is a betrayal, in a way, of everything we've lost. What right have we to carry on, to start over? My children, yes—they are blameless. But me . . .

23 April 1848

Perhaps there is no baby after all. It could just be I'm exhausted and anxious. I still don't sleep well here, with all the lights and the noises. The neighbors are so close you can hear them coughing, spitting, arguing, lovemaking. It's unsettling, all this aggressive intimacy.

But it's the crunching that troubles me most, in the nighttimes. Every night, it wakens me. If I could find its source, I might have peace. I have a terrible fear that it's coming from inside me, from my mind.

25 April 1848

Dear God, I killed her. I killed her. It is late now, and the children are asleep here, and I was awakened by that horrid crunching, and it was so vivid, the sound of it, that it brought me right back there. . . .

The cottage. That last day in the yard, under the blackthorn tree. I can see myself, almost as if from above. Like I'm that magpie in the tree looking down. And there's the other me down in the yard, the ferocious me. The baby is there. Maire is watching. Oh the horrors my poor daughter has seen in her short life.

I'm holding the hurley bat in both hands, and I'm swinging it down over my head. How does my face look in this instant? Is it pained, twisted, demented? Demonic, with the power coursing through me? I am about to take a woman's life—a woman who was only kind to me until this last day, these last moments.

She is dead now.

Would that I could wish myself back to that moment, and stop it there. To drop that hurley bat to my feet, to hear its soft clatter in the dust. But instead there's an almighty crack like thunder as I bring it down on her skull, and she drops, heavy like a bag of clean, dry praties. The baby nearly falls with her, but I catch him, I catch him, by one dangling arm. Her eyes and her mouth stay open, and Maire's eyes, too, wide open at my back. Her voice is windy. She calls me mammy.

There are shards of the blue Wedgwood china on the ground, and they crunch beneath my feet, like the sound of bones snapping. Maire's cheeks have gone a sickly white. There are pieces of the pale blue china strewn through the dead woman's hair.

Why I remember this crunching, above all else, is a maniac question. Perhaps it's easier than the rest, than Maire's intrepid voice, and the baby crying after. It stays in my ears like a disease, that crunch. It robs my sleep.

God forgive me, God forgive me. I can still see her dead and ghastly face.

I close the book with a snap and throw it down on the bed, but the damage is done. I will never sleep now. I pick up the monitor from the nightstand, and a feeling of dread creeps over me. I'm almost afraid to look, afraid I will see a hand pass across Emma's face, a shadowy figure lurking by the rail of her crib. I hop down from the bed, and hurry through the hall to check her again in person, without the void of technology between us. I hold my hand beneath her nose until I can feel the moist guarantee of her breath against my knuckles.

I retreat to the kitchen, where I top up my wine and then pace to the front window. It's almost eleven o'clock. Emma will be up for a feed in a little while, Leo home not too long after that. I don't sip the wine; I gulp it. I shouldn't really have more than one, but surely an extra half glass won't hurt? I bring it to the office, where I set it on the desk while I google *Ginny Doyle*, and get a bunch of LinkedIn and Facebook profiles. I don't bother clicking through them. They don't have what I'm looking for. Facebook can't tell me how I'm related to some lunatic murderess from the eighteen hundreds. And maybe I don't want to know. Maybe it's best not to trace that line back too carefully, not to seek hard evidence of my shitty maternal genetics. I would like to believe that I can, one day, be a good mother. Or at least a not-terrible mother. What kind of a woman kills someone in front of her own daughter? With something called a "hurley bat"? And what the fuck even *is* a hurley bat? I google *hurley bat*, and then shudder at the flat, heavy thickness of the wood, the violent images that flood my mind. Who could do this? Who could crack open someone's skull with a cudgel? Some great-great-grandmother of mine, I guess. Fan-fucking-tastic.

Maybe we're all doomed, Emma and Leo and me. Maybe you can't outrun catastrophic DNA. Maybe Jade is just more honest than I am. I shiver, and shut the computer down, then dial my parents in Florida.

"Hey, Dad, is Mom home?" I pace around the house while we talk.

"Hey, kiddo," Dad says, and I hear him sipping his beer. "Nah, she's out with the girls. It's martini night at the clubhouse."

I look at the clock on the oven. Eleven seventeen. My mother has never been out past nine thirty in her adult life. What has gotten *into* them down there, in Florida?

"Okay, Pop, just tell her I called, will you? I'm just curious to know if she's found anything out about this Ginny Doyle person, in her genealogy searches."

"Sure thing, honeybunch," he says. "How's everything else?"

"Good," I say, because I know he doesn't want a bunch of details. "It's fine. It's been a crazy day, but Leo will be home before too long."

"That's good, I don't like the hours he keeps," Dad says, for probably the seven millionth time. "I wish he was home with you at nights. I don't like you and that baby there on your own."

Then why the hell did you move away? I do not say.

"We're fine, Dad."

"All right, I'll tell your mom to give you a shout in the morning."

"G'night, Dad. Oh hey, Dad?"

"Yeah."

"One more thing—did you ever hear crunching in this house?"

"Crunching? Nah, what kinda crunching?"

"I don't know, just a regular crunching. Like a *crrrrrrrrrrk* sound. Usually upstairs, in the bedroom or bathroom, but sometimes in the living room, too."

"Nah, never heard crunching," he says. "You gotta mouse."

Chapter Twelve

IRELAND, MAY 1847

It was still strange for Ginny, waking up in that enormous, lavish bed, with the midmorning sunlight streaming in through the tall, stood-open windows, and the song of the sheep out in the pasture, below. It sometimes took her a moment to remember where she was, but today the ache of fatigue in her body was acute. Yesterday, her baby boy was born. Raymond's and her little son.

Her eyes popped open, and she rightly sprang up in the huge bed. The baby, where was the baby? Ginny yanked back the folds in the sheets. She could still see the impression, the little dent in the blankets where she'd made a nest for him, to sleep in beside her. *Mother of God, please don't let him have rolled off the bed,* she thought. *Please God, please God.* She stumbled down from the mattress, already with bile in her throat and mouth. She ignored the tenderness in her lower body as she loped to the far side of the bed. Nothing. She dropped to her hands and knees to make sure.

Jesus, God, he's not here. He's not here. Where is he? Where is my baby?

She clutched the side of the bed, and hauled herself to her feet. She was bleeding, but not much. She could feel fluid trickling down the insides of her thighs. She threw open the door, and staggered into the corridor. Should she scream? Should she call for help? Halfway down the corridor, the door to Alice Spring's chamber was ajar, and a soft and drifting note of song broke through Ginny's panic. Who was singing? It was a lullaby in minor tones, and the sound of it stopped Ginny's feet beneath her. She came to a halt outside Mrs. Spring's door, and she pushed it in without knocking.

Mrs. Spring was sat at a rocker by the window, facing out. She had the baby in her arms, and Ginny could feel her whole body flush with relief. Her shoulders collapsed down, and tears filled in behind her eyes. She leaned against the doorframe and listened. She laid one hand against her breast, and felt the rigorous thrashing of her heartbeat beneath, winding down, slowing to a more normal tempo. But she was not yet at her ease. She waited for a break in the song, and then she cleared her throat. Mrs. Spring turned from the window, and her face opened into a warm smile.

"Ginny, you're awake," she said.

"I am, Mrs. Spring, and I got an awful fright when I couldn't find the baby."

Mrs. Spring stood up from the rocker, but continued the swaying motion from her arms and hips. Raymond was bundled cozily inside.

"I'm dreadfully sorry," she said, walking him toward his mother in the doorway. "I didn't mean to startle you. I heard him crying during the night—I knew you were awake with him a bit. So I came in and collected him this morning, and I thought to let you sleep some more. I looked in on you only a few minutes ago, and you were fast asleep."

Ginny reached out and touched the gathered blankets around Raymond's ears and chin. Such a beautiful wee boy he was. He had Raymond's nose, Ginny's full lips.

"You're very kind," Ginny said. "But I'm up now, I'll take him," and she reached to scoop him out from Mrs. Spring's arms, but the woman pulled the baby away from his mother, just out from beneath her grasp. Ginny's eyes snapped to Mrs. Spring's face. What was she playing at?

"Nonsense, back to bed with you," Mrs. Spring said. "I'll carry him in." She was gesturing at Ginny with her head, shooing her out of the doorway. But Ginny wasn't leaving without him.

"Come, now, I'll bring him directly," Mrs. Spring said, and she walked with Ginny into the corridor. "Anyway, you shouldn't be lifting him just yet. The doctor said."

"Doctor?"

"Yes, Dr. Spangle. I sent for him this morning, to come and look at you, to check on the baby. He'll be here at midday, he sent a note. Said just to keep you off your feet until he arrives."

"Mrs. Spring, I don't need a doctor, I'm grand. Fit as a fiddle. I'm ready to go back to work." She nearly said, *None of my other children had doctors. I've never needed one before,* but she caught the words before they flew out of her mouth. They were drawing near to the doorway of Ginny's chamber.

"I won't hear of it. It's your time of confinement. You must take your rest."

"I don't want to be a burden, Mrs. Spring. It's vital to me, this job. I'm not comfortable lying up in bed. I'd rather be working."

Mrs. Spring wasn't listening. She walked Ginny and the baby over to the huge bed as if she was their mother, as if she was going to tuck them in. It was tremendously awkward. She laid Raymond gently back into his nest among the blankets.

"Go on," she said then, to Ginny, who had no choice but to climb in dutifully beside him.

Ginny laid her hand on his bundled little self then, and was so glad for the anchored weight of him there. What a gift.

"Mrs. Spring, I . . ."

"Auntie Alice," she interrupted.

Ginny found she had no earthly idea how to respond to this new absurdity. Mrs. Spring leaned down over Raymond on the bed, and her voice piped up to a singsong.

"You tell your mummy there's to be no more of this *Mrs. Spring* business," she squeaked into Raymond's little face. "I'm Auntie Alice now."

Ginny watched in supreme astonishment. Alice Spring stood up from her position over the baby and went to the door.

Her voice dropped back to normal. "I'll send Roisin up with tea and toast," she said.

Ginny nodded, stunned. "Thank you."

"Auntie Alice," she instructed again.

"Thank you." Ginny faltered, but then recovered. "Auntie Alice."

When the doctor came, he urged Ginny to keep to her bed for a week, but she managed to talk him down to just two days. She was back in the kitchen with Roisin by week's end. They made a tidy little basket for Raymond, and he sat atop one of the broad barrels while they worked. She was still staying in the guest chamber with Raymond, and Mrs. Spring had wheeled in an ornate little cot, all valanced with ribbons and bows for the baby, but Ginny couldn't bear to put him in it. It stayed empty, and Raymond slept in bed with his mammy. Their proximity to Mrs.

Spring's chamber made it more difficult to sneak out in the nights to see Seán, but they managed.

The children were grand, Seán assured Ginny. Maire had everything well in hand, and Michael was *delighted* to finally have a brother. God, how she missed them. Even more now, with the baby. He was a balm to Ginny in many ways, but also a reminder of everything she was missing.

"Maggie's lost her first tooth," Seán told her, and Ginny asked him to bring the tooth to her—a piece of her daughter that she could hold and keep.

"They haven't heard from Raymond at all?" she asked Seán. "Or his brother, Kevin?"

Seán shook his head. "I'm sorry, Ginny. Nothing."

Mrs. Spring gave Ginny the Sunday afternoon off, to go and have the child christened, and she permitted Roisin and Seán to accompany her, for to stand up as Raymond's godparents. She even allowed Seán the carriage, to drive them. It was the first time Ginny had ventured beyond the gates at Springhill House since her arrival so many weeks before, and she studied the fields with great interest as they passed them by. The potato stalks were just beginning to lift their hopeful green heads, and from the carriage window, Ginny couldn't see any sign of blight. There was no stink in the still air; there was no spring breeze to speak of. All the country seemed to be holding its breath.

"The early potatoes will be ready in a few weeks' time," Ginny said to Roisin, who was seated across from her in the bumpy carriage. "Perhaps the worst of it is over, and the new crop will be healthy."

Roisin gazed out across the fields as well. "Please God," she said, and then, in a momentary lapse from her usual carefree manner, she whispered, "But how many countless dead in the meantime?" They both crossed themselves hastily while the carriage bumped along beneath them. Ginny held Raymond tighter in her arms.

Seán had gotten turnip seed, for the children. He'd urged Maire and Michael to prepare the other fields as well then. And Ginny didn't know how he managed to get seed potatoes for them, because her own wages would never stretch as far as that, she knew. But he had, and now the seed was all in, planted. Their neighbor, Mrs. Fallon, had sent her two grown sons to help with the sowing, God bless her.

The children knew the land. They helped every year, every season, with the work. Maire and Michael knew how to prepare the soil, how to sow the seed, and when to harvest. Maggie was old enough to be of some real help as well. But Poppy would only be in the way, and it was enough work for a whole family anyway, even when Raymond and Ginny had been there together. Ginny couldn't imagine how the children had managed it all on their own, even with the help of the Fallon lads. Still, sitting in that carriage, looking out over those spring fields, all buoyant with cheerful green splendor, she felt a rushing thrill of hope. If they got a good crop in, she could leave Springhill House. She could be home in time for the harvest, and she could wait with her children then, together, for news from New York. If the crop was very fine, Raymond could stop worrying about finding work, and start thinking instead about making his way home.

Father Brennan was none too pleased with Ginny when she turned up at his door with baby Raymond in her arms. He hadn't got past her leaving the children alone so she could go to work at Springhill House. But he would never turn a child away from the house of God.

"Bring him in, we'll do the job," he said, and then, to baby

Raymond, he whispered, "It's not my decision anyway. You belong to our Lord and Savior Jesus Christ."

"Thank you, Father," Ginny said, as they filed into the church.

She had never been to the baptism of any of her other children. It was usually the father's job to do that, or the godparents'. But these were unusual times. The ceremony was quick, informal. They lit no candles. There was no song, no gathering. Her son was made Catholic, and they all traced the sign of the cross on his bald little head.

"I wish his father was here for this day," Ginny said afterward, and that made Father Brennan soften to her a small bit.

He put his hand on her elbow. "It is a shame he can't be here, Ginny," he said. "An awful shame."

"Would you wait for me outside?" Ginny asked Roisin and Seán, and they didn't even answer her. They just vanished quietly out through the door.

"Father, I'm sick with worry. You know we haven't heard yet from Ray, and we should've got word by now, weeks ago. He's an awful long time gone."

"Nine months, it must be," he said, touching the baby's soft hand.

"Will you write me another letter, to Kevin?" she asked. "I know we've sent two already, but we should let them know about the baby, anyway. That he's here and healthy. His name and all that."

"I will of course," he said.

"I fear the worst, Father," Ginny said, and as the words came out, she realized how true they were. Her throat constricted with terror.

He nodded.

"You haven't heard anything at all?" she asked.

"I haven't, Ginny, you know I would tell you."

"Have you had word from anyone else in the parish, who went out around the same time?"

She rummaged all through his face for clues, but he only shook his head.

"Father, surely you understand now why I had to leave the children?" He folded his arms in front of him. "Please, Father, I had no choice."

"So you say."

"They would have starved."

"Ginny, you made your choice, and it's worked out grand. I don't know why you need my blessing over it."

The church was filtered through with the hushed colors of stained glass, but they stood in the arched doorway, where the brightness from outdoors pooled in around them.

"I want to be in a state of grace, Father," Ginny pleaded. "Raymond is gone, I'm all on my own. I took the decisions I had to take, to save my children, but that doesn't mean I feel good about them." She could feel tears welling into her eyes. "She doesn't let us out, Father—this is the first time. I haven't seen Maire and the others since March." And now the gathered tears loosened themselves onto her cheeks.

Father Brennan was shaking his head. "I know, Ginny, I know you found yourself in a terrible, difficult position. But you are their *mother*. You belong with them. Whatever happens is God's will, you can't just abandon your station in life."

Ginny was trembling. Little Raymond quivered in her arms. Maybe Father Brennan was right. She gazed down at her baby's lit face and made a terrible confession. "I hardly remember their faces, Father." She began to cry harder. She tried not to hiccup.

"Listen, there's no sin in it," he said, trying to calm her. He always was a man made uncomfortable by a woman's tears. "There's nothing for you to confess here. It's only my own belief: you belong at home. Look at you, the pain you're in. It's unnatural for a mother to be rent from her children this way."

"Father, please," she begged him, she clutched at his sleeve. She needed him to sanction her choices, to tell her it was all right, what she'd done. He placed a hand across her knuckles.

"There, there," he said. "It'll be all right, Ginny. Gather your strength, child."

Strength. She sniffed, wiped her face. She had been strong for so long. She had felt blessed. They were surviving; her children were surviving. But here in this church, where she had taken Raymond for her husband, where Father Brennan had christened all six of her children, even the one who didn't make it, where she'd attended mass every Sunday of her married life until the hunger happened, she cracked. She felt vulnerable again. There was a deep and sudden yearning for the strength of that union, her marriage. She didn't want to do this on her own anymore. She didn't want to go back to the lucky working life at Springhill House. She wanted Raymond back. She wanted their family.

"Here, just hang in there a bit longer," Father Brennan was saying. "I'll write the letter to Kevin. I'll let them know about the new little Raymond here, what a fine young fella he is. I'm sure we'll hear back from them in no time."

Ginny nodded her head, wiped her face with her sleeve.

"When the packet arrives from Raymond, you can call it a day, hah?" Father said. "Once he starts sending money back? You can go home to them and make everything right. You can forget all about Springhill House, forget it ever happened."

Ginny nodded some more, tried to recover the courage that had leached from her in this beloved, familiar place. She dipped her fingers into the holy water well beside the door and blessed herself, blessed Raymond.

"Thank you, Father," she said, squeezing his hand.

She was already out the door when he called her name. She turned back to face him where he stood, his hands in his pockets, his eyes downcast.

"You probably did the right thing, Ginny."

Ginny smiled gratefully back at him, and then turned to her waiting friends. Seán offered to drive her home to the cottage in Knockbooley to see the children.

"We have an hour at least before Mrs. Spring would expect us back," he said.

Ginny looked at Roisin, who was already up in the carriage, waiting. She handed Raymond up to her friend, and then stood in the churchyard with her hands on her hips, her face still damp from her spent tears.

"No," she said.

"No?" Seán looked at her like she was daft, but she shook her head adamantly.

She knew she didn't have the strength for it, that if he took her there, she wouldn't be able to leave again. She thought of Maire, her fine, fearless face. She thought of the gap in Maggie's mouth where her tooth had been. She imagined Poppy mooning over the new baby, and Michael watching everything silently, taking it all in. How could she leave them again? How could she pry their baby brother from their arms, walk past Maggie's majestic cairns in the side yard, and wave them good-bye? By now they had got past the worst pangs of their mother's absence. They were settled in their routines, growing accustomed to their self-sufficiency. It wouldn't be fair for Ginny to come home for an hour and undo all that.

"You sure, Ginny?" Seán asked.

"I'm sure," she lied.

He gave her his hand. She was still rather delicate from the birth. He helped her up the steps into the back of the carriage.

"Springhill House, then," he said, and he started the horses off on a trot.

When Raymond was a few weeks old, Roisin and Ginny were interrupted from their cooking one afternoon by a footstep on the stair. After a moment, Alice Spring swept into the room, all perfumed elegance in a neat red gown. Her golden hair was gathered up off her neck and looped dramatically with black ribbons. Roisin immediately began wiping her hands on her apron and fussing about nervously.

"Where's our little Raymond?" Mrs. Spring asked, looking at Ginny.

"He's just there." Ginny gestured to his basket atop the barrel. "Dreaming, I'd say."

Mrs. Spring's crimson skirts swished beneath her as she crossed the room to the baby. "He is such a gorgeous little thing," she said, peeking down over him. His mother smiled. "Would you mind if I took him out for a constitutional?" She turned and looked at Ginny earnestly. "I don't like to think of him down here the whole day, and you working, unable to tend to him. I'm going out anyway, and he'd be fine company for me on my walk."

Ginny left Roisin at the worktable, and went over to where Mrs. Spring stood next to Raymond's basket. He was awake and blinking up at them. "Well, I don't have a perambulator, I'm afraid," Ginny said.

"I have one!" Mrs. Spring answered quickly, and then she changed her voice and her pace; she slowed. "I mean, I happened to come across an old one stuffed into the back of a wardrobe in one of the upper chambers. I had Katie haul it out last week and give it a clean. It's all ready for him."

Ginny nodded. Perhaps it would be good for him then, a bit

of fresh air. "Well, that would be lovely," she decided. "If you're sure you don't mind."

"Oh no!" Mrs. Spring said. "It's no trouble at all. I'm so fond of our little Raymond."

Mrs. Spring scooped him easily out of his basket and up onto her shoulder. She was so natural with him, and Ginny could see the longing in every gesture of her body, how keenly she wanted a baby of her own to love.

"You have a great knack with him now," Ginny said. "All the practice you're getting."

"Ah, we're great friends, aren't we, mister?" Mrs. Spring said to him. "I'll bring him back in a while."

"I'm only after feeding and changing him," Ginny said. "He should be grand for a couple of hours, but if he gets fussy, don't hesitate."

Ginny watched his wide eyes peeping over the top of Mrs. Spring's shoulder as she disappeared up the stairs with him. When they were gone, Roisin sat down heavily on one of the stools beside the worktable. She looked awful shook.

"What's the matter?" Ginny asked her. "Are you unwell? You look pale."

"In my four years in this house, that woman has never set foot in this kitchen," she said, shaking her head. She stood up then, brushed the flour from her hands. "I hope she's not planning to make a habit of it."

Ginny laughed lightly, and for the first time, she saw something of a sour look pass across Roisin's usually jolly features.

"My goodness," Roisin said, "but that made me awful nervous altogether."

"Well," Ginny said, returning to the onion she'd been chopping before the disruption, "she's gone now. We survived."

Roisin was sifting flour for a spice cake. "She's grown very attached to young Raymond," she said. "Very attached indeed."

It became customary, after that, for Mrs. Spring to spend a couple of hours each afternoon with Raymond. It was early June, and the weather was fine and clear most days, so they often walked out in the gardens together, and when it rained, she would bundle him into her arms, and sing to him beside the big fire in the drawing room. She brought him extravagant gifts, fine little suits of clothes, an exquisite silver and ivory rattle, sweets he was too small yet to eat.

Ginny told no one of her plans to leave Springhill House if the crop came good at home, not even Seán, though she was sure he suspected. She couldn't risk upsetting the comfortable balance they had all settled into. She knew it would distress Mrs. Spring to be parted from baby Raymond when the time came, but that couldn't be helped. In truth, Ginny was growing fond of Mrs. Spring, too, despite her peculiarities. How could she not, with the way the woman doted on her son? When they got out of here and went home, when Raymond was back from America and the crop was strong again . . . when Ginny's family was whole and all of this was a distant memory, she would welcome Mrs. Spring into her home in Knockbooley. Of course she would. Mrs. Spring could visit young Raymond whenever she liked.

Ginny and the baby still slept cuddled up together in the four-poster bed in that silked, striped room, which seemed to have become a permanent arrangement, despite Ginny's repeated insistence that they were well able to return now to the servants' quarters in the attic.

"It's too drafty up there for him," Mrs. Spring would argue, fussing over Raymond. "Besides, this room is only sitting empty anyway, gathering dust. He's the most delightful houseguest we've ever had at Springhill."

So they stayed.

Late one night while all the house slept, Ginny was nursing little Raymond when she heard a clatter at their window, which was frightful, being that they were on the second story of the house. She thought some bat or night bird had hurled its poor body against the glass, and she arose from her bed with Raymond still at her breast, to look out. Seán was standing below, his features upturned and glowing ghostly in the moonlight. She opened the glass, clutched the baby tightly, and looked out.

"Oh, thank Jesus that was the right window," Seán said, replacing his hat on his head. "Come down, Ginny."

Her heart skidded. "I'll be right there."

Raymond whimpered when she pulled him off the breast, as he was only halfway through his feed and still hungry. He kicked angrily at the blanket his mother swaddled around him.

"Shh, shh, it's just for a minute, love." She kissed the top of his head. She had no housecoat, and she could hardly go down to Seán in her nightdress, so she slipped into her shirtwaist and skirt as quickly as she could. She tried not to wonder, but she knew something must be very wrong at home for Seán to come in the dead of night like this. He had been to see the children earlier, and he must have gotten some urgent news, to risk disturbing the house.

"Please God, don't let it be the blight," Ginny said. "God keep that crop clean and strong."

She hoisted the baby onto her shoulder and fled down the corridor, her heart racing. Raymond squawked in her arms, and she tried to shush him, but it was too late. The door to Mrs. Spring's chamber was opening, and she was peeking out.

"Is everything all right?" Mrs. Spring asked. "Nothing's wrong with the baby? Is he ill? Shall I send for the doctor?"

Ginny's mind was flipping and racing, but she managed to go to Mrs. Spring, to feign calm. She reined steadiness into her voice. "No, no, we're grand," she said. "I just need a bite to eat. He's hungry, and I haven't enough milk for him, so I'm going to make myself a cup of tea. Go back to sleep."

Alice Spring yawned, her face anxious beneath her cotton nightcap. For a moment, Ginny was afraid she would insist on joining them. Ginny took a deep breath, faked another yawn herself. "I'm going to be quick, and straight back to bed. I'm exhausted," she said. "We'll see you in the morning."

"Good night, sweet Raymond," Mrs. Spring said, her voice still thick with sleep.

The door closed with a click, and Ginny flew to the staircase and down as quickly as she dared in the dark, with the baby on her shoulder. She opened the small green door across from the stable, but Seán was nowhere to be seen.

"Seán," she whispered.

The bushes next to her rustled.

"Shh!" he said. "She was looking out. Mrs. Spring was at the corridor window a few minutes ago."

"Is she there now?"

The bushes wobbled some more.

"No," he whispered back. "I don't see her now."

Ginny opened the door a bit wider. "Get in, quick!" she said.

"You'll need tea," Seán said, and she could feel her face drain of color.

They went down to the kitchen, and Ginny unloaded Raymond into Seán's arms while she filled the kettle and started a fire in the high hearth, for to boil the water. She lit a single lamp on the worktable, and then sat down on one of the high stools beside it, to steel herself for whatever he had to say. Seán was awkward with the baby, and tried to hand him back to her, but she shook her head.

"I can't," she said. If there was a shock coming, she didn't want to drop him. "Is it the blight? How is the crop?"

They had started hearing sporadic reports that the curse was returning, that it was marching, more slowly this time, but just as decisively, across the land. Hope was still the order of the day, but now it was tinged with alarm. If the crop failed again, the starvation would be endless, the misery complete. There was no mercy coming from the landlords. They had proved themselves more pitiless than ever in the time of Ireland's greatest despair. This time, it might not be absurd to think of the absolute extermination of the Irish. How could they possibly survive another failure, another whole year of nothingness?

"The crop is fine so far," Seán said. "Maire has been checking it daily, for signs of decay."

Ginny breathed. Raymond squirmed in Seán's arms.

"Raymond?"

Seán looked at her, confused. "He's grand, he's here."

"They didn't have word from America?"

"Oh," he said. "No, no."

"So what is it, then?" One of the children. Something was wrong with one of the children.

Seán cleared his throat. "It's Michael."

Ginny sucked her breath into her and trapped it there. She found she couldn't breathe out again. Her knuckles were hard and white, her cold fingers curled over the edge of the worktable. Her knees trembled on the stool beneath her, and she could feel her bowels loosen.

"What about Michael?" she whispered, but her voice came out warped, louder than she intended. She already knew what Seán was going to say. He was ill, her son was unwell.

"He's ill," Seán said, and Ginny dropped her head into her hands.

"How bad?"

Seán paused, then conceded, "Bad."

She could hear the water boiling for the tea, but she didn't move from the stool. Seán handed her the baby, and went to lift the kettle from the fire. He spooned some tea leaves into the waiting teapot, and poured the steaming water in over them. Raymond was stretching and mewling, but Ginny barely registered him. In her mind, she was already home.

"In what way is he taken ill?"

Seán cleared his throat, swirled the water in the teapot in front of him. He didn't want to say any more, but he knew he had to.

"High fever, headache. He's not himself at all. He's very poorly."

"When did it come on him?"

"Only yesterday he was fine, Maire said. It was very sudden."

"Anyone else ill, nearby?"

"One of the Fallon boys fell ill during the week. The mother thought it was the dread famine fever."

"And?"

"Died last night, Maire said."

Ginny gasped, and it felt like a punch to the stomach. She rocked herself and her baby on the stool. Her hand was moving frantically beside her face, like a small bird, like it didn't belong to her.

"Has he any rash? Michael?"

Seán nodded. "Along his abdomen, and up under his arms."

Ginny knew the danger of that rash. She knew what it meant. The worst kind of fever. Her stomach plunged. She stepped off the stool and fell down on her two knees in prayer. Through her muddled shock of grief she could hear Seán's voice, clear like a bell cutting through the din. "Ginny, you need to go to him."

Chapter Thirteen

NEW YORK, NOW

In the morning, Leo lets me sleep in, and it's strange, waking up to my own biology, without the frantic urgency of Emma's cries to retrieve me from my dreams. It takes me a moment to figure out where I am. Sometimes in sleep, I think we're still in our tiny Manhattan apartment, and I'm still thin and modestly glamorous. Waking to this new life is still a confused adjustment to me.

I sit up, and realize that my pillow is wet, and so is my face. What was I dreaming? I can't remember, but I have an awful, unsettled feeling in the pit of my stomach. Ginny Doyle's diary is sitting on my nightstand. I take a deep breath, reach for it, and flump back against the pillows, but before I can crack it open, Leo's face appears in the doorway. He has Emma tucked into the crook of one arm, and a plate of pancakes in the other.

"I got you maple butter and honey!" he sings, but then I guess he catches a glimpse of my face, and his expression falters. "What's wrong?"

I shake my head. "Nothing, I don't know. I think I had bad dreams last night but I can't remember."

He sits up onto the edge of the bed, and nestles Emma into the canoe of my legs.

"Yeah, you were very restless in your sleep," he says. "I almost woke you."

I yawn, stretch, and toss the diary onto his pillow beside me.

"But that should make you feel better," he says, gesturing at Emma like he is Vanna White and she is the prize. "And this." He gestures back to the stack of buckwheat pancakes he set on the nightstand.

I reach for the plate instead of the baby.

"These are my favorite," I say, stuffing a towering bite into my mouth. "So good."

He smiles at me. "Try not to drip food on your daughter," he jokes. But I do not laugh.

The buckwheat and honey go dry in my mouth, and suddenly I can't chew, because I'm crying instead. For fuck's sake.

"Hey. Hey," Leo says, leaning forward, and taking the plate from me. He sets it back on the nightstand. "I was only joking. You can spill all the food you want on the baby. Maybe she likes maple butter. She needs a bath anyway."

God love him, he's a good sport. He's trying to joke his way out of it. I finally manage to swallow the enormous bite, but it sticks in my throat halfway down, because I didn't chew it enough. Leo is holding my hand.

"It's not you." I sniff. I thought I was ready to talk, but my lips feel hard against each other, and my throat is taut. I wave my hand in front of my face—why, I have no idea. It doesn't help. "God, what is the *matter* with me? I'm such a mess."

Leo doesn't push. He waits until I can breathe deeply, and then he says, "Listen, take it easy on yourself, Jelly. You're not a mess. I hate it when you say stuff like that."

I breathe again, and Emma rises and falls with my breath even though she's on my legs, because my body is now so spherical and interdependent that any activity going on in one part of my anatomy causes fallout around the globe. I'm planetary like that.

"I know," I say. "I'm just not used to being so emotional. Gah. It's awful. I'm so sick of all this weird, random crying. It's like I suddenly have no self-control."

This must be what it feels like for people who have incontinence. Like, *Oh dear, would you look at that. I just pooped my pants again!*

"I know it's hard," Leo is saying, "but it's totally normal. I was just reading about postpartum depression on WebMD and—"

"You what?" I interrupt.

Leo looks up at me. Caught.

"I was just, I mean, I was just looking around, not like I was specifically looking for information about postpartum depression, but . . ."

"Good, because I don't have that."

"No, I know, that's what I'm saying."

My tears have vanished now, and the weird, desperate sadness I felt a moment ago has been entirely replaced with anger. I have switched gears unequivocally, like only a proper psychopath could do.

"So why were you looking up postpartum depression?" I say. "Do you think I'm falling apart?"

"No way."

I lift my chin. "So then why?"

"I was just reading about different kinds of postpartum experiences," he says. "And I think yours is perfectly normal. The hormones racing through your body during this time, they're just . . ."

I can tell he wants to say *crazy* or perhaps *insane*. He casts about for another word.

"Overwhelming?" I offer him.

"Yes." He snaps his fingers. A look of unadulterated relief settles over his face. "Overwhelming. Even if you didn't have the sleep deprivation, the big life change, all the stress of caring for a new baby. Even without all that stuff, just the dips and spikes in your hormone levels alone are enough to make you feel supersensitive."

My favorite pancakes are getting cold on the nightstand, and Emma, as oblivious to my emotions as ever, has fallen asleep on my legs.

"You're very sweet, Leo," I say, even though I feel slightly annoyed by this whole conversation. I *want* to think it's sweet. But instead, I feel like my very real, very personal emotions have been reduced to some safe, clean Internet diagnosis. "But you know, I think it's more than that."

I trace my finger along the contours of Emma's sleeping face.

"How do you mean?"

"I just—" Where do I even begin trying to explain all of this to him? "Yes, it's true, everything you've said is true. I'm hormonal and overwhelmed and sensitive. The change in my lifestyle has completely knocked the wind out of me, and I didn't expect that. I thought this would be effortless for me, that I'd be a natural."

"You are, you're so nurturing," he says.

That sentiment is so wildly wrong that I don't even bother contradicting him.

"Every effort I make seems to flop. I'm not used to that. I

succeed. I'm a succeeder!" And then I shudder, remembering. "Ugh, that mommy group yesterday. Even that girl Jade, from channel C...I liked her. I mean, it was awkward, but she seemed nice. And then I practically had to put her in a choke hold to get her to take my phone number. I'll probably never hear from her again."

Leo rubs a hand along my leg. "It will get better," he says. "You'll find people you click with. And you'll get back to work when you're ready. You'll find a rhythm."

"I know," I lie. I glance at the diary on his pillow, then reach back and grab it. "I was reading this last night, before bed. I think this is what upset me, gave me the nightmares or whatever."

"Why, what does it say?" Leo picks up the plate and takes a bite of my pancakes.

"She killed someone."

"No shit!"

"Yeah, in front of her kid."

Leo chews thoughtfully. "Wow."

"I know."

"Salacious!" he says, puckering his lips.

"Leo, this is not *Us Weekly*," I say. "This woman was related to me."

He sets the plate back down, and begins to nod his head.

"Oh, I see, I get it now," he says, and he brings his hands together in front of him, in this maddening professorial gesture he uses whenever he's theorizing about something. "So because your, what was she, like your great-great-great-aunt's uncle's cousin's grandmother? Because she was a bad mother, because she killed someone in front of her kid, somehow this trickles down to you?"

"It's not as crazy as you make it sound," I say.

"Actually, it kind of is, Majella."

"No, it's not," I say. "Think about it, Leo. You know my mom. She's not exactly the warm, fuzzy type. She flees the scene at the first sign that she's about to become a grandmother. She's incapable of talking to me about anything more serious than a hammertoe. She's totally emotionally vacant."

"She is not, you're too hard on her."

I grip the diary hard in my hands. Leo's mom died when he was seventeen. She was diabetic, and she more or less ate herself into a doughnut coma, from which she never recovered—speaking of emotionally healthy women. He and my mom have always loved each other, and even though he understands my exasperation with her, he can't help but take her side from time to time. And it's not even like I can really blame him. She is a tremendously charming woman. Just ask the receptionist at her accountant's office! Everyone loves her. Maybe that's why I don't feel like she's really *mine*.

"She is vacant, Leo. You don't understand." There's nothing I hate more than the sound of my own whininess, so I reach for a note of concession. "I know she could be worse."

Leo snorts. "You have no idea."

"But she could be better, too." I revert to whining. "This is not the relationship I want to have with her. She's totally closed off to me."

"She's just a phone call away, Majella."

"She is in *Florida*," I say, as if this is the grandest, most obvious proof that she's unreachable. Why doesn't he understand? "I'm just saying, it comes from somewhere, the way I'm feeling. We learn how to be parents by watching our mothers."

"Yes, and then we *choose* whether to emulate them or do things differently," he argues.

"Yes, that's what sane people do," I grant him. "But what if you can't choose? What if it's coded deep into your genetics, and you can't outrun it? And what if I'm just part of some inescapable genetic cycle of failed nurturers, and I'm about to fuck up our baby, too?"

I am crying again now, and Leo bites his lip. The poor man is utterly defeated. I feel so sorry for him. I'm terrified, in this moment, that he is wishing he married someone else. Someone more stable and light, someone more like I used to be. I reach for his hand, and I squeeze it, but not to reassure him. I wish I were that selfless. I'm afraid to let go.

"You could never fuck up our baby," he whispers.

Please let that be true. He touches my face, and then we both look down at Emma, asleep on my legs. I'm so glad she's not old enough to understand any of this. I hope I'm better by the time she can. I so want to be that strong, steady woman Leo thought he married. Didn't I used to be that woman?

"Leo?" I whisper, and now I am truly shaking, because against my better judgment, I'm about to confess something that I had no intention of telling him. I can feel the words unfurling inside me, and I wish I knew how to stop them, how to swallow them, but out they tumble, unbidden. "You know I love her, right? I do."

"Of course."

And then there's a long gap of silence, when I think I might actually be able to thwart these words before they appear. I might be able to conquer them. But no.

"I don't know if it's enough," I whisper. "I don't think I love her the way I'm supposed to."

The silence that descends over the room now is beastly. Heavy. I can feel it on my chest. Leo's face is broken. He pushes breath up and out of his lungs. I can see his cheeks puff as the breath leaves his body, but there is still no sound. He takes the diary from me, thumbs through it without reading anything, and then stands up from the bed.

"You should throw this fucking thing in the fire."

"What?"

He's shaking his head. "It's ridiculous, you getting yourself into this kind of state over some stupid, prehistoric diary."

"It's not about the diary. . . ." But he won't listen. He's found his comfortable scapegoat. He needs this to blame, instead of me. He is shaking it at me.

"This has nothing to do with you, do you understand me? Nothing." He is actually pacing, like some thwarted soap opera lover, and his voice is loud. He's going to wake Emma. "Whatever crazy-ass thing some whackjob lady did in front of her kid some two hundred years ago *has nothing to do with you.*"

Emma's eyes pop open, and she immediately begins to cry. Leo stops in his tirade and tosses the book onto the bed at my feet. He reaches for her, but I get her first, lift her onto my shoulder. She stops crying, and it is a bona fide miracle. I kiss the side of her head. Leo watches us. His hands hang helplessly at his sides.

"Look at you," he whispers, and then he comes and holds us both for a long time. "I wish you could see what I see."

I take a long shower before I head downstairs, and I expect Leo to be ready to walk out the door to work. Shoes on, jacket. But he's not. He's sitting on the couch with a cup of coffee, the PlayStation controller in his hand, and his socks up on the coffee table. Emma is doing tummy time on the yoga mat beside him.

"Aren't you going to be late for work?" I ask from the kitchen.

I'm rummaging in the cabinet for a mug while I inspect the coffeemaker, as if my powers of deduction alone are powerful enough to tell whether it's decaf.

"It's half-caf," Leo says from the couch. "And I called out."

I have the coffeepot in my hand now, but I stop pouring midstream, and turn to him. "You what?"

"I called out. I'll probably go in later, for the dinner rush. Mario can handle the prep. Thought I'd spend the day with my girls."

"On a *Saturday*?"

In the seven years I've known him, Leo has never called out of work. Not once. The idea that he would do it on a Saturday, on the restaurant's busiest night, is actually unthinkable. He has worked through migraines, fevers, flu symptoms, and, one extremely foolhardy time, even food poisoning. Something is extremely suspicious here. Does he want me to believe he just called out on a whim? Just because he got a hankering for some family time? I turn back to my mug and fill it up before I join him on the couch. I sit on the far end, as far away from him as I can get. I look around the unfinished room.

"Yeah, you wanna spend the day getting a jump on some of these projects, then?" I say. "Maybe we could install some of the wood flooring?"

Our renovation efforts have come to a screeching halt since Emma was born. Steam curls up from my mug and around my face. I sip. I am laying an ambush. I am about to pounce.

"Yeah, maybe," he says, focused on his game. The buttons click beneath his thumbs.

"So what, you don't trust me with her now? You can't go to work and leave me alone with her?"

He glances at me for just an instant, but it's long enough to distract his on-screen quarterback, who throws an interception.

Leo throws the controller down on the coffee table, and it hits his coffee mug, which sloshes.

"You know what, Majella," he says, standing up. "Maybe you are fucking crazy." He grabs his coffee and stalks into the kitchen. "Is that what you want? Someone to confirm it for you?"

I set my mug down on the table. I can't tell who's wrong. I draw my knees up in front of me, and it doesn't hurt. My incision is painless. Maybe it's becoming a scar. Leo gulps some coffee and dumps the rest into the sink. Then he comes back and stands in the doorway.

"I just thought you could use a little extra support today," he says. "You seemed like you were shook up. I know you're having a hard time here, Majella, but I'm not going to be your punching bag. I'm trying to *help*."

I rest my elbows on my knees and nod my head. After a moment, he comes and sits back down on the couch, but not close to me.

"Maybe you should call Dr. Zimmer," he suggests.

I'm astonished. Flabbergasted. Does he think I'm that unhinged? That I need to call my therapist for an emergency appointment?

"It's Saturday," I answer lamely.

He shrugs. I reach for my coffee. Sip. All I wanted to do was vent. Now I have killed my husband's patience. I wish I could go back an hour, and unsay everything, back to a time just sixty minutes ago when he believed in me. Even though his faith was misguided, it had been a comfort, a hope. How had I won him over to my own doomed perspective so convincingly, so accidentally?

"Maybe you should think about taking something," he says quietly, and his words feel like an unwelcomed injection, a sharp prick that leaches beneath my skin.

"Like happy pills?"

"Just something to help balance your chemistry, until you're feeling better. You're not yourself at all."

He won't look at me. This could be the most disappointed I have ever felt in my entire life. I have let everyone down. This is not the mother either of us expected me to be. This failure is incalculable. With monstrous effort, I push myself to my feet.

"I'll call Dr. Zimmer."

I wear one of Leo's baseball hats, and I pull it down low over my face so I can cry all the way to Dr. Zimmer's office on the subway. When I get there, she is wearing Saturday clothes, some high-waisted jeans and Nikes, which totally throws me off. I wonder if I called her away from her kid's soccer game or something, if my bad motherhood is having a knock-on effect, making her a bad mother, too—the kind of woman who abandons her child's soccer game to go be with a patient instead. In my mind, I see her daughter scoring the winning goal, her hands held aloft as she celebrates, her brown ponytail swinging behind her as she searches the cheering sidelines for her absent mother.

"I'm sorry to call you on a Saturday."

"It's fine," she says. "Part of the job." She smiles at me, and I don't remember for sure, but I feel like this is a first, too, that her smile is only enabled by the Nikes. "So what's going on?"

I shake my head. "I don't know. Yesterday I had a good day. I mean, I went to the worst mommy-group in the world, but ended up going for coffee with one of the other moms, and it was cool. I had a good day with the baby, Emma was happy. She seems not to be crying as much these days. Everything was fine."

"And then?"

"And then, remember that diary I told you about?"

"The one from your Irish ancestor. During the famine?"

"Yes."

She nods.

"Well, I read more of it last night, and it was awful. It made me feel really awful. I think it gave me bad dreams."

"What kind of dreams?"

"I don't remember. But I woke up in a really wicked mood."

"So why do you think it was the diary? What did it say?"

"She killed someone. This woman, my ancestor, killed another woman. She smashed her skull in with a cudgel."

"Oh dear."

"Yeah, and she did it in front of her kid."

"Her own kid, or the victim's kid?"

"Her own kid. Her daughter."

"Well, I can see why that would disturb you."

"Yeah." I rub my hands nervously along my thighs. "And I just hate that, I hate that I'm related to this person. I feel like it confirms all my worst fears about myself, as a mother."

Dr. Zimmer is nodding, frowning.

"Like if this is the stock I come from, well, no wonder I'm coming unhinged. Maybe it's just in me, to be like that."

"To be violent?" she asks carefully. "I've never heard you mention anything violent. That seems like quite the leap to make."

"I don't know, maybe not violent," I say. "But at least crazy. And a shitty mother."

"I notice you're using pretty vivid language. *Wicked. Unhinged. Crazy. Shitty.* Is that how you're really feeling about yourself?"

I shrug. Then nod. Then whisper, "I kind of hate myself right now. I feel like I'm letting everyone down, like I've committed false advertising. Like Leo and I both thought I would be this wonderful, easy mother, and now I'm *this* instead." My eyelids feel puffy and swollen, my nose completely blocked with tears. I am wretched. "Leo and I are at each other's throats. I feel like I've exhausted his patience. I thought his patience was infinite, but I think I've found his threshold at last. He's so fed up with me. He's the one who suggested I call you this morning."

"Oh?" She raises her eyebrows. "You didn't want to come in?"

"I don't know. He thinks I need to take something. Like a prescription."

"And how do you feel about that?"

I fold myself over my knees and weep until I think I must *finally* be done weeping. Seriously. Good God. Dr. Zimmer says nothing. She's still waiting for me to answer her question. Wasn't that fresh round of uncontrollable sobbing answer enough?

"I don't want to take some fucking pills that are just going to turn off my brain, squelch my emotions. I want to learn how to *handle* them. How to cope."

"There are plenty of options today that are very light-handed," she says. "You don't have to be a zombie."

"But isn't this normal, what I'm going through?" I ask. I so want it to be normal. "I mean yes, I'm sleep-deprived and I'm super-hormonal. I cry every ten seconds. But don't lots of new moms feel like this?"

"I don't think you're experiencing anything *abnormal,*" Dr. Zimmer assures me. "But that doesn't make it any easier, does it? If it's becoming more severe, a temporary prescription might really help." She looks at me and smiles again, and for some reason, that makes me feel worse. "Part of the difficulty of being a new mother *is* the fact that your body chemistry is doing lots of crazy things, and that *can* make it harder to sleep, harder to focus. It can really take away your ability to function normally."

I look for a nail to bite, but I've already scalped them all. "Have you ever heard of a drug called Ativan?" she asks.

I shrug. "I don't think so."

"It's not an antidepressant. It doesn't change the way your brain functions. It simply helps with the relief of anxiety. It helps you relax."

"Like Valium?" I ask. "Or beer?"

"Well, it's lighter than Valium," she answers, ignoring the beer remark. "It's not something you take every day; it's just the sort of thing that's good to have in the medicine cabinet for days like this. When you're feeling overwhelmed or anxious, it can help you achieve calm."

"Okay," I say noncommittally.

Dr. Zimmer stands up from her red chair and moves behind the desk I've never seen her use. Where is she going? When I said, "Okay," I meant, "Okay, now I understand what Ativan is," not, "Okay, I'd like some Ativan now, please."

"What about breast-feeding?" I ask, mostly as a stall tactic.

Dr. Zimmer is flipping through her old-fashioned rotary Rolodex. I didn't even know they made those things anymore.

"I think it's safe," she says, stopping on the Ms. "But the prescribing doctor will go over all of that with you. There's a guy right here in the building, Dr. Maledon, unless there's someone else you'd rather use?"

I shift uncomfortably in my seat and don't answer her. I don't even look up.

"Majella, it won't take you fifteen minutes. What's the worst that could happen?"

"What if he doesn't take my insurance?"

"He takes your insurance."

"Oh." How did she just happen to know that off the top of her head? How does she even remember who my insurance carrier is? What is she, some kind of insurance zealot? She interrupts the silent character assassination I am conducting against her by clearing her throat.

"You don't even have to take the medication, Majella," she says then, with intractable rationale. "Sometimes, just knowing you have the option helps. It certainly can't hurt, right?"

Damn all these rigidly logical people in my life. They are so exasperating! She sits down behind the desk and awaits my verdict.

"Okay," I finally whisper, with deep, irrational shame.

I cry quietly while she fixes an appointment for me with Dr. Maledon. Oh, calling his answering service was unnecessary because—joy of joys!—the doc just happens to be in his office until noon today, and no, he has no openings, but yes, he will squeeze me in because he is a stand-up guy, and it is his heroic vocation in life to save New York City from crazies like me.

Dr. Zimmer locks up her office, and then directs me to Dr. Maledon's office on the third floor. Fifty-five minutes later, I am standing on the subway platform at Third Avenue, waiting for the L train, with the crumpled Ativan prescription shoved deep into the back pocket of my jeans. I can feel it there.

I get off the L train at Myrtle and Wyckoff, and hop on the almost-empty, late Saturday morning Q55 bus. I get off two stops before home so I can go to a pharmacy I've never used before, where no one knows me. I'm pretty sure the young, ponytailed pharmacist smirked when she saw my prescription. I wait on a hard plastic chair while she fills my prescription. My knees jiggle nervously beneath me. I text Leo: *Be home soon. We need anything?*

After a few minutes, the phone beeps, and I check the messages, but there's no text from Leo. Instead, a voice mail from a number I don't recognize. Maybe Dr. Zimmer is just checking on me, to make sure I haven't offed myself. I press *play*, hold the phone up to my ear.

The first thing I hear is a baby crying, and then a door slams and the cry becomes muffled. Then, hurried footsteps and a breathless voice. *Hi, Majella, it's Jade from next door? I went for a coffee with you yesterday, after that soul-sucking mommy meetup?* She pauses, and it seems like she's distracted by something. My knees have stopped bouncing against the hard plastic chair and my body is stretched, motionless. I'm straining to hear her. The baby is still crying, but it sounds far away now. Jade's voice is echoey, like she's locked herself in a shower or a stairwell. *Anyway so yeah, I just wanted to say hey. It was nice meeting you, and I thought maybe we could do it again sometime. Okay.* There's more noise in the background, and then nothing, like she's hung up, or muted me. Then she's back, and the baby is crying loud again. *Okay, so just give me a call sometime.*

The message cuts off, and I turn my phone up as loud as it will go so I can play it again, listening for clues like a twenty-first-century Nancy Drew. What is going *on* in that apartment? The chaos that is Jade's life makes me feel comparatively sane and balanced. I'm halfway through playing the message for the third time when the pharmacist startles me by calling my name. I pocket the phone and approach the counter.

"You're all set," she says, and she tries to make eye contact with me, but I lower the brim of my hat to intercept her curiosity. "Just sign here." She points to a line in her notebook with a square, tangerine fingernail. A fingernail that has clearly never known the dark misfortune of baby poop.

I scribble my name and I'm outta there. On the sidewalk, I stuff the prescription into my diaper bag and check the phone again. There's the text from Leo: *Take your time. Don't have to be at work till four. Pick up lunch? And butt paste.* I text him back: *Sounds delicious. See u soon.* And then I go back to Jade's message, and hit *call back.*

Maybe her life is even more chaotic than mine. And maybe we

have nothing in common except that we both cry all the time and we're terrible mothers. Spending time with Jade might be awkward, even potentially unpleasant. But anything is better than the prospect of spending a sunny Saturday afternoon alone in our half-renovated house with my crying baby and a bottle of stigmatic pills.

"Hello?"

"Hi, Jade! It's Majella."

Chapter Fourteen

IRELAND, JUNE 1847

Ginny didn't remember Roisin coming into the room, but there her friend was, sat at the long worktable with baby Raymond in her arms. There were two more lamps lit, and the kitchen was in brightness, like it was daytime. Ginny's tea had gone cold in front of her, and she was standing, then sitting, then standing again. She didn't know what to do with herself. Her arms and legs felt loose from her body, and she had a mad compulsion to run.

"I figured it was you," Roisin was saying to Seán. "I knew someone was taking the food to her children, but our Ginny here was very discreet. Didn't want to get you in trouble, I reckon. Still, who else could it have been?"

"Well, I'm not sorry, even if it does cost me the job," he answered.

"Nobody's asking you to be sorry."

Ginny sat down again beside Roisin, and lifted the baby into her arms. He still hadn't finished his feed.

"He's hungry," Ginny said. "I'll have to feed him before I go."

"Go where?" Roisin asked.

Ginny looked at her. "Home, of course."

Roisin took a deep breath, and nodded her head. "It's true that you need to go home."

"Don't bother trying to talk me out of it," Ginny answered.

Roisin raised a hand. "I won't. But just think carefully. Let's plan it through before you fly off and do something you'll regret in a few days' time. Let us help you. It's so easy to act rash when you're in a fluster."

Ginny tried to slow down in her brain, but Roisin was right. She was in an awful panic. She couldn't think straight. Seán set a fresh cup of tea down in front of her, and this time, she tried sipping at it. It was hot and bitter going down.

"I just need to get home, I have to get home." Ginny shook her head.

"And you will," Roisin said. "But listen, if you leave now, this morning, you'll have to tell Mrs. Spring everything, including how you found out that your son is ill."

Ginny glanced at Seán, but he made no eye contact. He only arranged himself on his own stool.

"It's not only your own position you'd be jeopardizing," Roisin said, with sacrosanct reason. "You'd have to tell her that Seán was the one who brought you the news."

"Never mind about that, Ginny," Seán put in, waving his hand. "I'll take you home. You should get home. I'll be grand. If she gives me the boot, so be it."

But Roisin answered him back, "And if she does give you the boot, then what? You can take your savings and nip off to America, and what will become of poor Ginny and her children then? If you're no longer here to supply for them?"

Seán drew his mouth into an irritable line, folded his arms in front of him. Raymond fussed and wriggled in his mother's arms. Ginny took another swig of the tea.

"There's a bit of the spice cake left in the larder," Roisin said, rising to her feet. "I'm peckish."

She tottered off, and Seán and Ginny looked at each other. He bit his thumb.

"*Ochón!*" Ginny said. And a tear sprang up in her eyes. She blinked hard to chase even the notion of crying away. There was no time for that sort of luxury. Her heart was racketing around in her breast. "I'm awful sorry, Seán," she said. "I never meant to drag you into this."

"You didn't, I was happy to do it. I'd do it again." But she could sense that his bravado was hollow.

Roisin was coming back from the larder now, the wrapped chunk of spice cake in her hand. She had a bit of a nighttime limp, a slow crookedness about her body when she longed to be still tucked up in her bed. She set the cake on the table, and broke off a piece for Ginny and then one for herself.

"I'll make up a story," Ginny said without touching the cake. "Or I won't even tell her. I'll be gone before she wakens. Then, when Michael is on the mend, maybe I can come back. I can tell her there was an awful emergency. Something with the baby."

"That might work," Seán said. "And then I could still bring you provisions, as you need them."

"It might work," Roisin conceded. "But why would you risk it? Mrs. Spring is an unpredictable woman. Just because you're in her good graces now doesn't mean you'll stay that way after a stunt like this. And God forbid she gets it into her head that you had anything to do with the fever! She would never let you back into this house, neither of you."

Ginny cradled Raymond in one arm, and scraped her free hand up over her face, through her loosened black hair.

"Listen, Michael has only been ill for one day, right?" Roisin asked, looking at Seán.

"Yeah, that's what Maire said, that he was grand yesterday."

"So"—she reached over and placed her hand on Ginny's—"what about this? What about you stay here today . . ."

Ginny was already shaking her head.

"Just hear me out," Roisin said. "Just stay here today, only for the day. We'll work. I'll be here with you, and everything will appear like normal to Mrs. Spring. She can visit with yourself and Raymond in the morning, after breakfast as she always does, and then she can take him out in the afternoon as well. Just stick to the regular routine so she won't suspect anything. We'll wait until nightfall then, until she goes to bed. And then you can go off, and Seán, you can take Ginny on horseback, right, and I'll keep Raymond with me for the night, after you give him his last feed in the evening, Ginny. You can go out to Knockbooley then, and be with Michael until the baby needs his next feed in the morning."

Seán was studying Ginny, waiting for her reaction. Roisin kept on with her plan.

"If he's well, if he's turned the corner by tonight, you can just spend a few hours there, and comfort him. Mother him. Doctor him. And you could still be back before daybreak, before anyone even misses you. Nobody would ever be the wiser."

"And if he's not? If he doesn't . . ." Ginny couldn't bring herself to finish the thought. All she could think about was that baby who'd died in her arms, that tiny coffin. She didn't think she could bear that kind of loss again.

"Well, if he's as bad as all that," Roisin said, "then I'll send baby Raymond along home to you. Seán can come back and collect him, and you'll be home with your children, and we'll figure out the rest of it then, what to tell Mrs. Spring."

Ginny looked at Seán, but he was giving nothing away. He only stared at her.

"I don't know what to do," Ginny whispered.

In all her weeks and months of wishing for Ray, she had never longed for him as much as she did at that moment. *Please God, tell me what to do*, she thought. She closed her eyes. Squeezed them shut.

"What time is it?" she asked.

"I don't know," Seán said. "I'd say it's an hour at least until dawn."

Ginny opened her eyes and looked at them both. She looked at baby Raymond, who was sucking on her finger.

"Maybe you're right," she said. "Maybe I should wait until nightfall." But even as she said it, she felt it was not possible, to stay parted from Michael for the length of this day that was stretching out in front of her. She felt a wicked horror in her bones.

Seán started nodding his head. "I think it's a good plan. We can leave this evening, as soon as the house is quiet. You meet me beyond the south pasture, by that stand of trees. If we get out in good time, we'll have six hours at least, before we'll have to be back in the morning."

Ginny breathed deep. She tried.

"That's loads of time for you to heal young Michael." Seán smiled. "If he's anything like his mammy, he's a fighter. He'll be back on his feet this time tomorrow, tearing round the place."

God, how she wanted to believe him. And she knew it was possible, anything was possible, with the fever. Just as many survived it as not, she reckoned. Or nearly. She tried not to picture that spreading rash along Michael's soft and prickled skin. She could still see his pale, bony knees sticking out beneath his red petticoat. She wanted so much just to tear out of that madhouse and run to him. Her baby boy.

"All right," she breathed.

"Grand." Roisin nodded, patting the table in front of her. "So that's settled. You'd better feed that baby of yours before he eats your finger. I'm going to do my best to get another hour's sleep, and I suggest you do the same. Close your eyes, at least. It'll be a long day ahead of us."

"Yeah, I'm off for a kip myself," Seán said, pushing back from the table to stand up. "You right, Ginny?"

She forced herself to nod. "Grand."

There are no words to describe the torture that day was to Ginny Doyle. The hollow endlessness of it. After breakfast, Mrs. Spring sat with her as usual, while she breast-fed the baby. Ginny wasn't capable of conversation, and she felt uncomfortable, exposed, sitting in the quiet with the baby at her breast. But Mrs. Spring didn't seem to mind. She didn't even seem to notice. Ginny spent most of the rest of the day working in the kitchen, by Roisin's side, but all she could see was Michael's pained and frightened face. Every hour, she questioned herself. She put the knife or the rag or the brush down where she stood, and she turned in circles, ready to bolt. She had nearly convinced her brain that it was best, to wait until nightfall, but her body was having none of it. Her legs were twitchy and slack. She felt unfastened from the ground, her head floaty and detached. The hours of that single day were longer than the months since Ray had left. They were longer than the years of her marriage, the decades of her life. In the afternoon, when they heard Mrs. Spring's footstep on the stair, Roisin hurried Ginny into the larder.

"It's best if she doesn't see you, the way you're looking now. You're awful peaky," Roisin said, as she shooed her friend away.

Ginny stood inside, wrapped her arms around herself, and shivered. She leaned her head against one of the cold shelves, and waited. She could smell the sharp, heady tang of cheese all around, and it was too much. She held her breath. Outside, she could hear Mrs. Spring talking.

"Here's Auntie Alice," she said, in the singsong voice she only ever used with the baby. "Where's your mammy now? Are you ready to come out for your fresh air with Auntie Alice?"

"She's just in the back of the larder there, doing some clearing out," Roisin was saying. "She said it was fine for you to take Raymond out, whenever you came down."

"Ah, lovely," Mrs. Spring said. "And aren't you looking dapper today, my little man? Oh, you're getting so big!" Her voice changed with the weight of him in her arms.

In the larder, Ginny leaned her elbows onto a lower shelf, and turned into it, let the wood dig a mark into her forehead. She picked at a loose splinter, and listened until she couldn't hear footsteps anymore. She tried closing her eyes, but all that was there was Michael's face, the damp brown hair sticking to his feverish forehead. She opened her eyes, shook the image out of her head. Roisin's face appeared instead then, around the doorjamb.

"She's gone, dear."

Ginny nodded, and made to step out of the larder, but Roisin came toward her instead, put a hand against Ginny's forehead. Ginny let her.

"I'm fine," she said. "I'm not ill."

"No," Roisin agreed, "you're just shook-looking. You're awful pale altogether."

"I suppose . . ." Ginny trailed off insensibly.

"Sit down and have a cup of tea, dear. You do need to keep your strength up, for tonight. You look as if you could fall right down."

She shook her head. "I can't sit. I need to keep going, keep working."

"Right so," Roisin said.

That was what they did.

After the dinner was served and the kitchen was cleaned and cleared, Ginny retired early to her room with Raymond. Her nerves were too shattered to feed him properly, but she had to try. He was too young yet, for cow's milk, and if Ginny was thinking of leaving him with Roisin for the night, he would have to be full up before his mother went. She lay down on the bed, on her side, and unbuttoned her shirtwaist. She tucked him in along her body where he could lie beside his mammy and suckle, and then she propped a pillow under her head.

She closed her eyes, and the tears came at once. She had held them in check all day, she was so close now. Another hour, perhaps, until Mrs. Spring retired for the night. Until Ginny could steal out into the dark, and down to the moonlit stand of trees beyond the south pasture. Seán would be waiting for her. With a good, fleet horse, they would be in Knockbooley in a quarter of an hour. She bit her lips. Raymond sucked sweetly and noisily at her breast.

"Eat up, little man," she said. "Or you'll be hungry till morning."

He was just finished eating, and she was walking him round the room, rubbing his back and squeezing him gently to bring up his wind, when there was a rapid knock at the door. Ginny opened it at once, and Katie stood in the corridor. She wouldn't look at Ginny.

"You have a visitor in the parlor." The girl turned on her heel. A visitor?

"Who is it, Katie?" Ginny called after her, but she was gone, scampering down the corridor into the dark.

Ginny slammed the door and set Raymond on the bed, and then went mad buttoning up and tucking in her shirtwaist as quick as she could. Her hands were shaking, but her mind was mercifully blank. No catalog of harrowing possibilities presented itself to her. No image of a tiny coffin impressed itself upon her vision. Before today, her mind would have gone directly to Ray. News from New York. Something dreadful. But now, there was nothing, only a petrified and hurtling urgency. To get to the parlor. Her hands shook violently as she lifted Raymond from the bed and onto her shoulder.

"Please God, keep my legs beneath me," she said, as she took to the grand central staircase in a terror for the second time today. Outside the parlor door she paused, just for an instant, she paused. And she wished that she could suspend that moment, that she could stop her life right there, that she could remain the person she was before she had to turn the knob and open that door. Before she had to walk into that room and face whoever, whatever, was waiting for her.

Ginny clung her face into Raymond and breathed. When she opened the door and stepped into the room, Katie was already fussing around a tea tray at the sideboard. Father Brennan was standing in front of the fireplace. Father Brennan. He turned toward Ginny as she entered the room, and when she caught sight of the grim pallor of his face, she knew at once. She felt her legs wilting beneath her.

She cried out because she knew she was going to drop, and she was in terror for the baby. Katie's head snapped up and she saw Ginny tilt; she lurched fast across the room to lift Raymond out of his mother's arms. Ginny gripped the back of a chair, and then Father Brennan was beside her, his arm around her waist, holding her up. He helped her to the settee, and she crumbled into it.

He sat down on a chair across from her, and leaned forward. He started to speak, but Ginny waved her hands to stop him. Whatever he had to say, if he didn't say it, then she wouldn't know.

"No," she said.

"Ginny . . ."

"No! No."

He shook his head, folded his hands in his lap. His face was awful stern, but his eyes were wet.

"No no no."

"I'm sorry, Ginny."

She folded her body down over her knees, and wrapped her arms over her head.

"Michael is gone, Ginny. He's gone. He went quick and peaceful."

Everything fell out of her then, every good thing that had ever been. It all came up into her throat and stopped beating. Her breath wouldn't move in her lungs. The keen that came in at her breast was too big to unleash. It was trapped. She couldn't speak, couldn't move. There was a violent stillness in her.

"He didn't even know you weren't there," Father Brennan was saying. "He slept into his death. It was peaceful."

She rocked. Something elemental rocked her. Back and over, on the settee, back and over. Like a baby in a cradle she rocked. And then that same something elemental breathed for her, it kicked in at her lungs, and she gasped loudly for air. She rocked.

"He's gone to God, Ginny," Father Brennan was saying. "Michael's in a better place now. He's with Thomas. There's no suffering. No famine in the kingdom of God."

His hand was on her back, and she wanted to wrench it off, to slap it away. But she couldn't move. She could only rock.

In a moment, Ginny was aware of Mrs. Spring in the room.

She heard the woman's high and watery voice. She heard her say Michael's name. Her baby boy's name. And then she heard Roisin as well, beside Mrs. Spring, begging a moment's privacy, leading her out, and out. Ginny flew at her.

"You! You told me to stay!" Ginny screamed, and her voice was like something beastly. Demonic. "I should have gone. I should have been with him." She was suddenly on her feet, and the air was strangulating around her. "You told me to stay."

And then Father Brennan's hands were on Ginny's elbows, and he was sitting her down, and she was rocking again on the settee, and she could see Katie's shoes, the black toes of her shoes, and she could hear a clatter and a clink as the girl set the teacups down on the table before them. Ginny lifted her head.

"Where is my baby?"

Katie swallowed and stammered, "I . . . Roisin . . ."

"I want my baby!"

And now the teacup was in Ginny's hand, and now it wasn't, because it was airborne, flying, and the streak of tea came liberated from it, and hung in the air like a hot, black splash, and now the teacup wasn't a teacup anymore, because it smashed against the wall. And now it was all in pieces. It was all in pieces.

And then they were in the yard, by the stables, and it was twilight, and it was warm. June.

"What is the date today?" Ginny asked.

"The date? Why . . . ?" Father Brennan was asking.

But Seán was there, and he broke in. "It's the twenty-fourth of June, Ginny."

"The day . . . June twenty-fourth." She nodded. She wanted to remember it. The day Michael died.

Roisin was gone, she was disappeared, she was vanished. Katie and Mrs. Spring stood by the back of the carriage. Katie was still and stared at her shoes, but Mrs. Spring was swaying from side to side. She was wringing her hands. Raymond was bundled into his mother's arms, and he not knowing anything was different in the world. Just an ordinary day. Father Brennan climbed into the carriage, and Seán was there at Ginny's elbow, to help her up.

Mrs. Spring stepped forward, clapped her hands vigorously in front of her. She shook her head primly, pressed her thin lips together. Ginny felt the woman's effort, her vicarious grief. Her eyes were dreadful.

"I'm so sorry," Mrs. Spring whispered, and then she embraced Ginny, and Ginny barely registered the clinch, but she heard Katie gasp behind them.

Mrs. Spring squeezed Ginny's hand then, and leaned down over Raymond's face, to leave her perfumed kisses along his nose and forehead. She started to draw back, but then she stopped herself. She clutched Ginny's elbow.

"You could leave him with me," Mrs. Spring said, her voice low and forceful. "I could mind him for a few days. You'll have your hands full. You'll have so much to . . ."

Ginny started, and pulled away from her. She answered her directly. "Mrs. Spring, I can *never* be parted from a child of mine again."

"But think of his health," Mrs. Spring said, stepping in even closer to Ginny and the child. There was a panic about her movements. "Think of the *fever*, Ginny. Don't bring him to that place!"

Ginny stepped back and handed Raymond quickly into the carriage. Father Brennan took the baby, and Ginny watched as Alice Spring's arms followed him up. Her soft, delicate hands fluttered in the air and hung there, beseeching.

"I thank you for your kindness, Mrs. Spring, but I belong with my children," she said quietly. "And they with me."

Mrs. Spring stayed where she was in the yard, while Seán closed and fastened the carriage door. Ginny didn't look back as the wheels began to roll and crunch over the gravel. She didn't see Alice Spring standing there, beside the stables, her arms still stretching after them in the twilight.

There was still light enough to see the cottage when the carriage crested the hill approaching, and it glowed out faintly white against the dark riot of green in the fields. The potato crop was thick and tall, and the western sky hung still and purple above it. In the yard, Maggie's cairns were enormous. The cottage looked tiny between them. Defenseless. How had she left her child here? How had she left them?

"God forgive me," Ginny whispered.

"Ginny, there's nothing to forgive," Father Brennan said. "You did what you had to do, for your children. There was no sin in it."

"I abandoned them, Father."

"You did the very opposite."

"Michael . . ." She shook her head.

"He might only have died sooner, and more wretchedly, if you had stayed."

But his words were useless to comfort her. She was ruptured, entirely. The cottage door was standing open, but then the road wound downhill, and they descended behind the ridge at the bottom of the lower field. The height of the rock wall overshadowed them.

"How will I ever tell Ray?" Ginny said, as the carriage stopped beside the lower field.

Through the gate, she could see them, her daughters: Poppy and Maggie stood together at the top of the ridge. They were so tall, the two of them. They stayed there as their mother opened the gate. They didn't run to greet her as she imagined they might.

258 · JEANINE CUMMINS

Seán and Father Brennan hung back and waited, awkward around the carriage behind her.

"We'll give you a few minutes," Father Brennan said.

And when she turned to look, Seán was picking some imaginary grass from the spokes of the back wheel, and Father Brennan was studying the rusted hinge at the gate. As Ginny approached the crest of the hill, Raymond wiggled in her arms, and Poppy broke from beside her sister to run to her mam. Ginny dropped down to her knees, and caught her youngest daughter heavy against her shoulder. She was big. She was so big. Her golden curls had thickened and dropped; the ringlets hung down to her shoulders. Ginny stroked the back of her head, and she could feel her small body trembling. Poppy wrapped her legs around her mother's hips, and Ginny struggled to stand, holding the two of them now, Raymond and Poppy both. Maggie had scampered away, down to the cottage door.

Poppy tucked her head under her mother's chin, and her voice piped out of her, softly. "I thought you weren't never coming back, Mammy."

Ginny gripped on to her so tightly then that she nearly crushed her. "I'm sorry, love. I'm sorry."

"Michael died, Mammy," Poppy said. "We tried to make him better, but he was sleeping with the rash and the fever, and then he died."

Ginny nodded her head. She breathed. She quivered. But she couldn't answer her daughter. At the cottage doorway, Maggie blocked her path, her face hard and her arms crossed in front of her. There was no greeting here for Ginny, who stooped to set Poppy down. Maggie's eyes glittered, but the rest of her face was fixed—all the roundness was gone out of it. She was all tough and rigid lines. Her mouth was entirely straight, but she lifted her chin as she spoke.

"I suppose you want to see him, now that he's dead." She was like an angry little sentry in the doorway. "My brother."

"My son," Ginny reminded her. She looked at her daughter evenly, and shifted Raymond's weight in her arms. "I know you're angry, Maggie. I know."

Maggie's face grew darker, stormier. "You shouldn't have left us."

"I know, love," Ginny said. "I made a mistake."

She thought about touching Maggie's chin. She longed to feel the softness of her daughter's face beneath her fingers, but Maggie turned away, leaned her back against the doorjamb. She still wasn't letting Ginny in.

"I didn't know what else to do, *mo chuisle*." Ginny didn't bend down to her. She wouldn't, until she knew her daughter was ready. "I know now I shouldn't have done it, I should never have gone. Maggie?"

Maggie dropped her arms and looked at her mother. The hardness in her little face was only a veneer, and Ginny could see through it, to the tenderness behind. At last, she bent down, and drew her face close to Maggie's.

"You don't have to forgive me, but you are my daughter," she said. "And that is our boy in there. He is *ours*, do you understand me?"

Maggie nodded, and when Ginny reached for her daughter's tough little fingers, Maggie didn't pull away. The warmth of her hand was like melting butter against Ginny's palm. Together, they stepped into the cottage, and then Maggie flitted quietly into the sleeping room by herself.

Maire was inside by the fire, her shoulders sloping down, her chin folded low. Her back was to the door.

"Maire," Ginny said, but her daughter didn't turn to face her. "Maire."

Poppy was sitting on the stool inside the door. "Will you hold your baby brother?" Ginny asked her.

Poppy smiled up at her mother, and bounced.

"Now you have to sit still, love."

"I will." Poppy held her arms out, and Ginny placed Raymond in them. His eyes locked onto his sister's face at once.

"Hallo, baby!" Poppy sang. "What's his name?"

"He's called Raymond."

Poppy looked up. "Like Daddy?"

"Like Daddy. Hold on to him tight, now, love. Don't drop him."

"I won't, Mammy. I have him."

Ginny bent and kissed her golden head, and then she turned to Maire, who was still sat on her haunches at the fire. Ginny touched the back of Maire's shoulder, and her daughter winced. Ginny moved around to Maire's side, went down on her knees, and drew in close to the fire so she could see her daughter's face. Maire wasn't a girl anymore. There were bald tears in her eyes, and she wouldn't look at Ginny.

"I'm sorry, Mam," she said quietly. And then her face stretched and contorted, and she drew her hands up to her cheeks, and the tears came running through her fingers. "I'm sorry, I thought I could . . . I did everything, I . . ."

"Maire, stop!" Ginny gripped her by the two shoulders, and turned so they were facing each other. "Maire, look at me."

But she wouldn't. She covered her face with her two hands, and she sobbed. She collapsed her body all into Ginny then, and Ginny mothered her.

"Oh, my brave girl," Ginny said, "this is not your fault. Do you hear me?"

Behind them, Poppy's eyes widened, rimmed with tears.

"Mammy, why is Maire crying? Why're you crying, Maire?" Poppy said.

"Because she's sad, *mo chuisle*," Ginny answered.

"But Maire never cries."

Ginny nodded. "I know, love. How's the baby? What do you think of your baby brother?"

"He's gorgeous, Mammy. Look! He's sucking my finger! Look at his little gums, Mammy!"

Maire's cries were growing soft and measured now. Ginny pulled her daughter's hands away from her face, and they knelt together in front of the fire, their knees touching. Ginny lifted her apron to dry her daughter's face, and Maire shuddered in front of her. Maire shook her head.

"Everything was working so well," she whispered, and Ginny could hear the choked grief in her voice. "We did everything. Did you see the field? The crop? Michael was so steady and smart. You'd have been so proud of us. And then this . . ."

She leaned over again, the hands over her face. She dropped her head into her mammy's lap, and she wailed. It was the sort of cry Ginny hadn't heard out of her daughter since she was a baby, and it split her right open. Her grief now was for her daughter, what had she done to her daughter? God above.

"It's all right, Maire," Poppy was saying, while she tickled Raymond's chin. "When Michael gets born again, he can go back in Mammy's belly, and then he'll be a baby."

"Do you know any songs you can sing for little Raymond?" Ginny asked, and Poppy went off dutifully on a lilting tune.

Ginny leaned over Maire and rubbed her back.

"I'm so proud of you, Maire. This doesn't change any of that. There was nothing you could have done. Father Brennan said it was famine fever."

Maire sat up again, from Ginny's lap, and she wiped at her damp cheeks. She looked over at Poppy and the baby, and she tried to collect herself. She breathed deep.

"But why *now*?" she said. "When we were almost through it? You could've come home—do you see that crop out there? Daddy could've come home." She looked up at the ceiling and breathed deep, back into her shoulders.

"Here," Ginny said, standing up, and helping Maire to her feet. She put her arms around her daughter, and held her close. Maire was nearly as tall as her. "Come and meet your new brother."

Maire stepped slowly across the room, and looked down at the baby. She went down on her knee beside Poppy and touched his nose.

"Isn't he lovely?" Poppy said. "He likes me best." And then loudly, "I'm your big sister."

Maire laughed softly through her tears.

Chapter Fifteen

I order burritos on Myrtle Avenue, and while I'm waiting for them, I flip through my online recipe box, looking for some vegan cookies I can make for Jade. I asked her to come over when Leo leaves for work around three. It's a really warm day, for October, so maybe we can sit outside in the backyard and drink lemonade and eat vegan cookies while the babies hang out on a blanket together. Maybe it will be relaxing and enjoyable, like my ridiculous prenatal fantasy of what motherhood was going to be like.

The vegan snickerdoodles look good. Not really. I mean, how good can a cookie look without eggs or butter? But I want to be optimistic. I'm willing to try. I pay for the burritos and then stop at the market on the way home to purchase something called "Earth Balance," which I'm supposed to use instead of butter, and then some fake-egg stuff. If I'm nonjudgmental, maybe they will be delicious. I also buy Fritos, which—*guess what!*—are arguably vegan, even though I would never serve Fritos to a guest, vegan or otherwise. I can hardly fathom eating them myself. But they're in my basket, and I grab peanut butter, too (also potentially vegan). And then butt paste for Emma. And condoms, because eventually I'm going to have to do it with Leo again, and if I get pregnant again right now, I will probably die. This is, without question, the strangest combination of items I have ever purchased at one time.

I dump everything onto the counter beside the cash register, and await the rampant judgmentalism of the cashier, but it turns out she's far too bored to judge me. I lug everything home, the heavy plastic bags cutting their marks into my fingers. Leo's waiting and he's hungry.

"Oh hey," he says, "burritos." But he says it like, *Oh hey, head lice.*

"Yeah, it was just quick. It was on the way."

I try not to sound defensive, but I'm wearing maternity pants again, and one of those awful Empire-waist tops that the woman at Motherhood Maternity convinced me were flattering. That kind of outfit would make any woman combative.

Leo takes the burritos in to the coffee table in the living room. Emma is cooing beside him on the floor, and something else: she is staring at her hands. She is studying them as they flutter and swoop through the air above her.

"Hey, look at that," I say.

Leo is busy, unhappily unwrapping the burritos. "What's that?"

"Emma," I say, "she's watching her hands."

"Hey!" Leo abandons the burritos and goes down on his knees beside her. "What do you see?"

While he's distracted, I stuff the bag with the condoms, Fritos, and peanut butter down deep in the pot drawer. Then I cover it with a loose lid, just in case.

"What else'd you get?" he asks.

"Just, you know," I say. "The butt paste and stuff."

"Cool."

"Yeah."

"And how'd it go with Dr. Zimmer?"

His voice is careful, but the question is loaded. He wants to ask about the pills, if she gave me a prescription. I sigh, and take two glasses down from the cabinet. Ice cubes. Seltzer. I watch the glasses fizz up, and then I join my small family in our living room.

"You seem like you're feeling better," he tries again.

I shrug. "I just had a bad morning. It was nice to go in and talk to her, though. It was good."

"Well, good, then," he says, and puts an arm around me, leans in to kiss the side of my head.

I wait a moment to make sure he's not going to ask, and he's not. He's leaning toward his burrito again. He folds back the foil and takes a bite.

"Do we have any sour cream?" he asks.

"I got a prescription," I say, and then point to the burrito bag. "Check the bag, they usually throw some in."

He pauses in his chewing, leans his hand into the bag on the floor, and returns with two small plastic cups of sour cream with little lids on them. One more dip into the bag produces a plastic knife.

"Okay," he finally says.

"She said that everything I'm going through is totally normal, but that the drugs could still help, just temporarily. Just to balance out my chemistry a little bit until things get back on track."

Leo has popped the lid on one of the sour creams, and is smearing it on his burrito. He nods. "So basically what you're saying is that I was so spot-on, I'm practically a mental health professional."

"Yes, that's exactly what I'm saying."

"That will be three hundred dollars, please," he says, taking a huge bite of the burrito. Emma is kicking her little heels into the yoga mat beneath her. She's doing calisthenics. "But seriously, that's great," he says with his mouth full. "How do you feel about it? Are you okay with it?"

"I don't know, no. Not really." I unzip my boots and kick my feet up onto the coffee table next to my untouched burrito. "I mean, I got it filled. I stopped on the way home and went to the pharmacy, and I have the pills in my diaper bag, but I'm just. I don't know. I don't want to take them. Especially while I'm breast-feeding Emma. I mean who knows how that stuff might really affect the baby?"

"Fair enough," Leo says. "I'm sure the doctor wouldn't prescribe them if there was any risk to the baby, but one step at a time. At least you have them now, and you can think it over. Maybe you'll change your mind."

I reach for my burrito. "Maybe. Any sour cream left?"

He hands me the second little cup, and I pop the lid. We watch Emma like she's an expensive matinee, and eat the rest of our burritos in silence.

After lunch, Emma naps while Leo showers, so I start on the vegan cookies. I plug in my perky pink KitchenAid mixer, and start measuring out the ingredients. The Earth Balance stuff seems all right, but the fake egg shit totally freaks me out. It's a *powder*. That you add water to until it "foams up." I wonder if Jade will be able to tell if I put real eggs in the vegan cookies. Will she break out in hives or something?

"Fuck it," I say, but I'm only bluffing. I dump the fake egg powder bullshit into the mixer.

By the time Leo comes down from his shower, the cookies are in the oven, and they don't smell terrible. Neither does my husband. I'm at the sink, with my hands submerged in the hot, sudsy water. He stands behind me and his skin is damp, and I can smell his aftershave. I feel the clean shave of his cheek against mine.

"I love you, Majella."

I turn to him, but don't remove my hands from the water. "I love you, too."

"Prepare yourself, woman, because I intend to do incredibly sexy things to you when I get home from work tonight."

I laugh.

"You laugh," he says, "but that laugh will not save you."

I take my dripping hands from the water and flick them at his face, but that does not deter him either. He kisses me. Open-mouthed and everything. And the strangest thing happens: I *like* it. We make out by the sink for two full minutes like some horny teenagers deep in the stacks at the school library. He even goes up my shirt, over the bra. It's so exciting. And then my boob starts to drip milk.

"Gross," I say. Leo tries to keep kissing me, but it's over. "That is so not hot," I say.

He adjusts his jeans. "I beg to differ."

"Take it easy there, cowboy," I say, and I turn back to the dishes, plunge my hands in. The water is lukewarm.

"This is not over," he says, and he kisses my neck one last time. "I have to go do some damn work now. I must cook for the hungry city! But I will be back. And you will be mine."

When he's gone, Emma is still sleeping, so I retrieve the clandestine shopping bag from the pot drawer and place the Fritos and peanut butter on the counter. I take the condoms up to the bedroom, stash them in my nightstand drawer, and grab the diary. Then I take it, along with the monitor, Fritos, and peanut butter, into the office and sit down at the desk. My diaper bag is there on the floor, beside the desk, and the top of my paper prescription bag is peeking out. I lift the bag out, rip it open. The little orange bottle of pills falls out into my hand, and it's covered with stickers. *May cause drowsiness* on green. *Do not drive or operate machinery until you know how this drug affects you* on yellow. *Dizziness may occur* on pink.

I open up Google and type in *breast-feeding Ativan*, but then I don't even bother to click on any of the results, because I'm not taking these pills. I slap the bottle down on the desk, and I like the sound it makes, the crashing rattle. I google *genealogy Virginia Doyle* instead. There are something like ten million results, so I start clicking through. Right away I realize I need to find out her birth date before I can go any further. It's the only way to narrow down the information.

The orange prescription bottle is distracting me, so I open the desk drawer and toss it inside. *Rattle crash*, in among the pens and the stamps. I don't know what I expect to find on the Internet that will tell me more about Ginny Doyle than her own diary. But maybe there's something. Maybe there's a newspaper article from Ireland about the murder. But no. Because I guess if she got caught, she would have gone to jail, right? She wouldn't have ended up in New York then, surely, having more unsuspecting babies to infect with her crazy DNA.

I shudder. Maybe I'm being unfair. Maybe she wasn't as awful as she seems, in the diary. If there is some other, softer, more forgivable explanation for what she did . . . I don't know, then maybe redemption is possible.

The phone rings and it startles me. I glance at the caller ID. It's Mom, so I weigh my options carefully. I don't know how long I have before Emma wakes up, before my cookies are ready. Mom tends to be a little long-winded when she's the one who initiates the call. It's better if I call her and catch her off guard. Do I really want to hear about her neighbor's nephew's backpacking trip around Argentina? I pick it up.

"Hi, Mom."

"Majella!" She always sounds surprised to hear my voice, even when she calls me. It makes me wonder if she dialed me by mistake, if she was one button off on her speed dial. "How are you, how's everything?" she says, but before I can answer, she says, "You wouldn't believe the weather we're having down here—it's gorgeous! You wouldn't even know it's October. What's it like up there? Vera said it was warm."

"Oh, you were talking to Mrs. Wimmer?"

"Yeah, well, she had an operation on her knee last week, and I just called to see how her recovery was going, and I guess she's not doing too well. She's in a lot of pain, and the doctor said she has a contusion. . . ."

I tune her out, go back to clicking through the millions of Virginia Doyles, but I can't really concentrate on my research while Mom is talking. I open the drawer and look at the pill bottle. Talking to my mom on the phone makes me really consider taking the Ativan. Maybe it wouldn't be so bad, to stop feeling. Maybe it won't poison Emma's food supply. I slam the drawer, and make the decision to interrupt.

"Hey, Mom, I don't have much time, I'm having a friend over."

"Friend? Who's that, honey?"

"Just this new girl I met around the neighborhood. This girl Jade."

"Oh, that's nice," she says. She doesn't ask where we met, or how. She doesn't ask if she has children. She doesn't ask anything.

"Yeah. So she's coming over in like a half an hour, and I probably need to get cleaned up and stuff."

For a crazy half a second, I consider telling Mom that Jade is the woman from channel C, that she has twin babies, that she might have serious postpartum depression, that I am struggling, too, that I am seeing a therapist, that I have a bottle of Ativan in my desk drawer. And then I imagine her sitting in the clubhouse with her friends around a table of chef salads and gossip and carefully coiffed heads. She's telling them everything. And then she tells the butcher, the postal carrier, the stock clerk at the grocery store. *My daughter's on Ativan and she's breast-feeding. Can you believe that?* I shake my head. But maybe there is something else I can tell her instead, something real. Something that might pique her interest enough that she'll listen.

"Hey Mom, I meant to tell you, though, you know that diary I told you about, Ginny Doyle's diary?"

"Yeah, oh—I have some information on her, I've been doing some digging."

"Great," I say, "but listen to this, Mom: she killed someone."

"She *what*?"

"Yeah, I know. It's true."

"Well, wherever did you hear that?"

"It's right in her diary." My mother is outstandingly silent. "She wrote about it. She killed this woman right before she left Ireland to come here, and she did it in front of her daughter. I guess it really haunted her because she seems totally obsessed with it, in the diary. It seems like she feels terrible about it, but it was awful, and super violent."

"Well." One word, from my mother—an unprecedented one-word response. I think she might even be speechless. This is the best thing that has ever happened to me.

"I know, it's amazing, right?"

"It's awful," she finally musters. "Majella, she was my grand-mother's grandmother."

Shit, that's even worse than I expected. "Your mom's mom or your dad's?" I ask, as if this can save me.

"Mom's."

Double shit. A direct maternal line.

"Her daughter Maire was my great-grandmother," she says.

"Maire, yeah," I say, "that's the name in the diary, her daugh-ter's name. She witnessed the murder."

"Oh." My mother sounds flustered, deflated. I don't think I actually like this new, wordless mom. "Maybe it was a misunder-standing?" she tries. "Maybe you misunderstood what you read?"

"I don't think so, Mom, it was pretty clear." But she seems so disappointed and sad that I don't want to push it. "But who knows, right? I mean it was like a hundred-and-sixty-something years ago."

"Do you have the diary there?" she asks. "Would you read it to me?"

I'm reluctant, because reading it once was awful enough. But I do it, because my mother is asking to *listen* to me, and it is the first time in my life I can remember that happening. I read: the crunching, the blackthorn tree, the hurley bat, the baby falling, the daughter's windy voice, the pale blue china, the dead woman's hair. My voice shakes and my mother is silent, listening. When I'm finished, I can hear the electric hum of Emma's monitor on the desk. That's how quiet my mother is. I can smell the vegan snick-erdoodles, browning in the oven.

"God, that's appalling," she finally says.

"Yeah."

"But, you know, maybe it's just, maybe there's more to it than what you can read on the page."

"I mean it seems like there must be," I agree.

"Why would she *do* such a thing? How could anyone do such a wicked, violent thing?"

"And in front of her kids," I say. "I feel like that's almost the worst part. I mean, it sounds like the woman was holding the baby when Ginny Doyle struck her."

"Horrible," Mom says. "Read that part again, about the baby."

I flip back to the previous page, to where the entry began, and I read, "*The baby nearly falls with her, but I catch him, I catch him, by one dangling arm. Her eyes and her mouth stay open, and Maire's eyes, too, wide open at my back. Her voice is windy. She calls me mammy.*'"

Mom makes a disgusted sound. "Just imagine, that girl was my great-grandmother. She watched her mother commit murder. The poor girl."

"I know," I say, and I feel sort of sick to my stomach. That burrito is sitting in there like a rock.

"Still, I guess every family tree has at least one crooked branch, right?" Mom says, determined to return to her usual, dogged flippancy.

"I guess so," I concede. "But you said you found some other stuff about the mother, right? About Ginny Doyle?"

"Yes, there's quite a bit about her, and her children," she says.

"Do you know what year she was born?"

"Let me pull up my records," she says, and I hear her desk chair scrunch beneath her as she sits. "I already have the file open. I was just looking at it this morning."

I open the desk drawer and reach past the Ativan to pull out our scratch pad and a pencil.

"Eighteen seventeen, she was born, in the parish of Doon, in the County of Mayo. She was an only child," Mom says, "which was very unusual in those days. And she died in New York City in 1904."

"So that made her what, about eighty-seven?" I ask.

"Something like that," Mom says. "A ripe old age for a murderess."

"And what about her daughter Maire, your great-grandmother? Did you ever meet her?"

"No, she died before I was born."

There is some new and unfamiliar quality to my mother's voice. It might be thoughtfulness. Or self-reflection—that would certainly be new. Maybe she's wondering about the genetic line of disappointment. Perhaps she feels it, too, that we have all let each other down. That she hasn't been the mother I've wanted her to be. Maybe she understands my terror, in this moment, that I will disappoint my baby, that I am disappointing her even now. Maybe she's thinking about descending from Ginny Doyle, what it means to be the direct lineage of a vicious murderess. The oven timer begins to beep. The vegan snickerdoodles are ready, but I ignore it. I want to share this quiet moment with my mom. If she were here, I might hug her. But her other line beeps in.

"I'd better run," she says.

"Yeah, cool, Jade's on her way, anyway," I say, but she has already hung up.

I take the vegan cookies from the oven, and scrape them onto a cooling rack. *Scrape* is the right word, because they have the texture of thick tar on a hot day: pliable, but just barely. I sniff them suspiciously. Then I break one in half and wait for it to cool. I blow on it. And taste. It is not the most disgusting thing I have ever put in my mouth. It tastes like cinnamon and sugar, and beneath that, I don't know. The fake, powdered egg. Yuck. I throw the rest of it in the garbage, but save the others. Maybe Jade will be used to that nondescript chewy-chalkiness. Yes, it manages to be chewy and chalky both. I shake my head and return to the office. I'm still full from the burrito anyway.

I need to clean myself up, change my milk-stained top, and put on some lip gloss, maybe some blush. I go back to the office for the monitor, and that's when I remember the sneaky snacks I bought. There they are, waiting for me. Quiet. Obedient. I know they will be exactly what I expect them to be.

I twist the lid off the peanut butter and peel up its inner seal. Oh, the smell of a fresh-cracked jar of peanut butter! My heart soars. Then I grip the Fritos bag right at the top, and pull it open. The metallic bag squeaks beneath my fingers, and I breathe deeply, oh the fried and salted glory! I reach in and grab the first chip, dunk it deep into the waiting peanut butter. I rupture the smooth, inviting skin of that Jif without remorse. I am committing food pornography.

My inner foodie is aghast, ashamed, alarmed. I am a fraud. The last article I turned in to *Gourmet* before my maternity leave was about how best to achieve balance using fig in your holiday meals. Fig! People used to remark to me that it was curious and impressive, the way many food writers tend to be rather slim. "It's all about the palate," I would respond obnoxiously. "You just train yourself to enjoy the healthy foods, and eventually that's what you crave."

Fritos and peanut butter. Oh holy God in heaven. I close my eyes, and I crunch, and I chew, and I moan. I eradicate the memory of that vegan snickerdoodle, entirely, from my taste buds. My life has always been Fritos and peanut butter, Fritos and peanut butter. It is so, so good. I dip another one, and chew. And then another. Then I eat two at once; I make a sandwich out of them with that smear of depraved peanut butter in the middle.

I stand at my desk and do this. I don't even sit down. I eat and I eat until the waistband on my maternity jeans begins to feel somewhat compromised, until all the Fritos are gone. When the bag is empty, I tip it up, and deliver its unholy crumbs onto my waiting tongue. My fingers are covered in salty Frito grease, and I lick every one of them, until all that remains is the thoroughly assaulted jar of Jif. It is ridged and striped with the hostile craters of my attack. I collapse into my desk chair, and it rolls a few inches beneath my weight.

"Oh my God, that was so good," I say out loud. I tip my head back and close my eyes.

I don't wake up until the doorbell rings. Shit! Jade is here. I meant to get up, to wash, to do something with my hair. I spring up from the rolling desk chair, and I'm itchy from where some of the Frito crumbs have fallen down my cleavage and lodged themselves disgustingly inside my nursing bra. I unsnap the top hooks quickly, and brush at my boobs beneath to liberate the crumbs. I smooth my hands over my hair as I run for the front door.

Jade is outside with a baby on each hip. She is swinging like a human seesaw. Both babies are gummy, smiling.

"Hi!" I say manically. I wonder if I have peanut butter on me anywhere, so I brush one hand across my mouth and chin.

"Hi," Jade says. She has her low-maintenance canvas diaper bag hanging from one shoulder.

"Can I help you?" I reach for one of the babies, the closer one. Madeline, I think.

"Sure," she says, and she shrugs the baby off easily. There is no hesitation, no tormented deliberation. The baby reaches her chubby hands toward me, and I heft her into my arms. She is so heavy, so substantial, compared to Emma.

"Come in." I back away from the door, and Jade comes into my house. I close the door behind her. "The baby's asleep, but she'll be up any minute," I say. She is following me down the long front hallway, past the stairway, and toward the kitchen. "I fell asleep, too," I say, mostly because I want her to know why I'm so disheveled. "I meant to get cleaned up, change my top. Next thing I knew, the doorbell was ringing!" I laugh, but Jade seems concerned.

"Are we early?"

I glance at the clock on the stove. "No, no. We said threeish. It's almost three fifteen." The poor girl has only been in my house for thirty seconds, and I've already made her feel uncomfortable. This is hopeless. "No, it wasn't you at all," I try again. "I'm just so *tired*. This newborn thing, you know? We're still up with Emma two or three times a night." I yawn. "Tell me it gets easier."

She stares at me without answering.

"So hey, can I get you a drink?" I ask. "Seltzer, Diet Coke, coffee? I might make lemonade."

"Coffee's good," she says. "Thanks."

She holds Max on her hip and examines the kitchen with naked admiration. She bends to gaze into the glass doors of the Sub-Zero. "That is one fancy fridge," she says.

"Yeah, we're into food," I say. "My husband's a chef."

"You said that."

I remember telling her that I was a food writer, but I guess I was bragging about Leo, too. I can't remember. My brain is so slushy these days. I fit a filter into the coffeemaker and dump the grounds in on top, fill up the tank with water. I can do all of it with one hand, because Madeline clings on to me like a monkey. Her limbs are lithe and strong, and I barely have to hold her. She's so easy. The coffeemaker begins to gurgle at once, and Madeline laughs at it. She claps her hands. Jade steps to the living room door and peers in.

"We're renovating," I explain. "We've really only finished the kitchen, so far."

"Yeah," she says, stepping through to the living room. "Is this whole place yours? The whole house? Or it's a two-family?"

"No, it's all ours."

"Cool. Nice to have so much space." I feel like she's casing the joint. I've never seen anybody so unself-conscious about checking out someone else's stuff. Oh. I left the empty Fritos bag and the peanut butter on the desk in plain view, just through the open doors to the office.

"Yeah, it needs a lot of work, but we'll get there," I say, sweeping into the room and closing the office doors, hiding my paraphernalia inside. "It's got great bones, this house. I grew up here, actually."

"What, like in this actual house?"

"Yeah, it was my parents' house. Leo and I bought it from them last year, when we found out I was expecting. They were moving to Florida anyway, so we moved in."

"Wow."

"Yeah."

I flick the yoga mat out on the floor, lay one of Emma's blankets on top of it for the babies. We really have to get the wood floor installed, and an area rug.

"Living in the childhood home," Jade says ominously.

"Yeah."

"Cool," she says, but that is definitely not what she means.

I am so relieved to hear Emma cry out on the monitor.

"She's up!" I say. "Back in a minute."

Chapter Sixteen

IRELAND, JUNE 1847

When Michael was two years of age, before Maggie and Poppy came along, Ginny gave birth to a little boy who was unwell from the very start. He just wasn't right. He came a few weeks early, and was quite small, had trouble getting a proper breath into him. Raymond and his brother, Kevin, took the baby straightaway to the church, when he was only a few hours old, where Father Brennan christened him in great haste. They called him Thomas, and they expected he wouldn't live to see the light of his first dawn. But he did, he survived. He ate little, but he fought so doggedly that Ginny allowed herself the terrible comfort of hope. And with each morning that she awakened to find him squirming and struggling—growing stronger, she thought— beside her, that crazy hope flourished. Until the morning of his ninth day, when he finally grew still in her arms. And he died.

Ginny remembered the howling depth of her grief and despair. Her rage was such that not even young Michael could comfort her. He, who'd been her baby only two weeks before, seemed suddenly garish after the death of his tiny brother, a big and clumsy boor of a child who squealed and crashed around the cottage, oblivious to his mother's anguish.

They waked Thomas in the house, as was their custom. Raymond brought in enough *poitín* for the whole of the parish, and it was a good thing, too, because they all came. Every man, woman, and child in Knockbooley came to the Doyles' door to console them. But it was difficult all the same, to manage the festive mood of a proper wake, because there was so little of Tommy's life to celebrate. Nine days. There was no one, really, to grieve the loss of him, only Ginny, and then Raymond. The women of the parish did their best, though. They keened for him. And when they brought in the tiny coffin, Ginny was horrorstruck by the sight of it.

She went down on her knees and begged God to take the pain away from her, to take her along with her child into the grave. She remembered thinking that no matter what life held in store for her after that, she would never see a day worse than that one. She was wrong.

Michael was laid out on his parents' bed in the sleeping room. He was the only one of Ginny's children who seemed not to have grown while she was away. He looked pale and tiny on the bed. His skin had an awful grayish hue to it, and his lips were blue and parted. His eyes were still open because Maire had no copper farthings to place on his eyelids for to close them. Ginny fell down on the bed beside him and swept him up in her arms. His frail body was not yet cold. His limbs were still loose, his little fingers soft and pliable. She could nearly breathe life back into him, that's how recent he was. Ginny's child.

Maggie stood beside the bed and watched her mother weep. Ginny tried to do her crying quietly, so's not to frighten Poppy in the next room. But the tears came up from her rib cage, from her bones. And soon all her face was wet with them, and they were running through Michael's hair and down his fragile white arms. Maggie stepped in to her mother quite forcefully then, and took her hand. And Ginny was suddenly overcome by the sense that she had come very close to floating away, that she'd been in danger of actually disappearing until Maggie took her hand and saved her. Tethered her. Maggie gripped her little hand around Ginny's knuckles and she squeezed. So that after some time, after some awful storm of dark and bottomless minutes, Ginny was able to lay Michael's lifeless body back onto the bed. She was able to arrange him tenderly, reverently, the way Maire had done before her. And then she was able to gather up Maggie and hold her instead. Gorgeous little Maggie, all grave and warm and full of suffering. Sweet Maggie of the cairns.

Ginny heard Seán and Father Brennan coming in by the outside door, and without setting Maggie down, she rose to greet them. Maggie was nearly too big for it, but she clung her legs round Ginny's hips, her little arms knotted tightly around her mother's neck. Ginny wanted never to let go of her again. She didn't bother wiping the tears from her face. Why should she? She didn't look back at Michael on the bed as she stepped into the main room of the cottage, but she didn't have to, because she had memorized him—the sight of him, the way he looked there, laid out on the bed. The smell of him gone, faintly sweet and sick. The soft rumple of his hair beneath her fingers. Those memories would never leave Ginny, not for a moment, not for the rest of her days.

Maire was standing with baby Raymond in her arms, and the room was cast in the cheerful glow of the turf fire. Poppy was hanging round her big sister's skirts, and Ginny was struck then, by how tall Maire had got, the high grace of her, her long neck.

The way Poppy hid beneath her skirts, Maire could nearly be her mother. If Ginny hadn't been so laden with misery, she might have gasped.

"Poppy, come here, sit down by the fire," Maire was saying, and Poppy obeyed, crossed her little legs beneath her, and waited faithfully for Maire to place baby Raymond in her arms.

Poppy took the weight of her brother happily, and rocked him on her knee like he was a baby doll. Maire dipped a cup into the water pail for to offer the guests a drink.

"We'll need to make arrangements for the burial," Father Brennan was saying.

But Ginny's child was still warm in the bed beyond. Her hand flew uselessly to her breast. Of course, the burial.

"Tomorrow?" he asked.

So soon. She wasn't ready. Her eyes flashed to Maire, who spoke up.

"We'll need one more day at least, Father," Maire said. "For to wake him properly."

"You needn't go to all that ritual in these times, Maire," he said softly. "You know that no one will come."

Maire threw another sod of turf on the fire. "Move back a small bit, Poppy," she said, and then to Father Brennan, "All the same, Father, the custom might be a comfort. For my mam."

And Ginny felt that they had traded places for a moment. Maire was mothering her. How entirely had Ginny failed her daughter, that she felt the need to do this, that Maire knew her mother was incapable?

Ginny found her voice, and with tremendous effort and the help of God, it sounded strong, deliberate. "She's right, Father. Give us a day to wake him. What day is it, today? Tuesday?"

"Wednesday," Seán said.

Ginny crossed the room and set Maggie down on the floor

beside Poppy and their baby brother. Maggie leaned over the two of them, reached out and touched Raymond's head. "So we'll bring him Friday morning, Father," Ginny said.

"Grand."

"I suppose we'll need to arrange for a coffin," Ginny said, and she remembered the horror of that other small coffin in years gone by.

"I'll take care of that for ye," Seán said.

Ginny nodded.

"Did he get the last rites?" Ginny asked.

"He did," Father said. "Just."

They had managed to get Father Brennan here in time, but not his mother, not his father. Dear God, why had Ginny listened to Roisin, instead of her own instinct? She would never forgive herself for that, for not being here.

"Were you here in the end?" The strength in Ginny's voice was faltering, and a strangled note of hysteria was creeping in. She swallowed it.

"I was, Ginny," Father said.

"Did he . . ." She blinked. She tried to breathe, but her lungs were immovable, concrete. Father Brennan was shaking his head.

"It was very peaceful," he reassured her. "He slept into it." He'd said that already. She wanted more. She turned to Maire.

"Did he ask for me?" she said.

"He did before," Maire said. "In the night, last night, when Seán was here. But he was all right, Mammy."

Ginny couldn't stop the tears then. Maire crossed the room to her mother, and she spoke quietly into her ear.

"He thought you were here, Mammy, in the end," Maire said. "With the fever, when it got bad . . . he thought I was you. I held him in the bed. Until he slept."

Ginny took Maire's face in her hands then, and they leaned

their foreheads together—Maire was tall enough Ginny could do that now. She leaned down to her daughter, and she closed her eyes. "Thank you," she whispered. Maire took her mother's hands in her own and held them tight, but she did not cry.

After a moment, baby Raymond grew fussy, and Poppy started singing loudly to him. Maggie was stone-faced beside them. Ginny went over and lifted Raymond from Poppy's knee.

"He's all right, Mammy!" she said. "I have him."

"It's all right, love. He's hungry," Ginny said. "I think Mammy needs to feed him."

Her face fell. "Why can't I feed him?" Poppy said, and she lifted her shirtwaist to try and locate her breast. She poked uncertainly at her belly button instead.

Ginny pulled the shirt back down over Poppy's tummy. "We'll talk about that later," she said, kissing the top of her daughter's head. "Only mammies can feed their babies."

Ginny bounced Raymond on her shoulder, tried to comfort him with movement until Seán and Father Brennan left. They were already moving toward the door, and Ginny went out with them, into the yard. There was still plenty of light in the sky, the hopeful, lingering yellow of a summer sunset. She had one more question for Father, but she didn't know if her voice would manage it, if her body would permit the words to come.

She stopped him with her hand, and he waited, patient. She blinked carefully. Raymond wriggled on her shoulder, and she felt as if her whole body might break open, as if the words might cleave a fatal wound all through her. She heaved them out.

"Do you think . . . can we bury him in beside Tommy?"

Father Brennan nodded, and squeezed her hand. "We can of course," he said, and then he placed a warm hand on Ginny's forehead, and one on the back of Raymond's little head, and he whispered an ardent prayer over them, a balm and a shield.

Michael's wake was pitiable, wretched. In the morning, Seán brought Ginny a Belfast linen cloth, a gift from Alice Spring for the burial. Maire helped her mother spread the cloth out beside the fire in the main room, and they laid Michael out there, so that the firelight could warm the lovely contours of his face. But they had no money to provide food or drink; there was little to offer the mourners. And anyway, there were no mourners. What few neighbors were left were afraid to come into the Doyle house now, for fear of the fever.

Mrs. Fallon came, God bless her, and she looked as beleaguered as a standing-up body could be. Her hair had turned peak-white, and her skin was washed out, too, so that the only color left in her was the mournful brown of her gaping eyes. She had shriveled from her shoulders to the ground, so that you'd nearly be afraid to touch her, for fear she might crack and shatter in front of you. She keened with Ginny, she kept vigil. God, Ginny was grateful for her, for the recognition between them. What a terrible thing they had in common now: the attendant ghosts of their children.

Maire stayed with the grieving mothers while they keened, but Maggie and Poppy spent most of that day out of doors, away from the sorrowful rituals they didn't understand. Baby Raymond's needy rhythm kept his mother going. He needed feeding, he needed changing and mothering; that didn't stop just because Ginny had lost her son. She had to keep going. They all did.

The next day, on the twenty-sixth of June, 1847, Ginny Doyle buried her son in the church graveyard in Knockbooley, in the same grave his baby brother had gone into eight years before. His father wasn't there to mark the day. His neighbors and friends didn't gather to see him off with song and drink and the memory of laughter. It was just his sisters and new brother, and his mother,

Ginny, stood lonesome and hollow by the fresh, damp soil of his gaping grave.

Father Brennan spoke solemnly, but Ginny couldn't hear the words that came out of his mouth, couldn't make any sense of them. Maire was courageous and solid. She held Raymond, and her nose was red, her eyes puffy. But she never let go a tear. Maggie held on to her mother's hand, and she wailed and cried when they threw the dirt in over his coffin, and Ginny did, too, God help her. Poppy stood somber and quiet, clinging on to her mother's hand. In her innocence, she wanted to know why Michael was in the box, and how he would get out again when he wakened up.

For her part, Ginny couldn't believe that no one was there, no one came. Their parish had emptied of its people. They had all starved or fled. Ginny and her children were alone.

"Be grateful you were able to bury him," Father Brennan said to her. And those seemed like the emptiest, most abhorrent possible words he could offer a devastated mother.

"Is that meant to be a comfort, Father?" Ginny said incredulously. She tried to keep the anger out of her voice.

"I only mean to say that, in times of atrocity like these, a proper Christian burial is a blessing," Father Brennan said. "James Madigan walked all the way here only last month, so weak from the hunger he could barely stand upright, and he carrying the last two of his children dead in his arms, and he struggling all that way for to see them buried. He died when he reached this gate, Ginny. I had to bury the three of them together, and not a soul left to mourn their passing."

Ginny glanced at Maire beside her. Only a few months past, she would've shielded her daughter fiercely from a story like that. She would've distracted her and hurried away. Now Maire didn't even blink. She crossed herself.

"God rest them," Maire said. "I'll say a prayer for them, Father."

"Do."

And then Ginny remembered, with a start: walking the road into Westport town all those months ago with Ray and the children, when the blight had first struck, when things already seemed dire and frightening. Little had they known how much worse it would get. They had seen James Madigan that day, met him on the road outside his farm, sitting up on the stile beside his ruined field, wringing his hands in terror. Grieving already for the children he knew he would lose. Ginny *had* tried to shield Maire, on that other day, from the poor man's passionate dread.

In the churchyard now, Ginny crossed herself as well.

"I don't expect that to be a comfort to you, no," Father Brennan said kindly. "Of course not, Ginny. Only God can do that for you, and He will. In time."

Ginny didn't believe him, not in the slightest. The only comfort to her now would be her own death, and even that would mean abandoning her children again. So there was no possibility of comfort, never again. Ginny tried to lift breath into her breast, but she only shuddered.

"I suppose we should write to Kevin again," she whispered. She tried not to imagine Raymond, sitting at a table in some faraway New York City tenement room with his brother, Kevin. Some neighbor or priest reading the letter out to them. She tried not to picture Raymond's face.

"Let's give it a few days," Father Brennan suggested. "With all the upheaval in Ireland now, it's little wonder we haven't heard from your Raymond yet. I'd say his letters have gone astray, but you keep faith, and one will find its way to us soon. We can answer him then. We'll give him the news soon enough."

They walked home then, Ginny and her girls and the baby.

Ginny spent the whole of that day trying not to think of Ray. Hope was a wicked thing, and she knew she'd be better off without it. Ginny had heard stories of men fleeing to America to save their starving Irish families, only to arrive in New York and forget all about them. Some drank away their grief and their earnings. Others spent them on a new wife and children, a fresh start. Ginny knew her Raymond wasn't capable of that sort of monstrosity. She knew he was a good and honorable man, that he wasn't temptable or changeable. He loved his family. But then she remembered the willful amnesia of Springhill House, smack in the middle of the famine and wholly oblivious, and she feared that anything was possible. Perhaps New York *would* be seductive enough to make Raymond forget. Or maybe, even the revulsion of that possibility was just easier for her to imagine than the alternative.

Saturday was the first morning wakening up in the cottage without Michael, and the absence of him felt heavier and more shocking than Ginny could ever have conceived. All those weeks after Ray left, when Michael had stayed silent, hoarded his voice into himself, stolen time from Ginny—she wanted every one of those days back, every minute. She wanted to hold him and heal him and make him whole. She wanted to repair him back to the living boy he had been before that wicked blight had come into their lives, and robbed all the happiness out of his small world.

Seán came to the cottage that afternoon, and he brought a basket of food that Roisin had prepared: some fresh bread with a noggin of butter, cold boiled carrots, and a meat pie in one of Mrs. Spring's blue Wedgwood china pie plates. There was a jug of buttermilk as well. A feast, compared with what Ginny had been stealing to send to the children all these months. A glimmer of guilt pulsed through Ginny for how cruel she'd been to Roisin at the house, how she'd blamed Roisin for everything. God bless her. It wasn't her fault; Ginny had made up her own mind, after all. Roisin had only been trying to help.

Also tucked into the basket, and wrapped in a thick and perfumed lavender paper with a gray ribbon, was a gift for baby Raymond—a little book of children's verse.

"Mrs. Spring knew you were coming?" Ginny asked.

Seán nodded. "She sent me. She still doesn't know that I've been coming here all along, that I was bringing food. Or at least she hasn't asked."

"Is she not worried about the famine fever?" Ginny asked.

Seán shook his head. "She doesn't seem to put it all together."

"I suppose it was all quite shocking to her. She doesn't exactly have a rugged constitution," Ginny said.

"No," Seán agreed.

Ginny looked at the lovely cream-colored book in her hands. On the cover was a tangle of flowering vines, and a little rabbit wearing a waistcoat. Poppy touched the rabbit. She hopped on the balls of her feet and clapped her hands.

"Will you read it to us, Mammy?" Poppy said, climbing up on Ginny's knee and backing herself in against her mother.

Ginny flipped through its pages. They had never owned a book before.

"*Mo chuisle*, I can't read it," Ginny said. "Maybe we can ask Father Brennan when he comes again. But we can look at the pictures and make up our own rhymes, right?"

"All right." Poppy tried not to sound disappointed.

"I can read it to you," Seán said.

Maire was brushing the ashes from the hearth, and she stopped to raise her eyebrows.

"Fancy," she said, and Seán laughed.

"Hardly," he answered. "Just lucky."

"Indeed," Ginny said, and Seán sat down on the stool beside them, where she handed him the book. Poppy didn't climb up on his knee, but she did stand, enthralled, by his elbow, while he read, and every now and again, she interrupted.

"Is that one there Hector?" she would ask, pointing to one of the frogs.

"This one, with the blue hat," Seán would answer. "I think that one with the red bow is Millicent."

He read the whole book to her, and when Maire was finished cleaning, she joined them. Maggie sat beside the fire and pretended not to listen. Ginny lifted Raymond from his cradle, and brought him into the sleeping room to feed him. In the privacy and quiet, she allowed herself a lurching of simple tears while Raymond suckled. She dried her face after, but her eyes were still swollen when she came out again. Seán was preparing to go.

"Thank you for bringing the food," Ginny said, walking him out to the yard. "Hopefully we won't need your help much longer. The crop seems to be coming good."

"Thanks be to God," Seán answered. "There were reports again in Westport this morning that the blight is spreading rapidly. People are beginning to panic."

The two of them stepped out toward her strong, flowering plants. It was late June. The turnips and early potatoes would both be ready for harvest soon, in the next weeks, and there wasn't the slightest sign of decay in the fields.

"They look grand so far," Ginny said.

"Touch wood," Seán replied. He fixed the bit in his horse's mouth, but before he climbed up, he turned to her. "There's something else."

Inside the cottage, Ginny could hear Poppy singing to her baby brother. She shivered, and folded her arms across her chest.

"Mrs. Spring is leaving," Seán said.

Ginny's mind wheeled. "Leaving how?" she said. "Back to London?"

He shook his head. "New York."

Ginny's mouth might've fallen open, but she didn't know how to respond at all.

"Apparently, her husband has taken a temporary appointment there, and he sent for her to join him."

Ginny's stomach roiled. "New York," she whispered. "I thought . . . I mean Roisin always thought their marriage was finished, that he would never send for her."

Seán shrugged. "I suppose even a bastard like Stuart Spring has some well-emaciated sense of duty. I think Murdoch's been pressuring him to get her out of here, telling him how bad things have got, and that they might get even worse again now that it looks like the blight is returning. Murdoch doesn't want to mind her anymore, but Spring doesn't want her back in London either. He probably has another woman there now, and he wants to keep wifey out of the way. So when he got the post in New York, I guess he saw a chance to get her out of Ireland without having to compromise his freedom, his new life in London without her."

"So you think he'll just set her up in New York and then abandon her there, too, whenever his business is finished?"

"Of course," Seán answered. "She's only an unwanted responsibility to him now, nothing more."

Ginny thought of Ray, and Seán's words racketed around in her head: *an unwanted responsibility.* But that couldn't be Ginny; it couldn't be her children. No.

"It's so horrible," she said, wrenching her thoughts back from her own husband to Alice Spring. "I know she's a bit touched, but she's kind, she's a kindly woman in her way. Not to mention beautiful."

"I hadn't noticed." Seán smiled. He fitted one boot into the stirrup and hoisted himself up to the saddle. The horse stood still beneath him.

"So what will happen to Springhill House?" Ginny said. "How soon is she going?"

"Murdoch is arranging for her passage. He wants to get her gone as quick as he can, in the next couple of weeks. He'll need to get her down to Cork, I'd say. I'll probably have to drive her down, myself. All the good ships sail from there. They wouldn't be great ones sailing out of Westport."

"Right," Ginny said, even though his words were rushing through her, and she couldn't grab on long enough to make sense of them.

"So they've already dispatched Katie. Roisin begged for her to be able to stay on, but Mrs. Spring refused. There's no need for her now."

Ginny gasped. "But where will Katie go? Aren't her parents dead? She's too young to be all on her own."

Seán shook his head; his face was stern.

"I don't know," he said. "Roisin is tight-lipped about it. She's in an awful state. She'll barely speak now, these last days. She'll stay on to cook for Murdoch, and keep the house, even though it will only be the two of them left in it. And then most of the grounds staff will stay. They still need to work the land."

"And what about you?"

"They won't need me anymore," he said. "I'll go when Mrs. Spring does." At those words, Ginny caught the terrible whiff of a nightmare memory in the air. The stink of something putrid and rotten.

"Go where?" she asked.

"I don't know yet," he said. "I've enough saved for my own Atlantic crossing. I might . . . I don't know. I've no land here. No prospects. Know any rich folks looking for drivers?" He laughed, but Ginny couldn't.

New York. Where Ray was. Now they were all going. The little company she'd come to rely on, the people who, over these last weeks and months, when all of the world had crumbled and decayed, had come to be her unlikely friends. They were going off across the sea now to New York, to Ray.

Ginny would miss Seán. But she should never have grown so fond of a man who was not her husband. She should never have grown so dependent on him. When she tried to breathe, it felt like water was seeping into her lungs. They walked to the top ridge, Seán on the saddle, and Ginny strolling alongside the horse, until they reached the highest point of Ginny's land together. She turned back toward the cottage then, and looked out across the dips and folds of the winnowing fields, her little home tucked snugly among them.

"Please God, let the crop come good," she said. "Let *one thing* come good in our life. We need this."

And they really did. If the potato failed again, there would be no salvation this time. On the ridge looking down over Raymond's cairn, Seán froze on his horse, cocked his head sideways as if he were listening to something in the distance. A high breeze whipped through his black hair, and he patted his horse's neck beneath him. Then he lifted his head again and took a deep breath in through his nose.

"Do you smell that, Ginny?"

Chapter Seventeen

"So how do you take your coffee?"

"Just black," Jade says, "unless you have soy milk?"

"Black it is, then," I say. "I did make vegan cookies, though. Snickerdoodles."

Jade is sitting cross-legged on the floor beside the yoga mat, but it's too small, and the twins keep rolling onto the unfinished subfloor. Emma is watching from the bouncy seat.

"Maybe we should move out back. It's beautiful out," I say, bringing a plate of the vegan cookies in to the coffee table. "And sorry about the floor. I'm not used to mobile babies, and we just haven't been in a rush to do the flooring yet, because Emma doesn't really get around much."

"Yeah, I guess not," Jade says, deadpan.

She is unimpressed by my sparkling wit.

"I'll just make some lemonade first, and we can go outside," I say.

"Cool."

I squeeze the lemons in silence. Emma is vibrating in her little bouncy seat, and Jade just sits there rolling her babies back onto the mat whenever they get near the edge. She doesn't talk to them or tickle their feet or kiss their armpits the way I do to Emma whenever she's defenseless on the yoga mat with me. She just watches them silently, rolls them away from the edge.

I have never squeezed lemons so fast in my life. I add sugar, water, ice, and some crushed mint leaves. I carry the pitcher, some glasses, and the plate of awful snickerdoodles out to the back porch, and then return to grab Emma's whole bouncy seat.

"Ready?"

"Sure," Jade says, getting to her feet.

She lifts Madeline and her mug of black coffee, but leaves Max on the floor. I frown at him.

"Hmm, guess we can't carry everything," I say, thinking that perhaps it's the mug of coffee she should leave behind.

"He'll be fine, he can't get very far," she assures me. "I'll come right back for him."

I guess there are certain risks you learn to take when you have twins.

"Okay," I say, and I lead her to the back door and down the five steps.

As soon as we're outside, I recognize the fatal flaw in my plan: there is no grass here, nowhere soft to set the babies down. Not yet, anyway. Leo and I have plans to cut back the jungle beyond the porch, but like with most things on our renovation list, we haven't gotten to it yet. Jade looks around desperately, and I cringe.

"I'm sorry," I say. "Gosh, we just haven't gotten to this stage yet, with Emma, where we need a baby-proof environment. I guess I hadn't thought . . ."

I set Emma's vibrating seat down next to my own chair at the wrought-iron table.

"It's fine, you can't expect the whole world to conform to your babies' needs," Jade says, with the grace and wisdom of Yoda. "I wouldn't have thought of it either, before they were this age. I'm only starting to baby-proof my own place. But they sit up all the time now. Until they fall over. They really need somewhere soft to land, because the falling part is inevitable."

"Well, here, let me take her, anyway," I say, because all I can think about is Max, still inside on his own. We've been out here for almost a full minute. That kid could be down the front steps and halfway to Myrtle Avenue by now. Jade hands me her baby, disappears inside, and returns after a minute with Max.

"I could run next door and get my Pack 'n Play," she says.

She is not leaving me alone with these three babies again. No way, nohow.

"Oh, we have one! You can use ours. It's still in the box. We registered for it, but haven't used it yet."

"Cool," she says, and then I realize that I'm going to have to go inside and upstairs to get it out of the hall closet. I'm going to have to leave Emma here alone with her. I take a sip of my lemonade to stall. Jade sits down at the table and balances Max on one knee. I settle Madeline on the other knee, and then I kneel down over Emma.

"Mommy will be right back!" I tell her. "Don't go anywhere!" I have the idea to pinch her while I'm down there, to make her cry, so that I can track her little voice the whole time I'm inside. And then I realize that this is probably another symptom of my crazy, so I leave it. Jade is hardly going to kidnap her, anyway. Why would she want *another* baby? And how far could she get in thirty seconds with all three of them?

As soon as I pass the kitchen door, out of Jade's line of vision,

I break into a dead run. I ignore the dull pain of my C-section scar as I take the steps two at a time. I throw open the door to the hall closet with a bang, and I haul the Pack 'n Play out onto the floor. I pry at one end of the box with my fingers, but it doesn't budge. Shit. Why is baby-product packaging so stubbornly resistant to being opened? This could take entire *minutes*. I bend down, and drag the whole box into Emma's room, where I can see out the back window into the garden. Jade is holding both babies on her lap with one arm, and sipping her hot coffee with the other. Emma is looking straight up at the window. Can she see me? I wave.

After several moments of intense cursing and sweating, I finally loosen the thick staples from the cardboard flap on one end, and the box gives way. I upend it, and the Pack 'n Play slides out onto the floor. It's fairly lightweight and tidily bundled. I lift it by the handle, and lug it quickly back downstairs. Jade hands me only one of her babies, and sets up the Pack 'n Play in approximately ten seconds. I couldn't even get the bloody thing out of the box. She is the most accomplished human being I have ever met, and that includes my cousin who was in a boy band that was huge in Poland in the nineties.

"Wow," I say.

"Yeah, it's easy once you get the hang of it. These things are great. You'll use it so much when Emma's bigger."

I don't believe her. It's like a tiny jail. She plops Max inside, and he rolls happily onto his back, and begins chewing one foot. Then Madeline goes in beside him, and starts chewing his other foot.

"Gosh, they're so good," I say. "They never cry."

Jade snorts.

"I mean just compared to Emma. She seems to cry an awful

lot. Sometimes she just goes on these crying spells, and they can last for hours, when *nothing* comforts her. It drives me insane."

Emma sighs theatrically in her bouncy seat.

"Yeah, well, who doesn't cry for hours sometimes, right?" Jade says. She leans back in her chair, and twists at a couple of the blond spikes that stick up from her scalp.

"It's hard, isn't it?" I say. "Becoming a mother? I mean, it's amazing, too, but it's so exhausting. Even with my husband, with one baby, it's exhausting. I can't imagine how you do it on your own with two of them."

Actually, I know exactly how she does it. She leaves them in their cribs for hours, and the three of them cry all day long. That's how. I look over at her babies, happy in their padded cell, and then I look at Emma, whose face has fallen, whose lip is threatening. She is squirming, her face turning that telltale magenta. Soon, she will let loose with her most impressive, most harrowing cry. The hunger cry.

"I gotta grab the Boppy," I say, and I run inside and grab the nursing pillow off the couch.

I manage to get Emma out of the seat and attached to the boob before the cry rears its ugly head, which makes me feel almost as skillful as Jade, with her Pack 'n Play magic tricks. She is staring vacantly at her babies. I have absolutely no idea what to say to her.

"You know, you're so impressive," I decide. "I hope I can make it look as easy as you, when Emma's that age."

This time she does not snort. She does not respond at all.

"I'll get the hang of it, right?" I say, and I brush the side of Emma's face, her ear, with my fingertip.

This conversation is really not leaping out of the starting gate the way I had hoped. I can't ask about the father; he's not in the picture. There's no family here. She hates her job. And then asking a new mom about her own interests seems almost cruel, a reminder of her lost life. I'm out of options. Jade sniffs, and when I look up at her, I realize with horror that she has tears in her eyes. She has turned her face as sideways as she can, to try and hide them, but it's unmistakable. She stands up from her chair in haste and turns her back to me. She leans over the Pack 'n Play, and pretends to play with the twins for a minute, but she's unable to recover herself. She crumbles.

"Hey," I say.

Yep, that's what I go with. The perennially helpful *hey*. Jade sounds a loud sniffle with an undercurrent of grunt, and then she sets about wiping her face. She knows she's been caught. "I'm sorry," she says, and when she turns back, her face is wet and red. Her cheeks are splotchy.

I shake my head. "No, no. Not at all, there's nothing to be sorry for."

She sits down on the edge of her chair, reaches into her bag, and retrieves a tissue.

"Hey, I cry like that about ten times a day," I say. "Like, for no reason at all."

She takes a deep, shuddering breath, and flumps back in her chair. She honks her nose into the tissue and rolls her blue eyes up to dry them. "I do it about ten times an *hour*," she whispers, and then she tries to laugh, but it comes out flat. "The only time I don't cry is when I'm at work. God, I can't even wear mascara anymore, because my face is all in stripes every ten minutes. It's so embarrassing."

"It's not," I say, "not at all." Even though we both know it totally is.

"Maybe we should go," she says, standing up. "We can try it again another day, when I'm feeling better. I'm just so tired. They

haven't been sleeping well the last week. I think they're teething."
And then she really disintegrates into tears. She plomps back
down in her seat, and it rocks beneath her as she cries. Max and
Madeline have stopped chewing on his feet, and have both turned
toward the sound of their mother's weeping. Their little faces are
opened right up to her.

"No, please," I say, lifting Emma off my boob and up to my
shoulder to burp her. "Please stay."

Jade blows her nose again, waves her hand in the air.

"I'm sorry," she says again.

I shake my head. "Please, stop apologizing," I say. "Here, wait
here. I want to show you something. I'll be right back."

I walk with Emma up the back steps and in through the
kitchen and living room. I fling the French doors to the office
wide open and descend the two steps. I open the desk drawer and
pull out the bottle of Ativan with my name on it. I take it outside
and set it down on the table next to Jade. She seems to have recovered herself for the moment. Her eyes are red, but her breath is
steady. She picks up the bottle. "What's this?"

"Crazy pills," I say. "I've been having a hard time, too. I've
been crying a lot. Like a lot. Just trying to adjust to being a new
mom, you know? It's sort of not what I expected. So I've been seeing a therapist, and you know. She sent me to a psychiatrist, who
gave me these pills to help."

"And do they?" Jade is studying the bottle. "Help?"

I shrug, and Emma burps loudly in my ear. I lean back in my
chair and unsnap the bra on the other side. She latches on.

"I don't know yet," I say. "I haven't decided if I'm going to
take them or not."

Jade breaks the seal on the bottle and opens it without asking
me. She tips the bottle up, shakes one little white pill out into my
hand, and then pops it in her mouth. She swallows it back with

coffee while I watch. Perhaps I should feel affronted by this, or at least surprised. But I'm not.

"I'll let you know," she says.

"Cool," I tell her.

It's quiet then, for a few minutes, but the silence is less awkward than before. She runs her hands through her hair. She rubs her face. And then she tells me this story:

"I started going to church on Sundays, right down here at Saint Pancras. I wasn't raised anything. My mom was Catholic, but she never brought me. I don't even think I was baptized. So I just started going after Paul left because Sundays were so long and empty. Mass took up an hour, and people there were nice to us, when they'd see me on my own with the two babies. And then like a month ago, I was there, and they were asking for prayers for this young couple whose five-month-old baby died. He had some awful disease, and he died, and the mother was just inconsolable. That baby was the same age as my twins. And all I could think about was finding that couple, and giving them one of my babies. Or maybe both of them, if they wanted them both."

Jade looks at me to gauge my reaction to the story, and I'm careful to keep my face plain and open.

"I don't mean that I thought about it in some theoretical, kind of abstract way," she says. "I mean I actually *considered* it. I thought about which one to give them, if I gave them just one, and I settled on Max, just because Madeline is easier." She glances over at the twins. "Cover your ears, Max," she says, and then she blows her nose again. "I don't even know what stopped me. I don't know. I could still do it. It would be so easy, to only have to worry about me again."

I don't say anything, don't press her. I just wait for her to talk it out.

"Do you think I'm a terrible person?" she finally asks.

"Not in the least," I answer honestly. "I told someone my baby died."

She laughs, and somehow that laugh does not offend me. It sounds like salvation. I laugh, too.

"You what?"

"Yep, told a guy she died," I repeat. It sounds so absurd now, with the taste of mint lemonade on my lips. "I didn't mean to. I was telling him about a dream I had, and he misunderstood, but I didn't correct him."

Jade pushes the orange pill bottle across the table at me. "I think you're going to need these," she says. And then we both laugh, and I love her more than I have ever loved another human.

When Emma is finished eating, I consider putting her in the Pack 'n Play with the twins, but they are both so big and strong, and it looks a little crowded in there. So I tuck her into my elbow instead, and she stays awake and looks at us. Jade sits back in her chair, and folds her legs beneath her. She finishes her coffee, and smiles at me. It is the first really genuine smile I have seen from her. She is beautiful.

"Mind if I grab another cup?" she says.

"Of course not, help yourself."

Jade and the babies stay all afternoon, and we talk about everything. She tells me more about deadbeat Paul, who now works as a production assistant for some shit reality show in L.A.

"That just means he fetches coffee and tampons for the trampy women who come on the show to find love while he waits to get discovered," she explains. "Pathetic."

"Discovered for what? He wants to be an actor?"

"Yeah," she says. "That's why we came to New York, really. Or that's half the reason."

"What's the other half?"

Jade shrugs, and I can sense her reluctance, but it's much fainter than it was before, and she brushes it aside. "I wanted to be a writer," she admits.

A writer! So I was right when I detected a well-concealed interest in my career yesterday. I am careful not to betray too much excitement.

"Oh?" I say coyly. "What kind of writing are you interested in?"

She shakes her head. "It's stupid."

"It's not stupid at all, what are you talking about? Why should it be stupid? Plenty of people are writers."

"Yeah, but I want to be a novelist," she says shyly. Her cheeks pinken, and she suddenly looks years younger. "I'm a huge sci-fi and fantasy buff."

"That's terrific," I say. "So have you done a lot of writing?"

"I have a finished trilogy, and I'm working on book one of the next series," she says. "But I don't know. When I first came to New York, I was temping at publishing houses, but they pay so little. And then I started temping at this law firm, and they offered me full-time, and since I was expecting, I felt like I had to take the job. But I still really want to write, and the best thing about the law firm is that I can sit at my receptionist desk and write all day. As long as I answer the phones and greet everyone who comes in, they don't care what I do. Actually, one of the partners said he loves me writing because I look so busy when the clients come in."

"So it sounds like a perfect arrangement."

"Yeah, I guess it is," she says. "It just seems like such a pipe dream now. Like maybe it's time to grow up and start living in the real world."

"Well, if being a receptionist at a law firm isn't the *real world*, I don't know what is," I say.

Jade smiles again. We spend the next hour passing the babies around, and discussing the relative merits of Tolkien versus Lewis. I tell her I can forward her trilogy to an agent I know, and she seems carefully excited. Before I know it, the sun has passed behind my house, and the late-afternoon light is leaking quickly from the back garden.

"Hey, you guys want to stay for dinner?" I ask. "My husband is working until late. Maybe we could order something in?"

"Yeah, why not?" she says. "Cool."

It is dark by the time we have finished our falafel pitas. The babies are all fed and drowsy, and I feel like I have known Jade all my life. I wish we could put on some footie pajamas and make popcorn, stay up late watching trashy television and talking about boys, but she has to go home and put her babies to bed. I leave Emma's bouncy seat beside the front door, and I follow Jade next door, so I can hold one of the babies while she unlocks their door.

"This was really fun," she says.

"Yeah, I can't believe you were living right next door to me this whole time," I say. I kiss Madeline on top of the head, and give Jade an almost-not-awkward hug before they disappear inside.

It is the best second date I've ever had. On my second date with Leo, he took me to a car show at the Javits Center, where a lot of bimbos stood around in tight red dresses, rubbing their booties along shiny, revolving cars. It was so awful I almost turned down date number three, which turned out to be a day at Coney Island, and then a romantic dinner, followed by the world's greatest make-out session under an awning during a summer downpour. I don't expect that kind of chemistry the next time I see Jade, but I'm so excited about our budding friendship that I can't rule anything out.

I skip back up the front steps to my house and wake Emma, who needs a bath before bed.

"We can't let Daddy see that I dripped tzatziki on your head," I tell her.

After she's tucked in, I change into pajamas, and then flop down in front of the television. I flick through the channels, trying to guess which awful show Paul works on, which desperate women he caters to for a living. I wonder if he's even met his beautiful babies. I wonder how much production assistants make, and how often he sends Jade money. Emma cries out briefly, arcing a bright red spike on the monitor, but she's only talking in her sleep. I am asleep on the couch when Leo comes in around two o'clock.

"Hey, Jelly," he says, sitting down on the coffee table and leaning over to kiss me. "What are you doing up?"

I sit up. Yawn. "I wasn't really up," I say. "I guess I fell asleep down here. How was work?"

He is walking into the kitchen and taking off his jacket.

"Good," he says. "Busy night. How about you?"

"Great!" I say. "I have terrific news!" He fixes the jacket on a hanger and then comes back to the doorway. "My scar is just a scar now," I announce. "It's not an incision anymore."

He laughs, and then disappears to hang the jacket in the closet. "How do you know?"

"I just do," I said. "I ran upstairs today and everything. I'm almost back to normal. Except for being enormous, I mean."

"You're not enormous," he says, coming back to sit beside me on the couch. "You're beautiful."

I decide not to contradict him, but it's only for the sake of peace. I lean my head against his shoulder, and hand him the remote. He flips to ESPN.

"Hey, did that girl come over today?"

"Yeah, Jade," I say. "Her name's Jade."

"How'd that go?"

"It was amazing," I say, and then I try to temper my reaction, and I'm not sure why. Maybe I'm afraid Leo will caution me, somehow. That he'll ruin my euphoria. So I go with a noncommittal, "She seems like a really nice girl. I think we have more in common than I originally thought."

"That's good," he says.

"Yeah."

We watch a couple of men make conflicting predictions about tomorrow's football games and then, during the commercial break, Leo asks me, "Did you think any more about the pills?"

I pick at some nonexistent fluff on the afghan I have draped across my knees. "Yeah," I say. "I'm not going to take them, at least not yet. Not now." And then I lean away from him reflexively. I prepare for a battle.

"Good," he says. Which totally throws me off kilter.

"Good?"

"Yeah, maybe you don't need them," he says. "I mean, I think it's great you have them, and there is nothing wrong with taking them if they help. But just . . . I was thinking about it all day. I was thinking about *you* all day, how amazing you are."

"Well, it's true that I'm amazing," I laugh.

"You are. And maybe if I was just a little more supportive when you need me to be . . ."

"Like when I freak out crying and stuff?"

"Exactly, you freakazoid," Leo says, but then his face turns serious, and he says, "I don't know. Just maybe all you need is for me to listen more, without making my own judgments about what you're going through."

"Leo, you're so wise," I say suspiciously. "It's almost like you've been watching Dr. Phil or something."

"Dr. Phil wishes he were as wise as me," he says. "Dr. Phil can kneel at the temple of my superior marital wisdom."

"Leo, Dr. Phil is an idiot."

"True. But there's something else I keep thinking about. That conversation I had with my brother last week, when I told him that life hasn't changed that much, since we had the baby?"

"Yeah," I sigh. I've really been trying to forget about that.

"I get how unfair that is," he says. "It's sort of ridiculous. When I stop and think about it, I can see how much everything has changed for you. I have to remember that. Just because my life is still the same: I get up, I go to work, I come home and play with Emma . . . I don't know—it's hard for me to appreciate how much everything has changed for you."

I look hard at him. Does he truly comprehend this? I don't want to be fooled. He taps on the side of his head.

"I have a lot of time to think now, with my long commute," he explains. "I know it's not just moving to Queens and the hormones and the sleep deprivation. It's everything—it's your whole routine, your work, your friends, your whole life has been upended."

God bless him. Maybe he does get it.

"Sometimes it feels like my life isn't even my own anymore," I whisper, "because every moment of the day revolves around Emma now."

"I know," he says.

"But I don't even really mind that so much. It's more than that. It's like my sense of identity has just dropped out from under me. Like I'm not even a writer anymore. My palate is shot." For a harrowing moment, I consider telling him about the Fritos, but I press past it. "I used to be such an overachiever, but motherhood has kind of obliterated that. I'm not super good at this. I'm not even sort of good at it. And then, my body and brain are both out of control. It's like I don't know who I am anymore. I feel like I've kind of disappeared."

I can see Leo struggling with all of this. I can see him battling his own irritation. He wants positive thinking only.

"I know you don't like to hear me talk like this," I say, "that it bothers you when you think I'm being hard on myself. But instead of arguing with me, or trying to convince me I'm great, and everything is fine, maybe I just need you to listen. And empathize."

Leo nods. "And maybe it will help when you get back to work, too. Instead of me reminding you how awesome you are all the time, maybe you need to remind yourself. You feel ready to start writing again?"

I shake my head. "Not without child care. It's impossible. I don't have the headspace."

Before Emma was born, we had these crazy ideas that our professional lives were flexible enough that we could work around her, that we might not need child care. We had delusions of me fitting in my research and writing around Leo's work schedule and Emma's sleeping. We failed to account for an actual live, human baby. There is nothing part-time about her.

"Yeah, we're going to need at least part-time child care, huh?" Leo says.

I feel like it's Christmas—no, better than Christmas. Between falling in love with Jade, and now Leo's dawning enlightenment, this could be the best day of my entire life.

"If we want me to make any money, we are."

Then we make out on the couch until Leo wriggles out of his checkered chef pants. I guess I did tell him that my incision was a scar now. He probably thought that was code for something.

He's tugging at my pajama bottoms, but I'm nervous. If he thinks I'm doing this without birth control, he is insane. He's kissing my neck, and I have to admit, it feels good, even though his hair smells like meat frying, with a nuanced hint of vegetable steam. I dig my fingers into his shoulder blades, and remember the new package of condoms in my nightstand drawer.

"Let's go upstairs."

Chapter Eighteen

T he blight came slow into the fields. At first they could only smell it, and Ginny knew that calamitous odor like a sinner knows the devil. But the crop looked so verdant and promising under the midsummer sky that she postponed her despair. She put it on the long finger.

They dug up the earlies, and they were sound, if small. They harvested the turnips as well then, and ate like kings during the first weeks of July, without a whisper of charity from anyone. Seán visited regularly, though Ginny tried to convince him there was no need of that now that she was home with her children. And though she wouldn't have admitted it to anyone, she was glad he ignored her protestations. Dread was seeping in through the back of her mind, its presence growing, like the familiar stench that impressed itself more firmly into her consciousness with each passing day.

It was the eighteenth of July when they noticed the first visible stripe of brown creeping serpentlike through one corner of the potato field. Maire saw the black spots on the leaves first, and she screamed out for her mother. Ginny remembered the date precisely because they were down on their knees in the field studying the stinking, cancerous sores when Father Brennan appeared over the ridge at the top of the field. Ginny hadn't been expecting him, and when she rose to greet him, she noted that he had a white envelope in his hand. Her heart skittered, and she felt a shivering weakness in her hips and knees. She grabbed Maire's hand and helped her daughter to her feet.

"Go on in, and get your sisters a drop of water," Ginny said. "See is Raymond up from his kip. I'll be along to give him a feed shortly."

She met Father Brennan halfway across the yard. Her voice was high and tight in her throat. "Did you open it yet, Father?"

He shook his head. "Sure, it's not mine to open," he said, and he handed her the letter. "It's postmarked New York."

She lifted it to her nose, and sniffed it, to see could she catch a hint of Raymond on it, any remainder of him. Or failing that, perhaps a whiff of exotic New York or the Atlantic salt between. She handed it back to Father Brennan.

"Will we go inside?" he said.

Ginny glanced toward the open cottage door. Maggie was standing there, but when she caught her mother looking, she scampered back inside.

"Better not, Father," Ginny said. "Until I know what it says."

"Fair enough. Will I open it?"

Together they stepped around the larger of Maggie's cairns, so that they were hidden from view of the cottage. Ginny breathed as steady as she could, and clasped her hands together. She nodded, and all the joints in her body went loose and shuddery.

"Go on, Father." She trembled, and he pulled a delicate piece of lined blue paper from the envelope. Some American dollar bills were tucked inside, and they fluttered to the ground, but Ginny let them go. She would pick them up after. She held her hands up below her chin, clutched and twisted her fingers together. She could hardly breathe. Father Brennan cleared his throat and began to read.

7 April 1847

Dear Ginny,

    I hope this letter finds you well, and in good spirits, for I fear that the news I have will come as a shock.

Father Brennan stopped reading long enough to glance up at her, and she could already feel that her face was drained, that life was slipping out of her. Her children were just inside the cottage. The blight was beginning to eat their field. She could smell it, the rot. Father Brennan carried on.

    I'm sorry I didn't write sooner, to respond to your letters, but I was waiting in hopes that I might have better news. I've been trying to track Raymond's ship, to get some news of his passage, but I could find nothing until a young man came to me at work last week on the docks, and he asked me was I Raymond Doyle's brother from Knockbooley in Mayo. He said he was on the ship with Raymond coming over, and that conditions on board were dire, that fever broke out when they weren't two weeks under way. Scores of people died on the passage, Ginny, and this young fella, he said Raymond was very brave, that he hung on mightily. He spoke of his family the whole time, he said, and of his beautiful wife back home in Mayo. This young fella knew all of your names, even the baby one, who ye call Poppy, even though I only ever knew her to be called Pauline.

He held onto ye until the very last, and I hope that is some small comfort to you in your coming time of grief, Ginny. My brother, your devoted husband Raymond, died three weeks before they made landfall in New York. He was buried at sea. Meagan and I will send what we can, to help ye, until you're back on your feet. I know it won't be easy for ye, the way times are, and you on your own with the children. We're enclosing a few dollars here. Please God we'll all be together again some day. It would be a beautiful thing to see your face, and to kiss my little nephew and nieces. Meanwhile, kiss them for us, and you'll be an auntie soon enough yourself. Meagan is expecting our first wee one this summer.

May God provide you peace in your time of sorrow, Ginny. God bless,

Always your faithful brother,
Kevin Doyle

Father Brennan folded the blue paper solemnly, and slipped it back into its envelope. He leaned down to collect up the fluttering dollar bills that had scattered by their feet. He looked up at Ginny and pressed the money into her hand. She took it. She folded it into her pocket. She caught her breath.

She didn't know what he expected of her at that moment. She didn't know what she expected of herself. And to be sure, there were tears, hot and fast, slipping down the fallow field of her face. But she surprised herself and Father Brennan both, nonetheless.

"Read it again, Father, please," she said softly.

It's hard to describe the shape a grief can take, when there is nothing but sorrow left in the world. It's difficult to imagine that devastation can be liberating. Perhaps Ginny had known, deep down, for some time, that Ray was dead. She thought that was right, that she had felt his emigrant absence more deeply than an ocean's crossing. Perhaps her soul had perceived the passing of his. In any case, the hope of him had been like an imbecile yoke, and she hadn't understood the guilty weight of it until it was lifted from her.

Father Brennan was standing beside her in the yard, and he was calling out her name, but his voice, it sounded like gravel. And she turned to look out over her fields. Their homeplace. She stared out into the wind, and as she watched, all the colors separated, one from the other, and she could suddenly see the world as it was truly made up, as of tiny, whirring grains of sand. And she thought, how easy it would be, to walk into that decaying corner of the potato field, and simply scoop out all the brown bits. To leave only green behind. How easy it might've been, to scrape the wicked fever out of young Michael's body, and leave him whole and well. How easy it would be even now, to walk farther into that as-yet-untouched portion of the field, to stand beneath the slow summer gloaming, to lift her hands to the sky, and dissolve. To go to her husband. Her two sons. To go to where they were gone.

"Ginny." Father Brennan's hand was on her sleeve, and as she looked down, it snapped into focus, his knuckles as solid as the roots of the blackthorn tree.

Ginny blinked her eyes very slowly. The wind in the fields whipped the grief clean out of her. The stench of the blight was growing. She felt her chest caved in, in a way that she felt certain was permanent.

"Are you all right, Ginny?" Father was asking her.

She laughed.

Ginny lost track of how many days passed between that and the day Alice Spring came to call. She knew that the blight had gathered speed and resolve. Their field was rotting where it stood. The earlies in the pits were beginning to collapse and stink, too. Maire and Ginny were doing what they could to dry them and save them, but their efforts were proving largely useless. It was exactly the same as last year, only Ray was dead and gone. Michael was dead and gone. There was no cow to sell, no hog or hens. Their resources were exhausted, entirely.

It was midmorning, and Poppy was singing to baby Raymond. Her baby lullabies sounded so awful eerie now, her unblemished voice all full of sweetness amid the rot. Maire was stood in the doorway looking out when Ginny thought she heard carriage wheels approaching. Maggie pushed past her sister and went out to stand in the yard. She ran up to the ridge to see who was coming. She would chase them down and ask them for money. She was bold like that, Maggie was. She hadn't learned to give up yet. The carriage wheels slowed as they approached the gate, and Ginny and Maire caught up with Maggie atop the ridge.

After a moment, behind the rock wall that lined the road, they could see the extravagant purple feather of a hat cavorting merrily along. The feather paused as the head that bore it approached the gate, and Alice Spring's face came into view. Seán stepped before her and opened the latch on the gate. Ginny turned to Maire.

"Go in and see to the baby. Make sure he's shined up for his visitor."

The gate swung in, and Seán stood aside to hold it open for Mrs. Spring, who gathered up her skirts in both hands and traipsed into the little lane like she was the Queen herself. The brilliant purple of her gown was visible beneath an elegant velvet traveling cloak that she wore buttoned up, despite the clammy warmth of the day. Her golden hair was plaited and wrapped into a tightly calculated chaos. She loosened the folds of her skirt, and the purple fabric swirled around her legs. Maggie's little face fell open with wonder as she watched. Alice Spring's smile was dazzling, even at this distance, her teeth white like the pearls strung tightly round her straight, tidy neck.

"Here, Maggie," Ginny said, holding out her hand to her daughter. Maggie turned to her, and shied herself in behind her mother's petticoat while Alice Spring stepped up the sloping lane toward the ridge. Behind her, Seán swung the gate closed, and disappeared into the road behind the wall. Alice Spring began climbing the slope, and as she approached the top of the ridge, she held her gloved hands out to Ginny. Her eyes were blue like a cornflower, lit bright by the outdoor light, the fresh and clear summer sky. It was so strange for Ginny to see Mrs. Spring now, after everything that had happened, all the stunning grief she had endured since her departure from Springhill House. This woman was like an apparition from another life. Ginny nearly felt she couldn't place her.

"Ginny!" Mrs. Spring called, gripping Ginny's hands, while Maggie hid behind her mother. Mrs. Spring kissed Ginny outlandishly on both cheeks, like they were old friends or sisters. "You're looking well," she said. "What a beautiful home you have. Such a quaint little cottage. And the land here." She turned to look out over the fields. The purple taffeta swished dramatically around her. "What a gorgeous view!" She was breathless.

"Thank you," Ginny said flatly.

"It's all rot," Maggie said, poking her head out now, and stepping boldly away from her mother to look at Mrs. Spring.

"Maggie, whisht."

"Well, it is, Mammy, can she not see that? It stinks."

"Maggie, go inside and check on your brother."

Maggie rolled her eyes, and then stamped her feet beneath her, but in a moment she scuttled down the hill and in through the door. Alice Spring turned back to face Ginny.

"I suppose you heard the big news!" she said.

"Seán mentioned . . . you're going to New York?"

Her smile broadened. She had a shallow dimple in her right cheek that Ginny had never noticed before. The exhilaration suited her. She looked younger than before, like a girl in the first blush of love.

"Isn't it exciting?" she said, stepping closer to Ginny, and taking one of her hands again. Her gloves were impossibly soft.

"I'm delighted for you," Ginny managed to stammer.

"New York City!" she said.

Ginny swallowed.

"Isn't that where your husband is?" Mrs. Spring said abruptly then. She stepped in so close that Ginny could smell her, stronger than the acrid tang of the blight in her fields. A powdery honeysuckle with lavender. The sweetness was cloying, like Poppy's lullabies. "I thought perhaps I could look him up for you, if you have an address? Perhaps he simply hasn't had the means to contact you. I know you've been anxious for word from him."

She was staring intently at Ginny's face, but Ginny couldn't meet her gaze. Instead, she looked past her visitor, at the shapes of Maggie's cairn behind her.

"I was," Ginny said.

"Were?" Mrs. Spring prompted.

"I was. Anxious."

"Oh!" She clapped her gloved hands. "So you received word, then? You've had a letter?"

Ginny nodded.

"Oh." Her expression faltered. "Oh dear." She placed one scarlet glove rather delicately across her breast.

Ginny cleared her throat. "A few days ago, I had a letter from his brother, Kevin, in New York."

Mrs. Spring trained her piercing blue eyes on Ginny.

"He didn't make the passage," Ginny said quietly.

"I don't understand. What does that mean, *he didn't make the passage*?"

Ginny cleared her throat and tried to answer, but found her voice to be quite faulty in her throat.

"He died." She hadn't intended to whisper it.

The red glove was in front of Mrs. Spring's mouth now, and the corners of her eyes turned down. She was very pink in the cheeks, and with the purple of her dress, the pearls, the rich velvet cloak— she was a riot of color there beside the bleakness of the cairn.

"But how . . ."

"There was fever on the ship. Many died on the passage. He wasn't the only one. Many died."

"Oh." Mrs. Spring's voice was clear and loose. "I'm so sorry." But her compassion felt artificial. Ginny stared at the bobbing feather on her visitor's hat.

"Here, come inside anyway," Ginny said, turning from her. "We haven't much to offer you, but Raymond will be happy to see you."

Ginny heard the heavy taffeta rustle as Mrs. Spring stepped down the slope behind her, and into the cottage. Maire had stoked the fire, and Maggie and Poppy were sitting with their backs to it, where they could see Mrs. Spring when she entered. Poppy's eyes grew wide as she took in all the finery. Ginny tried to imagine what this lady must look like to her daughter, an exotic bird or opulent cake. And then, as quickly, she wondered how her life, this cottage, must appear to Mrs. Spring. She looked around her modest home, one of the nicest tenant homes in the whole of the parish. But it was smaller than the kitchen at Springhill House, smaller than Mrs. Spring's bedchamber even. Still, it was clean and warm, Ginny's children bright and beautiful despite everything. Maire was sitting on the stool with Raymond on her knee and the little book of verse opened in front of him. She was pointing out the various pictures to him, but Raymond only squirmed and kicked his feet.

"Look, there he is!" Mrs. Spring sang. Her voice was like a trumpet in the cottage, her accent shrill. Maggie looked pale, and winced at the sound of her. Ginny went to Maggie quickly, and placed a hand on her little forehead. She felt warm.

"Maggie, come away from the fire there, love," she said. "Come and sit beside the door for a few minutes, get some air." Maggie stood to her feet and went to lean against the doorway.

Maire stood up and swung Raymond on her hip. "You can sit down there, missus," she said, pointing to the stool.

Mrs. Spring looked at the seat distastefully, but then caught herself, and forced a smile. "Thank you," she said, as she made a great show of seating herself and arranging her skirts around her. When she was comfortable, she removed her hat and gloves, and then opened her arms to the baby.

"Come to Auntie Alice!" she called.

Maire glanced at Ginny, who nodded. Maire stepped across the room, and deposited Raymond carefully into Mrs. Spring's waiting arms. Mrs. Spring stared down at the baby, and the light in her eyes grew brighter. She rocked him lightly on the stool.

"Dear little Raymond," she said, her voice finally quieting to fit the room, "how I've missed you."

Raymond cooed, and his little hand flew out from his swaddle and locked onto her finger. He gripped her.

"Oh!" she laughed. "Look at him, Ginny! My, he's grown so big since I saw him last. So strong. You're a proper little gentleman now, you are."

Maire looked at her mother uneasily, but Ginny twisted past her and retrieved a cup of water to offer their guest. She needn't have bothered.

"Thank you anyway," Mrs. Spring said, "I'm afraid I can't stop for long. Jarvie wants to make Galway by nightfall."

It was so strange the way she called Seán *jarvie*. Ginny wondered if she even knew his Christian name. Roisin said that Mrs. Spring had called her *cook* for the first three months of her employment. But Alice Spring had called her *Ginny* from the very start, from that first moment in the garden, outside the French doors. How much had changed since that day. That day felt like someone else's life.

"I only came to take my leave." Mrs. Spring was talking dreamily, more to baby Raymond than to Ginny. "I couldn't go off to New York without saying good-bye."

She leaned down and touched her nose to Raymond's. It was such a tender and intimate gesture that it shocked Ginny from her reverie. Something in her stood up. The hair on her arms prickled, and she waited for Raymond to fuss. He would be hungry soon. But he only stared gummily up at Mrs. Spring, their eyes locked onto each other. Poppy watched in awe. Maire went to stand in the doorway with Maggie, who flumped in against her big sister. Maire stroked her hair. The quiet in the cottage was an uneasy one. They all watched Mrs. Spring with Raymond, and when she rocked up and away from him, Ginny could see, in the firelight, that the woman's face was wet with tears.

"Oh, how I will miss you, my darling boy!" she said, and her voice was taut with an anguish that Ginny recognized.

"Ah, now," Ginny said, setting the untouched cup of water on the table, and reaching for her baby. "You're all right. It's not the end of the world, now, is it? You'll hardly even remember us when you get to New York."

Alice Spring's body tensed as Ginny lifted Raymond from her arms. Ginny watched her go rigid and pale. She straightened herself from the spine and neck, but her fingers went crooked and stiff. She cleared her throat, and contrived a grin with her teeth.

"And anyway, you and Mr. Spring will have your own little one before you know it, when you're reunited." Ginny turned her back to Mrs. Spring for a moment, sheltered Raymond from the woman's sight. "A little American, right?" she said, turning only her face to Mrs. Spring.

Alice Spring's smile twisted, her lips lurched. She stood quickly, and knocked the little stool out from beneath her. She didn't bend to retrieve it, but Poppy stood up from beside the fire, and righted it onto its three legs.

"Thank you, dear." Mrs. Spring smiled down at her. Poppy didn't respond. "Oh, I nearly forgot! How could I forget?" she said then, snapping her fingers. She lifted the flap of her cloak and reached inside. She drew out several small, brightly colored paper sachets, each tied with a gleaming ribbon. She handed the first to Poppy, who took it, but then plopped it down on the table. Poppy curled her fingers over the table's edge, and set her chin there, between them, where she eyed the sachet suspiciously.

"What is it?" she said.

"They're sweets," Mrs. Spring replied, holding the other two sachets out to Maire and Maggie in the doorway. Maggie flew across the room at once, and snatched the gift from Mrs. Spring's fingers. She tore into it.

Maire took hers graciously in hand. "Thank you," she said.

Mrs. Spring nodded at her, and then bent down to convince

Poppy, who looked up at her without lifting her chin from the table.

"They're called caramels," Mrs. Spring explained. "And they came all the way across the sea on a boat, from London!"

Poppy frowned.

"They're gorgeous," Mrs. Spring said. "Try one."

"If they're so gorgeous, why aren't you eating them?"

Mrs. Spring laughed. "Well, a lady has to watch her figure. You'll know all about it when you're bigger."

Maire's mouth fell open a small bit, but she said nothing. She went back to the hearth, and set her unopened sachet down beside the fire. Raymond watched everything from his mother's arms, unblinking.

"Girls, thank Mrs. Spring for the lovely gift," Ginny said.

Poppy and Maggie both mumbled their gratitude while Mrs. Spring nodded in condescension. An uncomfortable silence descended on the gathered party then, and Alice Spring endeavored to chase it away.

"I suppose it's time I was on my way," she said, clapping her hands together, and crowding in against Ginny in the doorway. She stood in close beside Raymond, and smoothed her hand over his forehead. She was holding her hat and gloves in one hand, and when she leaned in to kiss him, her hair grazed Ginny's cheek. Ginny led her out through the doorway, and her daughters followed. Maggie was sucking on one of the caramels.

In the yard, Mrs. Spring hesitated. She hadn't said a word to Ginny about her husband, about Michael. As if Ginny was so far beneath her that Mrs. Spring couldn't conceive of her grief—the way that Ginny couldn't know how a bitch might suffer when she loses a pup. Death was so common among the Irish now that perhaps Mrs. Spring thought they couldn't *feel* it anymore. Perhaps she thought they'd developed an immunity to suffering. In any case, her condolences were careless and cursory, and now here she stood in Ginny Doyle's yard, with audacious tears in her eyes. Taking leave of *Ginny's* child. For a moment, Ginny thought of plucking one of the larger stones from Maggie's cairn, and hurling it at her. She just wished Mrs. Spring would leave now, quickly, while the impulse remained only in Ginny's head, and not in deed.

Go now, Ginny thought. But she lingered. Twice, she turned in circles, and then drew in close again to gaze at Raymond. Ginny's daughters watched as Mrs. Spring affixed her hat over her careful hair. She stuck a pin through one of her plaits, and then dropped her arms to her sides. Poppy was holding the scarlet gloves. She was petting them. She handed them back to Mrs. Spring, who pulled them delicately over her pale knuckles. There were tiny pearl buttons at the wrists. When there was nothing left for her to dawdle over, she finally squared her shoulders and sighed.

"I guess I'm off, then!" There was a split in her voice.

In the yard, the stink of the blight seemed to have gotten stronger just in the space of minutes. Ginny could taste it in the back of her throat. Alice Spring's face was creased in the sunlight; a line of frown ran down her forehead and her nostrils flared.

"Good-bye, then!" She kissed Raymond once more, and Ginny thought the smell of her perfume would linger over him, that it would never go. "Take care of your mummy and your sisters!"

Ginny hoisted him onto her shoulder, and Mrs. Spring rubbed his back. "Safe journey," Ginny said, but she couldn't muster a smile for the traveler. She just wanted her gone. Gone.

Alice Spring nodded, and whirled around to face the ridge, but before she could go, Maggie piped up.

"Sweets won't do us any good," she said, stepping out away from her sisters and mother.

"What's that?" Alice Spring turned, but only slightly.

"Maggie!" Ginny snapped, but she ignored her mother, and went toward Mrs. Spring.

"Our crop is rotting in the field, missus," Maggie said. "My father is dead, and now my mam has no job because you're leaving."

Ginny could feel a blush creeping over her neck, but it wasn't shame, or at least not for Maggie. Maybe it was shame for herself, because all her daughters were braver than she was. Alice Spring was blinking furiously.

"That baby can hardly take care of us if there's no food to eat, can he?" Maggie taunted. "If you like my brother, if you want him to survive, you should give him some money, some food. Not sweets. Not stupid books with pictures of pigs wearing shoes."

Maggie was folding her thin little arms across her chest. Behind her, the cairn was so much taller than she was. Ginny wondered how she had got the rocks up that high, if she'd had to scale her own mountain to balance the uppermost ones on top. Raymond's hurley bat was usually stored in the shed, but now it was propped against the base of the cairn. Michael must have gotten it out when the weather started to warm, before the harvest. Before the fever. He might have played a bit of hurling with the Fallon lads. Ginny wondered if he was as good a shot as his father. She had wasted so much time at Springhill House. She had missed so much. All for nothing.

Mrs. Spring was at a loss, but only for a moment; she recovered herself quickly. "Of course." She looked at Ginny, and then back to Maggie. "I'm sorry, I didn't . . . I just . . ," She was shaking her head.

Maggie shook hers, too, and then turned and walked back inside. Maire followed her, but Poppy stayed beside her mother.

"Of course, I should give you some money," Mrs. Spring stammered.

There was a time when Ginny would have protested. Now she only lifted her chin.

"I could be Raymond's benefactor," Mrs. Spring explained to herself, warming to the idea of her own generosity. She smiled. She was pulling off her gloves again. "And then one day, when he's bigger, perhaps he can come and visit old Auntie Alice."

Ginny nodded. "Perhaps." Her heart was barely beating. "Or it may be you'll come back."

Folly.

No one ever came back.

"Or . . ." Mrs. Spring turned fully back to face Ginny now. Her cheeks were beginning to flush. There was an eruption of excitement across her features. "Oh, Ginny!" she said, and she gripped Ginny's arms where she was holding Raymond. Ginny could feel the fingers digging hard into her flesh. "Ginny, I could take him with me. Yes! Let me take him to New York."

And now the pounding came into Ginny's heart like mad, a deep booming, thundering thud. "What?"

"Think of it, Ginny."

"Poppy, go inside." Ginny shooed her daughter away from her skirt, tousled the back of her head. "Go on."

"Think of the life he would have with me, in New York City. He'd be so well-off. I would take care of him as if he were my very own, you know I would. You know how I love him so. He could have an education, everything. He could have everything."

Ginny was shaking her head. She was shaking. Mrs. Spring's face was so eager, so awful and pleading, all screwed up with some voracious kind of hope. Ginny could see all of Mrs. Spring's bottom teeth. Her tongue poking out, her eyes wild. Ginny felt the weight of Raymond's little head against her shoulder.

"I can't." Ginny shook. "I can't."

Alice Spring tightened her grip on Ginny's arm. Her voice tilted and dropped, reached an unholy pitch.

"I will pay you for him," she said.

Chapter Nineteen

NEW YORK, NOW

Jade and I sit across from each other studying our enormous seventeen-page diner menus. Emma is asleep strapped into her car seat, safely tucked between the booth and the table, and Max and Madeline are strapped into matching sticky high chairs at the end of our booth. I'm trying not to be a germ-prude, but Max is chewing on the corner of Jade's menu, which is totally grossing me out. How many people have sneezed on that menu? I shudder.

"Ah, here we go," Jade says, flipping the page. "Vegetarian Delights."

Max flails his arm as his mother turns the page, but then he patiently guides the peeling corner of the new page into his slobbery mouth. I guess I'm cringing because when Jade glances up at me, she looks at her baby, and says, "Max, ew, don't chew on that."

Max turns purple with rage and begins to scream.

"Wow, that is impressive," I say. "Did you see how he changed colors?"

But Jade is not listening. "Okay, okay, fine," she tells him, and she hands him back the menu. "But don't come crying to me when you have mouth ulcers."

Madeline sticks her finger in her brother's ear.

"What are you gonna get?" Jade asks me.

There are so many terrible, terrible deep-fried, cheese-drenched choices. How's an ex–food writer to choose?

"I think maybe just a burger," I say casually, though I am practically paralyzed by the sheer quantity and variety of the burgers on offer. Pizza burger? Texican burger? What even *is* a Jumbo BBQ Crunchburger Deluxe? I'll have three of those, please.

"Yeah," Jade says, "maybe I'll try the veggie burger."

Poor Jade. She closes her menu and relinquishes it to Max.

"So what's new, how's work?" I ask.

"Ah, it's the same old thing, it's fine. But I wrote almost a whole chapter of the new book today, after lunch."

"Wow, that's great," I say, with some measure of actual envy. Not that I want to work for a bunch of self-important douchebag lawyers, or commute on a bus and two subways every day with twin babies, but you know—the writing part.

"Yeah, it's cool," she says.

And then there's an awkward moment when we have nothing to say to each other, and I fear that our burgeoning friendship was all an illusion, that I imagined the whole thing because I'm so lonesome and pathetic.

"How about you?" she asks.

I shrug. "Yeah, you know. We had a pretty exciting day. Emma pooped twice."

Jade whistles, and the twins both snap their heads up to look at her. "That *is* exciting."

"Yep. The second time, there was so much poop I had to change her entire outfit, and throw out the onesie. It wasn't salvageable."

"Love those poops," Jade says knowingly. "Those are the best."

The waitress is approaching, so it's probably time to can the poop-talk.

"You ready to order?" Her pen is poised over her tiny notepad.

"Yeah, I'll have the veggie burger," Jade says, as she tries to pry Max's little fingers from the wet menu. He starts to howl. "You mind if he keeps it?"

"Nah, that's fine," the waitress says.

"Cool."

"How 'bout you, hon?" she asks, turning to me.

"What's on the Jumbo BBQ Crunchburger Deluxe, exactly?" I ask. I am equal parts mortified and titillated as this question escapes my lips.

"Oh, it's a half-pound burger, with cheddar cheese, bacon, and barbecue sauce, and then some crispy fried onion rings on top. And it comes with cheesy waffle fries and a side of guacamole."

Oh my God.

"That," I say, without shame. "I'll have that."

I snap my menu shut and hand it to her. Jade's face looks like mine did when I noticed Max chewing on the menu, but I do not care. It has crispy onion rings on top. For the love of God!

"So tell me more about your family," I say, mostly to distract us both from the abomination of food I have just ordered. "Any brothers or sisters?"

"I have a half sister, but she's much younger than me," she says. "She's eight, and still at home with my crazy mom. Poor thing."

"Oh, you have a crazy mom, too?"

"Totally."

"Like what kind of crazy?"

"Like, she doesn't know who my dad is, crazy."

"Oh." That's not really the sort of crazy I expected.

"Yeah, she was a real party girl and got pregnant with me when she was super young, but she didn't let me slow her down. We just partied together," Jade laughs. "She was kind of a groupie for a couple different bands in the late eighties. My dad might be some famous has-been."

The *late eighties*?! Good God. I might be closer to Jade's mom's age.

"I don't think I had a full night's sleep in my life until Paul and I moved to New York," she says. "Mom has hot pink hair. Thinks she's Cyndi Lauper."

"That is . . . wow," I say profoundly.

"Yep. What kind of crazy is your mom?"

Well, after that, she sounds kinda boring. "You know, maybe she's not totally crazy, just . . . normal mother-daughter stuff, I guess. She drives me nuts."

"Yeah," Jade says, but she's not really letting me off the hook. "How?"

I glance down at Emma, like I shouldn't be talking about it in front of her. "Well, for one thing, she's super sociable," I say. "Everyone loves her. She could talk to the wall, you know the type?"

"Sure," Jade says. "Paul was a bit like that. Whenever we went anywhere, he got us free upgrades."

"Yeah, she's exactly like that. Everyone thinks she's their best

330 · JEANINE CUMMINS

friend because she talks nonstop. And she's a great storyteller.
Everyone loves her stories. She's funny. But you can't get a word
in. And the thing is, with all that talking, she doesn't actually *say*
anything."

"Ah," Jade says, but something in that syllable sounds like she
really *knows*. She understands. She has taken a sugar packet from
the bowl, and is flicking it back and forth.

"She'll tell you about the most mundane, trivial shit," I
say, "but then she'll neglect to mention that my dad had chest
pains last week, and had to go for an EKG. It's insane." I can
feel my whole body tensing as I talk about it, even though I
wonder if it sounds insignificant compared to Jade's slutty
rocker-mom.

"So she's one of those people who glosses over all the important stuff?" Jade says.

"Exactly."

"And she fills in every conversation with fluff, to preempt you
from trying to talk about anything real?"

"Yes."

"Because talking about real stuff, like fears or feelings, would
make her uncomfortable?"

"I guess so," I say.

"You've never tried it?"

"Tried what, talking to my mom about fears and feelings?"

"Sure, why not?" she says, ripping open the packet of sugar
and dumping it into her iced tea.

"Talk to my mom about fears and feelings," I say again, because it is the single most absurd suggestion anyone has ever
dared make to me.

"You could try asking her about it," she says. "You never
know." I watch her sip her iced tea. She smacks her lips. "I'm just
saying, usually when people are like that, there's a reason."

I pick up my own glass, and stir the ice with my straw.

"There's usually some super-deep reservoir of hurt under there that they're trying to hide," she says. "And they spend their whole life doing jazz-hands so that nobody will notice the gushing wound of pain behind the curtain."

I sip through my straw, and try to be open-minded. I hope Jade doesn't use phrases like *gushing wound of pain* in her trilogy. Can we still be friends if it turns out she's a terrible writer? She's so smart. I try to consider her philosophy, but end up shaking my head.

"I don't think my mom has a gushing wound of pain."

She shrugs. "Maybe not."

The swinging door from the kitchen opens, and the waitress backs out with our plates. My Jumbo BBQ Crunchburger Deluxe is approaching. I can smell fried beef and cheese and bacon. I can hear angels singing.

After dinner, I can hardly move. I have to waddle down the diner steps to where we have parked our strollers. I have eaten so much that my scar feels taut, stretched.

"I think I need to walk for a while," I tell Jade when we get to our street. "I probably need to walk for like seven weeks, to work off that dinner."

"That was some burger," she admits.

"You wanna walk?"

"Nah, I should get home," she says.

"Okay. I'll see you later."

"Cool." She turns the double stroller hard left and crosses the street toward home.

It's fairly dark, but Leo won't be home for hours, and Emma is awake now, content in the stroller. She is watching the leafy canopy go by overhead. Sometimes when she's in the stroller, I squat, and then turn and look up, just to see what things look like from her vantage point. I push her stroller along by the cemetery fence that runs down Myrtle Avenue. I think about going in, but the sign on the gate says they close at sundown. The sun is down now, and it's still open.

"All we need is to get locked in a cemetery for the night, Emma," I say.

But then I remember being a kid here, maybe ten or twelve years old, hopping the fence with friends and playing flashlight tag amid the headstones. Maybe it wouldn't be so bad. Emma opens her mouth, but then closes it again without answering. My phone is ringing in the diaper bag, so I stop and fish it out from beneath the stroller. It's Mom.

"Hey," I say.

"Majella!"

"Hi, Mom."

"Listen, I found something I thought you'd want to know about," she says. "I've been combing through the genealogy files and I found some really interesting stuff." I begin to walk again, slowly now, pushing the stroller with one hand. "The woman whose diary you found, Virginia Doyle?"

"Yeah."

"She had several children, and it turns out that one of her sons, Raymond Doyle, lived to be one hundred and one years old."

"Wow."

"Yeah, he didn't die until 1947."

"What year were you born again?"

"In 1949. Anyway, the really interesting thing is that, apparently, he participated in some Irish-American folklore project at the New York Public Library in the thirties."

I stop walking.

"What, like an oral history or something?"

"Exactly. There was some famous professor who wanted to record people's folk memories of the famine before they were all gone."

"That's amazing," I say. "Can you read it online, what he had to say?"

"No, but you can do even better," she says. "You can go to the library there and listen to it. I think it's an actual recording. I'm looking at the library Web site now, and it says it's a spoken-word CD, and that it's for in-library use only. I guess that means you can't check it out."

"Yeah."

"Still, that sounds amazing, don't you think? To be able to hear Raymond Doyle's story in his own words?"

"Definitely," I say. "I wonder if he knew what happened, about his mother."

"I don't know," Mom says. "It seems unlikely. He must have been just a baby when they left Ireland. Why would she tell him a thing like that, that she killed a woman?"

"Did you find records of their crossing?"

"Not yet, but I'm still looking."

I pull the phone down from my ear so I can check the time. It's almost seven thirty. I wonder how late the library is open tonight, but it doesn't matter anyway. I can't go now, not with Emma. She needs to go home and get to sleep. I stick the phone back to my ear.

"Maybe I can go tomorrow," I say.

"Oh, I wish I was there to come with you," Mom says. "I'd love to hear that CD."

I stop walking and take a deep breath. She wishes she was here. Not so she can spend time with her daughter and new grandbaby. But so she can hear some dead great-uncle tell stories on CD at the library. I remember what Jade said, about the reservoir of hurt, and the curtain and the pain and the jazz-hands, and I decide that it's definitely bullshit.

But then again, what have I got to lose?

"Hey, Mom," I say, because I am determined to make a change. I will force her to have a real conversation with me. I am going to make this happen. "Mom, I have to tell you something."

I hear her take in a quiet breath, and I feel so powerful, when I can make her quiet, even just for a moment. That conversation we had on Saturday—about the diary, the murder, Ginny Doyle—it's true that that conversation ended the way they all do: with her disappearing, and me feeling sad and exasperated. But before that, there was something in there, some nugget of potential. I think it was fear that quieted my mother and bound us together. Maybe I can find that scab again, and pick it. If Jade is right, if I can locate my mom's wounds, then maybe I can make her bleed. I can make her *feel*.

"What is it, honey?" she says.

"I don't know." I really don't know. I want to tell her everything. The crying, the therapy, the pills. I want her to know all of it. But what if she doesn't listen? What if her other line beeps in? "I miss you."

"Aww, Majella. We miss you, too, honey! But you would just love this place, you and Leo both. . . ."

"No, Mom, that's not what I mean. *Listen!*"

My mom goes quiet.

"What was it like for you, when you first had me?" I ask. "How old were you?"

"Oh, I was old, by the standards of the day. I was thirty. Over-the-hill!" she laughs.

"And how was it? Was it hard, having a baby? Or were you just a natural at it?"

"I mean, it's always hard, Majella. Being a mom is the toughest job in the world."

She sounds like a frigging greeting card.

"But was it hard for *you*?" I say. "I don't want to know about your generation, or your friends, or society back then. I want to know about *you*. As a person. How you handled it. How you *felt*."

I pause. Will she answer? Will she dodge? It's like waiting to see how many pins your carefully launched bowling ball will take down. It teeters at the gutter. Mom clears her throat.

"I don't know," she finally says. "It was a different time then. We didn't talk about our feelings. There wasn't all of this postpartum mumbo jumbo. We just got on with it."

I feel like my bowling ball glanced. I got maybe two or three pins, which is all you can really hope for your first time out, right? But maybe I can go for the spare. After all, she did say the word *postpartum*, and that seems like evidence of something.

"Well, we talk about our feelings now, Mom," I say. "It's not too late for that, you know. People do that."

"What people?"

"Other people. Lots of people. Me!"

"Oh, don't be silly," she says, but I interrupt her to push my silliness a step further.

"I'm going to therapy," I say.

My mom gasps. It's a bona fide gasp. I think she would've been less shocked if I'd confessed a heroin addiction and a lesbian affair.

"That's ridiculous," she says. "What do you need therapy for?"

"Are you kidding me?"

"You're fine, Majella, you don't need therapy. How absurd. Tell me one good reason you would need therapy."

"How about because I can't stand my mother!" I bark. I am standing on the side of Myrtle Avenue with my fists clenched in the dark. The lit-up Q55 bus rolls past and farts exhaust at me. Jesus God, what did I just say to my mother? She is quiet on the other end of the phone. "I didn't mean that, Mom. Mom?"

She doesn't say anything, but I move the phone away from my ear, and I can still see the seconds ticking by. I can hear *Jeopardy!* coming on in the background. She hasn't hung up.

"I'm sorry, Mom," I say. "You know I didn't mean that. I don't hate you."

She's still quiet, and I hear her take a shuddery little breath. Emma takes a matching one in her stroller.

"I love you, Mom. I just hate the way our relationship is sometimes," I say, "the way we communicate. I just want to be honest, I want us to be closer. I feel like we never talk about anything *real*. I have so much on my mind right now—I'm so scared I'm going to be a bad mom, there's so much I don't know. And I don't feel like I can talk to you about it. I feel like you don't really listen to me." But she's listening now, isn't she?

"Mom?" Still nothing. "The truth is, I started going to therapy because I'm crying a lot, like all the time. And I feel really overwhelmed, with Emma. It's not like I thought it would be. It's so scary."

I hear Alex Trebek being charmingly pretentious in the background. My dad laughs. I hear a noise like a sliding glass door opening, and then the sounds shift and change. The door closes, and *Jeopardy!* is gone.

"I cried a lot, too," Mom says. I hold my breath. "Your father and I always wanted a big family." She stops talking for a moment, so that I begin to wonder if that's all she is going to say, but then she sniffs, and I realize that she is crying. My mother.

"What happened?" I ask softly. "How come you only had me?"

"There were others." Her voice is high and tight. She exhales a squeaky breath. "I had five miscarriages before you."

I clutch the handle on Emma's stroller. *Five miscarriages.*

"My God, Mom."

"The last one was a boy," she says. "We thought he was the one. We made it all the way to almost thirty-five weeks, and then my labor came early. . . ."

She stops. She is pushing these words out for me. She is delivering this terror because I made her. Because I told her it was what I needed.

"It's okay, Mom," I say. "You don't have to talk about it."

"No, no, it's good," she says. "You should know. You had a brother. But he was born gone. He was already gone. They let me hold him."

Tears are running down my face now. Snot is collecting beneath my nose.

"Oh God, Mom, I'm so sorry." I can't imagine anything worse than laboring to give birth to a dead baby. It is literally the worst thing I can imagine.

I hear her crying, softly, tenderly.

"We called him Jimmy, after your grandfather."

I don't know what to say. I wish I was in Florida, on that stupid condo balcony with my mom, overlooking the golf course. I can hear cicadas.

"After that, it was hard," she says. "I mean, I couldn't have loved you any more, Majella. You know that, don't you? I love you so much."

"Of course, Mom."

"But it was hard. I was still grieving. I felt guilty for loving you so much. Like I was cheating on that first baby, all of those first babies. Like I shouldn't be so happy, when they were gone, when Jimmy was gone." She takes a deep breath. "I always remembered his little body in my arms. How still he was." Her voice is ragged.

"I'm so sorry, Mom."

"I don't talk about it," she whispers. "Not even with your father. Never."

I look down at Emma, who kicks her foot at me like I'm a horse that she wants to get moving. I mop up my snot and tears with my free arm, and then begin pushing her down the street again.

"Mom?"

"Yeah?"

"I really love you. I love you. I'm sorry."

"I know, Majella. I love you, too."

After we hang up, I feel incredibly fat and rattled. The Jumbo BBQ Crunchburger Deluxe is sitting like a stone in my gut. And the cheesy waffle fries and the guacamole. Emma and I stride through the darkened streets of Glendale in a vain attempt to outrun the damage I've just inflicted on my body. And my mama. When my baby begins to whimper, we head for home.

I look at the microwave clock as we walk in. It's a little late for Emma's bedtime, but she'll be fine. As long as I feed her and bathe her, and swaddle her tightly before bed, she's happy. I've left the monitor on the kitchen counter. I thought they'd be asleep by now, but on channel C, Jade and her babies are all crying.

The next day, Leo doesn't have to be at work until early afternoon, so I'm waiting alone on the library steps when they open at ten o'clock. Well, not alone exactly—there are plenty of caffeinated undergrads and some sneaker-sporting tourists waiting with me. It dawns on me that after living my whole life in New York, I can tell the tourists from the locals without even trying, and I accidentally sort people into these groups at a glance. There is a young, ambitious tourist on the steps beside me, and she's trying to fake everybody out. She wants to be a New Yorker. She wears all black, and she's vigilant about keeping her hair lightly mussed, her giant sunglasses perched just so on her nose. She impersonates disdain well, but she's only wearing it; it's not real. And is she really alone? Aren't those her criminally embarrassing parents posing with the lions? She looks like she wants to crawl inside her clean Armani handbag. As soon as she's old enough, she will move here. She will run.

When the doors open at ten o'clock, I follow the grad students up three flights of steps to the Rose Reading Room. I grab a call slip and mini-pencil, and fill in the information that I looked up on the Internet last night. I even have the call number on a crumpled scrap of paper in my pocket, because I am a professional. When the serious, bespectacled librarian hands over the CD a few minutes later, he reminds me to use headphones when listening.

"Yes, sir," I say.

He nods solemnly.

In the South Hall, I find an empty table and open my laptop. I pop in the disc, plug in my earbuds, and sit down to listen. It's a collection, and the files are listed first by county and then by surname. There are hundreds of Irish voices here. So many stories. I scan the list until I find Mayo. R. Doyle is the fourth file. I take a deep breath before I click on his name.

There is static, like the sound you used to hear when you would play old records, and then the time-warped voice of a young American, the famous professor.

"Just start with your name there. Don't worry about the microphone, no need to lean in."

"How's that?" Raymond Doyle's voice flashes brightly into my brain.

"Perfect. Now. Your name?"

He clears his throat. "My name is Raymond Doyle, sir."

"And where are you from, Mr. Doyle?"

"Originally from a place called Knockbooley, in the County of Mayo, sir. In Ireland."

His voice is weathered, throaty, full of living. His accent is broad, gorgeous New York, one hundred percent. There's no trace of a lilt or a soft *T.* Nothing Irish about him. I don't know what I expected, but it wasn't this. This is better. He sounds like an aged gangster. I have goose bumps on my arms. I draw his mother's diary out from my backpack, but don't open it. I set it on the table, and place my hand over it gently. It feels like a heartbeat.

"Very good, Mr. Doyle, and would you mind telling me your age, sir?"

"I believe I am ninety-three years of age or thereabouts. I was born at Springhill House in County Mayo in Ireland, in the year of our Lord eighteen hundred and forty-seven."

"Springhill House?" the famous Irish-American professor asks. "An estate house?"

"That's correct, sir."

"You were born into the landed aristocracy?"

"No, sir," Raymond Doyle laughs, and I can hear the years of accumulated smoke in his lungs. I wonder what he did for a living. "My mother was under their employ, at Springhill. She was a chambermaid to the missus, Mrs. Alice Spring."

"Ah. And your father?" I can hear the pencil-scratching of the famous professor taking his notes. I close my eyes so I can hear everything better, sharper.

"He died before I was born. Died on the passage over to America, on the coffin ships."

"As so many did, so many," the professor says. There seems to be a note of anger in his voice, more than in his subject's. "And when did you make the passage yourself, Mr. Doyle?"

"I was only an infant. To be honest, I remember nothing of Ireland, only my mother's stories."

"And that's why we're here, Mr. Doyle, to collect your stories."

"Not my stories," Raymond corrects the famous professor. "My mother's stories. The famine stories."

"That's right," the professor concedes.

"She was a saint, my mother. Ginny Doyle was her name."

I open my eyes, rub my fingertips across the diary. *A saint,* I think, and I shake my head.

"She saved my life more times than I can count, God rest her soul." The reading room is beginning to fill up with people. I turn up the volume on my laptop, and close my eyes again. I wish I could *see* him. "It started before we ever left Ireland. Before I was born, even."

"She saved your life before you were born?" the professor interrupts.

"She did," Raymond says.

"How so?"

"Did you ever hear of any babies being born in the middle of the famine?"

The professor grunts, but makes no real answer.

"I nearly wasn't. Nearly wasn't born. We were starving, all of us, starving after my father left and died on the coffin ships. I was starving in my own mother's womb. My sister Maire would tell it better, before she died, God rest her. She remembered. She was the oldest, and she saw all the babies born. She saw how a woman ought to look when she has a baby in there, but she said I wasn't growing at all, inside, until my mother went out and got the job at Springhill."

"She went there when she was pregnant?"

"She did."

"And they employed her?"

"They did."

"Highly unusual," the professor remarks.

I click *pause* on the file, so I can stop and try to take this all in. I need to imagine it. Being pregnant, having—how many?— other children at home already, and Leo being dead and gone, and there being no food at all, to feed my children. My God. I breathe deep. I click *play*.

"It was unusual, but that's how it happened," Raymond says. "I was so small that she wasn't even showing she was with child, so she left the other children at home, with my sister Maire. She had no choice, you see, because Dad was gone already, and there was nobody else to mind them. Sure, Maire was only a child herself at the time."

"How old was she?"

"I don't know. Eleven? Twelve? She was young."

"And how many other children were there?" the professor asks. "How many brothers and sisters?"

"When I was born, there were four. One had died when he was a baby, before I was born. That was Thomas. And then I had an older brother, Michael, who died around the same time I was born, or shortly after."

"Did he die of the hunger?"

"Typhus." Raymond clears his throat again, coughs out a smoky rasp. "And there were two other little girls besides Maire. One of them died on the passage over—Maggie, she was called. I don't remember her. So there was only three of us left by the time we got to New York: myself, Maire, and Poppy. My poor mother, she lost three out of six of us. And our father."

The professor makes a sympathetic sort of a noise, and I imagine him shaking his head. There is a whacking noise then. Perhaps Raymond is smacking the table. He is sitting up, beside the microphone. He is grieving for his broken mother.

"Would you tell me more about her?" the professor prompts.

"Your mother? You said she saved your life more times than you could count."

"She did."

"Tell me some of those stories."

Raymond pauses. There is a clicking noise. I can nearly hear my own heartbeat in the earphones.

"How about I just tell you the big one?" he says. "How she got us the hell out of the famine."

Chapter Twenty

IRELAND, JULY 1847

"I will pay you for him," Mrs. Spring said again, her voice wild and strained. There was something feral about her, in that moment.

She loosened her grip on Ginny's arm and grabbed on to Raymond's blanket instead. Ginny backed away from Mrs. Spring, who let go, but stamped her feet beneath her billowing purple gown like a spooked stallion. The feather flapped windily from her hat.

Behind Ginny, Maire came back into the yard carrying the blue Wedgwood china pie plate.

"You forgot this, Mrs. Spring," Maire said, stepping toward her mother and the visitor.

Neither of them answered Maire. Instead, they stared at each other. Maire looked from her mother's face to Mrs. Spring's and back again. She asked nothing; she didn't say a word, but she went to Ginny, and she took Raymond from her mother's arms.

Ginny's hands were shaking, and when Poppy peeked out into the yard, Maire told her to go back inside and close the door.

Ginny didn't turn, but she heard the cottage door squeak and then slam. Raymond started to fuss, so Maire tucked the china plate beneath her armpit so she could rock him up on her shoulder. She shushed him and patted his back, but her eyes stayed locked on the two women in front of her. Finally Mrs. Spring broke the edgy silence.

"Think of your girls, Ginny," she said. "Look at your fine daughter there."

"I have a name," her clear voice rang out. "It's Maire."

Alice Spring turned her faulty smile on Ginny's daughter, but Maire's face was as grim as the blight.

"Maire," Mrs. Spring said. "Perhaps you should let the grown-ups chat, dear."

Ginny stepped forward, between them. "My daughter is more grown than you'll ever be," she said.

Mrs. Spring's face betrayed shock, but she wasn't ready to kill decorum. She still had hope in her wild scheme, so she let Ginny's insolence go.

"I didn't mean to insinuate . . . ," she said. "I only thought perhaps it would be better for us to discuss the matter in private. To come to an arrangement."

"There's nothing to discuss," Ginny said. "There will be no arrangement."

Ginny looked at Maire, who was staring intently at her mother, and bouncing her brother softly in her arms.

"At least hear me out!" Mrs. Spring pleaded, her voice rising again. "Don't be so hasty. I'm not asking you to abandon him. The very contrary, dear! I'm offering you an opportunity. Think of it. Look, look!"

Mrs. Spring pulled back her cloak again, and revealed a thick silver chain that was looped across her shoulder and through a hidden belt inside the cloak. She drew on the chain until a large mesh purse appeared from behind her back. It was bulging, heavy, filled mostly with gold coins. She opened the clasp and pulled out all the notes at the top of the purse. She held them out to Ginny.

"Take it!" She stepped forward. "It's money. Take it, I'll send more!"

Raymond was beginning to cry loudly. He needed a feed. There was that awful stink in the air. Alice Spring stepped forward again and grabbed Ginny's arm. She pressed the folded bills into Ginny's hand and forced her fingers to curl around them.

"There is fever here," Alice Spring reasoned. "You've lost one child to the fever already. Will you risk this one as well, when you have a chance to save him? You can get him out of this misery."

Maire's eyes widened as she watched. She looked younger, suddenly, than Ginny had seen her look since her father left. Alice Spring was still talking.

"You have blight here, even the little one said it. What will you feed your children when your crop is gone again? How will you feed little Raymond, if you can't nourish yourself?"

Ginny could feel her breast rising and falling erratically. She was shaking her head, shaking her head. She tried to shake all the reason and outrageous logic loose from her ears. Instead, she would hold only to the sound of her baby's cries. His hungry voice.

"And how would *you* propose to feed him?" Ginny said, but her words were deficient of the bitterness she felt. She could see a glimmer of triumph in Alice Spring's eye. "He's hungry now." Ginny's voice was defeated.

"I'll get a wet nurse."

"No, no!" Ginny said, finding her strength again. "I am his

mother!" She beat her fist against her chest, but then fell silent. She was so worn down by fear and anguish. She was so wholly exhausted. "If you want him, you will have to bring all of us," she said resolutely. "*I* will nurse him."

"Hah!" Alice Spring huffed, her face incredulous. "Don't be preposterous. I can't show up in New York with an entire ragtag family of Irish beggars at my heels."

Maire's face pinkened, but she held her tongue. Ginny stepped forward and opened her fingers, threw the matted wad of bills back in Alice Spring's face. They rained down around her like summer snowflakes. Her eyes and mouth popped open in shock. She was still holding her purse in one hand. She had locked the clasp over the weight of gold coins inside, and now her fingertips yellowed beneath her furious grip.

"You fool!" Alice Spring screamed, and she swung the purse wildly, hitting Ginny hard in the side of the head. The weight of gold made a sickening clunk against the side of Ginny's head, and she half buckled, but then recovered herself. She could hear nothing of Mrs. Spring's continued rant, only a loud ringing in her right ear. She clutched the side of her face, and turned to Maire, who was backing away now from Alice Spring. Maire was shielding the baby boy in her arms. Ginny lurched for them, but she was dizzy from the blow, and she collapsed down on one knee. Alice Spring was bulging with rage. Everything felt slow and contorted. Ginny couldn't hear past the ringing. And then there was a sound like air being sucked from a balloon, and Ginny could hear Alice Spring again, shrieking like a madman.

"Damn you, I will have him!" she was screaming. "He belongs with me!"

Ginny staggered to her feet and listed forward, but she couldn't get to them in time. Maire clung tightly to Raymond. She kept one hand over his head, and pitched her own head low to cover him. Alice Spring was pulling at his blanket, wrenching Maire's arms. The Wedgwood pie plate came loose in the struggle and Alice Spring bobbled it, then caught it secure in her fingers. Ginny could see the veins throbbing in Alice Spring's hands as she lifted the pie plate overhead. Maire cowered beneath the lunatic, shielding Raymond. And then Ginny's own voice flew from her like a woeful, animal thing—a curlew.

Ginny saw the Wedgwood bludgeon coming down slow over her children, a violent streak of blue against the morning sky. Her voice flew out around them and her body hurtled forward, but she was too late, too late. There was a crack and smash as the plate shattered down over her daughter's head, and Maire dropped to her knees, but she never let go of Raymond.

"My God!" Ginny was shrieking now, too, though there was nothing of God in her heart at that moment. Her daughter was on her knees. Maire crumpled into her mother, and Ginny caught her. Alice Spring caught Raymond. She lifted him triumphantly into her arms.

"Maire." Ginny was on her knees now, too, down beside her daughter. Maire's eyes were open and she latched them on to her mother. Her mouth was slack and her cheeks were pale, but there was a bright red ribbon of blood running down from a wicked gash in her hairline. She was moving her lips. Ginny held her daughter's face and kissed her. She kissed her.

"I'm all right," Maire said, but her voice had a terrible windy quiver. She was garbled. "I'm grand, Mammy. Mammy, Raymond. Get Raymond."

She pointed to Alice Spring, who was stood looking down at them. She had baby Raymond in her arms, and a demented tiny half smile on her face. Ginny's soft confusion snapped and diffused. Maire sat up, and Ginny stood to face Alice Spring, who lifted her chin.

"It didn't have to be like this," Mrs. Spring said, and there was a crazy brilliance in her eyes.

Raymond was crying, and she was squeezing him, too tight. She would wind him.

"Give me my baby," Ginny said to her.

"He's coming with me. He needs to come with me."

"He's going nowhere with you." Ginny bent quickly, and lifted Raymond's hurley bat from beside Maggie's cairn. She held it loose by her side, and stood above her daughter. "Give me my son," she said again.

"Look. Look," Mrs. Spring cried, and real tears came quick to her eyes. Her voice warbled, and she shook her head urgently. "Don't make me hurt him. Let me take him with me, let him go. God, I love him so dearly, don't make me hurt him. I will." She was trembling. She had the fingers of one hand splayed awkwardly across his tiny head. She held him slippy in one arm and his head was lolling back. She could snap his neck. She could hurl him at the ground. She was capable of anything. She was barking mad altogether. She backed away from Ginny slowly. "Don't make me hurt him," she cried again softly.

"Mammy!" Maire's voice was in a panic. "Mammy!" she screamed.

Ginny was so quick then. She didn't falter. She didn't think. She lifted the hurley bat behind her with the fast certainty of a god, and she heaved it without conscience. With all the might in her spent body, she hurtled forward and brought that cudgel down. A bloodcurdling crack split Alice Spring's waiting skull.

And she dropped.

It was so slow, the way Raymond came loose from Alice Spring's arms, sickening slow. Ginny reached out for her baby when Alice Spring fell, and she saw him tumbling, the tuck of his blanket unrolling, unraveling. He came free from the blanket, and he flew, his ten little fingers splayed out in terror. Ginny sprang, she leapt. Her fingertips grasped his in the naked air, his arm wrenched.

She caught him. By one dangling arm, she caught him.

And then the wind and the blood and the blight were all coursing through her, ferrying remorse and relief both all through her blood, as she folded Raymond's tiny, twisting body into her arms, and stepped through the scattered blue shards of china. They crunched like bones beneath her feet. The purple hat had come loose from Alice Spring's head, and it skittered across the yard now like a frightened bird, its sole feather waving manically. The loosened money, too, flapped along the breezy ground. A few bills caught in Maggie's cairn, and more clustered around Alice Spring's fluttering skirts. Her blue eyes were open to the sky. The bloodiest horror of the head wound was hidden beneath the soft golden loops of her hair. My God. What had Ginny done? She put her hands over her baby's face and closed her own eyes.

"God forgive me," she whispered.

Raymond howled and cried, from the shock, Ginny hoped, but his little arm was hanging at a queer angle. Maire was crying softly behind them. Her voice was windy. She called out, "Mammy." Ginny turned to look at her daughter, at the blood beginning to clot and dry in her hair. Ginny took two crunching steps to where her daughter sat trembling, still pointing at Alice Spring.

"Mammy," she said again.

"Here, we'll get you inside," Ginny said, and she stooped to lift her daughter.

Maire put an arm around her mother's neck and struggled to her feet. At the door, Maire turned back to look at the body, but Ginny stood in her way so she couldn't see.

"Mammy, the money," she said.

"Don't worry, Maire. I'll take care of it."

Inside, Maggie and Poppy were all round eyes and mouths. They were all silent astonishment.

"What happened to Maire, Mammy?" Poppy whispered.

"I'm grand, Poppy," Maire said, but her voice was still shaking. "I just fell and hit my head."

"Oh." Her little sister nodded reverently.

"And I'm going to clean it up for her," Ginny said.

"That's good because it looks disgusting," Poppy said.

"How do you feel?" Ginny said, settling Maire onto the stool. "Are you dizzy?"

"No."

"Maire."

"A little," she admitted.

"Listen, I'm going to clean you up, but I have to take care of some things outside first, right?"

Maire tucked in her lips.

"Maggie, come here and hold your brother."

"Why does Maggie get to hold him?" Poppy whinged.

"Because you have to hold me," Maire said.

"But you're too big for me to hold."

"You have to hold my hand," she explained.

"Oh," Poppy said. "That's all right." And she stood in beside the stool, lifted Maire's hand, and gave it a squeeze. "How's that?"

"Perfect."

"Don't get up," Ginny said to Maire. "If you're dizzy, I don't want you falling again."

"All right, Mam."

"I mean it. Promise?"

"I promise," Maire said.

"Why is he crying like that, Mammy?" Maggie asked then. Raymond's little cry was frantic, his lungs squealing out all the volume he could manage.

"He's all right, Maggie," Ginny said. "Babies just cry like that sometimes. It's nothing to worry about."

But Maggie didn't look convinced.

"I think he hurt his little arm," Ginny said, bending over the baby to inspect him. "You just hold on to him tight there and make him cozy. I'll be back in just a few minutes to feed him."

Maggie nodded, but her face was still creased with worry.

"It's no worry if he cries, love," Ginny said. "It's good for him. Just keep this door closed until I get back."

"Why?" Maggie asked.

"Because there's a monster outside," Maire said. Poppy's eyes widened. "Don't worry, it can't get in as long as we keep the door closed."

"But what about Mammy?" Poppy asked, tears threatening.

"Oh, it's not a grown-up monster," Maire said. "It's a baby monster. It only eats babies and little children. Mammy will be fine."

Ginny closed the door behind her and leaned against it. There was blood in the yard. Maire's bright red blood, all scattered through the china. And then Alice Spring's blood, pooling dark and mortal beneath the twisted wreckage of her body, her legs akimbo beneath her splendid gown. Ginny clapped her hands across her face, and wept at the sight of Alice Spring, the damnation of her soul.

When Ginny was able, she ran. She reeled up to the ridge, and down the other side, all the way down the lane through the bottom field and over to the gate in the rock wall. She pawed frantically at the latch on the gate. It loosened and the gate swung in. Mrs. Spring's carriage was parked in the road beyond. The two horses stood still and quiet, and behind them, Seán sat up with his feet propped high on the footboard and his arms crossed in front of him. His chin was dropped to his chest, and he was snoring lightly.

Ginny walked to him directly, and took hold of his boot. She shook him.

"Seán, wake up."

He snorted and sat up. "Hah? Oh, I wasn't sleeping. Just resting a . . ." He stopped short, lifted his hat to scratch beneath. "What are you . . . Where's Mrs. Spring?"

Ginny stood back from the carriage and looked down the road. She looked back up at him then, and tried to form words into a sentence that she could say to him out loud. She couldn't do it. He hopped down from the carriage and leaned in to her face.

"Jesus, Ginny," he said. "What happened? Are you bleeding?"

She looked down at the sleeve of her shirtwaist, the shoulder. It was smeared with the brightness of Maire's blood, where she had leaned against her.

"No," she said. "No, it wasn't me. It was Maire."

"Oh God."

"No, she's grand, I think she'll be all right. I may need to give her an old stitch-up."

"What happened?" he asked again.

Ginny shook her head. "She went mad."

"That doesn't sound like Maire."

"No, Mrs. Spring," Ginny said. "She tried to *buy* Raymond."

"She what?"

"She gave me all this money, she wanted to take him with her."

"To America?"

Ginny nodded.

"Where is she now?" he asked.

Ginny turned and started walking back toward the gate, and

Seán followed, but she stopped before they got there. She gripped his arm before she said the words out loud. Her voice was a wobbly whisper.

"Seán, I think I killed her."

His jaw flickered and his eyes gave a start, but he said nothing.

"I think I killed her." She said it again, but she hoped it wasn't true. She knew it was.

Seán was shaking his head. "You couldn't. You couldn't, you maybe just . . . what happened?"

She closed her eyes. "We were fighting. We were arguing over the baby. Maire was holding the baby, and she gave me money— Mrs. Spring did. She gave me all this money, and said she was going to take him, and I told her no. I threw the money back in her face, and then she went for Maire. She hit Maire over the head with the pie plate while she was holding Raymond."

Seán took Ginny by the hand, and backed her in against the rock wall so she could lean into it.

"All right," he said. "All right. Where are the children?"

"They're inside, they're all inside."

"And where is Mrs. Spring?"

Ginny took a deep breath and heaved her body away from the wall. Together, they went to the gate, and she hadn't latched it. It was hanging halfway open. "She's there," she said, pointing uphill.

Seán pushed the gate in and stepped up the slope in front of Ginny. When he reached the top of the ridge, he could see the small heap of purple taffeta beyond.

"My God," he said.

He returned back down the slope to the gate, where Ginny was waiting. He stared back up the hill.

"She had Raymond," Ginny said. "She said she was going to

hurt him. She said *Don't make me hurt him. Let me take him.* And she had his little head in her hand like a nut. I thought she was going to kill him. Seán?"

He turned to face her.

"I didn't mean to kill her. I didn't think. I just. I hit her with Ray's hurley bat."

He stood staring at her for what felt like a full minute. Then he stepped past her and back out through the gate. Her heart hammered after him. Where was he going? She wheeled on her feet to follow him.

"Where are you going?"

He strode to the carriage and reached beneath it. He pulled out a horse blanket and handed it to her. Then he hefted out one of Mrs. Spring's trunks. Ginny followed him back to the gate, where he tied the blanket across the hinges and the latch, so no one would come in. He closed it behind them.

"The times that are in it, Ginny," he said. "God help us, but who will notice another body? Who will miss her?"

Ginny was stunned. She tried to take it in, what Seán was saying. "Well, I have to tell . . ." She shook her head. "I don't know. I can't go to the constable. But Father Brennan at least."

Seán cocked his head at her. The tears were back in her eyes. She blinked them away.

"God forgive me," she whispered.

"Ginny." Seán grabbed her arm. "Never mind all of that right now. Listen." He gripped her roughly by the shoulders and looked her full in the face. "You did nothing wrong. You protected your children. It was a horrible accident."

She nodded. "So then, Father Brennan . . ."

"If you need to confess it to clear your conscience, you may think of that later, but for now, you should not involve Father Brennan."

"But if you really believe . . ."

"No matter what I believe, Ginny. The damned English have already hanged half a dozen Irish for killing landlords this year. What will happen to those children if you're the next?"

Ginny dropped her breath in her chest and closed her mouth. He was right. They climbed to the top of the ridge and then down the other side, Seán carrying the heavy steamer trunk the whole way. When they got into the yard, he set it down beside Maggie's cairn. He went down on one knee and unlatched the trunk, pulled out a silken, lemon-colored gown that was all stitched and embroidered with golden threads. He handed it up to Ginny, who gathered it into her arms. It weighed more than her baby.

"Go in and take care of the children. Stitch up Maire, if she needs a stitch. Then pack whatever ye need for the journey, and put that on." He nodded at the flood of silk in her arms.

He was still rummaging around in the trunk, and now he pulled out an envelope stuffed with documents and more money. He stood up.

"You're Alice Spring now. You're going to New York."

Chapter Twenty-one

Why didn't I bring Kleenex? I should know better than to travel anywhere without Kleenex nowadays. In the Rose Reading Room, I click *pause* on my laptop, and unzip every empty pocket on my backpack. There is no Kleenex. I shrug off my jacket and then dab at my eyes with my shirtsleeve, try not to sniff too loudly. Under no circumstances will I look up, in case I make eye contact with another human. I look up. The young, black-clad tourist from outside is standing by the History of Civilization and Culture shelves. Without her enormous sunglasses, she looks impossibly Midwestern and fresh. She is staring at me. I am red-faced and puffy; my cheeks and armpits are damp. I am an authentic New Yorker. She reaches into her black Armani bag and pulls out a tidy packet of Kleenex. She pulls a few loose and steps forward, hands them to me.

"Thanks," I say, without removing my earbuds.

She shrugs and only half smiles. Her mom is standing behind her, and when she turns back, the mom reaches and squeezes her hand. The daughter doesn't pull away. She doesn't shrink. They walk like that, holding hands, past the catalog room and into the North Hall.

I clean myself up before I turn back to my laptop. I click *play* again. Raymond Doyle has just finished telling the professor his mother's story.

"What a remarkable tale," the professor says, and his voice has dropped its academic armor. He sounds truly full of awe.

"My mother was a remarkable woman," Raymond Doyle says simply.

I sniff loudly, and a man who is sitting at the other end of my table shifts uncomfortably, but doesn't look up.

"Indeed, indeed," the professor says, and I can feel him casting about for a thread to follow. There are so many questions.

"So she assumed Mrs. Spring's identity then?"

"Only for the passage over," Raymond says. "As soon as we were off the boat, she ditched the traveling papers, and we disappeared into the streets of the New World. She was always Ginny Doyle after that."

So that's why my mom couldn't find evidence of their passage in her genealogy records.

"And did anyone ever discover what had happened to Alice Spring? Did her husband go looking for her?"

Raymond sighs heavily. "I donno," he says. "I never really cared to find out. Seems unlikely, though."

"And your mother took this secret to her grave?"

"Not exactly. I mean she told the authority that mattered to her. She made it right with God. But that's not to say she ever forgave herself. She lived with an awful weight of guilt on her, the poor woman."

"If you'll forgive me saying, it seems odd that she would've shared the story so freely with you, if she was as ashamed as you say she was. Are you certain she wasn't proud of herself, in some way? That she got away with it?"

"Nah, no way. She never spoke of it. Never once in her life. She was haunted by it. She hated what she did."

"So then, how was it that you come to know the story?"

"My sister Maire would tell it. She always thought Ma had a tremendous heroics about her, after that. They were very close. But it wasn't only Maire. Seán would tell it, too. He was a little more reluctant because he knew it made Ma uneasy, but he knew everything."

"Yes . . . Seán," the professor says. "What became of him? Did he accompany you, then, on the passage? He stayed in touch with your mother?"

"You could say that. They were married not long after we arrived in New York. He was a good man. Taught us all our letters, and that was no small thing in those days. He even taught Ma how to read and write."

He taught her to write! Of course—the handwriting. On the table, I open the diary to its inside cover and trace my fingers along her name, Ginny Doyle, where it is written fourteen times in that childlike scrawl. She wasn't crazy; she was practicing.

"Seán worshipped my ma," Raymond Doyle says.

"Did they have any more children?"

"Three more. My two younger brothers and one sister."

"Are any of them still living?"

"Only my baby sister, Alice."

"They named her Alice?"

"They did."

"Fascinating," the professor says. "And have you any family photographs? Of your parents?"

"Nah, that was for rich people back then. There wasn't any photographs."

360 · JEANINE CUMMINS

"But they must have been well enough off, with all of Alice Spring's money."

Raymond snorts. "They hardly had all of it, Professor. Most of her money was in the land, in Ireland. Or it was with her husband, in New York or London, or wherever he was off gallivanting. It's true that she had some traveling money, and then Ma was able to sell the horses and the carriage in Galway. But she used most of that to buy us traveling clothes, to disguise us as rich kids, and then buy our passage over. There wasn't much left when we got here, only enough to get us on our feet. She worked hard."

"Mm," the professor says. And then there is a long pause and the static takes center stage. "It's been such a pleasure to talk with you. Is there anything else you'd like to say, anything you'd like to record, before we finish?"

"Yeah," Raymond says, and he clears his throat. "You know, growing up in Queens. I remember getting into scraps with some of the other kids around. I remember one time a kid taunting me, saying how much the Irish loved their mammies. He said it like it was something shameful. *You Irish boys love your mammies.*" Raymond's voice grows clearer and stronger for a minute. I imagine he is sitting forward in his chair. He sounds younger. "They had no idea. What we went through, what our mothers went through. In those famine days."

Raymond clears his throat again, or he tries to. He sounds strained now, and tired.

"That is something that has always stuck with me," he says quietly. "My mother, she did penance for the rest of her life. She could have been a wounded soul, she could have crumbled. But she didn't. She didn't let all that guilt and sorrow defeat her. I never knew such strength, never saw the like of it in another human being, not even in my own beloved wife, God rest her soul. Even after everything Ma lost, everything she suffered—she carried on for us. She lived life. For us. Everything she did was for us."

I try not to sniff, not to irritate my tablemate. I breathe deeply, use the Kleenex to sponge the tears out of my eyes before they spill.

"Raymond Doyle, thank you," the professor says. "It has been my honor and privilege to talk with you. Thank you for sharing your stories."

Raymond Doyle says, "Yeah, sure," and then the static stops. The earbuds fall silent. I lean forward and rest my forehead on Ginny Doyle's diary at the edge of the table. My tears splatter softly onto the red tile floor beneath my feet. I take the earbuds out without lifting my head. I dry my eyes, sit up, and open the diary to the passage that has haunted me. The passage that convinced me that Ginny Doyle's malevolent DNA would make me a terrible mother. I read.

25 April 1848

> *Dear God, I killed her. I killed her. It is late now, and the children are asleep here, and I was awakened by that horrid crunching, and it was so vivid, the sound of it, that it brought me right back there. . . .*

> *The cottage. That last day in the yard, under the blackthorn tree. I can see myself, almost as if from above. Like I'm that magpie in the tree looking down. And there's the other me down in the yard, the ferocious me. The baby is there. Maire is watching. Oh the horrors my poor daughter has seen in her short life.*

> *I'm holding the hurley bat in both hands, and I'm swinging it down over my head. How does my face look in this instant? Is it pained, twisted, demented? Demonic, with the power coursing through me? I am*

about to take a woman's life—a woman who was only
kind to me until this last day, these last moments.

She is dead now.

Would that I could wish myself back to that moment,
and stop it there. To drop that hurley bat to my feet,
to hear its soft clatter in the dust. But instead there's
an almighty crack like thunder as I bring it down on
her skull, and she drops, heavy like a bag of clean, dry
praties. The baby nearly falls with her, but I catch him, I
catch him, by one dangling arm. Her eyes and her mouth
stay open, and Maire's eyes, too, wide open at my back.
Her voice is windy. She calls me mammy.

There are shards of the blue Wedgwood china on the
ground, and they crunch beneath my feet, like the sound
of bones snapping. Maire's cheeks have gone a sickly
white. There are pieces of the pale blue china strewn
through the dead woman's hair.

Why I remember this crunching, above all else, is a
maniac question. Perhaps it's easier than the rest, than
Maire's intrepid voice, and the baby crying after. It stays
in my ears like a disease, that crunch. It robs my sleep.

God forgive me, God forgive me. I can still see her
dead and ghastly face.

I close the cover of the book softly and clasp it to my chest. I
misjudged everything. I lean back in my chair, place the earbuds
back in, close my eyes, and listen to Raymond Doyle's story all
over again.

"You seem different," Dr. Zimmer says, leaning back in her red
chair.

"I feel different," I say.

"So is the Ativan helping?"

I nod. "Maybe it is."

Dr. Zimmer doesn't respond.

"Okay, it's probably not, because I'm not taking it," I say. "But maybe it's like you said. Maybe just knowing it's there is helping? Like a safety net?"

"That could be," she says. "It could also be that your hormone levels are beginning to shift back to normal on their own. Or that you're just getting the hang of your new life, that you're beginning to adjust."

I shrug.

"You don't think so?" Dr. Zimmer asks. "You know you're very hard on yourself. You're much more judgmental toward you than you are toward other people."

"Only out loud," I say. "In my head I'm hypercritical of everyone. I'm a total bitch."

Dr. Zimmer smiles. "Did you just call yourself a bitch?"

"Dammit." I hate it when I prove her point.

"So give yourself a little credit," she suggests. "That could go a long way. If you feel like you're doing better, that can become part of your new narrative for yourself, and you can build on that. You are healing. You're doing it yourself."

"Maybe," I say.

"You think it's something else?"

"You know the diary?"

"Yes," Dr. Zimmer says.

"Well, I found out the whole story about that ancestor. One of her sons did a folklore project at the New York Public Library, and I went and listened to the whole thing. He told her whole story. And she wasn't awful at all, that Ginny Doyle. She was like this amazing, heroic woman who saved her kids, and then felt guilty for the rest of her life because of what happened."

Dr. Zimmer is frowning. "But there was a murder, yes?"

"No, no, it wasn't really a murder. It was totally self-defense. She was just protecting her kids. It just seemed like a murder, the way she wrote it in the diary, because she felt so guilty."

"Mmm." Dr. Zimmer seems less than convinced, but I don't really care.

"Anyway, I just feel like I know the truth now. Like maybe I'm not so destined to fail after all. Maybe that sort of maternal malfunction isn't hard-coded into my genetics."

Dr. Zimmer nods. "Sometimes we have to make these sorts of discoveries for ourselves in order to truly believe them. And how *did* you make this discovery? How did you find out about this, what was it, a recording?"

"Yeah, it was a recording. My mom called and told me about it."

"Oh?"

"Yeah, I don't know how she found it. She's really into the genealogy stuff, and she found out about the recording, and called to tell me."

"So you've been talking to your mom about all this?"

"Yeah, a little." I shrug.

"And how is that? Does she listen?"

"Yeah, she does."

"That's good. Very good."

"Well, she's interested in it," I say carefully. "It's not like it signals a sea change in our relationship. But something else might."

Dr. Zimmer raises her eyebrows and waits.

"So I have this friend Jade, this new friend. And she was telling me this theory that when people talk all the time like my mom does, but don't really listen, it usually means they are hiding a bunch of pain about something, and they're trying to distract you from sniffing it out."

"Jade sounds like a psychiatrist."

"She's like a maharishi, except she cries all the time."

"So you think your mom is like that, that she's trying to conceal some deep pain?"

"She is."

"How do you know?"

"I asked her."

"Wow."

"Yeah, I was pretty surprised, too. I didn't really plan it. I sort of pushed her into it during a moment of frustration, but she copped to all of it. She's been through some horrible shit. Stuff she's never talked about. I had no idea."

"And this makes you feel closer to her?"

"I think so. I mean, it definitely makes me feel like I understand her more, so that's a start. I don't think our relationship will change that much. She'll still be the same woman. I don't expect her to suddenly open up all the time, and start talking to me about all kinds of deep stuff."

"But she might, now that you've opened the door," Dr. Zimmer says. "Could you handle that, if she did?"

"Of course, yeah," I say. "But I don't need it. I think it might be too hard for her. It's just not who she is."

"Okay, so what will you do with your new understanding of your mom?"

"I think I can just be more patient with her. Not get so frustrated all the time. I can know that it doesn't mean she doesn't love me."

"That's a lot of double negatives," Dr. Zimmer says. "Say it plainly."

"She loves me. My mom loves me."

I don't know why this makes me cry, but at least there is Kleenex here, and these aren't the discomforting, strangulated tears I've become accustomed to anyway. They are looser, somehow. Welcomed. Like they are washing something unclean out of me.

At home, Leo and I lay out all the floorboards in the emptied living room. There is something tremendously satisfying in the way they fit together, the way their surface grows, transforming all the light and colors in the room.

"Hey, now that it's getting cold out, maybe we can cut back the garden, too, while everything is dead for the winter."

"You're ambitious," Leo says.

"You love it."

Leo leans up on his knees to stretch his back. "I'm almost ready to trust you with gardening shears, I guess."

Emma is watching from her bouncy seat in the doorway, like a superintendent. She kicks her feet and bats jerkily at the low-hanging monkey overhead. She is so full of energy now, and movement. Like me, she is stronger every day.

"Hey, how'd your checkup go?" Leo asks, sitting down on the finished section of our new floors, and leaning his sweaty back against the wall. He props up his knees and uncaps his Coke to take a swig.

"Good, the doc said the incision looks good."

"I thought it was a scar now."

I shoot him a look while he sips his Coke. "Don't push it. Oh, hey, you won't believe what else!"

"What else?"

I can't believe I forgot to tell him this. "The crunching!" I say.

He doesn't answer. He has a look on his face like maybe the Coke is flat.

"You know I kept hearing that crunching? You thought it was a squirrel? Dad thought it was a mouse."

"Yeah, and you thought it was a ghost or something," Leo says.

"I did not. Well, maybe," I say. "Anyway, the doctor . . . okay, this is totally disgusting, but fascinating."

Leo sits up in his sweaty T-shirt. *Disgusting* has him interested. "Go on," he says.

"So the doctor looked in my ears today, just as part of my checkup, and he asked me if I'd been having any trouble hearing. I told him no, and then he asked if I'd been hearing any funny sounds, like rattling or anything, or if things sounded muffled lately, so I told him about the crunching."

Leo is trying not to smile.

"What?" I say.

"No, nothing!" He feigns innocence.

"Well, I am not crazy," I say.

"Mm-hmm."

"He said that women's bodies do so much weird shit when we're pre- and postpartum—"

"He said *weird shit*?"

"I believe that is the scientific medical term, yes," I say. "Would you quit interrupting?"

"Sorry."

"He had another patient who heard a high-pitched squeal in one ear during her entire pregnancy. The day she delivered, it stopped."

"So is there like a scale of crazy, from rattling to squealing?" Leo asks. "Where does crunching fall in line?"

"Man, you are on *fire* today, with your hilarity," I say. "You should take that on the road."

"Stop, you're too kind."

"So, ready for the gross part?"

"Hit it."

"He flushed my ears out with a syringe, and there was so much wax in there, we could have built a hotel out of it."

"Mmm," Leo says. "Sexy."

"I know, I'm like a porn star, right?"

Leo looks over at Emma in the doorway. "Hot mommy's a porn star," he says.

I wince. "Okay, we're going to have to knock it off with the sexy baby talk."

Leo is frowning, too. "Yeah, I sensed that."

"Glad we're on the same page."

That evening, when the floors are finished, it only takes us a few minutes to unroll our thick new area rug, and move the furniture back in. The transformation is extraordinary. It's like a new house entirely. It's amazing what a floor can do. I can't wait to lay Emma down on the plush carpet. I take her out of the bouncy seat while Leo orders dinner, and we hit up some tummy time together. Her chubby little fingers splay along the carpet, and her head bobbles along. I make a spidery-hand, and I walk it over to her face. The spider-hand kisses her nose, and she smiles.

She smiles. Emma *smiles*!

"Leo!" I scream. "Come here! Emma just smiled! She smiled!"

Leo leans in from the office doorway and points to the phone at his ear. He holds up one finger.

"Yeah, the massaman curry," he is saying.

The spider-hand kisses Emma's nose again, and she grins with her whole face, her eyes, her tremendous set of gums. She has dimples. My daughter has dimples! Oh my God, she's so beautiful I could eat her.

After the curries and a bath and a feed, Emma sleeps, and Leo and I stand in the kitchen together for a long, long time. He holds me. His arms are wrapped full around me, my forehead tucked beneath his chin, against his neck. We are listening to channel C. Harrowing, weeping, wailing channel C.

"I don't understand," I whisper. "She's so incredible. She's such a better mother than me. I mean, she doesn't seem a hundred percent bonded with her kids, but she totally has the hang of it. And she seems so strong. And smart. About everything."

We watch Max and Madeline writhing in their cribs. They both clamor for Jade, who stays just offscreen. Her sobs are wrenching. They would knock the breath clean out of you, just from the sound of them. Leo is shaking his head.

"Yeah, this is not . . ." He doesn't know what to say. "Not good."

"Nothing like what I'm going through, right? Even in my worst moments?" I ask, just to make sure. Because it seems extreme to me, but familiar at the same time. I really can't tell.

"No," Leo agrees. "Nothing like your crying. She . . . she sounds like she needs help, Majella."

I pull away from him. I lift the monitor from the counter and hold it in my hands.

"I'm going over there."

"What, now?" he says.

"Yeah, I think I should."

"Are you going to tell her we've been eavesdropping over the monitor?"

I shrug. I think. "Maybe."

Leo nods. "Okay. Take your time. I'll be here when you get back."

I turn off the monitor and take it with me, because maybe it will be easier just to show it to her, instead of trying to explain. Maybe she can think of my eavesdropping as accidental, or at least incidental.

I stand at the front door of the six-family and study the various bells. There's no way to know which is hers, so I take a guess. The first one warrants no response. The second one results in a grumpy Polish lady leaning out her second-story window to shake her fist at me. I lean back and wave up at her.

"Sorry, wrong bell!" I say.

I ring bell number three. A little kid answers.

"Hello, who's there?"

"Hello, I'm sorry, I might have the wrong bell. I'm looking for Jade?"

"This isn't Jade, it's Franklin."

"Franklin, hey! I know you! It's Majella. I saw you in the window a few weeks ago—I live next door. Remember, you heard me say a bad word?"

"You said the *F word*!" he whispers.

"That's right, Franklin, that's me! The F-word lady!"

Franklin giggles.

"Franklin, do you know which apartment Jade lives in?" I ask. "With the twin babies?"

"Oh yeah, she lives on the first floor, in the back."

I frown. "Do you know which bell is hers?"

"Nope."

Damn.

"Franklin, do you think you could let me in?" I ask, knowing that I shouldn't. Knowing that I am asking this kid to break every rule he should follow in life, in order to stay alive and unmolested in New York City.

"Sure," he says, and he buzzes me in.

I ascend the three steps to the lobby, and walk through the echoey corridor all the way to the back. There are two doors, and one has a painted pumpkin on it that says *Franny's Fun Factory*, so I knock on the other one. Nothing happens. For a long time. I knock again, and then start to envision calling the fire department to break the door down with an ax. Or at least turning the monitor back on, so I can see what is happening in there. Why won't she answer the door? I'm about to knock a third time when I hear footsteps inside, and then the *shick*ing sound as she pulls back the cover from the peephole.

I hear her hesitate, but I know she's in there. I know how alone she is. And maybe I have at least an inkling of what she's going through: the way those hormones can bear down on you like a chemical wall of tears. The way you can feel the torrent coming, but you can't outrun it. The way you have to sit powerless and wait for that wall to pound down over you. The way you pray for it to end. The way some days, you want to scream at your baby *What the hell do you want from me?* just to make her stop crying. There's a reason they make you watch those anti-baby-shaking videos before you leave the hospital. Because if you didn't know how dangerous it was, *everyone* would do it at least once. This new-mama shit is no joke. No one should have to do this alone.

"Hey, Jade, open up," I say to the peephole.

There is only silence.

"Jade."

Another beat.

And then finally: the flick of the chain lock, the clack of the dead bolt, the twist of the knob. The door swings open.

"Hey."

She lets me in.

I am standing in the arrivals hall at LaGuardia, and it's hot. It smells like soup. There's another woman waiting, and her toddler has sprinted gleefully past the sign that says STAY BEHIND THIS LINE while the mother watches helplessly, bound by the rules of society in a way her kid is not. The mother has a Baggie of gummy bears out now, and she's shaking them softly at her moppy-haired daughter, trying to entice the child back across the line. Security is approaching, and the mother becomes frantic.

"Olivia, come back here this instant!" the mother hisses, her cheeks paling.

"Ma'am, you have to keep your child behind the line," the security officer says, his thumbs tucked idiotically into his belt.

"Yes, I know," the mother says, stabbing him to death with her eyes. "Olivia, get over here!"

Olivia lunges for the gummy bears and when she's close enough, her mother snatches her by the arm. I wonder what family member they're waiting for, what happy reunion Olivia is determined to ruin by getting her mother arrested. She gobbles the gummy bears joyfully, and the mother holds her hand so hard that her knuckles turn shiny and yellow. Olivia doesn't notice. She is dressed like a strawberry, because today is Halloween.

Emma is in her stroller, and she's wearing a frog costume that is so cute it would make your eyes bleed. She is kicking her legs, making the giant frog feet bounce. Olivia's mother smiles at me, but not because of the frog feet. That smile is an apology. Olivia is doing the twist in her strawberry costume, still holding her mama by one hand while she chews her gummy bears with her mouth open.

"It doesn't matter," I say.

I lift my phone from the stroller's cup holder and check the time. Eight weeks ago right now, Leo and I were in a taxi, racing along Sixty-eighth Street, pulling up in front of Weill Cornell Medical Center. The taxi driver was freaking out. He kept screaming, "Don't you have that baby in my car! Not in my car!" I could have reassured him—there was no way she was going to fall out on the floor of the cab. I wouldn't have that baby for another twenty-eight hours. They would have to hack me open to get her out.

I pull back the hood on her stroller, and she looks up at me. Her frog feet bounce. She flashes her fleeting, elusive, miraculous smile. That kid has my heart in a hammock.

And now people begin to appear from behind the line, behind a partition—tanned and wrinkled people, pulling their rolling luggage behind them. Olivia the strawberry tries to make a run for it again, but her mother yanks on her arm and holds fast. I hold, too.

I hold my breath.

My mother is here. She is here. She went to the airport in Tampa, and faced her worst fear. She boarded an actual airborne vessel. To get to us. My baby and me. And now she is here, she is walking toward us in the arrivals hall at LaGuardia. She sees Emma, and her face is so happy that she doesn't even smile. She has tears in her eyes. But she doesn't go to the stroller first, to bend down and greet her only grandchild for the first time. Instead she comes to me. She drops the handle of her suitcase and she leans across the rope and she puts her arms around me. I fall in against her, against the sound of her voice in my ear.

"Baby," she says.

Acknowledgments

I want to thank: Claire Zion, Doug Stewart, and Carolyn Turgeon for making me a better writer. Everyone at Penguin, especially Norman Lidofsky's phenomenal sales team. Dr. Mary Daly at University College Dublin for her historical expertise and generosity. My invaluable mama-friends: Brenna Tinkel Sniderman, Nikki Stapleton, Evelyne Faye-Horak, and Charlotte Jack, who lived a couple of hairy scenes from this book with me. E.C.—I have come to depend on your brilliant levity as a potent antidote to any frustration I might encounter.

I wrote about half of this novel in the Theatre Café on Metropolitan Avenue in Queens. They have excellent turkey wraps, and didn't make me buy extra stuff while I sat there for hours, writing.

I thank my parents, Gene and Kay; my brother, Tom; my sister, Kathy; and all manner of Kennedy, Matthews, and Cummins for their unfailing support. Especially, my unspeakably beautiful baby daughters, Aoife and Clodagh, who patiently teach me every single day how to be their mama. And my outstanding husband, Joe, who, despite all of his pragmatic and sensible inclinations, chose to marry a writer. I'm so lucky he did.

You are invited to join us behind the scenes at Tinder Press

TINDER
PRESS

To meet our authors, browse our books
and discover exclusive content on our
blog visit us at

www.tinderpress.co.uk

For the latest news and views from the team
Follow us on Twitter

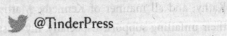 @TinderPress